Broken Sea

Broken Sea

A story of Love and Intolerance

NIGEL PEACE

Nigel Peace © 2018

All rights reserved

No parts of this publication may be reproduced, stored in a retrieval system, or transmitted in any form or by any means whatsoever without the prior permission of the publisher.

A record of this publication is available from the British Library.

ISBN 978-1-910027-23-3

Typesetting by Wordzworth Ltd
www.wordzworth.com

Cover design by Titanium Design Ltd
www.titaniumdesign.co.uk

Printed by Lightning Source UK
www.lightningsource.com

Cover images:
Background *The Ninth Wave*, Ivan Aivazovsky (1850).
Ivan Aivazovsky (1817-1900) was a Russian Armenian marine artist. The original of this painting is in the *State Russian Museum, St. Petersburg*. Foreground Soviet T-55 tank.

Published by Local Legend
www.local-legend.co.uk

For Hana

Věnováno Haně

This Book

Broken Sea is a novel, a story of love and of personal identity. It is based on the author's experience but all the characters are fictionalised; the political events are, however, described accurately.

The story begins in the summer of 1968 when two young people meet by chance and fall in love. But their struggles to understand the depth of their feelings are confounded by international politics, the Warsaw Pact invasion of Czechoslovakia. The emergence of these young people's inner worlds, in the face of profound personal challenges of the outer world, is mirrored by the struggles of a newly democratic nation, not tolerated by its neighbours.

Roy and Eva commit to each other, yet every character in this story will be radically changed by the year's events…

The Author

Nigel Peace's career path has seen him move from engineering to tourism to Mathematics teaching, with several byroads along the way. He has degrees in Science and Philosophy, and a lifelong interest in parapsychology.

In *Broken Sea* he returns to his youth to tell a story he had personal experience of, in the hope that the leaders of nations may wake up to the consequences of their actions – and inaction.

"We must learn from our history," he says, "both personal and international, if our lives are to be judged worthwhile."

Nigel lives in north London, UK.

Previous Publications

Nigel Peace has published five books of mathematical investigations and puzzles, and has contributed many articles to magazines on a variety of subjects from paranormal experience to nuclear Physics. His recent books are:

Spirit Revelations   ISBN 978-1-907203-14-5
Local Legend Publishing
An account of precognitive dreams and synchronicities, also available as an eBook. This book was national runner-up in The People's Book Prize.

Signs of Life   ISBN 978-1-907203-20-6
Local Legend Publishing
A comedy novel set in the afterlife, runner-up in the LLP national writing competition.

Lighting the Path   ISBN 978-1-907203-26-8
Local Legend
A companion to the I Ching, describing how to use and interpret this ancient Chinese oracle. Also available as an eBook.

Contents

Act 1	Uneasy Innocence	1
Act 2	Growing Pain	21
Act 3	Birth	41
Act 4	Violation	63
Act 5	Frontiers	87
Act 6	New Ways	111
Act 7	Moving On	133
Act 8	A New Year	157
Act 9	Reality	179
Act 10	Breaking Down	203
Act 11	Spring Rites	225
Act 12	Spirit	247
Act 13	The Examination	267
Act 14	Family	287
Broken Sea		301
The Players		303

ACT 1

Uneasy Innocence

E… A… C… B… His index finger hesitantly picks out the notes of A minor. Each one seems to question the last. Again. This time the C hovers, resonant in the still evening air like a small furry animal nosing out its path through woodland shrubs. The B waits but is defeated by the soft rush of waves across the beach forty yards away and in the gathering dusk the only sound is the tinkle of pebbles, chattering anxiously as they're swept together and left out to dry. E… A… C… B… he tries again, but can get no further yet.

    He shivers but not just with the chill. There are waves running through him, though he is too young – or perhaps it is that the story hasn't yet quite begun – to put his finger on them. So his hand flattens on the guitar as if to reassure him that the notes are still there, locked within the sound box. He only has four notes but at least they are the right ones and the rest will come with time. Ha! He has no idea how far and to what depth the music will have to go before the song is complete. How could he? He is just eighteen. So for now he sits on this grassy mound staring out to sea and watching young shadows hop and leap and settle on the waves. His thoughts are carried on the ebb, disturbed by what is to come, as he listens for one of these waves to whisper the next few notes; but each one is just broken on the sand.

Eventually, he stands and stretches, holding the guitar by the neck. To anyone watching – and there are a couple – his silhouette has a grotesque fist clenched in absurd salute. He is handsome enough and well-made, this boy, though his strength is untried and his studious brain untested by real life. Until tonight, life has been quite satisfying. Now there is a tear in his eye, but it's probably just the wind. So tossing back his centre-parted long, dark brown hair, he turns away from the beach with a wipe of his face and sets off across the campsite, stumbling one or twice in the darkness over rabbit holes and guy ropes.

A pale light filters from the caravan window, stabbing weakly at the outside air, as he pauses on the step to watch the looming hills beyond the small Welsh town disappear. Tiny cottage lights blink back. Turning one last time, across the waves other lights are burning intensely, but soon to be summarily extinguished. And there is a steady, insistent drumming somewhere in the world's ear, an inflammation of ideas, the sore throb of many feet withdrawing far too slowly from their exercises. It is 1968 and a disease is about to break out in the world's mind as a boy in Wales somehow, innocently, catches wind of it.

Φ

"Not bloody beans again? Chrissake, Paul, didn't your mother teach you anything except opening tins?"

"I can boil eggs too," Paul replies, matter of fact, half turning from the small cooker to see Roy framed in the doorway. "Shut the friggin' door, will you, you'll blow the gas out. It's already low." A gust of wind catches him and he trembles, sending a drop of red sauce flying from the outstretched spatula to smear against the yellow wall. It will stay there. Roy closes the door and moves through to the lounge area where he leans the guitar carefully in a corner.

"And whose fault is it that the gas is low already?" he grumbles.

"I like to think of it as a sort of natural phenomenon. You know, burning gas for your dinner tends to use it up. Mathematically, gas used equals space in bottle or, as Descartes would have it, I cook ergo – hell!" He snatches a burning piece of toast from the grill.

"I bet Descartes wouldn't've stood for baked beans every other evening for his dinner, even with the odd shrivelled sausage thrown in."

"Well, when you attain the same rhetorical heights I dare say you'll be able to command something better. Though a couple of A Levels and a place at Manchester is hardly promising." He pauses to ladle out the beans and bang them down onto the enamel plates. "It might help to be French, of course. 'Garçon, avez-vous les jambes de grenouilles? Eh bien, sautez dans la cuisine et trouvez quelque chose meilleur à manger.' There –" Paul brings in the plates and sets them down with a flourish on the unsteady table, "– food for thought."

"And what thoughts…" Roy mutters to himself, staring at the already congealing mass. "Anyway," he ventures, "if your French are so cerebral and civilised, what was all that up-the-workers crap in Paris last month?"

"The inalienable right of the citizen to demonstrate is –"

"To riot, you mean."

"– is fundamental to democracy. They were protesting against capitalist consumerism and –"

"This is the same workers who produce the consumer goods, then?"

"– and social conditions imposed by the government –"

"Which they then re-elected with a bigger majority."

"Yes, well, that does seem a bit odd. Here…"

Roy takes the tea that his friend offers and clasps his hand around the mug to warm them, his gaze disturbed by the rising wisps of steam. Some inner thought catches his attention and it turns beyond the scratched Perspex window, across the spikey dune grasses to the darkness of the breaking sea. Oblivious, Paul is already well into his meal, hungry and untroubled.

"Good stuff." He chews and nods, reassuring himself. "Eat up. We'll have to get used to this at uni, I hear it's all they have in the Refec. Government policy, beans for energy. And wind of course. Both necessary for advanced study."

Before long he pushes his empty plate away and almost in the same movement lights a cigarette, blowing the smoke across the table without thinking. Paul is a mobile boy, shorter than Roy and unathletic, yet his body moves with economy and confidence. He has quick eyes and friendly, open features framed by short, fair hair. He is also very clever but unaffected by others' moods; the atmosphere three feet away from him now is unimportant. It is an irony not lost on either of them that he is to study Modern History and French while Roy reads Engineering; then, the young middle class of suburban England these days are painfully immature in their decisions.

Without a word, Roy clears away the table and returns with a spoon and a tin of rice pudding, eating slowly with his knees drawn up in a corner seat near the guitar. After a few silent minutes, Paul tries to lift the mood.

"So what's eating you this evening? Not still in love with Carol, are you?"

"Eh? She was two years ago and anyway… No, just something in the air."

"Yeah, I always said this campsite was too close to…" He doesn't finish the sentence, realising at last that banality is inappropriate. "Did you write anything, then?" He gestures towards the guitar.

"Four notes," Roy replies with his mouth full. "EACB. Repeated. Eight notes."

"Well, that's something. I read that Bernard Shaw once spent an entire morning rubbing out a comma and putting it back in. Or was it Johnson? Those stories are usually one of the two. Still, not a lot is it, eight notes? You were out there an hour and a half with me sweating over a hot cooker so you can do your creating. I mean, that is the idea of this holiday, isn't it? One day on, one day off."

"Yeah, well I wrote eight notes. Sorry, I'll try to do better the day after tomorrow." Suddenly animated, he springs up and moves to the kitchen to throw the tin away before lighting a cigarette of his own and standing to stare out of the small window, fingers drumming on the worktop. Paul just arches his eyebrows.

"You've been working too hard," he says, picking up the creased copy of Playboy from the shelf by his head, flicking through the pages and occasionally turning the magazine upside down.

There is a lapse into silence except for the soft throaty gush of the two gas lamps mounted by the main window, the flicker of moths at the glass and the distant rattle of pebbles on the beach. The wind is getting up now, rocking the caravan slightly, and then a thin sheet of rain lashes the window and a familiar drumming begins on the roof.

"So much for summer," yawns Paul. "What's for breakfast?"

"Loaves and fishes."

"'For Chrissake,' said the five thousand, 'not bloody sardines on toast again?'"

Φ

At the open window of his suite in the Hradčany Palace, Svoboda stands in his pyjamas looking out silently, determinedly, at the distant dull flare of streetlights shrouded by city mist. He is acutely aware that these buildings date back almost eleven hundred years, before even Wenceslas, and bear virtually every architectural style of that millennium. But what is their future and that of the other great buildings in this most beautiful of all European cities? This is Svoboda's city. This is his nation too, almost to a man and woman, and a shudder of fear for them passes through him.

This night holds the most awesome fears and no-one can tell what morning may bring. So he doesn't sleep. He is a man faced with the unthinkable, not even sure that the sun will rise tomorrow and the Vlatava will continue to flow, so he tries not to think at all. After all, there seems little point, as ancient Prague stands passively between Slav and German at the crossroads of history and the whim of self-interested dictators. The Republic is approaching its fiftieth anniversary in three months' time, but celebration is not on the President's mind. Almost imperceptibly his hand lowers and fingers weakened by fatigue let go of the letter from the Five Communist Workers' Parties. Ceauşescu and Tito are standing firm, but the letter slides to the carpet under the weight of the other allies.

Instinctively – and, as it will turn out, forlornly – Svoboda's gaze turns absently westwards. He cannot know, and it would not concern him anyway, that several hundred miles ahead of him a young

Englishman is also approaching his own crossroads. Still less can he know that in a tiny, top floor Welsh hotel room a Czech girl is returning his gaze, her every thought with him.

Φ

Eva Kubíčková is twenty-one. She is not beautiful but her Slavonic cheeks and lips appeal to the mind and her nose often wrinkles with pleasure, somehow touching the heart. It is the eyes, a little close, that really hold the key by their clarity and resilient confidence. They are green.

Tonight, she is utterly afraid although no-one will see it. In the morning she will set the tables and carry the toast and the eggs out to the early risers, she will smile and chat with them as she passes the morning newspapers over to them, and they will not guess that she is not with them at all or that the headlines actually matter here. But alone now in her room, the yellow streetlamp picking out the absurd flowery wallpaper, she sucks a finger. It is the only private sign of a desperate inner space, a part of her forever unfulfilled.

"Do you think we should stop her doing it?" her mother had asked, looking up from the ironing board and wondering anxiously whether the two-year old crawling among the magazines on the floor will ever be unafraid. "Is it natural?" she had asked a year later, and then again. Her husband had folded his newspaper and considered the matter seriously.

"Eva," he had said sternly, "don't suck your finger. That's for babies and you're growing up now. It's alright when you're asleep, not in the daytime." So the little girl learned that fear belongs in the night. But she continued to suck her finger and argue her case in the stubborn way of all Czechs, who cannot be criticised, and by the age of five had learned resistance.

"I'll stop if you don't tell me to," seemed perfectly logical.

Tonight she replaces the finger with a cigarette, first licking the end before lighting it. It's a habit learned to soften the coarse first drag of dark Bulgarian tobacco, perhaps retained for the sake of a private idiosyncrasy or perhaps just to feel a little closer to home. And so thoughts fly across dark, deserted Bohemian fields back to her parents, full of anxiety as theirs must be for her, while grateful that she is safe.

Of course she had hurt them, and even deliberately, but that was their own fault for they should have realised that the affair with Josef was just a phase. She'd known it herself, so why hadn't they? She'd met him three years ago in Prague, in her first year of studying English. A journalist who called himself a writer, an ideologist who called himself an idealist, he was forcing his way into the reform movement as he had forced his way into her life. Neither his convictions nor her sensibilities were overly considered, both merely of use in forging a career in the shambles of the nation's collective destiny. He would even survive the coming onslaught virtually unscathed, despite his participation in the fateful Fourth Congress of Czechoslovak Writers.

"Gymnastics is a Leninist tool," he would say, as if quoting. "You're pandering to their warped cultural propaganda when you show off your body to them. When your muscles are flexing on the beam, and when you spread your palms and legs – and that ridiculous posing – you're exercising the Russians' muscles. The fascists love the perfect body, too." The argument was as logical as liking cats on the grounds that Hitler feared them. All the same, she'd gone along with the tide and stopped going to her classes despite the years of pain and sacrifice given to the work since childhood, the torn ligaments and the bones broken in falls from the bars. It was sad and she knew that it was. She had loved the achievements, the vitality surging through her that so few experience. She'd loved the balance, the harmony, the flight and, yes, the applause. There wasn't a lot of balance or harmony in Eastern Europe and precious little to applaud either, until Svoboda.

But this man had come along and had to be followed for a while. It was all part of education. Eva's bemused father had even almost cried as he threatened and pleaded with her, and she'd perfectly understood why. If only he had understood. So she'd been defiant and grown more distant, her resolve strengthening even as her heart cried out, "I'll stop if you don't tell me to…"

The appearance of the Writers' Manifesto in '67 only hardened the family split, mirroring as it did the flowering of her own independence far away at university in Prague. She was meeting foreign students and debating truth and justice in corner cafés, all this being necessary for its own sake. In bourgeois Czech society there might never be another chance. The ideas hardly mattered. Josef hardly mattered. But censorship of her life mattered.

"We do not want to interfere in your affairs…" the Warsaw Letter began.

"But you're not the girl we used to know…"

"There must be no change in the balance of power…"

"We cannot permit you…"

"Anti-socialist and revisionist forces have taken power…"

"You've begun to ignore us…"

"Mass media exert real moral terror against those who stand firm…"

"We may be growing old, but we have brought you up…"

"The situation is absolutely unacceptable to the Socialist countries…"

"You must see that we cannot accept…"

"Every Communist Party is responsible… to the international working class… we therefore think that the fight… is ours too."

"You are a woman now, but we are still responsible. We cannot just stand by…"

And as Svoboda turned towards the inner chamber, leaving the letter on the floor, a voice somewhere inside his head is saying, "It would all have been all right, if only you'd have stopped telling me what to do…"

Of course, Josef had not protested at the strength or perfect form of Eva's body when she had spread her palms and legs for him that heady summer. He had taken her as a matter of fact, neither gentle nor aware of the wonderful prize he had won. But somehow she hadn't really minded. It didn't matter that much, hardly counting in the bigger picture. Even when she'd met Aleš the engineer and had been reunited with her parents, she'd known that her life still hadn't happened yet.

And of all the places, hanging heavy with expectancy, where the world's fate unfolds, she is in this small room with its absurd wallpaper, damp with growth beneath the sink. She sits sleepless on the hard, wooden chair and watches, through the shimmer of her cigarette smoke, the rain lash the window.

Ф

"What shall we do today?"

"I don't know. What do you want to do?"

"I want to throttle you. That's what you say every time I ask what shall we do."

"I'm dependable. You like that. Anyway, what do we always do?" There's silence for several moments, broken by a soft curse from the kitchen. "Are you going to be much longer? I'm starving here. And it's after nine-thirty, the papers will be sold out."

"The papers are never sold out in this place. Bugger!"

"What's the matter?"

"Just having a bit of trouble with the eggs."

"I thought it was supposed to be sardines today. It is Wednesday, isn't it?"

"Haven't got any."

"Well, good job you weren't in charge in Palestine. 'Sorry, Lord, fishes are off. Will a couple of eggs do?'" Paul wanders into the kitchen area and peers over Roy's shoulder with an air of amused satisfaction at the thick yellow sauce he's stirring. "Too much milk," he observes.

"Yes, I'd worked that out," mutters Roy, breaking another egg into the pan and stirring furiously. There are five broken shells on the worktop now. "And by the way, these Christ jokes are getting a bit wearing, you know."

"Eh? Since when did you get religion back? I thought you'd stopped going to church yonks ago."

"Yeah. I did. But it's respect, isn't it? And it's getting to sound like you're trying to convince yourself you're really an atheist."

"Sorry I spoke, I'm sure. Seems you're still mardy from last night." He goes back to the living room. It's still untidy from the night before with blankets strewn on the couches, the ashtray overflowing and acrid. He picks his way through, slumps in the corner seat next to the guitar and plays Roy's four notes, repeated. EACB. It doesn't sound the same at all. "Not very promising," he observes, and plays Dylan's It Ain't Me, Babe instead. His voice is pleasant though the key wavers a little and he doesn't make the high note. Still, it's early morning.

Paul is quite creative in his own right and actually there's nothing unpleasant in him at all. To the tolerant and peaceful mind, he has very few faults. It's just that, at eighteen and a few months older than Roy, he has already accepted many of life's limitations. He is a steady and easy personality. Roy is not. But anyone watching from the dunes, their grasses still damp but shaking themselves dry in the fresh breeze, seeing Roy's face framed in the caravan's square kitchen window and his expression lifting like the morning clouds over the surrounding hills as the eggs finally scramble, would observe that something is sleeping in him and just beginning to stir and stretch.

"We need to get this straight," Paul insists, "so it's not embarrassing."

They've left the campsite now, passed the miniature railway station, and are entering the promenade. It's the long way round but they always go this way, just as they always do the same thing at the end of their walk. There's a sense of security in habit. He lights a cigarette, cupping his hands around the match against the wind, then passes the packet and the lighted cigarette to Roy who lights his own. They always do this. They know one another very well.

"What are we talking about?"

"What are we always talking about? What's the one thing on both our repressed juvenile minds from the moment we wake up until the last dregs of your awful coffee? Probably most of the night, too, in your case."

"Oh, sex."

"Oh, naturally. So what are we going to do about it?"

"Not a lot we can do until we find a couple of beautiful women, is there? And since we've been here ten days without the slightest hint of beauty in this town, there doesn't seem much point in having this conversation every day. Grief, why did we come to this place?"

"Because we're broke and my uncle's caravan is free. Anyway, you never know, do you? I mean, when fate will strike."

"Look, fate doesn't just leap out at people from the bushes. Not people like us, any road. And if it did, neither of us would know what to do with it, would we? That grammar school's got a lot to answer for. And because we wouldn't know, it won't happen."

"Is that Sartre or John Locke?"

"Laws of Physics."

"Well, I'd still like to get it straight, what we do if we ever get the chance. You never know. There must be a bored housewife or an aching nymph about, even here."

"Then let's hope they're not too choosy. Anyhow, I don't know that I want an aching nymph, sounds incurable."

"You know, you've got really pious lately. Doesn't suit you."

They lapse into silence again along the promenade, its pavements still patchy with rain although the day is beginning to brighten up. The tide is coming in, all cold rush and rattle, and the beach is empty except for a couple of hardy, dutiful families determined to do the proper seaside thing. Any other visitors will be snapping up china dogs and horse brasses in the souvenir shops or writing their cards in hotel lounges, preparing for the next fifty weeks until they can do all this again.

"But just supposing…" Paul tries again, fantasy preying on his mind. Roy pretends to be exasperated but allows himself to be drawn back in because he can't let go of it either. He has his own fixed, private image of who she will be and how it will be when it happens, as it must one day, an image shared only with Paul and then only after a couple of drinks. Neither of them is used to drinking any more than that, or to the excitement of it now that they're both of age, and in fact simply sitting in a bar is almost as heady as the alcohol.

She will be tall with long, straight blonde hair, willowy and with gentle, almost sad features, yet with an athletic body. He sees her at her best in an autumn cornfield or on the far shore of a mountain lake. She is nothing like Carol. When they meet – probably while both out walking on that shore and turning over poetry in their minds – they will have found all that is necessary. They'll hold hands, smile quietly and… well, the details haven't been worked out yet but naturally they'll make love quite soon and it will be a sacred thing. In a rickety yellow caravan? Heaven forbid. No, it would have to be in the dunes or beside that lake or deep within a forest… but then what if it's raining, or cold, or there are preying eyes?

"So I thought we'd agreed that whoever's first closes the kitchen curtains and is allowed three hours?"

"Hmm. Are you sure that's enough?" Paul is deeply puzzled. Neither of them has the faintest idea. And as the thought gets closer it brings a companion, a kind of cold fear, for neither of them is totally sure (despite the centrefolds) just what a girl looks like all over, front and back and all at once. Three hours surely can't possibly be enough. So the walk continues, past the gardens, the deserted bowling green and the Seaview Hotel.

The Seaview conforms to its name, orthodox and trite. Its plain, Victorian frontage has no distinguishing features whatsoever and but for its flaking green sign would be swallowed up by the rest of the terraced row that characterises this small town. Visitors come here because they ask for little, and that's exactly what's on offer, one hundred miles or three hours' drive with a short stop from the Black Country, for the convenience of those who live convenient lives. The place neither pretends nor demands, neither promises nor even goes out of its way. Certainly, those who come here are good people, the salt of the earth and mainstay of society; but they are the rest, when others have set the course of history.

Inside, the stiff white napkins are already folded into cones on stiff white tablecloths, even before the last of the late risers have finished their coffee. There is a high, mahogany-stained Reception desk unmanned in the threadbare Axminster carpeted hall, a half empty wall of key hooks behind it. On a low table beside glass double doors, heavy with wrought iron, sits a rubber plant and a selection of morning newspapers while in the lounge beyond the deep chairs are filling up with middle-aged fathers glancing at sports pages while they wait. Their wives arrive and sit with handbags on knees, unobtrusively studying one another in the long, gilded wall mirrors. From below stairs comes the distant, monotonous echo of table tennis balls. Children gradually emerge from various corners, quiet and well-mannered, and families heave themselves to their feet, fuss with their raincoats and set off in loose procession and at a fixed stroll to the outer doors. It is all very unenthusiastic.

"Crappy summer," Sally almost spits. She's pressed up against the window of the tiny top floor room, her head on one side with cheek squashed against an arm. She has long black hair and aquiline, freckled features. There is a dark attraction to her, especially as she is only wearing thin, pale blue pants and bra. The glass clouds with her breath and she draws a sad clown face on it with a lazy finger. "Hardly a wink of sun. Look at me, I'm completely white. It's crappy."

"You're supposed to be teaching me good English," murmurs Eva. She is also in underwear, sitting in the small armchair beside the bed with a newspaper on her folded legs. The radio is tuned, quietly, to pop.

"It is good English," Sally retorts. "It expresses exactly how I feel." In this sentence, we detect her slight Welsh accent. She peers down at the top of her breasts searching for some sign of tan, then laughs, singing along with the radio, "'If you're going to San Francisco you're gonna meet some gentle people there…' Oh, it's the same every bloody year here. Nothing ever happens and there's no-one to meet."

"Nothing will happen if you just sit here talking about it," Eva points out without looking up from the paper. "You have to go out."

"Where to? The Tulip Café? Miniature golf? Church? Anyway, it'll be time to start the lunches soon. Tell you what, though," her voice brightens, "we'll go out tonight, shall we? You're off after dinner, so we can have a few drinks – that place with the DJ, all right?"

"If you like, Sally."

"Yeah, we'll do that. Get you fixed up, eh?"

"Thank you, Sally, but I don't want to be fixed up, as you put it. Is that good English? Anyway, I'll be leaving soon. I have to go home."

"Well, I do even if you don't. And I can't go on my own so you can help me, isn't it?" She retreats into a broody silence and imagination. Her slim body wants so much to be given that it even hurts sometimes. Almost desperately, her quick eyes search the promenade in anticipation as Eva sets aside the newspaper and shakes herself out of her own anxious thoughts, getting up to stand behind her friend in time to see the two young men – not more than boys, really – who seem to pass every day at about this time on the opposite side of the road. Then they turn the corner and are lost from view.

"You never know, do you?" Sally continues. "I mean, there's billions of people in the world, everywhere's crawling with people, even this crummy place, and most of them are ordinary and boring like the guests here –"

"And like us?"

"– but you never know, do you? Maybe one of them's secretly really important, like a high-powered executive of a film studio with three cars and two mistresses, one for weekends and one for lunchtimes…"

"Oh, that would be Mr Arlington," says Eva, and they both convulse with laughter thinking of the short, very round man with a northern accent and equally stout, overbearing wife. As it happens, at this very moment the man is in the lounge below, longingly studying the picture of a surfer girl in a weekly magazine, his body tense as he keeps one nervous eye on the door. "See, you never know who people really are."

"You're right. There's that Miss Baines, always scribbling away. Said it's her diary when I asked, but she closed the book very fast. Maybe it's the latest chapter of a steamy novel about sadomasochism."

"Then she must have a very good imagination. Or a very long memory. She's about seventy."

"It takes all sorts, my Mam says. You never know. Look – see that car." She points out the lime green Chrysler as it turns slowly onto the promenade and follows it with a finger until it disappears. "Wow, you don't see many of them here. That'll be the Yank film director –"

"Or terrorist."

"– or baseball star –"

"Or KGB spy."

"Yeah, right, 'cause a small Welsh seaside town is the perfect place to go undercover when you're driving a massive American car. Yeah, right."

"So what about her?" says Eva, her own finger now on the glass pointing to the woman in a duffle coat, staring out to sea, long blonde hair tangled in the wind, hands thrust deep into pockets and legs astride in long black leather boots.

"Oh, she's obvious. Actress, Oscar-nominated for her tender bedroom scenes. Have you noticed how people in films always make love with a sheet between them? Bet she wouldn't, though. Now her marriage is falling apart and she's come here to get away from it all. In a minute her lover will suddenly appear across the road and they'll run into each other's arms –"

"And get run over by the film director in his big car." Eva turns away and starts to put on the white uniform dress before checking her make-up in the grimy mirror over the cracked sink. Sally leaves the window too and falls back onto the bed dreamily, willing life to arrive right now.

"All right, I know it's silly. But you never know, do you, I mean who's out there? Someone exciting. And I suppose everyone's a bit special in their own way. We've all got our secrets and dreams."

Eva stops what she's doing and turns to smile at her only British friend. "That's very wise, Sally. It's a good thought." She reaches a hand out to touch the other's hair gently and their eyes meet, for a moment each sensing the other's inner loneliness. "We'll go out tonight, then," Eva promises.

Φ

"I've just thought of something," says Paul, looking up from the crossword still sucking his pencil.

"About time," Roy replies absently, still reading.

"I mean, what if we both, um, you know, get lucky? We can't have three hours in the caravan at the same time."

"Logical."

"I mean, it would be very awkward."

"Definitely. And uncomfortable."

"So?"

"So what? It isn't going to happen. One more rhetorical question for the list." They're sitting at their usual table by the street window of the Tulip Café, ashtray and coffee cups on the green and white chequered plastic tablecloth. There are generic flower prints on the walls, a smell of burnt toast and the gurgle of a coffee machine. Tulip herself is at the counter filling an array of plastic boxes with sandwiches and home-made pies for delivery to local pubs. Today it's Paul's turn for the crossword while Roy studies the worrying front page, trying to get a grip of what's going on in another world while wondering whether he actually cares. They've done this same thing every day since arriving but neither is bored or dissatisfied; the accepting comfort of their friendship is mirrored in their routine. After all, university looms in a couple of months' time and who knows where that will take them. Breaking the strings of family, the stones of adolescence, is hard enough; knowing that even this uneasy innocence within must also soon break, they are grateful for an interval.

"But if you're first, what am I going to do for three hours?"

"Grief, Paul, use your imagination. Go for a walk."

"I've never walked that far in my life."

"It's the price of friendship. I'll leave the guitar outside for you, then."

"Nah, better not, you might need it. In fact, you'll probably need all the props you can get. EACB and all that. I'm stuck on five down."

Roy folds his pages and puts them down on the table, staring out across the sea as Mr Arlington and his wife pause outside to study the café menu. They look disinterested.

"Where is Czechoslovakia anyway?"

"Dunno," says Paul. "Turn right at Poland, I think. Why?"

"The papers are full of it. It was on the radio news this morning, too. Some sort of trouble."

"There's always some sort of trouble."

"This seems big. Aren't you supposed to be interested in politics? This is going to be your first lecture."

"Whatever turns you on." He drains his coffee and pushes back his chair. "What shall we do?"

"What do we always do?"

"Well, you say why don't I make any decisions then we have another cup of coffee and go to play golf."

There's only one small boy on the putting green behind the Seaview Hotel and he's running after his ball with every shot, keeping it moving and overtaking Roy and Paul. Roy takes a three at the ninth, retrieves his ball and stretches as if only now waking up. The day is stretching too, drying and warming. Paul hits his first shot within six inches of the hole.

"Another one to me," he observes, sliding the ball in with a foot and moving quickly on to the tenth. But Roy isn't watching, standing with his head on one side, towards the middle distance.

"You know when we passed the front of the hotel earlier? On the way to the café."

"What about it?"

"Well, I just happened to glance up at the top floor –"

"As you do."

"– and I'll swear there was a girl standing there with nothing on."

Paul slices his next shot but gets a hole-in-one at the third.

"Now you tell me?" He looks up and studies the rear of the hotel, its dirty brickwork and flaking black drainpipes, its yard strewn with rubbish. The lower windows are smoked grey and curtained. "Ever wondered what's going on behind curtains?"

"Another rhetorical one for the list."

ACT 2

Growing Pain

In an ornately panelled room high up in the Kremlin, the two men probably sat either side of a long, very solid oak table. They were watched over by a gilt-framed Lenin, a huge marble bust and by several stern images of Josef Stalin himself so there may be no mistaking his presence. It is his personal study. The other man was Winston Churchill. Otherwise alone, the two would have seemed almost insignificant here and in a sense they were. They were, after all, merely men who defecate in the morning, undress at night, eat bread, smoke tobacco, get ill and have private thoughts that they would rather no-one else knew about.

Of course, their power both personal and invested was greater than most others', the scope of their minds broader, their strategic instincts more developed. But these facts only make the depth of their stupidity that much greater. Like other men and women who have attained a certain age and independence, and who have quietly buried the ideals of their youth beneath the bathchair blanket folds of compromise and socioeconomic necessity, these leaders had learned the expediency of manipulating principles when faced with conflict. They would know that they could not be seriously questioned, for few would be glad to have their responsibility (and in any case would end up doing much the same). The difference with these two men was that for the sake of some transient security and the purchase of time, they were prepared to sign away the lives of millions of freeborn men and women and despatch the unborn to hard labour, like gamblers on a run throwing the numbers.

A large map would have been laid out on the table between them, a pall of tobacco smoke hanging over it as if over the battlefield that it was. This was May, 1944. Stalin and Churchill, in silent deep reflection, stared at boundaries and carved up Europe. One was mainly preoccupied with mineral rights, the other with the reaction of his Parliament. A blue crayon idly ticked off Bulgaria. Like some ludicrous, giant game of noughts and crosses, the edges were filled in and then they approached the critical centre. When Czechoslovakia was blue crayoned, Churchill would have shrugged; after all, it was not the first time a treaty had been broken.

A year later, Prague would be 'liberated' by the Soviet army and its people would resume their calm, cynical lives of hidden thought. That is, until June 1966 when a certain professor of Economics, leading an emergent intelligentsia, put in gear a movement that would claim the lives of a few score and irrevocably shape the souls of countless others.

Ф

In June 1966, Roy had been sixteen. He had bold ideas and was appallingly immature, never having experienced either freedom or discovery. At least he had a brain, he was working hard at school and thinking a lot. But then, there wasn't much else to do in the Midlands' suburbs, his family's home on the edge of town, far from the centre and a decent distance from the industrial heartlands that supported it. His was a cerebral, almost alien world of social ineptitude, without even the basic prerequisite of herd instinct (except briefly every fortnight at The Hawthorns); lacking any social foundations, his adolescence was proving painful.

It was a comfortable twenty-five minute walk around the estate, taken slowly, long enough to shake schoolmasters and the distant principles of Physics from his mind, and he took it most nights before bedtime. It was a habit. On these walks he also unconsciously learned the habit of glancing up at others' windows while imperceptibly slowing down in the shadows opposite Gaynor's house, for the sake of the silhouette.

On the other hand, lest this all seems too pathetic, and entirely without his realising it himself, Roy was developing independence, how to care for himself and how to remember his dreams. Their interpretation would come later. So at about this time, his guardian angels would probably have congratulated one another on getting him safely to this point and then sat back to wait for strokes of fate.

It probably wasn't fated that England should win the World Cup that summer, but it might as well have been because there were a number of important consequences. One of these was that English people began to talk to one another.

"I hear King Edward's beat us four nil on Saturday. The firsts could do with Nobby Stiles, eh? 'They shall not pass'."

"Yeah, but then he'd be in detention for a month."

"Still, we might win the odd match."

"S'pose. What's in your sandwiches?"

"Cheese and pickle. Wanna swop?"

"Haven't seen you around."

"I'm Languages. We live right on the other side of the field."

"Maths and Phys. Is that the NME you've got?"

And so Roy met Paul in the sandwich room at school one lunchtime. They began to do some folk songs together and Paul taught his new friend basic guitar chords. Apart from burdening the world with a few new songs it could do without, this discovery began slowly, creakily, to winch open the heavy gates of Roy's right brain hemisphere.

For another thing, the World Cup win enabled Roy to find out about girls from the waist up. To any football fan who saw it, that Final would remain in the memory as a deeply moving experience, a pulsating, edge-of-the-seat match (which the better team did not win). It was won by nationalism, by prayer, and by 96,924 surging voices singing out the desperate necessity of a small nation to achieve something that wouldn't even rate a footnote in another generation's history books.

In the Reeves' small front room with its green patterned carpet, brown striped wallpaper and glass animal ornaments (the ten inch giraffe was especially beautiful), sitting with Carol's family, Roy felt depths of joy and anguish and community that he'd never suspected before. Even Carol, who didn't like football, was touched by his reactions. So when her parents later went out, she decided to wash her hair and leave the bathroom door open. When Roy wandered in, on the edge of tears, she had embraced him and helped him with the clasp at her back. They held each other for five minutes. Nothing more. But the wonder of it! Nobody else before or since has ever scored a hat-trick in a World Cup Final.

These were days of music and flowers, beads and long hair, of reaction and rips in the social fabric (though not quite yet in the English suburbs). The newly pretentious student intelligentsia sensed that this was no mere ripple in the waves of evolution but a paradigm leap. The world began to crackle with the snapping of ties of deference.

Φ

Admittedly, there were few hippies in 1967 Prague, yet the Manifesto that followed the Writers' Congress was if nothing else at least an invitation. During the evening of October the 29th, in his small room off Karmelitska, Josef is in earnest discussion with Eva and an engineering student, Jan Hájek, about the expulsion from the Party of a friend who had spoken in Congress. Conversations about politics lead naturally to pessimism about the future.

"There isn't one," says Jan morosely. "Not for people like us. Me, you know, I've studied for five years and next summer I qualify a skilled man. And for what? They'll give me a job but no career. Sik will never get his way."

"I like the Manifesto," Eva offers.

"You don't believe that shit, do you? It's just paper. 'Incentives' and 'market economy'? It's capitalism in a bearskin. Your average cannon-fodder Czech wouldn't recognise an incentive if it crawled up his trouser leg and bit his balls. All he can see is food prices going up. I already know I'll be earning less than my cousin who's never spent a day in college."

"But these ideas –" begins Josef.

"Ideas don't work. And they don't put food in your mouth. The people who have them are all too busy playing chiefs and Indians and watching their backs to actually do anything with them. The rest of us just keep our heads down and stay quiet until it all goes away, `cause it will eventually."

"Don't be such a cynic," smiles Eva.

"I'm a realist." His invective is squashed out with his cigarette in the damp saucer they're using for an ashtray. Josef sighs and gets up, hands thrust into pockets as he wanders over to the window to survey the bitter early winter evening. He's silent for a few moments because he cannot believe what he's seeing, then there's a sharp intake of breath.

"Christ! Come and look at this – it's a march!"

The others are incredulous, at the window in a moment, then searching hurriedly for overcoats so they can join the students from the Strahovska hostel. Faces are fixed and determined within their wrappings, eyes narrowed against the mist, the mood as chilling as the air. Electricity has failed again and the students are cold and hungry and they cannot work. They wear neither beads nor flowers and carry nothing more offensive than lighted candles and textbooks as they cross the ancient bridge and move towards Old Town Square.

But they get no further than Jilska where the grotesquely masked police are waiting, lined up across the road, five to one. Josef pulls Eva back into the shadows; as a journalist, he has a pretty good idea what comes next and it does. Within seconds it has all gone wrong. The young man in the lead is Pavel Dušek, a student of English. He stops in surprise, raises an arm and calls out "Wait!" but a girl behind him pushes him forward towards the drawn pistols. A few other students try to break away in confused disbelief or just stand still in resignation, but none of it makes any difference. With an angry curse, the unthinkable is suddenly in full flood, ideas splintering with weapon butts on skulls, eyes streaming with gas and despair. Reality runs riot. Yet more police pour from the direction of the river to cut off any retreat, passing Josef and Eva, frozen and shrinking back hard against a doorway. Within minutes, the small, peaceful group is crushed. There are candles strewn absurdly across the street, some still flickering weakly, among crying and moaning bodies that can't get up. They're dragged away to the waiting vans anyway. Just one policeman remains lying there, his slipped mask revealing a human face, groaning with the ignominy of a torn knee ligament.

Jan is among those arrested. Clutching his useless arm, he is bundled away by four officers but still manages to turn back, eyes pleading not to see Eva. He will not, after all, qualify a skilled man next summer.

Φ

Soon after this, Eva left for England to study the language while supporting herself with whatever menial job her university could find for her. It was ironic, if nothing else, that their contacts were in Liverpool, a place with probably the strongest accent in the country. But the Party knows best.

And it was at the same time that Roy was having the first big, confrontational row with his father. It was a turning point, one more deferential tie broken, at last.

"Mooning about over some foolish girl –" Carol had broken up with him a few weeks before "– and getting your mother worried. Stuck in your room writing stupid songs. Going out walking alone at night. Don't you think there are more important things in life, like your A Levels and getting a weekend job? Money doesn't appear by magic, boy, people have to work for all this." He points one arm out towards the pleasantly decorated and carpeted hallway, standing belligerently at the foot of the stairs as if to follow his son up.

Roy stops and turns on the second stair, fortuitously now head and shoulders above his father. As his muscles tense and eyes begin to burn, he feels for only the second time in his life that strong, involuntary throb of the vein just above the left corner of his mouth. The first time he had felt it, a year or so before, the sarcastic bullying at school had stopped abruptly. It is a sign, small but unmistakable, of a rising power. His father now sees it too and turns away with a shrug even before the cold "Leave me alone" has ended. It is probably one of the shortest rows in history but nonetheless significant for that.

He has a long way to travel yet but at long last he is gaining that first priceless awareness of ego, the ability to affect others. It is the key to self. For most of his life he has felt awkward and distant from others, as if in the wrong place and time and probably the wrong family too. The world of Maths and Physics and engineering is no doubt good and valuable, and it is also familiar; he has never met any adult men who were not either teachers or engineers, and he has always been made to feel subservient to them. Now another person is emerging, one who need not be so full of fear, who is free to explore not only bookish achievements but interesting and possibly dark alternatives. After all, other people seem to make a living by growing vegetables or building houses, selling cigarettes or driving cars (Roy has recently started taking lessons). And whatever his father says, the beautiful guitar with its highly polished rosewood and resonant gut strings is becoming ever more important in this new order. Roy will never be a musician but he is beginning to appreciate something about being human that few people ever seem to: some ideas and experiences cannot be expressed in words.

It was a pity about Carol but he knows now that there'll be others. It was sort of a pity that he also found himself without religion, having recently stopped going to church with his mother – again, it was all too distant as well as boring – but oddly enough God seemed still to be hanging around in his mind. So like the melting cap of an iceberg running headlong down its own length, he is finding that his life needs to be wholly restructured. He'll have to do it alone too. Yes, he does have one very good friend, met in the sandwich room at school just over a year ago, but Paul is already content with his own life (in fact he always has been) and while he is more than happy to discuss philosophy it's not something that impinges on daily life.

Φ

Those who call themselves evolutionists and hold that the sine waves of history rise and fall in self-regulating and predictable patterns of social movements and ideas[1], sometimes erratic yet forging ever onwards, are far-sighted. They are also blind. For one thing, they tend not to see that each huge turning point in the affairs of mankind owes its life to an individual and these outsiders are remarkably few. So the patterns are neither continuous nor inevitable. Yes, there are certainly 'ideas whose time has come', say for example the discovery of the calculus simultaneously by Isaac Newton and Gottfried Leibniz, independently some seven hundred miles apart and the biggest game-changer for centuries in the development of Mathematics. But even this depended on the brilliance of an individual mind.[2]

For another thing, some would say, socialisation is the merest surface tension on men's vast, primeval swamp of emotions. It is hardly natural and barely necessary. At heart, Man is a suicidal fish eager to grasp any appealing hook that promises security. Being educated, he will follow where the school leads. And while his leaders play snowballs on mountain peaks, their ill-aimed efforts roll down onto the rest in avalanches. The 'patterns' of human life are brought about by sudden, small and fateful revolutions to which the herd willingly sign up.

---

[1] Perhaps the Russian sociologist Pitirim Sorokin, Paul thought? Rather ironically, he would die early the next year and Paul would refer to the fact during the holiday in Wales.
[2] Actually, to be entirely honest, neither of the above but that of the uncredited Reverend Isaac Barrow, Newton's tutor at Cambridge.

When change comes, its pace can be terrifying. In a strange, dark mansion of ignorance and confusion, Man flounders about a room, groping his way round the furniture until he happens to trip a switch. Immediately, the room floods with light and shadow, with images and perspective. The shafts of light lead through previously unknown doors to other rooms and other switches until at last the mansion is ablaze with light. Then what does he do? His eyes growing dim with the familiarity of it all, he leaves by the back door to seek another mansion. We die and we are born again a billion times.

As the light of dawn rises over Roy's personal desert island, others are rushing towards darkness. In December, a few weeks after the student rebellion, five hundred Communist Party officials in Slovakia petition one Alexander Dubček for the dismissal of Antonín Novotný, Head of State. The Praesidium splits. Troops move briefly towards Bratislava and Prague as the anger of intellectuals and workers alike flashes. On January 5th, 1968, Dubček becomes leader of the Communist Party and, as spring arrives, Ludvík Svoboda, national hero of two world wars, is President.

It isn't so much that an undercurrent of proletarian beliefs and ideals has now finally broken through the surface of public life, bearing on its crest natural leaders, more that the climate has actually changed. The nation and its people have changed. The swell soon becomes a tidal surge that ultimately can barely be controlled even by its own masters.

For the moment, at least, the pen is mighty and Josef grasps his opportunity eagerly. The loss of Eva has been a passing blow but hardly crippling. "Now," he confides complainingly to anyone who will listen, in the manner of one who has innocently suffered an unjust slap of fate, "I shall be associated with the West." Yet before long he finds himself amply compensated as press censorship is abolished and a golden age of the pamphlet dawns. His career is going somewhere. He doesn't meet with Jan when his old friend is finally released, for a chameleon never shows its true colours; instead, he moves with entirely new friends, treading the pavements of newly emerging routes. No human ideal, he reminds himself, can be both pure and practical. Now that there is freedom of travel, he does briefly consider the possibility of following Eva, making the dramatic gesture, the foreign crusade. But it is too much trouble. Moreover, here at home there are positions to be usurped in the new faith, there are disciples to be chosen, gospels to be edited and parables to be picked to pieces.

In England, to the despair of his parents and amusement of Paul, Roy is doing much the same thing. On one of his longer walks in January into the countryside near the family home, a soft glow of sunset above the elms, he pauses by a farm gate to look out across a field towards distant grazing animals and suddenly his whole being is touched by the natural beauty he is part of. It is not just a passing appreciation, such as that felt when gazing through the window of a speeding car. It is a moment of revelation. "I am a pantheist, then," he told himself. For the first time, he can feel the possibility of love. And just as all his peers are beginning to reject religion, Roy finds himself infested with it inside and out.

All revelatory moments have their own peculiar drawbacks. For one thing, this new and rather vague faith has no church to attend nor scripture to follow and definitely no parables to unpick. Regrettably, nor are there any other disciples in Roy's world. His gauche zeal is, however, undimmed. When the school Careers Master, intent on filling up his form, asks Roy's religion, the reply causes considerable perplexity. A senior Master is summoned and feels obliged to deliver a thunderous affirmation of Anglicanism. He is followed, at lunchtime, by the Chaplain who tries a more conciliatory and rhetorical approach. "How may God be everyone and everywhere? There are no pronouns to accommodate it." Notes are made in the backs of minds and the fronts of files, but none of it has the slightest effect on Roy. This is something that is necessary at the moment. Perhaps unconsciously his mind is responding, "I might stop if you don't tell me to…"

In a parallel world, when the New Revised Modern Language Edition of socialism, the April Action Programme, hits the streets of Prague, ministers of the Warsaw Pact draw their vestments tightly about them and convene a synod of the old ways in Dresden. Freedom of trade, of assembly and of expression, will surely turn the temple into a marketplace. As visitors stop coming, Dubček begins to feel a disease taking hold in the new body of opinion, and he pleads with his editors in vain.

In a similar way, though on a rather smaller scale, Roy now also finds himself even more ostracised from those around him than he has always felt. In search of company, he has only his own self and that's not much help at all. Pantheism – or whatever it will turn out to be – has no church but the fields, rivers, woods and sky. Its hymns are birdsong and the rustling of animals, foreign languages all. Moreover, it has no vestments whatsoever and little intuition is required to recognise how dangerous a love of the human body is in middle-class, suburban England, being some distance from Monterey. At the age of ten, Roy had been given some Marriage Guidance booklets to read and ever since then had found that his parents would unexpectedly turn off the television part-way through programmes. In school Assemblies there were vague references to something called "abuse" while the favourite jokes among the boys were always about lavatories and nipples. Roy might as well have lived on another planet.

But he is astute enough to realise that his nascent faith needs some kind of framework, even someone else's if necessary, within which to test out feelings and ideas. There have to be some axioms to climb onto, even if sometimes he falls and bruises his pride. So he begins to look for an acceptable name and social group, somewhere to belong that wouldn't mobilise others' armed forces. He takes himself to a Catholic mass one week and an Anglican service the next. In between, he finds that he doesn't enjoy the family roast dinner as much as he used to. He gives the Baptists a try and, to the evident delight of a bus queue, allows himself to be drawn into debate on the street by two Jehovah's Witnesses. Paul finds the whole thing so amusing and distracting that, at their next regular Saturday evening at the tennis club, he loses six straight frames of snooker despite an agitated Roy drinking too much.

Something of a breakthrough does come soon after, though, in a most unlikely small, cold and undecorated hall where a flock of about twenty apparently very ordinary, mostly middle-aged people are dotted about on decidedly uncomfortable chairs. There isn't one new hat to be seen. The organist twice plays the wrong tune and then drops her music onto the keyboard halfway through the reading, which is from de Chardin. But this is no Jesuit group. Instead of a sermon, a youngish woman with flaming hair and deep green eyes is apparently speaking with the spirits of the dead and passing on messages and advice to their relatives in the hall. Amazingly, some of these messages do seem to make sense to the flock. Not knowing of any dead relatives anyway, Roy watches it all with a detached fascination; at one point, the medium's eyes meet his and there is a brief flash of something between them – she will later tell him that they have shared a previous life together ("Ha, I bet she says that to all the boys," will be Paul's response) but she doesn't pass on any message to him. After this, there is an announcement about something called spiritual healing and then people drink tea together.

Marian, the medium, comes over to Roy and they chat for a while about this being his first awareness of Spiritualism, etcetera. He finds her vitality and simple conviction very attractive; she's quite sexy too, though considerably older than him, her eyes and mouth bearing lines of experience. Whether it's this, or others' welcome, he begins to feel more at home here than anywhere else. It may not be the most socially acceptable group – and it will arouse even more derision from his father – but it's an interesting compromise and there are some astonishing beliefs involved that are worth more than a second thought.

Φ

"Just suppose that what they say is true! Imagine that these things could really work out," Jan says animatedly to his brother Gustáv. His earlier cynicism is gone, replaced by an angry determination that was born on the night of the march. More than an arm had been broken then. "We have to give it a chance. There'll probably never be another opportunity like this."

"For what?" Gustáv drawls. "Cheap denims? Pornography?" He's only arguing for the sake of it, as brothers do in the mutual education programme of functional families. All the same, he is that much older and a respected married man with children and a job. Security is hard enough to come by and he speaks with the voice of one who has had to struggle through life but actually hasn't. "How can you ever win? Sooner or later they'll crucify you, one side or the other. Someone will. You just won't be… I don't know, allowed. People like us never are."

"But this isn't something that someone's just thought up and scribbled on the back of an envelope," Jan insists, leaning forward across their parents' white lace tablecloth. A cup of strong coffee grows cold beside his elbow while their mother silently busies herself at the greasy cooker behind him. Through the open kitchen door, the early summer morning still holds a slight chill. In the yard outside, Gustáv's young son kicks a football while his pregnant mother, in a shapeless, long black skirt and with a woollen shawl about her shoulders, cradles the baby and watches on. "It's really happening," Jan continues, "it's here and now. If we just give it a chance, it might work. Don't you see what that could mean? Dignity. Freedom. Something different."

"That's why," sighs their mother, without turning from the cooker, "it won't work."

Her daughter-in-law shivers, wrapping the shawl more closely about her, and comes to stand motionless in the doorway. Her shadow just touches Jan's shoulder. Even the boy seems to sense that some strange adult secret is in the air and comes to stand beside his mother, holding on to her leg, as his ball bounces aimlessly away across the yard. In the silent moment, Jan's thoughts flash to Eva, without his quite knowing why except that she would have understood what he was feeling now. She hadn't been his girl, but she would have understood. His hands clench the edge of the table tightly.

Eva takes another cigarette from the pack open on the canteen table, licks the end and lights it from the one offered by her friend. She blows a long, slow stream of smoke down across their empty plates and leans back limply with a heavy head, dropping the folded newspaper into the small pile of library books in front of her. Dubček's name is across the front page. With lowered eyes, she seems oblivious of the lunchtime bedlam around them, the rise and fall of chatter, the clatter of trays and cutlery, the criss-crossing of young angels in starched white uniforms. Nurse Mallory watches her across the table with genuine pity and finally reaches forward a hand to touch Eva's arm gently.

"You need a holiday, my love. You can't go on like this, so you can't. You're miserable and exhausted, and who'd blame you?" Her Irish lilt is at its best like this, quietly reasoning. "Anyway, a hospital kitchen's no place for you, up to your elbows in other people's dirt and leftovers."

"I have to work." Eva's voice can barely be heard. There's nothing moving within her. "The train home is expensive."

"Holy Mary, you're not going back there –" the words are enough to prompt a single tear from Eva's eye "– not yet anyway. It's dangerous."

"But I should. My family –"

"Your family wouldn't thank you. You're safe here, well off out of it so you are. And isn't it you're here to learn English, anyway? That's what they'd want for you, your Mam and Dad, a better life. Mind you –" she gestures around the canteen with one arm "– you could've picked a better place for it. This place is full of Paddies 'n scousers. We can hardly understand each other half the time." Eva smiles weakly and squeezes her friend's fingers.

"But I think I must go. It's where I belong."

"I get that, to be sure, I do. But not just yet, eh? No harm in a few more weeks, an' you need a rest, get away from here."

"I have to work," Eva repeats with a shrug as if it's programmed into her.

"Well…" Nurse Mallory casts about in her mind and suddenly a solution bites. She cannot imagine how big this catch will be. "Then it's a working holiday you'll be needing, and I've got just the t'ing for you. My old man knows some people with a hotel in Wales. By the seaside. Sure an' they'll take you on, they always need people this time of year. You might as well learn English there as here, and you'll get a bit of holiday too. How's that?" She slaps the table in triumph and that was that.

Φ

A Levels are over and the summer is still hot. Roy has passed his driving test first time and his father has bought him his first car, an ageing Ford, which he is now driving confidently through the twists and cambers of country roads. It's the family's annual holiday – the last that Roy will take with them – and his parents are following behind in the large Morris. Roy's thoughts are tumbling one upon another anxiously, changing direction with every shaft of sunlight through the overhanging trees.

He tries to explain to his younger sister sitting beside him, not that she will understand let alone sympathise but he just has to say it out loud. He'd called Marian and left a message but there had been no response. So maybe he'd been wrong about everything after all. It had felt natural, as though things were falling into place in his mind, but now he wasn't going anywhere. When he'd gone back to the little church – the only time he'd voluntarily gone twice to a church – the whole evening had been ludicrous. Some obese woman in a billowing floral dress had read interminably from the obscure sayings of someone called Silver Birch, and then embarked on a soliloquy on the moral depravity of modern youth, all the while shooting poignant glances at Roy whose long hair was held back with a purple headband. Then a thin, stooping medium had delivered excruciatingly banal spirit messages ("They are with you in the kitchen – be careful with that breadknife!") to three people, one of whom had to be prodded awake by her husband. The ripe apple of knowledge was riddled, after all, with maggots. The shining jewel was cheap plastic.

"Well, no wonder Mum and Dad are so annoyed with you all the time," remarks his sister, perceptively. "You're not like them, are you? And it does all seem a bit dross."

He cannot argue with that and is angry with himself for not being able to articulate his instincts. His sister puts a hand on his arm and he realises that he's driving too fast. At the same moment, there's a furious flashing of headlights from the road behind. So that won't help the general mood.

The family holiday is not a success. They've been to the same self-catering apartment in the same southern seaside resort five years in a row and there are no more discoveries to be made. The apartment is now too small for them anyway, there's no private space, so Roy cannot help being bored and needing to go for long walks alone on the beach, his mind racing with A Levels, Marian and Carol. He hasn't even been allowed to bring his guitar. Naturally, all of this only irritates his parents even more.

"You're worrying your mother sick," his father rages, his wife sitting tensely with a vacant expression, her face turned away. It's nearly midnight and Roy has just returned from watching waves. "If it's not one thing it's another. All these silent moods. Going off on your own all the time, playing at hippies. When you do talk it's psychic mumbo-jumbo. Plain selfish. All we've done for you and how do you repay us? I buy you a car and you drive like a maniac." This is not exactly a coherent argument but its force is unmistakable. "My God, you're going to university in a few weeks. Don't you think it's time to grow up? Meanwhile, this is a family holiday."

The vein begins to throb again slightly. It's another turning point. Roy looks his father in the eye.

"This is not a family," is all he says.

He drives home alone later, rather too fast again, wondering how God had come into it. He had left school only a few weeks before, with relief that the happiest days of his life were now over. All the leavers had been smiling, exchanging peace signs during the final Assembly, a few of them with a small flower tucked behind one ear, all full of bright optimism for the future. Now, already, shadows are closing in again.

"Jeez," he mutters next day to Paul, describing the debacle, "I need another holiday."

"Okay, then." His friend is quite good at ignoring a mood and thus changing it. "Let's see if we can borrow my uncle's caravan in Wales."

Φ

Elsewhere, there are other shadows closing in. The Warsaw Pact troop lorries had crossed the Czech border for "exercises" on May 30th and had stayed far into July because of "logistical problems" and "abnormal traffic". The arm of family friendship is turning inwards on itself. Perhaps this is not, after all, a family.

The workers' militia fails to take the hint. Jan's family stiffen at his side. Eva arrives at the Seaview Hotel and meets Sally. President Svoboda receives a letter from Warsaw. Soviet reservists are called up along the western frontier.

Two trains approach each other slowly, warily, on a single track at Čierna nad Tisou near the Ukrainian border with Slovakia, stopping a few yards apart. The two countries' railways have different gauges. The platform is invisible beneath a mass of heavy black boots as soldiers close simultaneously around Leonid Brezhnev, Nikolai Podgorny, Alexei Kosygin, trade union leader Alexander Shelyepin and the rest at one end and Ludvík Svoboda, Alexander Dubček and Josef Smrkovský at the other.

Much later in the evening, the place is deserted except for a solitary figure wandering beside the track with shoulders hunched, watching the parallel steel lines stretch away into the distance, never meeting.

"Why don't you sleep, comrade?" a gruff voice asks from the shadows of the office doorway when the figure approaches. The old railwayman steps forward to identify himself, wiping greasy hands on his blue overalls.

"I don't usually sleep until four," the other replies softly. He smiles weakly. "Too much to do now anyway."

"Will you have some coffee, then?"

He joins the small group of workers in the office and accepts a chipped mug. There aren't enough chairs so the youngest gives up his place out of respect.

"Going badly, then, is it?" asks another.

"Shelyepin's almost had me by the balls. Not a polite man," Dubček almost grins. "And Brezhnev's feigning illness, so I think he's upset."

"We heard that the troops are moving," stutters the young man nervously, now standing by the window. He's supposed to be getting married soon. Dubček nods tiredly.

"In Poland and the GDR, yes. But they're still on the other side of the border."

The old man laughs and claps his leader on the shoulder.

"Well, that's all right, eh? Shows we're important. All the same, comrade," his voice full of concern, "you look exhausted. You should take a holiday when this is over."

ACT 3
Birth

In the street, the jangling guitars of the Rolling Stones are muted behind the heavy oak-effect doors of The Willow and the leaded windows almost throb with the shouts and stamping of feet inside. Satisfaction. A glass smashes and a cheer goes up. It is one of those mock Tudor pubs with black beams and whitewashed walls and authentic Renaissance prints of monks on the walls. And a DJ at the weekends. Outside, a small herd of motor scooters graze together at the side of the road, their mirrors breaking the thin streetlight into a hundred pieces. The night is still warm, with an unthreatening blanket of cloud, and the ruddy horizon promises a fine tomorrow.

Noise explodes onto the street as the doors swing open revealing four somewhat unsteady silhouettes. Beyond them can be seen Phil, the landlord, leaning back against the bar. He is short and stocky, his sleeves rolled up over enormous hairy forearms, belly spilling over a thin leather belt. Narrow eyes survey his young, happy customers with transparent disdain. Still, they'll buy him a new car soon.

A young policeman strolls past and pauses but soon moves on. There'll be no trouble while Phil's around. The four figures emerge and gather into pairs, the doors closing behind them and swallowing up the noise. A solitary gull, up late, wheels and cries above them as they set off along the narrow street of souvenir shops and cafés, turning by the tree-masked churchyard towards the promenade. Eva watches in amusement as Sally, now ten yards ahead, half-heartedly pushes away the boy she's found and then wraps herself with an infectious giggle in his arm. He's not a film director, terrorist or KGB spy, though perhaps at the moment no less dangerous. The older youth sees Eva's smile and feels encouraged, a strong arm groping her shoulder and pulling her clumsily towards him, but she evades him. She's had plenty of practice. He's a bit confused but doesn't complain. After all, he has bought several vodkas so he has rights and will try again later.

As they approach the back of the hotel, Sally and the boy are welded together on the seventeenth green, backs arched as they push tightly together with hands beneath each other's jackets. They regroup by the back gate, broken and hanging from one hinge.

"Thank you, Carl," says Eva, "it was a nice evening." He leans at her again on unsteady legs but opens his eyes to see the back of her head moving away. "Sorry, I'm engaged," she says over her shoulder.

Sally and the boy don't speak. It would be pointless over the scream of their bodies. The girls let themselves in at the back door and feel their way through the dark kitchen, tiptoeing through the lobby past the night porter, dozing with a newspaper over his face. They hardly exchange a word at the top of the stairs.

"It was good music."

"Yeah. See you in the morning."

Within her room, Eva leans back against the door for a moment in the darkness, sadly waiting for the inevitable. It's barely three minutes before the soft tread of feet is just outside and the door of Sally's room creaks open. Her muted giggle can be heard as two people stumble inside. There is the light crack of knee on armchair, a low curse and hushing, and soon a rhythmic silence. Eva crosses to the window and looks out beyond the white horses. Her eyes returning to the promenade, she sees Carl mooching away beneath the insipid pool of a streetlamp, hands in pockets, kicking idly at the flowerbed. Half an hour later, feet pad away on the landing for the last time and soon there is a light tap on her door.

"Eva, are you awake?"

She has barely moved all this time and now crosses the room to let her friend in.

"Did you mean it? What you said." Sally's voice is wistful. "You said you were engaged. Is that true?"

"Does it matter?" Eva's voice is flat, tired. She pauses as if considering the matter and studies the fingers of her left hand. "No. Yes. Sort of. I was with someone back home."

"Oh, well, that's all right, then," Sally sounds satisfied. "See you in the morning." And with that she slips away to her bed and the warmth of fresh memories. Eva goes back to the window, breathes on the glass to mist it over and writes "Brzo".[3] But the letters run immediately.

In the caravan, with coffee, Paul is half asleep but he still wants to complain.

"Two days left, that's all. Two days. There won't be another chance like that. Those two girls were well up for it."

"You can tell these things, can you?" Roy is sardonic and has the advantage of feeling perversely wide awake. He is wired, his nerves on edge, knowing that there was an opportunity and he let it go. Yet he's also glad of that somehow.

---

[3] "Soon."

"You just sat there trying to make up your mind while they were well up for it. They saw us looking at them. But you let those two wallies get in first."

"Krauts."

"Eh?"

"They were krauts, not wallies. German. The master race."

"They were wallies. And so were you. Two days, that's all. Now, nothing."

"Poor you. Not even a bit of tit." He ducks but the pillow still catches him on the side of the head.

"Don't pretend you're not up for it as much as the next guy. Truth is, you wouldn't know what to do anyway, would you?"

"You're probably right," Roy nods, good humour in inverse proportion to his friend's frustration. "Fair enough. Though I guess everyone works it out for themselves when the time comes otherwise we wouldn't be here. But no, that's not why."

"No? Well what, then? Why did you sit there like a lemon when the thing we talk about every day was right there for the taking?"

Roy thinks back over all those juvenile conversations and asks himself the same question. The fact is, despite it all, he's feeling relieved. He's glad of whatever it was that kept him in his seat while a hovering Paul was looking him in the eye. For one thing, he'd never imagined it being like that, in a tacky pub with music pounding, alcohol swirling, everybody there with one thing on their minds and being watched over by Phil the gorilla. And for another thing… he finally puts his finger on it.

"Tomorrow morning."

"Eh? What?" Paul is genuinely incredulous.

"I was thinking about the morning. When you wake up. See, tonight it's all writhing limbs and hot skin, all sighs and groans –"

"Oh, thighs and groans…"

"– and the lights are out and you can't think 'cause you're pissed. That's what we imagined, wasn't it? Assuming by some divine stroke of fortune two attractive girls wanted it as much as we do, and that's not a given. But then there's the morning when you wake up and have to face her sober. Most people aren't very pretty in the morning. Well, I know you're not –"

"Thanks, I'm sure."

"– and people smell because they didn't bother to wash last night and your throat's like a camel driver's pants and your teeth are all silted up and there's dirty clothes on the floor and you've forgotten her name. So it's all embarrassing and I don't want it to be like that, just for the sake of it."

"You were thinking all that, were you? You know all about these things?" Paul is smarting but his brain is close to shutting down now.

"Stands to reason. There has to be a better way. I did us a good turn."

"Well forgive me for not thanking you." Paul kicks his shoes off and falls back onto the bed as he is, turning his face to the thin metal wall. "By the way," he mutters, "the dragons have long since had all the virgins."

The night is very still as Roy quietly lets himself out into it, carrying the guitar, a flask of coffee and a towel. The moon is riding high and the lights of a trawler blink slowly, dimly near the horizon. He picks his way carefully through the campsite, silently treading down the grasses and skirting the tents. There is light snoring and the rustle of bodies turning over in their sleep, but otherwise, here at least, he has the night's undivided attention. His head is clear and there is an inner pleasure in being the only one awake. He makes for the dunes and follows their line along the beach to the isolated hollow he'd found on the very first evening here, spreading out the towel.

For several minutes he does nothing, letting the evening's events and the conversation in the caravan slip from his mind as gradually the sea takes hold again. Then he picks up the guitar and has the next bar: A… C… E… D… moving with slow phrasing into D minor. Then A… E… C… D…

That's all for now, but the strength of the theme developing within him is lifting his spirit now. He sits back with eyes closed against the hollow and feels suddenly depersonalised, for some reason remembering childhood nights of dreaming that he was flying high above a desert of black sand whose every grain glistened as though it were a giant sheet of glasspaper. It had happened night after night, though he never knew where he'd gone or what it meant. Those days might be irrevocably lost but now, just for an instant, his every sense takes in the sand and the air, the mountain behind and the sea ahead, the rustle of grass and the slither of pebbles – one brief moment of realising the inconceivable, seeing the wind in empty space, being one with all and knowing that his instincts were right. There is such a thing as love.

Then it's gone as worldly thoughts inevitably intrude and he sits up feeling a little foolish, still too young to realise how much has to be abandoned.

He drinks some coffee from the flask and smokes two cigarettes, then noiselessly returns to the campsite. A few yards from the first tent he almost falls over a young couple hidden in the shadows of long grasses. The boy is leaning back on his elbows as the girl lies across his chest. Roy stops for a moment in surprise but they are not in the least embarrassed and simply look at him with amusement. A flush comes to his face for no good reason, except that he had been worlds away and is now back among others with no idea of how much time has passed, where he'd gone or what it meant.

Inside, he slips into bed and pulls the blanket tightly around him, still wakeful and watching the sky through a small gap in the curtain as it almost imperceptibly begins to lighten. He is not aware of sleeping but awakens to find the sheet clinging to him with sweat and sunshine streaming through the windows. He had dreamed that he was the captain of the ship about which folk singers say they have the strangest dreams. The vessel was pitching and rocking in waves that seemed as high as the clouds and he stood at a wheel that spun uncontrollably between his fingers as spray lashed his back. A small group of writers stood around him in a circle, examining his expressions and noting down everything he said to use for themselves. Finally, a figure dressed all in white and with a kind face had appeared beside him and said, "Life is a heady game, my friend. Make yourself ready, or you won't know when life has begun."

It's past eleven and Roy is annoyed with himself for having lost the morning. He is alone and on the kitchen worktop are the remains of Paul's breakfast, a greasy plate, an empty tin of beans and a saucepan of cold water. Whose turn was it this morning? He takes a pad and writes down the dream before washing, dressing and making some food for himself, only then drawing back the curtains. The campsite looks deserted. There's no sign of Paul. He considers trying the café and the putting green, but the routine has been broken now. So he makes another flask of coffee and takes towel, guitar and writing pad up to the lip of the grassy dune that overhangs the beach.

The night tide's crop of new stones lie in a swathe across the beach like mushrooms that have sprung up in the dark, the sea now distant. On the open expanse of sand there are several families setting about enjoying the unexpected heat of the day, the best of the summer so far. Castles are rising up, kites are flying and balls of every kind are bouncing. Roy's eyes track each group in turn, beginning to smile, his thoughts calming. Then as if to assert that he is back in this world, he stands and walks across the dunes down to the beach himself, spreading the towel, lighting a cigarette and inaudibly fingering the guitar.

Before long, Paul's unmistakable figure can be seen approaching, the day's newspaper under one arm. Somehow he walks from just above the knees with a low centre of gravity, grounded. There is a little uneasiness between them when he arrives, the conversation monosyllabic at first, but nevertheless Paul sits beside his friend and passes over the crossword page of the paper.

Soon it's lunchtime and as if at the silent call of a gong the families begin to gather their things together and drift away towards the promenade. Eva watches them go from the shelter of the overhang where she sits, a couple of open books spread beside her. It's Sally's turn to waitress the lunches today, despite her pounding head.

The beach now almost deserted, Eva stands and stretches, rising onto her toes and drinking in the sun's warmth through the pores of her athletic body. One cannot be lonely when the elements themselves are within, and in this moment she is at peace, a young girl again who wants nothing more than to perform, to jump and to swing between bars, to show off and prove that the training wasn't all wasted. Slowly and with perfect control, she steps forward with arms raised, cartwheels, stands and wheels again.

The movement catches Roy's eye and he turns from the newspaper, surprised and then transfixed. He cannot look away, his eyes following her as she steps forward and wheels again, the very slowness of it electrifying. Involuntarily, he raises himself on one knee, magnetised, some unknown voice within him shouting "Don't move!" Paul looks up briefly, stares, and then returns to the cricket report.

In that instant, Eva is aware of Roy's look – or perhaps she heard the voice – and she pauses with arms outstretched and body taut. She turns towards him and smiles shyly, then wanders back to her towel and books. Roy also sits again, but it has happened now and can never be undone.

When the embryo is in the womb, it is still possible to think of it as a strangely unreal medical phenomenon, a potential thing. But when the child arrives kicking and screaming in the world, nothing and nobody will ever be the same again. Roy's entire energy field has shifted. It is one of those days when the world briefly stands still, when you make a decision without realising that you have, when you end and begin and you look at other people and wonder at the gulf between you.

Like a man who has dreamed the winner of the Grand National and needs a witness to the name he is sealing in an envelope, Roy speaks slowly and deliberately to his friend.

"Paul, you see that girl?" He looks up from the newspaper briefly and nods.

"What about her?"

"I'm going to marry her."

Paul is used to his friend's naivety, the youthful idealism that borders on pathos at times, but he's never gone this far before.

"I see," he replies, and returns to studying the bowling figures.

Roy is aware of himself faintly trembling, not with joy or anticipation but actually with fear. What now? Maybe for the first time in his life he finds himself faced with a sheer fact upon which he must act, upon which everything suddenly seems to depend. Cigarette smoke curls across the table and everyone's eyes are upon him as God, wearing a black waistcoat and bow tie and holding a small silver ball, says, "Faites vos jeux, messieurs." Of course, Roy has one more chance to turn his back and leave, resume his life; but how many men alive could walk away from the table knowing that in a few seconds that little ball will be in the zero?

He stands and puts on a studied frown, ostentatiously checking his pockets in an act more for his own benefit than hers since she isn't even watching. Then as casually as a man wearing flippers on his three left feet, he wanders across the sand and pauses at the foot of her shadow.

"Er… I don't suppose you, um, would have a spare cigarette, would you? Please?"

She looks up from her book and their eyes meet for the second time. There's really no need for this charade but she may as well play along with it for a while, for his sake. She realises that she's a little older than him so she bears a certain responsibility in such situations.

"I beg your pardon?"

"A cigarette? Do you have one, please? I've run out and it's a long way to the shop." A sudden panic hits him. Good grief, what a stupid idea, asking a gymnast for a cigarette! Now when she says 'No' he'll have to walk all the way to the bloody shop and he hasn't got any money with him.

"Yes, of course. Take one." She offers the packet and he kneels down to take it as gracefully as trembling legs will allow. "But I don't think they're any better than yours. Actually, they're the same brand." She laughs gently and points to Roy's packet peeping from his back pocket. He feels the colour reaching his face and fights it back with a great effort of will; the tone of her voice tells him that everything's still all right. For the moment.

"Ah, yes. You caught me. Sorry. Um, you have a nice accent. Are you French?" The inner, sensible Roy beats him over the head again for being such an idiot. Of course she's not French, but it's the only foreign country he can think of.

"No, I'm Czech."

He is stunned into silence again by the enormity of the statement, as this week's front page headlines flash into his mind. Probably better not to mention them just now. So instead he asks another fatuous question.

"Are you here on holiday?"

What in any sane world would a Czech be doing on holiday in the backwaters of Wales at a time like this?

"Sort of. I'm working in a hotel. But I have some hours off today. I am lucky, yes, the sun is out?" She lays aside the book and sits up to light a cigarette herself, mesmerising him with the supple movement of her limbs and her soft skin only inches from his. "And you?"

This is going better than expected – she is actually talking to him – and Roy begins to relax a little. On the other hand, he's not very good at opening conversations with girls, not having had much practice, so he's going to have to learn fast.

"What? Oh, yes, I'm here with my friend Paul, over there. We're both starting university soon so this is the lull before the storm." Never had he spoken a truer word.

"I beg your pardon?"

"Ah, well, it's an expression that means… look, it's probably in here." He picks up the heavy library copy of Brewer's Phrase & Fable on the towel beside her. Actually, it isn't in there so he has to explain, which is good practice.

"This is my homework," she explains. "I am at university, too, in Prague, to learn English. And part of my course is to live here for some time."

"That's lucky," he says brightly, meaning that it is for him, then he compounds the mistake by adding, "I mean, there's some trouble over there, back home, isn't there?" He even surprises himself with the crass insensitivity of it but the game goes on despite him. Her expression fades briefly.

"Yes, it is true. I see that your friend has a newspaper." She may as well take over the initiative for a while before he ruins it. "Do you think I could see it, please?"

"Oh, yes, of course, yes. Please come over and join us," he enthuses, mightily relieved that he doesn't need to find any more excuses for the moment. "But I doubt –" he gestures at the rolled up paper in her bag "– that it says anything different to yours."

Paul looks up in some surprise as they approach. He hadn't expected things to get this far, but after twenty minutes even he can tell that this is no ordinary encounter.

"Shall I make us some lunch?" Roy suggests. Eva looks surprised so he gestures towards the campsite behind them. "We're in a caravan over there. Would you like a sandwich, maybe some salad?"

"It's my turn today," Paul observes, without looking up from the crossword that he's already finished.

"No problem," Roy says brightly, already on his feet. He needs a few minutes' break without thinking. He's not really used to facts, nor to relationships, at least not like this.

"Oh, shall I help you, then?" Eva is also momentarily confused, unsure whether to follow. So far they haven't had to think about the steps to be taken but it looks like God has moved on to His next task now and left them to it. Well, He must be very busy.

In the cool of the caravan, quietness descends. Unable to break it, they busy themselves with the food but it's not easy to avoid each other in the tiny kitchen. The air hangs about them, waiting impatiently, until eventually they both reach for the same knife and their hands touch. A switch is thrown and everything stops. Neither of them can move, their eyes locked, their bodies half twisted away painfully. Slowly, very slowly, Roy feels words gathering their shape in his brain and setting out on the long journey to his throat, pausing briefly to clamber over the spasm there. He couldn't hold back even were the knife at his throat instead of beneath his fingers.

"I… um…" is still all he can manage to begin with because he sees the single tear form in her left eye. With great effort, she stops it from falling and it only moistens her lashes. For Heaven's sake, she's thinking, didn't I already have enough decisions to make?

"Cut this," she says, moving again towards the kettle. Roy is still standing as if frozen, wondering what the hell has just happened and what the hell happens next, and looks down to find himself grasping a tomato.

A few minutes later, Paul is munching appreciatively on his sandwich, breakfast having been little more than adequate. Curious, he is now joining in the conversation.

"You were out late last night," he says, turning to Roy with his mouth full. "I didn't like to wake you this morning. You seemed to be enjoying another of your dramatic dreams."

"Couldn't sleep," says Roy. "Went for a walk."

"Along the beach?" Eva seems surprised.

"Uhu, over the dunes. I took a flask of coffee."

"Isn't it dangerous at night? We were always told we must never go out alone in England, especially at night."

"No, it's not dangerous. Least, I don't think so. I often do it. I like the night, the quiet, the sea... It's lonely, I can think."

"Are you lonely, then?" That was a bit direct.

"Not at all," he laughs, because now he isn't.

"And what do you think about, when you are alone with the night and the sea?"

"Ah, these days he's always thinking –" Paul responds immediately to the cue but Roy shoots him a telling look and he cooperates, "– about music. We write songs sometimes. How's the magnum opus coming along, then? Any more?"

"Eight notes last night. The second line," Roy says quietly, head bowed.

"Wow, that's real progress. Double productivity." He feels relaxed and doesn't try to disguise the friendly sarcasm.

"And are they good notes?" Eva asks gently. He lifts his head and nods gratefully.

Somehow they get through the afternoon successfully, talking easily and a little surprised by the easing of tension as time passes.

After much insistent encouragement, Eva shyly demonstrates a few more of her floor routines, to the obvious astonishment of a few families who have filtered back to the beach after lunch. She is not shy because of them, because she is oblivious to them. But although she has performed like this hundreds of times and is used to the effect that her body has on a thousand eyes, never before – even with Josef – has she been so aware of just one particular pair. She takes Roy's guitar and plays a short Bohemian folk song for them, without translating. She doesn't have an especially pure voice nor good fingering but, as Roy is quickly learning, everything she does faultlessly expresses her inner feeling at the time. She is transparent, totally honest. So this afternoon the music sounds beautiful and brings spontaneous applause from other couples sitting nearby. She laughs, embarrassed now, and passes the guitar to Roy but others' intrusion is enough to hold him back too.

At about four-thirty she tells them she has to go because she is on duty this evening so the three of them walk to the town together and there is the briefest of goodbyes on the hotel steps. Just before the heavy glass door shuts, Roy suddenly panics: there is so much that has gone unsaid and there is the whole of the rest of his life to be decided yet. They haven't even arranged to see one another again. She can't just disappear.

"Eva!" It's the first time he has used her name and she freezes. "Eva, when shall I see you – I mean, can I see you again? Please." She is surprised that he should even ask because it's already difficult to remember that some things understood still have to be said aloud. Tomorrow, she tells him, she'll be working all day but then free at about eight o'clock. Seeing that Paul is wondering whether to say something, she smiles and says she'll bring Sally along too. Then she's gone. Roy turns towards the sea but doesn't move yet, perplexed by the strange sense of relief he's feeling that the meeting is over. The last few hours have been on an altogether different energetic level than anything he's experienced before and he needs some normality.

"How about golf?" is all he can think of. Paul is delighted by this return of routine and to have his prodigal friend back. As they walk around to the back of the hotel he begins to chatter.

"Sally must be the one she was with at the pub last night, when those Germans moved in. She was rather nice, just my type don't you think?"

"Did we see them last night, then?" Roy is surprised.

They become totally absorbed in their game, back to their general daily banter, until on the eighteenth Roy suddenly remembers something.

"Christ! Tomorrow's our last day!"

"Yeah," agrees Paul enthusiastically, "the last chance." But he doesn't mean what Roy means.

Ф

"It is settled."

On a first floor balcony in Staroměstská Square, the Speaker of the National Assembly raises a hand to quieten the crowd's chants of "Pravda!"

"We defended our beliefs," Smrkovský continues, "and return with honour. We were successful. Čierna has once again brought us close to our friends and allies in the Bloc." There are a few muted cheers. These times are so strange and things are happening so fast, no-one is quite sure what to believe.

"Be satisfied," Dubček tells the people later, "that we have kept our promises. The path is chosen and we shall not lose sight of it. These people are our good friends."

It is perhaps the first time he has been so unequivocal before them, but perhaps it is not so deliberate; he is utterly exhausted, worn down by charge and counter-charge, by rhetoric and enormity. He hasn't smiled for days. But now, on the television screen, under the lights and make-up, he is still their leader and he will – he must – hold on a little longer until all truly is well. Okay, so they must shelve western trade for a while; well, there should still be plenty to go round. Okay, so the press must be more restrained towards their allies; well, that is a mere courtesy. After all, the Czechs need the Soviet Union. Or, to put it another way, the Soviet Union is a necessary fact of life. So now there is just the Communist Party Bratislava summit on the 3rd of August to get through…

Φ

"Hello, I'm Sally."

She is on time, bouncing confidently down the path and across the road to where the boys are sitting on the low promenade wall. Behind her, Eva appears briefly at the doorway of the hotel and waves before disappearing back inside. Roy stands and takes a step forward, looking straight past the bright, pretty girl approaching them with consternation written on his face. Has it all gone wrong so soon? Yes, it's true that he has spent the whole day convincing himself that there may well be nothing else for them and it was all a good and worthy experience for him that he probably, almost certainly, misinterpreted, this being Roy after all. But the lurch in his stomach betrays him. With great difficulty, he turns his attention back to Sally as she coyly offers a hand.

"Eva's sorry, she'll be late. Mrs Baggage the manageress – at least, that's what we call her – she wants Eva to do something and she can't get out of it. Then she's got to 'phone home. But she'll be along later. We agreed to meet in The Willow. Do you know it?"

"Oh yes," Paul chips in, "we were there the other night. We saw you and actually –"

"Look, you two go on and I'll wait here," Roy breaks in, his eyes searching the hotel windows.

"No, you can't. She said you'd probably say that and you're not to. Anyway, you'll only make the place look untidy. She'll be along later. Come on, then." And she takes each of them by an arm and sets off determinedly along the pavement.

At least Paul is well pleased by her easy familiarity and the early physical contact is promising. She also seems to recognise that they don't have much time. The pub is already filling up noisily under Phil's satisfied glare and the two of them take advantage of the impossibility of polite conversation by drinking fast and dancing close, as Roy sits it out with a fixed smile and tries to focus on the music. While Sally is away adjusting her image, a beaming Paul gets another round in and leans across the table to talk into his friend's ear.

"We still haven't decided anything."

"Eh?"

"About the caravan. Tonight."

"What? Oh, for God's sake. It's yours."

"Right-o, thanks. But, er, what'll you do?"

"I don't know. Go for a walk in the sea or something."

"What? Can't hear you."

"Nothing. Doesn't matter. Go for it, she's nice."

It's after ten when Eva finally appears and Roy is quite drained by the conflicting emotions and thoughts of the last couple of hours. She stands framed in the doorway against the darkness, looking around and through all the jostling bodies before she sees them and comes over.

"I'm sorry to be late," she smiles, sitting beside Roy and putting one hand on his. Her touch is unexpected yet so natural that he doesn't even notice until he realises with surprise that he's calm again. As if at some prearranged signal, the other two reach for their jackets and get up.

"Um, getting some air," Paul mumbles, somehow unable to look either of them in the face. "See you guys later."

As they make for the door, the younger of the two Germans who had been watching sullenly from the bar moves across to stand in their way. He seems to be remonstrating with Sally.

"She'll just tell him that Paul's her brother," says Eva. "It will be all right, I think Sally is used to this kind of thing." Sure enough, Sally now leans forward to kiss the young man lightly on the cheek and he stands aside. Paul turns back towards the table with a raised eyebrow and a look of incomprehension, but is then dragged outside into the night and on to meet his fate.

"They go together well, I think," Eva laughs, squeezing Roy's hand as she turns back to him. "Do you agree? They really like each other."

"Uhu, I guess." This is now another new situation that he must learn to handle. He is a touch disappointed to notice that she is wearing make-up that's a bit heavy around the eyes, though this is not a criticism: her bright smile and tone of voice belie something else, something that's changed in her. Or something has happened today. As they chat about what he has been up to and what Mrs Baggage insisted on, she has one drink.

"Let's go," she says then, taking the fawn leather jacket from the back of her chair. "Let's go and walk. Oh, by the way –" she has seen Carl start to move "– you are my fiancé, okay?" Roy is long past trying to understand what's happening to him these last thirty-six hours and just nods weakly.

"Fine. Suits me."

"Hello again, Eva." The voice is low and full of menace. "So you are engaged to this young one, are you, or is he another brother?" There's a certain kind of man who believes that buying a girl vodka leads naturally to sex, and this stereotype's head is thrust forward on a rigid, muscular body. There are also times when even a young man doesn't need to understand what's happening because some primitive instinct simply takes over, the heartrate rising as the adrenaline flows. There's something in the aura too, and we can all feel it. The dancers nearby stop to watch.

In the blink of an eye, the naïve adolescent gets the whole reality of what he experienced on the beach yesterday. This woman by his side, who is now watching his face intently, is all he could have hoped for, the meeting-place of all his unformed ideas. Without knowing how or why he could have deserved it (whether or not that's relevant), he has found something that every man searches for. This is a moment of grace, in which there is everything to gain and everything to be lost by what he does next. On the other hand, there really isn't any choice, any more than a new-born can re-enter the womb. And even if what he wants should turn out one day to be something different, there is no other way but to take it.

So the small vein throbs just the once, not this time with anger but with compassion. Carl looks into Roy's eyes and steps back. Nobody has spoken.

Outside, perhaps because there's a real chill in the air, Eva draws close to him with her arm locked around his, and they walk on slowly with nothing to say for now. Then they turn as one into the shadows of the churchyard and face one another beneath the weeping branches of the yew, holding more tightly while they still can.

"I, um, I have to leave tomorrow," he begins, leaning his forehead down onto hers. "Paul's relatives have booked the caravan… anyway, it's my mother's birthday and I'm due back at work… oh, I didn't tell you, I have this summer job and…" It all sounds like excuses.

"Yes," she says, as if she knew all of this already. She lifts her head and they kiss for the first time, lingering far longer than they need to. It's more of a shared breath. Then they walk silently to the beach and sit in the sheltered overhang at the edge of the broken sea.

And all the while Eva tries to justify to her torn mind what she has to do. There are so many expectations, and not just others'. But even her greater experience of life has not prepared her for this. When you've lived all your days in a desert, it's hard to recognise flowers or to trust running streams, your senses spun by heat and arid ambitions. When you've learned to walk straight, keeping your eyes on the immediate future and your ears strained for danger, it's hard to believe a big, flashing sign in front of you with its neon arrow pointing to A New Life. No, this boy, this thing whatever it is, belongs in now and in Wales. She belongs in Czechoslovakia.

Far out beyond the waves, the wind is gathering and the weather is changing. On the horizon, a small ship has dropped anchor and has settled down to wait, its green starboard light blinking in the haze. A pair of gulls cry as they wing inland overhead. Darkening clouds don't seem to offer any choice. They don't need to say much, both of them knowing at some level what is to become of them yet they must still go through with it as the storm approaches.

Back in her room, the suitcase half-packed, there is a light knock on the door and a breathless Sally falls in.

"Did you have a good time, then?" asks Eva, though her friend's flush gives the answer.

"Wheeee..." Sally spins round and falls backwards onto the bed, unzipping her jacket and undoing the two buttons that still hold her blouse together before allowing her arms to flop limply over the sides. She seems to have lost her bra. "Eva, you wouldn't believe it," she speaks to the ceiling between giggles. "Paul is –" She realises that one hand has hit the suitcase on the bedside chair and sits up again quickly, looking at Eva's pale, drawn face. "Oh no. The 'phone call, was it bad news, then?"

"Quite bad. Dubček – he's our leader – has been on TV telling everyone it's okay but nobody believes him. My parents say it won't be long now. They won't give way."

"So are you going home?"

"It's the right thing to do. I think I have enough time to go to Liverpool first. There is a good friend there I want to say goodbye to. She helped me a lot and…" But then the tears won't wait any longer and she sits beside Sally, one finger in her mouth, grateful for her arms.

The weak yellow light of the caravan window is in sight as Roy stops to light a cigarette, cupping his hand against the growing wind. He exhales, looking out across the whitening sea, and doesn't hear the quick movement behind him, gasping in surprise as the heavy fist bears into the small of his back. Then his breath is cut off by the strong forearm across his throat. More blows throb into his abdomen and he falls, eyes instinctively closing when the boot breaks open the corner of his mouth. Then there's some sort of German expletive and the sound of running feet. Roy opens one eye to see a middle-aged, very fat couple leaning over him with evident concern on their faces.

"Are you all right, ol' son?" the man says as gently as a Birmingham accent allows. "Thought I 'eard summat. We was just over there. What were all that about, then? There was two on 'em, furriners I think."

Roy props himself up on his elbows, his head clearing as he fingers the blood on his chin and then tastes it. The man helps him to his feet.

"Shall us call the police?"

"Police? Oh, no. Thank you." When he reaches the caravan door he still hasn't stopped laughing to himself that he is grateful to Carl. Now that his body really hurts, he knows that everything will work out. Inside, the gas lamps are burning down and hissing. Paul is asleep on his bed. The floor is littered with clothes. Silently, Roy picks up the pale blue bra with one finger and folds it neatly away with the rest of his friend's clothes in a drawer.

ACT 4

Violation

He never did like family parties. It is not just because he is shy – indeed, he knows he should get to know people better – but more that the people he has met have not been very interested in talking with him and the parties have not been the sort at which people enjoy themselves.

He stands by the small garden pool, a small vodka in one hand and willow leaves trailing over the other shoulder, watching the goldfish nose about beneath the pattering spray of the fountain. Behind him across the grass, the guests have popped up in threes and fours like grotesque, thin mushrooms planted by his parents in carefully chosen groups. The flowerbeds are organised, the curves of the lawn regular, and it is as usual a hot Sunday afternoon. The sun, if not other gods, has shone without fail on these birthday parties for over a decade. It seems to be some sort of natural law. Nevertheless, the men are suited and their women bonneted, with many a lace frond about ears hung with silver and gemstones.

A frog plops noisily from its lily pad and the fish scurry away. Roy's father is circulating with a tray bearing a punch of his own invention, enjoying himself on the fringes of the gathering while actually controlling it.

"Good party," says Roy dutifully as he passes, deftly exchanging his empty glass for a full one.

"Yes, I think so. Nothing's gone wrong. But I do wish you'd try to mix more. You'll be starting your training at the company soon and you need to get on with these people. I don't know why you're always on your own." And he is already onto the next group.

Roy is indeed alone. Eva is a hundred miles and three hours or perhaps a Channel and half a continent away. He might as well have dreamed it, except that this dream is still playing throughout his mind. To distract himself, he goes to the kitchen to help with the food. His mother is busy over canapés with Lucille, her token 'modern' friend. Petite and blonde, still caring about her figure, Lucille is always to be found where intrigues are being discussed and Roy can immediately tell that this time it's his.

"Isn't Paul coming?" his mother asks without looking up.

"He should be here soon. He never misses a free feed."

"Who's this girl, then?" Lucille never wastes any time.

"Hmm, what girl's that?" mumbles Roy, swallowing whole a tiny salmon and cucumber sandwich.

"Come on, Roy, the girl you met this week. Is it serious?"

"Don't be silly, Lucy," his mother interjects. "He's only known her five minutes."

"Her name's Eva."

"She's foreign, then?" Roy's mother puts down her small knife and stands rigid, as if her son had just confessed to GBH.

"Uhu. Czech."

"What? A Communist?" The crime has got worse. "You didn't tell us that."

"It's not important."

"Of course it is. Haven't you heard of the Cold War? They've got nuclear bombs aimed at us." Roy considers the obvious response then thinks better of it; he really isn't interested in this argument. "And anyway, there can't be any future in it, those foreigners always go home in the end."

"Maybe I'll go with her, then," Roy teases, instantly regretting it as he remembers that his mother isn't good with jokes. Fortunately, the front doorbell rings and this long day, which has dragged its feet interminably through all the preparations and arrivals and distribution of drinks, now becomes breathless.

"Sorry we're late. Happy birthday, Mrs Carter. Dad's just parking the car half a mile down the road." Paul ambles into the kitchen and helps himself to a canapé, leaning against a worktop next to Roy, his mother following. "Only we've just heard that my Uncle Harry's had a bit of a car accident. He's all right but they've taken him in to keep an eye on him."

Connections suddenly flash and a lightbulb explodes in Roy's brain.

"Isn't it your Uncle Harry who was going to the caravan?" he asks his friend as calmly as he can.

"That's right. A tyre burst just outside Welshpool."

"So the caravan...?"

"Oh yeah, I suppose so. For a few days, anyway. Yeah!" He's got the connections too now. The boys' excitement is contagious and the thing is agreed within minutes. Even Roy's mother is somehow briefly touched by her son, despite this being her day, though his father is less forgiving.

"Not this stupid girl again. When are you going to grow up?" He doesn't even know yet about her being a Communist.

In less than twenty minutes, Roy has kissed his mother on the cheek saying "Sorry" – she doesn't come to the front door, though – and Lucille has surreptitiously pressed a £5 note into his hand "For petrol" with a wink. They stop off at Paul's house to gather his things and then Roy is again definitely driving too fast through the countryside. Just outside Welshpool, Paul points out the old black Rover still abandoned forlornly in a layby.

"Good old Uncle Harry," Roy smiles. "I mean, I hope he's okay of course. We'll go and visit him afterwards."

"Yeah, s'pose so. Look, do you have to drive so fast?"

Roy only knows, without knowing why, that there isn't much time so Paul sits back, trusting his friend's instincts. He's delighted to be going back, too, of course; like a child who's discovered he can reach the top shelf, he's hungry for more of Sally. But he can't escape the feeling that he's in the wings of someone else's stage.

They finally pull to a juddering stop outside the hotel with the petrol gauge nudging 'Empty'.

"It's dinnertime. They'll be working," Paul points out as Roy slumps back in his seat and lights a cigarette. "Why don't we go to the caravan and unpack? Get some food? I'm starved, I only managed two canapés and a sarnie before you dragged me out."

"I'm waiting," says Roy with finality.

But his is not the reward. Within five minutes, Sally glances through a downstairs window, does a double take, then smiles and waves frantically. Another woman, frowning, stout and middle-aged, joins her and says something, and continues to peer disapprovingly though the twilight at the car as Sally disappears. Roy stares back at her impassively. Within five minutes Sally is on the back seat of the car with her arms round Paul's neck, her short red dress riding up. It feels like an age before she answers the unspoken question.

"Oh, sorry, Roy. Eva's not in. It's her evening off."

"Where is she?" His voice is cold and measured.

"Um, I don't really know. I expect she'll be back soon though, so –"

It's obvious that she's not saying all she knows so Roy instantly turns the ignition key, puts the car in gear and drums his fingers on the steering wheel impatiently.

"Right, I'll go to the caravan, then. See you two later."

Paul is a bit taken aback but gets the message, hands over the keys and levers himself out of the car with Sally still holding on.

"Okay. But what about –"

"About what?"

"Er, nothing. See you."

With painstaking control, Roy drives slowly to the campsite, his mind a mass of raging ideas and unbelievable scenarios. Surely he can't let go now? With measured steps he carries their bags across to the caravan and stops, frozen with incredulity, at the door. Entwined on the handle is a small blue flower.

He unpacks his bag and eats a leisurely dinner from tins, savouring every tasteless mouthful. He has not been wrong. He has resisted doubt and the dream continues to play. He clears the plates and washes up so that everything is tidy again. He undresses and has a wash, putting on clean clothes because it feels important to be renewed. He makes coffee and sits comfortably, patiently, to drink it with a cigarette. He turns on the small transistor radio and turns it this way and that to catch the signals.

The evening is calm with a light wind, both moon and tide full, and nothing seems to be moving outside. The radio crackles as pop music fades in and out again, so Roy rolls the tuning knob until an intelligible voice can be heard. It is the BBC World Service and Dubček is addressing his people.

Ф

"…in the Bratislava Trade Union House, the heads of the Warsaw Pact states met with your leaders to finalise a joint communiqué concerning recent events. There was some opposition, it is true, from the Polish and East German delegations, but it was agreed that the reforms of our Prague Spring may continue as long as we curtail the development of our contact with Western countries.

"Our national independence and territorial integrity are guaranteed. We thank our comrades in the Soviet Union especially for the concessions they have made. Comrades Brezhnev and Kosygin offered fraternal good wishes to the Czechoslovak people before they left for home and they assured me that all is now normal."

As huge crowds take to the streets to welcome the news, two men are considering their position in a dimly lit Prague cellar bar. Alois Indra, newly appointed Chairman of the Czech Communist Party, and Party Secretary Drahomír Kolder speak in low, earnest voices, their heads bowed close together. The beer is cloudy but it's only an excuse. The barman had recognised them with a little surprise, but had smiled in greeting and said nothing. After all, what is open democratic government if its leaders cannot enjoy a quiet drink together in a public bar? There is a new atmosphere of trust in the country. So the barman polishes glasses and considers trying his luck with the young woman sitting alone on a high stool. She seems to be waiting for something.

Ф

Roy turns off the radio, pulls the curtains and locks up the caravan, setting out to walk back to the hotel. Eva sees him sitting on the promenade wall immediately as she turns the corner and he too knows that she is approaching. It is as if their eyes belong to one another, focusing automatically whenever the other appears. His pulse jumps once and then quietens, pleased to realise that the figure beside her is too tall to be the German boy. He sees the pair pause beneath a streetlamp, as if to make things public, and shake hands before she puts the long buff envelope the man hands over into her jacket pocket. Then he turns to sit the other way and watch the waves.

She watches the man disappear the way they had come and then slowly crosses the road to stand just behind Roy.

"I realised that I hadn't given you my address," he says, feeling her presence, with his back still to her.

"You didn't need to, not yet."

Now he turns and their hands reach out to hold one another's fingers lightly.

"Hello."

"Hello."

"Thank you for the flower."

"I think it's nice to give flowers to welcome someone."

"You couldn't have known that I'd be coming back."

"Sooner or later, you would come."

There is still a touch of wariness between them, as though they still can't quite believe that this is happening. Perhaps it is because they are half expecting a big crossroads sign to appear suddenly on this unfamiliar road. So they walk quietly along the promenade to the steps and down to the stony beach, hugging the sea wall as the tide is just beginning to ebb, sometimes lapping at their feet. He notices the envelope that's too long for her pocket but says nothing about it or the man she'd met, deciding that he never will. Lovers shouldn't have to ask questions. Oh, is that what they are now?

Further along towards the campsite, where the promenade gives way to a high earthy wall and dunes as the beach widens out, Eva suddenly takes off her shoes and runs across the night to the water's edge with arms outstretched, a shoe in each hand. Her head is back, drinking in the Welsh sea air. Caught unawares, he soon recovers and follows her, kicking off his sandals, but the stones hurt his feet and he yelps in surprise. It is what they need to break the remaining distance between them. She runs to him, laughing, and throws her arms around his neck.

"Poor thing! We gymnasts have hard feet."

"I think I'm bleeding," he complains, inspecting one sole and leaning against her. His weight brings them closer and in a moment their skins are aware of each other's. In the midst of the stones, they kiss, and this time it's deeper. Still clinging together like wounded soldiers, they walk up and along the dunes, kneeling and then lying on the grassy mound where he had found his first four notes, without ever letting go, locked together by something primeval.

Roy is aware that he is losing both reason and bearings. Like an accidental tourist he has somehow wandered into a foreign country where he can't read the signs and people seem to have strange customs that no-one has ever told him about and whisper to one another in shadowy corners or behind locked doors. He is forgetting to breathe. True, the countryside is beautiful and the city architecture has clean lines with pleasing proportion. But there is always the slight fear that one might get lost and be unable to ask for help because the language here has a different root to one's own; moreover, he might not be welcome around the next corner.

With a pang of guilt, he realises that Eva's jacket is open and that his hand is moving across her breast, trembling fingers lightly brushing the material. He hadn't intended that. But she is not moving away and indeed her own fingers are slowly moving from one small white button of her blouse to the next until it falls open. He is desperate to stop but cannot help himself, astonished by the silky whiteness of her skin.

No painting or photograph could ever have prepared him for the beauty of this woman. Not even Carol has prepared him, that time with her the merest veiled hint of what could be. God only knows what has brought him to this place, but something in his spine tells him that he is close to the source – and that one must tread very carefully there. No-one has ever told him, but he would never have understood them anyway. It is all a matter of instinct from now on.

He leans down to touch her soft pale skin with dry lips, barely touching, in contrast to the tension he feels throughout the rest of his body. He is terrified, momentarily, of this strange land. Eva is feeling it too, surprised by where they have found themselves. A man's hands and lips are not strangers to her, of course, and others have been more knowing, more tactical. But never before has a man touched her beneath her skin, moving some inner organ that she didn't know existed. And this is not even a man. He is young, naïve and confused, yet somehow he knows something more than the others. So she must help him. She translates the signs, taking his hand and showing it where to go, letting him know that he's safe by touching him too. They lie together quietly like this, clothed and smiling, until all the fear has run away and time decides to step back into their lives.

"It's my turn to go. Tomorrow." Her voice is barely audible. "I have already packed."

He sits up, leaning on one arm and looking down at her face with fathomless feeling. This is why he'd had to drive so fast. This is why he'd read the front page of the week's newspapers before the sports stories.

A single cloud drifts across the moon and in the still night the only sound is a light breeze in the long blades of marram grass guarding the mound, waving like despairing fingers clutching at the air.

"Please don't ask why," she continues. "It's more than life's worth to… It's… my duty. They need me there."

"I need you too."

She sits up and takes his hand but cannot look into his eyes.

"And this is the only place I want to be. Believe me, Roy. But I have to."

"Will you come back?" Like a sand timer, everything that has brought him to this moment is slipping away upside down. He's turning a corner and finding those signs with their foreign words springing up again around him.

"I don't know. I'll try, but…" This time the tear escapes her lashes. "Things are going to be bad, Roy. I don't know if I'll be able to come."

"I'll be here."

"Yes, I know."

"I love you, Eva. I know I'm young and I don't understand much and all this is new," he waves one arm to indicate the two of them but actually taking in the whole world, "but I love you and wherever you go I'll be there, on every street, in every face you see."

"I know." She cannot say more.

Midnight comes and a chill wind with it sends shivers through them. They stand and brush each other down then set off back towards the campsite with hands tightly clasped. Neither of them notices the long buff envelope lying on the grass. Distracted by their own different thoughts, they almost fall over Paul and Sally sitting in a hollow with their legs hanging over the dune.

"Grief, where have you come from?" Paul exclaims, with equal annoyance and surprise. "We thought you were in the caravan. The curtains are drawn so we've been waiting for you."

"Well, we went for a walk," Roy shrugs, "and here we are." Sally giggles with the irony of it, which makes Eva smile too. "Let's go in and make some coffee."

"Mind you," Paul says later in the darkness, once the girls have gone and the caravan has settled down for the night, "the time wasn't wasted. And there's a lot to be said for sand, even if it does get into all the wrong places. She's fantastic, Sally, really fantastic. I have to thank you for dragging me back here. She says she'll come and stay with me in a couple of months once I've settled in at Bristol. The hotel will be closing up for a couple of months. Doing repairs or something."

"Uhu. I'm pleased for you." The familiar patter of spray on the windows has returned and the caravan rocks slightly with the breeze. Roy is wide awake and cannot imagine ever sleeping again.

"Twice, we did it. Twice!" He probably expects some reaction from his friend but there is silence. Roy doesn't understand. How can anyone feel this twice? It arrives and then it's there forever.

In the morning he collects Eva with her suitcase and drives her to the station. They kiss goodbye briefly and don't let the tears fall.

"You have my address, don't you?" he asks for the third time.

"I will write, I promise."

"Take care of yourself, please. We'll see each other again."

The train begins to move and soon picks up speed, leaving him alone on the platform. She takes a seat that faces forward, knowing that there's very little chance of that. But then, when you grow up in the Eastern Bloc you're quite used to people appearing and then disappearing and you learn not to look back.

Back in the town, Roy drives slowly past the hotel. Paul and Sally are on the putting green.

"You never know, do you," Sally is saying, "who might be driving past? Maybe it's someone really important, like a high-powered executive of a film studio with three cars and two mistresses, one for weekends and one for lunchtimes…"

"I s'pose."

"…or who's standing next to you in a pub. I mean, they might look perfectly ordinary but you never know, do you?"

Back at the caravan, Roy makes a flask and takes his towel and guitar back along the dunes to where they had sat. She isn't there, but the feeling of her is. What kind of fucking crazy world is this? Five minutes ago he was an educated boy who knew nothing, confused about just about everything; then he had discovered love, only to have it immediately snatched away by international politics. From absolute power to total powerlessness in a day. So does he now have to start again? Nonetheless, he is a little surprised to find himself soon calming down and within a few minutes, despite the calls of cormorants and shouts of children on the beach below, he gets the third line.

D… D… C… B…, A… B… C… B… The last note is waiting, questioning, like a fingertip on soft skin. And although he feels that he knows what follows, he doesn't want it yet. He's not ready. Instead, he plays through all three lines together now, linking them to get the timing right in his mind of all that's come so far. Suddenly he stops, noticing the envelope caught in the grasses a few feet away.

It's very wet with spray and dew, creased by their bodies lying on it, and the ink of the short, hand-written address on the front is smudged. Roy is surprised to find that it's not sealed so he opens it in case it's important to her and he should send it on. She's given him her parents' address. There's a single sheet of typewritten paper with an official-looking heading. There's only one paragraph but he cannot read it because it's in a strange script. He holds it for several minutes as if its meaning might filter through to his brain by telepathy. Then, without really knowing why, he scoops out a deep hole in the sand nearby and lays the envelope in it, covering it with small stones arranged to form her name and finally brushing back the sand over it all as if there's nothing there.

Φ

Outside the neglected grey stone building in Prague, the secretary stops to check her pockets and handbag, then turns to go back in. In the thickly carpeted first floor corridor all is quiet and deserted except for the chatter of a telex machine behind an open door at the end. Alois Indra looks up angrily from his desk when she enters.

"What are you doing here? Everyone has gone home." The girl is suddenly frightened by his tone, out of character, and her eyes are instinctively drawn to the papers on his desk. But they're too far away to make anything out.

"I… I'm sorry, Comrade. I forgot something here."

"Get out."

"I'll just be a few seconds." She takes one step forward.

"I said get out." And he stands, coming round the desk as if to block her way.

"Don't you think I should tell someone?" she asks her boyfriend later that evening as they sit in a small bar. "He was behaving very strangely. It felt, I don't know, dangerous somehow."

"Dangerous for you," he answers, taking his jacket from the back of his chair. "Who would you tell? And he'd make sure you lost your job too. Why worry about it? Come on, let's go." His mind has already moved on elsewhere. "Anyway, if you can't trust the Chairman of the Czech Communist Party, who can you trust?"

So an Invisible Letter, signed by Indra, Kolder and others and written in Russian, is sent on its way the next day. It is a call for help by all means possible to guard against the counter-revolution.

Ф

Hooked over the painted metal handle of the grimy window is a new sports jacket. It is green with a light brown check and leather elbow patches. Insofar as it is possible to hate an inanimate object, Roy hates it; it is the uniform of stability, security and engineering company offices and his father – on whom he is still dependent – has insisted on the necessity of appearances. For now, at least, it serves the useful purpose of blocking out the view of the black, prefabricated foundry building.

Roy is feeling distinctly uncomfortable. This is a short training course intended to introduce him to the adult world but after little more than a week he is even less comfortable than when he started and convinced that life has made a ghastly mistake by placing him here. He doesn't belong in this strange land of noise and acrid air, belching chimneys and gliding forklift trucks, with its alien blue boiler-suited inhabitants whose breath is coarse with dialect and obscenity. Each night he falls exhausted into bed asking the angels please to put it all right tomorrow. And each night the angels patiently check their records and assure one another that indeed everything is as it should be.

As he sits at his drawing board he concedes that at least he has some talent for this and even technical drawing affords an opportunity for thought. A helical screw thread takes shape in front of him but he is on a beach in Wales, and as he carefully fingers the dividers they become open legs.

Mr Lloyd comes to stand at his shoulder. He is nearing retirement, none too soon, his life-blood spent for the company. Widely regarded with gentle scorn for his kind and sensitive nature, he doesn't really belong either. But fifty years ago there was no choice and then there was a wife and a baby and a Depression. So the least he can do for Roy is to understand.

"You have some talent, son," he says quietly, eyes twinkling as they always do even if he's asking for three pounds of potatoes, "but your mind's on something else, eh?" He points out that one of the rear turns is missing. "Is it a woman, then, you dirty young man? Well, mind on the job now. Summer's nearly over and we'll be settling in for the winter soon." The poor chap won't see the end of this one though; once you've given yourself wholly to a job, retirement becomes pointless.

Nearby in the machine shop, the hum of lathes and drills suddenly stops as lunchtime arrives and there's a rush for the washroom. Roy walks downstairs and joins the queue for the time clock, eventually feeding his card in and getting another corner chewed off. An eerie quiet has descended over the plant when he emerges into the daylight. The day is warm and the air as fresh as it can be in the Black Country; summer is not yet over. In every direction men are streaming out of holes in the ends of the huge corrugated metal boxes where they've spent their morning, their movement as mechanical and regulated as the machines they operate. From above they would look like so many blue corpuscles jostling along veins with a handful of bleached leucocyte women strutting alongside, arms folded across woolly cardigans. Nearing the Canteen block the veins converge and then split apart again, clotting at the various doorways.

After lunch, he considers half an hour at the snooker table but opts for sitting on the grass in the sunshine at the far side of the sports field. He cannot begin to imagine what it would be like to spend a working lifetime here. Yes, it is worthwhile and purposeful to forge steel into boilers and pipes and vehicles, building an economy and with it a social structure. The people are good and honest enough. Two workers stroll past, the one short and thick-set, late fifties – he nods a greeting to Roy – the other taller and younger. But with their overalls, their heavy accent and their tired eyes they are of one blueprint, one body that spans the generations. Roy cannot feel any idealism and his life seems as much to do with these men as a leveret finding itself in a family of lions.

Several pairs of people are now lapping the sports field to catch some warmth before disappearing back into their boxes, and two girls are following close on the men. One is Marcia, Mr Lloyd's short, plump secretary. She is bright enough to know that she is not attractive and has a grating voice but not bright enough to change these things, opting to accept her position and learn how to use her smile and her bottom instead. She gives it a swing for Roy as they pass and waves a 'hello'.

He smiles back although his eyes are transfixed on the other girl, whom he hasn't seen before. The contrast is almost funny. She is tall and slim with long black hair, high cheekbones and straight shoulders, and even her walk is different to the other's, elegant and with fingers clasped behind her back.

"She is beautiful, I think."

The clipped, correct voice beside him brings Roy back to himself. He hasn't noticed Nick arrive. He is Asian, his family recent immigrants from Kenya, and he's probably even more out of place here than Roy. Of course, it is not his real name but no-one can be bothered to try and pronounce that. He doesn't mind because 'Nick' is local and ordinary and might help him to settle in.

The siren wails and the new friends begin to make their way back to work.

"I thought you weren't supposed to have those sort of thoughts about women," Roy teases.

"Oh, I think Allah would understand. In any case, I know she's not for me. My marriage is already arranged."

"What? But you're only eighteen. Why would you want to get married?"

"It doesn't matter what I want. It is our custom. Our parents have arranged it."

"Surely you don't have to, though. Not now you're in England. You can do what you like." Nick slaps Roy on the shoulder and laughs aloud.

"My friend, you're very naïve if you believe that. I have been in England three months. Okay, I have a job and I speak the language… even if I don't understand half the people here." He waves an arm towards the factories. "But if I am here fifty years I shall not be able to do as I like. Nobody can. Not me, not you. We all have our destiny."

They reach the entrance to the drawing office and the time clock informs them that they are two minutes late and that their wages will be docked. Roy slots his card back into the wall holder with annoyance, but not because he cares about the money. Has he not already discovered lately that there are at least some things in life we have no control over whatsoever?

"Blimey, that was all I needed to hear right now. I seem to be surrounded by people who know exactly what life is all about and what's going to happen for the rest of it."

"Don't be such a pessimist, my friend," Nick smiles. "Of course we don't know exactly how our lives will turn out. But it's all for a purpose, even the bad things, and everything will be for the best in the end. This is what we are taught and it makes things a hell of a lot more peaceful – sorry about my language."

"So it's just your belief? You don't know that it's true, it's just something to get you through the days." Roy needs something to get him through the days. They climb the stairs and settle back at their boards.

"Everything has a purpose," Nick asserts again with a nod of the head. "Most of the time we don't know what it is but that doesn't matter. Maybe we'll know one day. Right now, I have no idea why I am supposed to be drawing this elevation of bloody pipework but someone has decided it's a good idea so why worry? It's not hard."

"Your English really is good," Roy smiles.

Φ

Eva is still in London. She has said her goodbyes to Nurse Mallory and the friends she made in Liverpool, expecting never to see them again, and is staying with her German penfriend Brigitte in Maida Vale. Her mind is in turmoil but she knows what she must do and has bought her ticket. She had been a little worried about the loss of the letter – it was nowhere to be seen when she went looking – but its contents are clear in her memory and she assumes it was blown out to sea.

Today she sat for an hour on the South Bank watching the tourist boats drift downstream past the Parliament buildings, before crossing Westminster Bridge and walking along the Embankment. She has bought gifts, a leather handbag decorated with yellow flowers for her mother and a blue denim shirt with silver buttons for her father, which he almost certainly won't wear.

She emerges from Warwick Avenue tube station and begins to walk along Clifton Gardens, aware of a heaviness in her chest when she sees the large, black saloon car without number plates parked near Brigitte's flat. A tall, fair-haired man in a dark suit, white shirt and sober blue tie, gets out of the passenger seat as she approaches and holds open the rear door for her. He smiles as he discretely shows her his identification.

"Miss Nováková? Please come with us. It won't take long, I promise." She knows that she has no choice – in any case, the driver is a huge man with a thick neck and short arms and whose broad shoulder is jammed against the side window – so she settles herself in the comfortable back seat with her shopping by her side. The other man turns in his seat to face her as they drive. "I am Inspector Peter Jones. We just need to ask you a few questions." She doubts very much that it's his real name.

"And who's the gorilla?" she wants to ask, but thinks better of it. She is frightened, of course, but then, living at the crossroads of Europe, Czechoslovaks have a friendly indifference to their own personal safety.

The radio crackles a couple of times as they drive and the gorilla murmurs back to it surprisingly quietly. It's not far to Harrow Road. Paddington Green police station is a banal, white building that could easily be taken for an office block. It is unfinished. They enter through a side door and pass along featureless corridors to an interview room where a female officer is already waiting; Inspector Jones waves Eva to a chair and offers her tea. So far he has been unfailingly courteous although as he leans forward with his chin on one hand she registers the cold blue emptiness of his eyes.

An hour later, the gorilla drives her back silently to Maida Vale.

Yes, she has confirmed several times, she is a student. Yes, she has been improving her English. ("In Liverpool and Wales?" He had actually smiled.) No, she has no contact with officials of any government. Yes, Prague University. No, she has no interest in politics. Well, yes, of course she is worried about "the situation", wouldn't he be if his family were…? No, she has not met anyone important. The boy? He is not important. How did you know about…? No, she does not want to stay in the UK. She has shown him her train ticket. He is satisfied.

Ф

"What's she like, anyway, this girl you're going to marry? Have you even met her?" The tea trolley has come round and they are both sitting back on their stools with mugs in one hand and digestive biscuits in the other.

"Of course," says Nick with his mouth full. "She is the daughter of one of my father's business friends. Well, they were in business before we came here. She is quite nice, pretty enough. She'll probably be a good wife."

"When's it going to be?"

"Not for a short while. She's only thirteen."

"What?" Roy splutters, only just managing to avoid spilling tea on his drawing.

"This is our way."

"But what if you meet someone else now you're here? Someone, I don't know, nicer, prettier?"

"I won't," he answers simply.

"There was that girl we saw at lunchtime, though. You liked her."

"So what?" Nick shrugs. "There's no point in thinking about her. She wouldn't be interested in me anyway, we're from different worlds."

"For Heaven's sake, Nick, don't you want to be free?"

"I don't know what you mean," the boy frowns. "I am free. I accept Allah's will. Actually, I think your way of doing things is very complicated, full of worries and uncertainties. My life is simple. I shall marry Asha, work hard and be happy."

"But," Roy has to insist, has to get to the bottom of this, "what if you don't love her?"

"You have a strange way of thinking, my friend." Nick seems genuinely surprised in turn. "Love is simply accepting one another and being at peace. Asha has been chosen for me, and I for her. We accept that."

Roy shakes his head, munches on his biscuit, and tries vainly to put himself in other shoes. Nick seems more at home, more at ease anyway, than he is. He wants to talk about what happened last week but knows there'd be no point since falling in love is senseless. Already, Wales and Eva are so far away from here and he's having to make a conscious effort to remember everything. Even her face is a little unclear. He'd had a camera but it didn't seem necessary to take her photograph. He feels stupid. And guilty. And surely he's not supposed to find other girls attractive now?

Arthur Morris is not like Jim Lloyd. In fact, if one had been given the task of creating a human being entirely dissimilar to Jim Lloyd, one could not have done much better than the Training Director. He is short and fat, with greased down hair and a cynicism in his eyes matched only by his natural disinterest in young people. How he got the job was a mystery to everyone. Now he is wandering about his fiefdom to assert his nominal authority.

"What'yer jawing 'bout, darkie?" He stands full square in front of Nick, hands in jacket pockets and belly thrust forward, an amused smile curling one corner of his mouth.

"Metaphysics, Mr Morris," the boy answers evenly, unconcerned.

"Metterwhat?"

"That's right, Mr Morris," Roy chips in, barely able to control his anger. But this man doesn't worry him. He had been at his parents' garden party and Roy had seen his large, hairy hand on more than one female bottom. "Perhaps you can help us out?"

"Uh?" Morris screws up his eyes and pulls out the spectacles from his top pocket to help him out. He has to be a bit careful with this one, his father being a director too.

"Yes, we were arguing about what Archimedes would think of this Hellenic screw I'm drawing." Morris grunts and moves off.

"Gerroff yer arses, lads, tea's done," he calls over his shoulder.

At five o'clock Roy wanders slowly against the flow of human tide across to the office block to wait for his father and a lift home. He nods to the Receptionist, sitting absurdly small and alone in the vast glass entrance lobby, and makes his way to the lift. Stepping out onto the fifth floor, one could be in a stately alien world where the purple carpets all but swallow the shoes and even the wallpaper is deep piled. The windows are triple glazed against the noises that have paid for the building. Up here, a man is judged by the length of his desk.

He treads silently along the deserted corridor towards the coffee machine, his attention caught by the whirring of an electric typewriter from an open door at the end. He pauses, noticing the mahogany coat stand just inside that carries a man's black umbrella and bowler hat and a softer, dark green velvet jacket. The young woman typing has her back to him.

"Come in, Roy," she says cheerfully.

"How did you…?" but then he sees that the walls are covered by long, gilt-edged mirrors.

"Waiting for your father?"

"Yes. I, er… Hello. I think I saw you at lunchtime. With Marcia?" He walks round to the other side of the desk and she looks up without pausing her fingers on the keyboard.

"That's right, she's my cousin, sort of, distantly. It was her told me about this job. I'm new here this week."

"Me too," he says with a self-deprecating smile.

"Mr Jackson's in with your father. I think they'll be a while." She is about twenty and lovely, a surprise here, a single blood-red wasteland tulip. Her voice still carries a Black Country trace but Roy has already unconsciously decided that he can live with that, especially as her blouse has a couple too many buttons unfastened and the gentle swell of her breasts somehow brings back to mind the rush of waves on a beach. She stops working and pushes her chair back from the desk, crossing her beautiful, slim legs. The red pleated skirt only rides up further. She smiles at him and decides to enjoy the effect she's having.

He is both fascinated and ashamed by his own reactions to this young woman. Having once touched and been touched, the penultimate chakra having been awoken, he simply cannot help the hungry instinct that can so easily violate innocence. Last week, he was both found and lost.

"Nice jacket," she says. Someone has to break the moment. "Is it new?"

"Oh, um, yes. Do you think so? I hate it."

"But it's good to look smart sometimes, isn't it?" Yes, she probably wouldn't have had the same effect on him in jeans and baggy sweater. Yet he's already imagining that and other situations with her. Is Eva already so far away and out of reach?

ACT 5

Frontiers

Eva is waiting at Victoria Station with a few minutes before the boat train. Putting her case down beside the telephone kiosk, she searches in her bag for the address book and then dials hurriedly, glancing over her shoulder towards the guard at her platform. There is no answer.

The intercom rings softly on the desk and the girl leans forward to depress a lever.

"Yes, Mr Jackson?"

"Come in, please, Kate."

"Yes, sir." She stands, straightens her skirt and fastens the blouse buttons before pausing next to Roy on her way out. She is almost as tall as him and her scent burns into him like acid. "It won't be long now," she says.

"Kate?" She turns, almost at the door, holding her notebook and with a pencil playing at her lips. "Can I… er, would you… shall I see you again?"

"I'll be here on Monday," she smiles. "And the day after, and the day after that."

Roy finishes his coffee and absent-mindedly leaves the cup on her desk next to the chrome-framed calendar. It reads Tuesday the 20th of August. A few minutes later he is sitting beside his father as they sweep out of the car park. Glancing to one side, he sees Kate climbing into Mr Jackson's Humber, laughing.

He has known for a long time that he was born into the wrong family and, though grateful for the opportunities given to him, he and his father are virtual strangers (except that strangers would feel less antagonism). However, at this point in life he needs a man's advice.

"Do you think," he begins hesitantly as they pull up to the traffic lights, "it's possible to love more than one woman?"

"What a daft question. What would you know about love anyway?"

So that's that and the rest of the journey passes in its customary silence. At the front door, Roy leaves his keys hanging and runs for the 'phone but it stops ringing before he can reach it.

Eva puts down the receiver and just makes it to the train before it pulls away.

He asks Marian the same question later that evening in The Mermaid. She has finally returned his call and suggested they meet here for a drink. The lounge is old-fashioned and comfortable, with walnut-veneered tables and leaded windows. There are maybe twenty people in. Roy and Marian talk like old friends, even though this is only their second meeting and there's more than twenty years between them.

"Of course you can," she answers, chasing the cherry round her third Martini with her tongue. "That's why I'm divorced."

"You're very, well, candid, aren't you," he observes, not sure whether she's being serious, "for a church sort of person, I mean? Don't you worry what other people think of you?" She tosses her long red hair, which is a kind of response in itself.

"After several incarnations," she says, "you stop caring what people think. Listen, Roy, when you start out on the search, the spiritual path, you leave a lot of people behind. A lot of people. Friends, family, lovers. Because you can never go back down the path. You might as well get on with it, you'll always be misunderstood."

"I heard a couple of people at the church talking behind your back. They weren't being very nice."

"But I'm popular enough for them to keep asking me back, aren't I? I don't tell them what they want to hear, that's all, just the truth. So if you're in it for popularity, you'd better find another friend."

"No, I'm sorry, I didn't mean that."

"Then say what you mean. Look, love," her voice becomes more gentle and she reaches over to touch his hand, looking disconcertingly straight into his eyes, "what happened in the last couple of weeks and what's about to happen has put you on a different level, a different road. There's no going back now. But it won't bring you any friends, not in this world anyway." He looks at her in astonishment.

"How do you know what's happened?"

"I'm a bloody medium, aren't I?" She laughs aloud and half the pub looks round at the happy sound. "I knew as soon as I saw you."

"So why didn't you say anything?"

"And spoil the fun? Anyway, it's not my job to tell people what's going to happen, just help them pick up the pieces afterwards. Mind you," she leans forward conspiratorially, "I don't know all the delicious details…"

"Time, gentlemen – and lady," intones the landlord Adam with a wink in their direction as he rings the bell. Outside, the night is turning cold and Marian wraps her fake fur jacket closely around her as she unlocks the door of her red MG.

"Don't be so serious, Roy," she says to him finally as she climbs in and winds down the window. "Enjoy your life and help yourself to everything that comes along. It's what life's for." So she has answered his question after all. "See you soon. And take care – there's something in the air tonight."

Φ

At almost the same moment, a huge Aeroflot Antonov 24 lumbers across the quiet sky and flops like a tired, fattened goose into Ruzyně airport. It taxis up to a group of large black cars and within minutes a handful of Russian army officers carrying identical briefcases have left the `plane and disappeared into the shadows. In the departure lounge overlooking the tarmac, a tall, swarthy man wearing a lightweight blue jacket and grey casual trousers watches the cars leave. He takes a last drag on his thin cigarette, finishes his coffee and nods to his six colleagues who all now stand. The old man who sweeps the floor curses as he is pushed aside and begins to remonstrate with one of them, but then stops, foolishly, and slides senseless to the ground with the blow of a revolver on his temple. Several tourists sitting nearby reach quietly into their sports bags and deftly clip together their automatic weapons. The bald man in a white apron behind the bar has his mouth and eyes wide open as he slowly sinks down for cover, while the young waitress carrying a tray of glasses melts backwards through the kitchen door and then runs for the telephone. She barely has time to shout before a large, gloved hand pulls her back by her hair as the other hand brings the revolver down first onto the back of her neck and then onto the telephone, smashing it into small chippings. The girl is dragged by the hair back to the bar and dumped next to her bald boss.

The control tower staff are relaxed, with no more traffic due for over an hour, so when the door bursts open only one controller reacts. He reaches for the intercom but spins back into his chair with a scream as a bullet rips into his forearm. It is followed by three more single shots and the lights on the control panels go out. One tourist crosses to the window and signals with a torch to the Antonov. Nothing else moves within the tower. There is barely a breath save for the quiet sobs of the injured man.

Then after about four minutes a faint distant hum grows to a roar as the enormous bat-like shadow of a giant transporter comes in low overhead, followed by another and another in a seemingly endless black stream.

Along the East German, Polish, Hungarian and Ukrainian borders, uniformed men with left hands holding telephones raise their right arms in signal. Fifteen divisions of tanks and infantry begin to crawl into Czechoslovakia, picking up speed and breaking down everything before them.

At home, Smrkovský puts down the receiver in slow motion, blank incomprehension on his face. The spell is broken by the scream of MIG fighters overhead. Fully awake now, he picks up the `phone again and is talking to Dubček.

"Sasha, are you awake?"

"Of course I'm damn well awake. I should think everyone in Prague is awake. What the hell's happening?"

"The Russians are happening. It's an invasion. I've just had a call from the airport."

"What? Are you mad? We only just signed the agreement with Brezhnev."

"I know that. You know that. But can't you hear the `planes?"

"It's an exercise. It must be. They wouldn't –"

"Sasha, listen to me. Did we sign an agreement for tank exercises at Ruzyně?

As he speaks, a huge infantry column carrying torches and automatic weapons is approaching the north-east suburbs along the Lenin Road from the airport. Their faces are impassive with not the slightest flicker of thought to be seen.

Roy tosses heavily in his bed, his whole body aching, unable to sleep.

"Well?" Smrkovský is trying his hardest to be calm.

"Well what?"

"Well, do we run?" There's about five seconds of silence on the line, broken again by a second wave of jets.

"No, my friend, we do not run. We face them. As it is, the people will probably never believe us again anyway. I'll meet you at the Central Committee offices. And call Černík." His voice is already tired, empty. As he replaces the receiver he sees that Gabriš has come in, wearing a dressing gown and old, worn slippers.

"Is it trouble, Sasha?" He speaks gently to calm his old friend. Dubček stands wearily and puts a hand on his shoulder.

"I have to go."

"I'll be with you in a minute, then." He turns to get dressed.

"No, I have to go alone."

"Sasha, I've always gone with you ever since we were little boys. I've driven your car, taken your messages, talked things through. I'm coming."

Dubček doesn't protest. He needs a friend right now. As a handful of cars race across the midnight city, the sky above Spořilov lights up with the fluttering confetti of hundreds of parachutes.

Hoffmann is ordering Radio Prague to shut down. In the same moment, Director-General Sulek of the Czechoslovak News Agency is ordering his staff to transmit to the world that Warsaw Pact allies have come to the nation's aid at the invitation of the new Revolutionary Government of workers and peasants. The teleprinter operators stare back at him blankly. Then as he moves forward raising his voice he is immediately surrounded and forced into a chair, guarded by the two heaviest men, while their colleagues spring into action broadcasting appeals for help to the world.

Around Říjnové Square, along Dejvická and Slovenského Národního Povstání, and even further now across the beautiful fourteenth century Karlův Most, the tanks are ripping up the cobbles and twisting the tram lines with a low, steady thunder. Lights are flashing on at windows throughout the city and the sleepy eyes of men, women and children alike are trying to focus on the lumbering forms below, wondering whether this is a grotesque collective nightmare or, more hopefully, a movie set. Jan Hájek dresses quickly, kisses his confused mother and slips quietly out into the dark street.

Ф

Eva is jolted awake as the train stops suddenly. Someone outside is shouting in German and a moment later the guard is sliding back the couchette door and saying something urgently. Two women sit up, startled, and clutch their blankets to their chests while an English girl, a student, interprets for Eva, stumbling over the words.

"There's… there's been a news broadcast. Prague. I… I am so sorry. It looks like… I mean, the Russians… they're invading. The train is stopping here. We have to get off. I am so sorry." She says it genuinely, as if it is the fault of her own country. Eva interprets in turn for the other Czech women, mother and daughter, and is shocked when the older woman claps her hands with a big smile.

"Ah, thank God the train is running late!" she exclaims. "They'll have to let us stay." But her daughter, about eighteen, has begun to sob in despair.

"What about Tomáš? And father?"

"Silly girl! Don't you recognise freedom when it's handed to you on a plate? Hurry up, get dressed."

Within ten minutes the passengers are standing in small, bewildered groups about the platform surrounded by their suitcases, next to the silent train. As her mother busies herself in gathering their things together and searching for their passports, the girl approaches Eva with an imploring look. She takes a creased photograph of a smiling young man from her pocket and scribbles on the back before handing it to Eva.

"Are you going on?" Without waiting for a reply – because Eva herself has no idea what to say – she continues, "Please, will you try to find Tomáš and tell him where I am? This is his address." Then she is dragged away by her still triumphant mother. The English girl has now disappeared too.

Eva takes her suitcase and crosses to a bench, sitting alone in Nuremberg station and wondering what in Heaven's name the world is demanding of her. "Roy!" she cries softly, and allows the tears to fall.

In his own warm English bed, Roy sits up suddenly with perspiration beading his forehead. He crosses to the bedroom window and opens it, seeing the early dawn light pick out the shimmer of the garden pond beneath the willow. Further away, the dark shadows of cows in a distant Sandwell Valley field are beginning to stir. He lights a cigarette and wonders what Marian had meant. All is still.

Φ

In his own bedroom in the Hradčany Palace, Svoboda has also lit a cigarette as he stands waiting at the window. In the courtyard outside, five tank gun barrels are trained on him, which he feels is a bit excessive. He turns away to enter his study and sit at the desk. Within a minute, there is a light knock and Alois Indra and ex-Premier Jozef Lenart are shown in. They seem surprised to find the President in striped pyjamas.

"We are sorry to wake you so early," says Lenart courteously. He has been trained to be polite to presidents and cannot break the habit even now.

"You didn't wake me," replies Svoboda calmly, "I just didn't think you were worth dressing for. What do you want?"

"May we sit down?"

"No. What do you want?" He looks at Indra coolly, right in the eyes, and the traitor is momentarily confused.

"I… er, that is, we… we wish you to sign this." He places a single sheet of typed paper on the desk and Svoboda draws it closer with a finger but doesn't pick it up. "It's a list of members of the new Workers' and Peasants' Revolutionary Government." Svoboda looks away, watching the pale pink light of a new day grow beyond the window. "Come now, comrade," insists Indra, Prime Minister designate. "The Spring is over. You've had your day, you and your reactionaries. You must have known it couldn't last." The president turns back very slowly to meet the others' eyes again.

"Get out of my office," he says quietly. Then he stands and brings a fist down hard onto the desk. "Get out, worm!" The two startled men back away as he picks up the paper between two fingertips and drops it into the waste bin. Indra turns at the door, his face flushed.

"All right, old man, have it your way. We'll just have to force you."

A few hundred metres away across the Vltava, a black limousine sweeps along the embankment with its trailing escort of armoured cars and into the square beneath the windows of the Central Committee offices. Dubček is already there, watching them come. Five men in dark civilian clothes get out of the car and advance, surrounded by troops, towards the entrance. The two guards, in a pointless yet heroic gesture of loyalty to their nation, step in front of them and are shot down even before they can make their challenge.

Now there are dead, Dubček can no longer hope for things to be otherwise and he hangs his head in deep sorrow. The men in dark suits are in the room in seconds and its four occupants – Dubček, Smrkovský, Kriegel and Gabriš – are thrown back against the wall and turned, their arms tied roughly behind them by the soldiers. Over his shoulder, Gabriš sees one of the Russians produce a hypodermic needle from an inside pocket and instinctively lunges back to protect his lifelong friend. But the man simply sidesteps and Gabriš falls heavily to the floor with a single bullet in his brain. Dubček doesn't even have time to react. Within a second of the injection he slumps down onto his knees and has to be carried out to the car with the others.

Soldiers announce their arrival at the Television Centre in the middle of the city with a salvo of shells, but the attempted intimidation is a mistake for it only alerts the crew inside. As the front doors are broken down, engineers and technicians are slipping quietly out at the back and racing for an outside broadcast truck. With them is a journalist, Josef, though he's not quite sure why he's running with them; perhaps it's some basic instinct he hadn't been aware of before. They make it to the truck and out of the yard, with two technicians hanging on grimly to one side, just as three soldiers burst from the exit and raise their weapons. Bullets spit into the dust around the wheels but somehow don't hit, and the truck is away towards the forest.

Ф

When Mr Carter comes downstairs for breakfast he finds Roy speaking slowly and loudly into the telephone with his free hand over the other ear.

"A bit early for this, isn't it?"

"Shhh," says his wife.

"Yes… that's right… on the news this morning…"

"Who's he speaking to for Heaven's sake?"

"Someone in Liverpool."

"We don't know anyone in Liverpool, do we?"

"Shhh, your breakfast is ready."

"…yes, tanks and everything… terrible… people dead…"

"I insist you tell me what's going on."

"It's Czechoslovakia, dear. The Russians have invaded."

"Oh my God."

"Shhh."

"…and did she leave any message? I see… well, thank you, Mary." Roy replaces the receiver slowly and turns to face his parents. His face is entirely white, fighting back tears. He needs them. "That was a friend of Eva's, Mary. Eva called her and gave her our number. Eva's already left. She's on her way there now."

In the car on the way to work, he feels an empty sickness churn and grip the pit of his stomach. What the fuck life is this? He turns on the radio.

"…and there are unconfirmed reports that Alexander Dubček is dead. In an official broadcast early this morning, the Soviet news agency TASS said that troops had entered the country in fraternal response to appeals for help from Czechoslovak government leaders. Lord Caradon is to make a strong statement…"

Mr Carter reaches across to turn the radio off, leaving his hand briefly on Roy's arm. It's probably the first time they have touched since the boy was a young child.

"Try to forget it, son. These things happen. And like your mother said, she was always bound to go back anyway."

Roy's head is spinning with the announcer's voice, his father's touch and sudden memories of the dunes and of a tall stranger beneath a streetlamp in Wales and of a letter in the sand. His stomach heaves and he tries to wind down the window, but it's too late and he is sick on the carpet.

Φ

A railway carriage can be a cold and lonely place, particularly if it is the last one of a train that is otherwise deserted. At a rural level crossing outside Freistadt in north-west Austria this early Friday morning, an unshaven farmhand stands, his collarless cotton shirt buttoned to the throat, watching the through train rock over the points and trundle slowly past. His chin rests on his forearms as he leans against an old wooden fence. The fence may be split and rotten, and for all his hard labour he may still be poor and have few decent clothes; but he is old enough to have seen rocks thrown down into valley streams and he had parents who told him about when those rocks had formed the walls of an empire. So now he watches the train roll towards Prague and is profoundly glad to be safe at his own insignificant moment of history.

Six, seven, eight carriages pass, all equally bare. A lot of people have passed this way in the last couple of days but all in the opposite direction. Nine, ten… His eyes widen and he stands to stare after the train as if to see through the receding metal the young woman in the fawn leather jacket, curled up alone in a corner of the twelfth carriage.

Eva hasn't seen him. A book lies open, unread, on the seat beside her. She barely notices the fresh morning countryside pass and cannot tell whether the mist is on the fields or in her own eyes. She is tired and afraid, wrapping the jacket tightly around herself, but for all her incomprehension and wishing things weren't so she is wide awake. She is about to need her wits as never before.

Leaving home had been difficult, momentous enough. But surely a homecoming was never so unknowable as this. For perhaps the twentieth time since her last illusion gave up its ghost a couple of days ago, she empties her left jacket pocket. A creased photograph falls out with a lilac handkerchief along with the envelope that Roy had given her just before the train pulled away from that Welsh station. She doesn't actually need to read the few lines on the paper, torn from a small notebook, that she now holds limply. They're clear in her mind.

"When will I see you, be you again?
Where does the sun blow?
What does the sand know?
You are my mind, in you I find
all thought and fear.
Let us both seek the Idea."

The grammar is not a problem and even the paper is all but unnecessary. She has loved before and others have loved her, in their ways, and most people would be satisfied with this. She might have been. But there is a certain group of cells buried deep within the folds of the cerebellum which, once awakened, can never again rest. Somehow, this awkward and strange young Englishman has contrived to disturb these cells and upset her previously mature world outlook. No longer will there be these few years and all they've been filled with between them. Perhaps there will never be anything between them again. This was not part of the plan. Her mind now carefully picks its way about its borders and finds them porous. There is, apparently, so much more to being, and what she has been seems barely important at all.

The train slows at last to a crawl and Eva finds herself once more at the frontier. Suddenly, she's not sure which direction is home but, either way, she is alone. As she steps out into the cold and walks towards the frenzy of the guard post her limbs weaken as if her gloves and shoes were leaden.

"Be strong," she tells herself. "Please be strong. Believe." In what? She doesn't know much about God but wouldn't it be just like Him to tear apart what He has so painstakingly put together?

This sleepy little border crossing has seen nothing like this before. It is accustomed to a trickle of tourists and some early morning traders who always return by evening. But political crisis is something it was not built for and now it throbs and creaks under the weight of the one-sided emotion passing through. The Czech army guards, sharing the refugees' loss, have dropped their mask of efficient suspicion and are only cursorily checking documents. They are the only calm amidst the clamour of cars, carts and bodies, waving them through as fast as decency will allow. Old women cry, men shuffle forward with eyes downcast, a few younger ones joke quietly to hide their feelings. Perhaps some are glad. One and all they get through and then stand aimlessly, homelessly, in little knots. Austrian army trucks, someone says, are on their way.

She has been standing by the guard's left elbow for five minutes before he notices her.

"Move on, then, girl," he urges gently.

"I want to come through," she replies evenly, offering her passport. Time and belief are equally suspended momentarily as he and a couple of others in earshot stare at her. Then he glances at the passport.

"You're Czech and you want to come back through?"

"Yes."

"Are you a journalist?"

"No. I'm just going home."

Without another word spoken the way is opened for her and she carries her suitcase back to the train, her head erect, refusing tears, with a couple of hundred eyes boring into her back.

Just over another border, in a Ukrainian mountain cabin barely four hundred kilometres from his roots in Uhrovec, Alexander Dubček is staring at wooden floorboards. He can do little else, for his head is unbelievably heavy and refuses to be lifted. His hands and ankles are tied back behind the chair, his bloodstained shirt open to the waist; the habitual lines of kind determination have vanished from his face. To either side, also tied, sit Smrkovský and Kriegel, half of whose face is already dark blue and etched with thin lines of dried blood. A little extra attention is often paid to Jews and, moreover, he hasn't had his insulin today. The rest of the cabin bulges ludicrously with ten huge Kalmyk soldiers, their hard, narrow eyes and automatic weapons trained on these three men, the embodiment of Czechoslovak idealism.

There is the crunch of wheels outside and then the sound of several steps, a couple of them less rhythmic than the others. The heavy wooden door swings open and Prime Minister Černík stumbles in, hands also tied behind him. He has come by 'plane and is a little stronger.

"A lovely day, comrades," he smiles weakly to his friends, "though I hadn't been planning a holiday just yet." He limps across to Dubček and kneels down to rest their foreheads together for a moment, until he is kicked away and also trussed to a chair.

"Oldřich, do you know what's happening?" asks Smrkovský.

"Nobody knows what's happening. Nothing's happening, I suppose."

"Shut your faces," a guard shouts in Russian. He is ignored.

"So Ludvík is holding out?" A gun barrel smashes down onto the side of his neck.

"I said shut up."

"He must be, since we're still alive." The gun is raised again but an officer shakes his head. "Ha, they can't afford to damage us too much yet. They might still need us, at least until Indra or Novotný are sworn in."

"And then?"

Černík shrugs as best he can.

"Remember Nagy in `fifty-six?"

There is a long pause for collective memory. An early morning sun begins to light up the green hills outside and warm the fresh, clear air.

"There's still hope, then. Imre wasn't executed for a good two years after the Russians went in."

"There is always hope." It is the first time Dubček has spoken and it's barely audible, his eyes still fixed to the floor. But it brings a smile to the others' faces.

Φ

In a corner alcove of the Social Club are displayed several silver tankards and small medals. The room is full, tables lost under beer mugs, bottles and overflowing ashtrays, as all eyes are fixed on the green baize and the two figures beside it. Smoke curls up in thin clouds up to and around the low overhanging light. It is Wednesday evening and the final of the company snooker tournament, one of the most eagerly awaited events of the summer. Beside the short, burly figure of Dave Steel, Pressings foreman, who's forty-one and might have been born in a bar, Roy looks absurdly out of place. He's young, tall and fresh-faced, he's trying not to drink too much and he still coughs sometimes when he smokes. But he's holding his own in the last frame and no-one, least of all the other trainees who have come to regard him as rather insular and wet, can quite believe it. The class structure, which dictates among many other things that shop floor workers are better at snooker than managers and their sons, is in imminent danger. The atmosphere is full of anxiety and not at all friendly.

Dave is on the attack, laying one trap after another, each one loudly cheered. Time after time, Roy looks, calculates and escapes, to a few polite claps and much shuffling of feet and bottoms. Then he flukes the blue and a groan ripples round the room. His few supporters dare not cheer. He takes sight on the long pink, hits it slow and cleanly, and it rolls up to the lip of the corner pocket, has a long think about the consequences of its actions, then drops. Everything now rests on the black and they chase it safely for three minutes.

There is the loudest groan of the evening as Dave Steel misjudges his angle and leaves the black dead centre of the table. Involuntarily, Kate squeezes Marcia's hand under the table, her heart jumping. Involuntarily, Roy glances towards her. Had she smiled back, everything might have been all right. The crack of cue on white is hollow this time, an unclear note, as the black flies towards the corner. But it knows better than the pink, catches the edge and spins back to cannon the white into the middle pocket. It's all over, the structure stands firm, and the sigh of relief erupts into a roar of triumph as Dave's men rush forward to lift him up bodily above their shoulders.

"Well done, lad. You done well," says Dave, offering a sweaty hand when he is eventually released. He knows he's only won by default but he's still won. Roy knows he's only lost through fatigue, worry and inexperience, but he's still lost.

Nick makes his way across the room to put a hand on his shoulder and say a few kind words, although Roy doesn't hear them. He is given a small silver tankard and, at last, some grudging respect, and a few minutes later is walking back to his car with Kate under the spitting rain and the hovering black shadows of the factories.

"Come on, now, don't be so upset," she says, taking his arm. "You couldn't help that. And you nearly won. No-one expected you to get past the first round."

"Oh, thanks for the vote of confidence."

"Other people. You know what I mean."

"I should have won. My game's better than his."

"Look, he must be over forty. He's been playing for years, probably two or three times a week."

"And I've got a Maths A Level. Better ideas. And I don't have a pot belly."

They reach the car just as it starts to pour down. Inside, she leans over to rest her head on his shoulder with instinctive comfort. She is warm, her hair soft, the skin of her scented neck white beneath the security lights. Coming to himself, Roy cannot believe where he is. In a matter of weeks his life has turned inside out and around. The schoolboy found love in the wings of an international political stage and now he is sitting beside the most attractive girl in the company and she is asking him to take her somewhere so they can be alone.

Ф

In his Hradčany office, Ludvík Svoboda sits at his bare desk. A whole long day and a whole long night have passed but he has not slept, wearing fatigue all about him like an overcoat. He stares at the door opposite then seems to remember something, unclipping a medal from his jacket. 'Hero of the Soviet Union'. He grimaces with the irony of it and then drops it into the bin beside him as the door opens. The Ambassador of the USSR is announced.

"Chervonenko," the President nods wearily.

"Good day, Ludvík. My, you look tired. Have you not –?"

"It's not the time for stupid pleasantries. Where are Dubček and the others?"

"They're safe."

"You mean they're alive, at least?"

"Of course, what do you take us for?" Svoboda stares back into the man's eyes with contempt. There is no need to answer. "Look, Ludvík, I have a plan."

"Another one or the same one?"

"I don't know what you mean."

"Come now, the whole filthy thing has been your plan. Then you brought Indra into it."

"You credit me with too much influence, Ludvík." The ambassador tries to look embarrassed, which he's quite good at. "I was asked my opinion, in my official capacity, and I said that I thought the country was in disorder."

"And the people would welcome some fraternal support?"

Chervonenko shrugs in an offhand way.

"There might have been an over-reaction, a slight miscalculation."

"A miscalculation?" Svoboda thunders, getting to his feet and standing face to face with the man before thinking better of it and crossing to the window with hands thrust safely into his pockets. It has been a long life, a good life, and he's had his three score years and ten and two more, but if he gives way to his personal feelings now it will all have been wasted. With huge effort, he softens.

"Stepan, there are people dying out there. Your fraternal army is raping us. And all because someone made 'a miscalculation'?"

"Then let's settle this as soon as possible. Get it over with. Just sign in the new government."

Svoboda turns to him, the spirit of freedom back in his eyes.

"I will not. And if I did, the people would never accept it. As it is, the country is paralysed by a general strike. You cannot name one man who would be acceptable to them. You cannot – or will not – even name one man who invited you in. No, comrade –" with ill-disguised sarcasm "– I will not sign. You do not yet hold all the trumps. So what is your plan?"

"What?" The other man is taken aback by the switch of mood.

"You said you had a plan. Or did you miscalculate?"

"Yes, right. Brezhnev wants you in Moscow."

"To compromise?"

"To… negotiate."

Svoboda pauses for several seconds as though he is considering his options. He doesn't have any.

"All right. We talk. I'll follow you."

As Chervonenko leaves, Ludvík Svoboda looks out again through the window across the beautiful, now scarred city. The Vlatava still flows peacefully but in the distance a pall of smoke hangs over Václavské, Wenceslas Square. With a deep sigh, he picks the medal out of the waste bin and fixes it back onto his jacket.

"It could be useful, I suppose," he says quietly to himself.

Within a few hours he is stepping from the black limousine with Leonid Brezhnev, who is beaming and waving back over the tail of the motorcade towards the cheering crowd lining the streets leading to the Kremlin. A banner across the road can still be made out: 'Long Live Soviet-Czechoslovak Friendship!' The evening is drawing in, the last of the sun glinting on the gold onion domes.

"Well, comrade," Brezhnev says to his guest as they enter the Grand Palace, lips still drawn back in a fixed smile, "let's talk."

"Is Dubček here, and the others?"

"No. Why should they be." It is not a question.

"Because I don't talk until they're here." As an afterthought, he adds, "Alive and well."

The General Secretary shrugs. The two men know one another well enough for him to realise that bullying is pointless. Besides, he needs Svoboda's legality.

"So kindly show me to my rooms," says Svoboda. "I'm rather tired."

The train creaks to a halt again and settles down with a judder. Eva jerks awake. This journey has been interminable, the train stopping frequently for no apparent reason as if doubting the wisdom of going in this direction. Automatically, she reaches for her passport again, expecting another checkpoint, but nobody comes. Loud voices can be heard outside though so she presses her head against the window to peer into the darkness, suddenly recoiling at the monstrous dark shapes of the tanks beside the track, brooding like thin-necked beasts. The train is passing a crossroads and the Russian reservists are obviously lost, all signposts having been removed. A young officer pores over a map by torchlight, which picks out the white paint by his feet: there's an arrow and the words 'Moscow 1500 km' but he doesn't know whether he can even trust that.

So it really is all true.

Along the road, an unsuspecting car approaches and stops just short of them, the driver realising too late what's ahead. The Russian walks towards him, revolver in hand, and an arc light on the leading tank is trained on the small, green car. The frightened young driver turns to kiss his girlfriend. She is attractive, with long black hair and a velvet jacket. Eva catches her breath, for the briefest moment believing that it's… but then the young man pulls away from his girl with a guilty look and winds down his window.

Ф

Roy turns the front door key as quietly as he can, hangs up his jacket, and makes for the kitchen treading softly past the open lounge door.

"You're back early," comes his mother's voice. "Did you have a nice time?"

"No," he calls back, switching on the kettle.

"A nice girl, that Kate," she says, assuming. Actually, he's been in The Mermaid alone nursing a pint all evening so he doesn't have to talk to anyone. "Your father says Mr Jackson thinks highly of her. You could do a lot worse." Roy stirs his coffee and pauses at the foot of the stairs.

"Well, there's no point anyway, is there? I'll be off to Manchester in a few days."

"There's the holidays. Nice girl. You should bring her home." This is not a conversation he wants to pursue.

"I'm going up. I'm tired."

"A bit early isn't it?"

"I'll read." He's on the fourth stair before she remembers.

"Oh, by the way, there's a letter for you. Came second post. We don't know anyone in Germany, do we?"

Roy retraces his steps and goes into the lounge where the envelope is on the side table. He picks it up in surprise, then recognises the writing even though he hasn't seen it before.

"It's not that girl, is it?" His mother is already tense, getting upset. "Why can't she leave you alone? What does it say?"

"I'll read it later. Goodnight." This time he makes five stairs.

"Nice girl, Kate."

In his bedroom, Roy sits beside the open window, reading by the thin light of his bedside lamp. It has stopped raining and there's a light breeze coming in. Maybe that's why the pale blue aerogram paper is shaking a little in his hands.

"When this is over,
when this dark night has flown
and the shadows are dead
and our souls are our own.
Will the candle still burn?
Will we know why it had to be
and will it ever be the same?"

"Goodnight, Eva." Roy smiles for the first time in days. Perhaps it is the greatest human quality that a few words can overcome tragedy and fire can be kept in by a single memory.

Ф

During the morning of Saturday the 24th of August, Svoboda has been treated to an hour's savage oratory by Leonid Brezhnev. He doesn't mind a bit, though, for Dubček, Smrkovský and Černík, suitably brushed up, are also listening.

"Comrades, it's your choice," he concludes, spreading his arms as if the whole business has always been their choice. The president manages a wry smile.

"And what choice is that, comrade? We forget what we believe in or you will kill us? One kind of death is much the same as another to me. Perhaps I should kill myself to save you the trouble?"

"I despise martyrs," mutters Brezhnev, standing to leave. "But in one thing you are at least right. We will do anything – anything – to defend socialist freedom. You have fourteen million people. Well, many, many more than fourteen million have died to defend socialist freedom in the last fifty-one years. You cannot win. You will simply be… absorbed."

As the Soviet entourage turns towards the door, Dubček speaks for the first time. His voice is weak but even.

"I seem to remember Stalin once suggested the same thing."

The Czechoslovak leaders sink back in their chairs, looking at each other across the long solid oak table. They are watched over by four armed guards, by the huge marble bust and gilt-framed portrait of Lenin in classic pose and by the several images of Brezhnev himself at every angle around the high, panelled walls. The men look completely insignificant.

"How is František Kriegel?" asks Svoboda.

"He's had a bad time," answers Smrkovský. "God alone knows what they're doing to him now in the name of 'treatment'. They'd have the Prague Spring as one big Zionist plot if they could get away with it."

"Don't worry," says Svoboda firmly, if wearily. Someone has to lead the leaders. "We won't leave Moscow without him."

"Are you sure we'll leave Moscow at all?" observes Černík.

"Well, at least Indra won't be leaving for a while. I heard that he's had what they're calling a heart attack."

"Oh good," says Černík, brightening. "He deserves one."

They do know, of course, that they have no choice if they are to save their people from further bloodshed. Having insisted on Kriegel's presence for the negotiations, the Moscow Protocol is signed three days later (though not by Kriegel, who refuses) and enacted by the new Czechoslovak Communist Party at the end of the month. They promise to protect socialism in Czechoslovakia, to denounce the 14th Party Congress and its resolutions, to restrain the media and to reject any interference by blah blah blah.

ACT 6
New Ways

Tom shuffles slowly through the backstreets of his Moss Side patch, the Lancashire night wind whipping up newspaper and market rubbish around his cloth-bound feet. Baggy trousers are tied at the ankle, the old army surplus greatcoat pockets bulge with bottles, and a yellow woolly hat perches like a lightbulb on his thick, tangled hair. A shambles. His brow is creased like a pile of wooden planks above eyes shrunken into dark caves. The rest of his face is lost beneath streaked, straggling whiskers.

A few minutes from the university, tradition ends here and relics begin: relics of the industrial revolution and of community, relics a hundred yards long with thirty front doors, row upon row of relics. And smelly relics with arms and legs.

He pauses beneath the halo of a streetlamp to pull out his left hand

and squint at the silver watch flashing in the light. He can't actually tell the time but he likes the flash.

"That's nice, Tom," says a low, disembodied voice from a shadowed doorway. He jumps nervously, hiding his wrist away. "Looks expensive, that. Where'd yer gerrit, y'bum?" Tom backs off at a lope and is still glancing behind when he meets the glare of the precinct lights.

"Hurry yourself, Tom, you old codger. There'll be none left." The duty constable greets him in a rough but friendly voice. Tom makes for the open rear doors of the Transit van parked half on the pavement, where the air is full of steam and chatter, and joins the short queue just as the church across the road begins to spill out its congregation. A few stop to stare at the shabby creatures dotted about the precinct with their bowls and bottles, but not for long.

"Thought you weren't going to make it tonight," says Roy as he scrapes the last of the congealed green soup from the tureen and ladles it into a plastic bowl. "Sorry, that's all there is."

Tom grunts and pads over to a wooden bench where Jonno is watching him arrive with quick glances from the corners of his guarded gimlet eyes. Nothing about Jonno is ever still. His eyebrows arch and his thin lips curl as he edges along the bench like a sparrow after crumbs. Tom chews on the soup with yellowed teeth and takes a piece of dry crust from his pocket to scrape the bowl.

"'ere," says Jonno when they've finished, offering his friend a whole cigarette. "Look as what I found. Tek it, go on. I got more." Tom inspects it ritually, holding it up to the light of the Chemist's window and sniffing it as though it's a glass of Bordeaux '58. They light up and both nearly bend double wheezing. Then Tom inspects the cigarette again with obvious appreciation before glaring around at the scene with distaste. A couple of students are moving around collecting the bowls and exchanging a few words with each pile of rags and string.

"Piggin' students," he spits. "Reckon as they'm clever cos they go to youniversiplace. It's their conscience, this, payin' their debt to society." He kicks his bowl towards the nearest youth.

"But we ain't society," says Jonno, frowning. Tom rocks forward with a hissing laugh like a deflating balloon.

"That's what's so bleedin' funny," he manages at last.

The constable pads around the benches and raised redbrick flowerbeds, wishing with all his heart that he wasn't here or at least wasn't police. Bums and students, both wastes of space. But at least it won't be long now and he can head off back to the station for the day's final paperwork. Within a few minutes the knot of students breaks apart, the Transit belches blue smoke and shakes away, and everyone is already merging back into the heavy black void from which they've come. It's a darkness that somehow clings like fog and gets into your pores.

Next morning, thin rays of autumn sunshine shaft through the tall windows of the Fallow Court dining hall as the last few of an untidy queue of students edge up to the serving hatch. Consciousness is doing its best to break through bleary eyes and bleak thoughts of work ahead. Graham pushes away his plate, beans and sausage only half eaten, and pulls on his navy donkey jacket. Pausing by the noticeboard and cigarette machine near the exit, he takes a letter from the post rack and glances up at the second floor closed curtains of Roy's room across the grassy quadrangle. Inside, huddled like a foetus beneath the single blanket, Roy is trying to decide whether he's awake or not. He fumbles for the alarm clock then catapults out of bed into his dressing gown and along the corridor to the washroom. In less than ten minutes he's leaping downstairs, out through the carpark and dodging the Wilmslow Road traffic to reach the bus stop where Graham is waiting. He just has time to catch his breath before climbing aboard.

"That was close," he says unnecessarily, clinging to the silver pole and adjusting to the swaying of the bus and the fact of morning. "No breakfast. You?"

"For what it's worth." A couple of people come downstairs to get off so the two race up to claim their seats. "Here, have a ciggie instead. Hey, I got a letter this morning, from Janet. Remember I told you about her, my bird back home?"

"Oh yeah, you did."

"She wants to come up for a couple of days. Can't live without me."

"Great. Good for you." Roy finds it hard to sound enthusiastic. They lapse into silence for a few minutes until Graham wipes a peephole on the misted window and peers down at the pavement speeding past.

"Well, there's the love of your life," he says as they pass the Art Gallery. "That old ratbag Tom. Probably making for the Union for a scrounge. Bloody disgusting, begging off us. Lazy bugger. You know he laughs behind your back if you give him something? 'Piggin' students' he calls us, I've heard him. And he's got that old fleabag with him again."

"Mary," Roy says absently. "Her name's Mary. You can always cross the road, you know."

"All right, Saint Roy, don't get pious with me."

The conductor sings out 'Butlins' and rings the bell. The boys hop down the stairs and join the throng of young people milling about on the Union steps like flies around a new smell before setting out in every direction for lectures.

"Look," says Roy, eyes downcast as though knowing his words will be ill-met, "I'm going to skip the lecture. Don't feel too bright. You go on, see you after lunch." Graham turns back to him in mid-stride with a cool look.

"You know, I don't know what you're doing here," he says. "I mean, you're not cut out for it, are you, engineering? You'd rather be writing songs and thinking about stuff than actually working. How long have we been here? You just spend every evening on the soup run or at some poncy Poetry Soc or something. What about coming down Maine Road or boozing with the rest of us for once?"

"Sure. You're probably right. I just don't feel up to it today." He looks down at his feet as if the conversation is over.

"All right, it's your life. But people talk, you know. People like to put labels on other people."

"Too bad. I'm going to get some breakfast. See you later."

He turns away up the worn steps, through the white pillars beneath the bronze eagle and into the Union. Graham's words have hit home but it can't be helped. So many things are just beyond control now. Janet didn't have to write the letter, Graham didn't have to mention it, Eva didn't have to leave, the bloody Russians didn't have to... But they all did. And no, he isn't an engineer.

The coffee bar has a scattering of students in varying degrees of trance, mostly sitting in groups. Roy picks up a newspaper and takes his coffee and cheese roll to a far corner. The table is strewn with colourful duplicated flyers for this or that society, this lecture at lunchtime, that march in London next weekend. The Politics Society is urging support for students in Czechoslovakia. Roy turns this one over and tries to sketch an outline of the country with his pencil but it keeps coming out like a face and he can't quite remember exactly where it is either. Perhaps he should be more involved.

"May I join you?" A young woman with tumbling blonde hair and wearing a dark green trouser suit has come over. Roy is lost in thought, listing Eastern European countries to himself. When he looks up he recognises her from some meeting he went to last week. An English lecturer, he thinks.

"What? Oh, sure."

"You look deep in thought." She sits opposite him with a herbal tea.

"Yeah, s'pose. Look at all this stuff." He scoops up a handful of flyers and drops them like falling leaves. "Everything's planned out, isn't it? Never a dull moment."

"It helps you to meet people at the beginning of the year."

"Everything arranged for us. You know, I've got this friend back home, a guy I was working with. Asian. He's got a fiancée who's thirteen – their families arranged it for them – and he'll be getting married before long. Life sorted." He glances at his watch. "They'll be having a tea break in ten minutes. And Kate will be taking dictation."

"Um, what are you talking about?" Her voice is probing but gentle and it brings him back to the present.

"Oh, nothing, sorry. Ignore me. I'm Roy, by the way."

"Yes, I know, I saw you last week. And I'm Deirdre. My inarticulate friends in English call me Didi. You're an engineer, aren't you? We don't get many of your lot at Poe Soc."

"You mean engineers are insensitive?"

"Hey, don't have a go at me. What's up? You had a go at that poor bloke in the meeting too, said his work was pointless, if I remember."

"Oh, yes, the hairy one. Well, everyone there was on an ego trip, weren't they, just itching to get up and spout their stuff. And his just didn't mean anything. Playing with words."

"I think you'll find a lot of student writing's like that, poetry, songs too – young people just trying to express themselves."

"Fair enough. But it still ought to mean something."

After a few minutes she has to go but she's brightened Roy up enough for him to slip into the back of his morning lecture. Nobody notices. The hall is packed with about a hundred and fifty students and the lecturer is so far away he can barely be heard. Roy squints at the coloured diagrams roughly sketched out on the white board; it's thermodynamics, though it may as well be Mandarin. He thumbs through the shiny new and unused textbook he's brought and wonders why he's living his life in all the wrong places. Possibly the wrong century too.

At lunchtime the next day, the previous evening having been spent copying Graham's notes ("You owe me a pint now."), he's arranged to meet Deirdre again on the way to afternoon lectures. They walk by the small boating lake in Platt Fields with their coats pulled tight around them against a cold wind.

"Summer's gone, then," she observes conversationally.

"Totally," he agrees. "And a lot more."

"Mmm. So are you going to tell me what's been eating you?" He doesn't answer and they complete their first circuit in silence until she tries again, gesturing to the water. "Do you think there's any fish in there?"

"I doubt anything could survive long in that. Haven't you noticed, even the ducks spend all their time on the pavement, walking round like us."

"I had one once."

"What, a duck?"

"No, silly, a goldfish."

"Doesn't every kid?"

"Ah, but Harriet was special. She was good company and I was a grown up. My early childhood was spent in West Africa. My parents were missionaries, would you believe, then I was sent over here to boarding school so I'm used to living alone – still do. A very quiet place, just a couple of rooms and a bit of a kitchen, all purples and blues and posters and souvenirs."

"And Harriet," he prompts, wondering what the point of this is unless it's to tell him about her rooms. She's ten years older and her voice is rather dry, academic, but she's attractive with a girl's figure. Another confusion for his mind.

"She was a bit faded round the gills but quite happy. I was convinced she was smiling at me every time she came round in her bowl.

Then some well-meaning friend told me it was cruel to keep fish like that so I forked out on a tank with plastic shells and snails and bubbles. Everything her little fishy heart could want. Do fish have hearts?"

"I guess so. They must have some kind of circulation."

"Ah, well, that was exactly Harriet's problem. Circulation. The poor old thing was so used to the bowl she just kept swimming round in circles and glaring at me accusingly. I even tried laying a trail of ants' eggs round the edges of the tank to get her used to it, but she was dead in a week."

"Probably got too fat to swim."

"Do you think so?"

"No, I think the whole story's leading up to some sort of wise moral. Lecturers do that, don't they? What is it, then, back to everything in life being organised? We all need routine, security? We can't handle change?"

She stops to light a cigarette, inhaling deeply. She seems stung by his words.

"I was only telling you about my fish. Heavens, is that the time? I must dash, got a first year Lawrence tutorial and if I'm late they'll start thumbing through the rude bits." The words come out in a rush and she's already turning away towards the road, tossing her cascades of hair. "I expect I'll see you again, Roy."

"Happiness is being satisfied with what you've got?" he calls after her. She stops a few yards away and looks back at him coolly, an odd look in her eyes. Two young mothers passing nearby with prams also stop talking and watch them, waiting for the reply.

"Happiness," she says slowly, "is whatever two people want from each other."

She disappears along the path and Roy turns back to the ducks and the pale northern sun reflecting on the dark waters of the lake. He knows he's upset her though he's not sure how. Maybe all the events of the last two months have actually made him less sensitive. Suddenly, the next line of the song comes to him although he isn't sure of the notes without his guitar. Standing still, an incongruous figure in the middle of the pavement outside the small café, he tries to visualise the fingering. It's something like… yes, E… C… B… A…, G… E… D… E… He looks up at the clock above his head. If he hurries, he can get back to his room to check it and still make the afternoon lecture. It's Mechanics.

Φ

In the even colder and now less picturesque Vrchlického Park in Prague, beside the railway station and between the shell-blasted Bohemian National Museum and Maksim Gorky Square, Russian soldiers continue to dig themselves into their command post. It is around midday and most of them have been awake over seven hours, time filled with emptiness. Some of them are writing letters home, some are bent over bowls washing underwear and socks, some are cleaning their guns, some just sit and stare at nothing.

By the broken-down perimeter wire at the Wenceslas Square end of the park, half a dozen T54 tanks and a few armoured cars sit huddled together like a herd of morose alien beasts. Their crews in padded black leather jackets are perched in the turrets staring down the large group of young locals who have gathered, as they do every day now. The spartan whipcord uniform and gaunt, close-shaven features of the soldiers contrast sharply with the long hair, denims and colourful jackets of most of the Czechoslovaks. Before long the discussion begins, as usual, and the soldiers can't help being drawn out of their vigilance into the argument. Sometimes it's in Czech, sometimes Russian, with one or another interpreting. The TASS cameraman scurries enthusiastically from angle to angle for his pictures of fraternal solidarity, soldiers ensuring that they're smiling as the lens meets them, locals ensuring that they're not.

"But comrades," says one Russian officer who doesn't look old enough to be out of school, "I love your country. Don't you?"

"With all our hearts," comes the reply. "That's why we want you to go away. And don't call us 'comrades' – we might have believed it six months ago but never again."

"Don't you understand that we're here to protect you?"

"Ah, so the fifty people you've killed so far were capitalist insurgents, then? Including the Palace guards, the nurse, the two children?"

"There are agents everywhere."

"Yes, another trainload of KGB arrived yesterday."

"Go home, scum, you're not wanted..."

"We were happy. We don't need you..."

As more voices join in and other soldiers are attracted to the debate, the crowd thickens and intermingles. At its fringes, souvenirs are changing hands surreptitiously: a red cap star for two packets of cigarettes, three live cartridges for a tee-shirt. A few girls stand deliberately, provocatively close to the Russians in short skirts and half-unbuttoned blouses.

"Shit," breathes one infantryman, turning aside to a bearded youth whose been interpreting, "I haven't seen girls like this for two years. Haven't touched one for even longer."

"Really?" says the youth. "Perhaps we can help." He whispers to two friends nearby who nod and jump onto a scooter, juddering away at speed over the broken road. In ten minutes or so they're back with a large cardboard box full of well-thumbed magazines, American, German and Swedish. Some are distributed free though roubles are demanded for the American ones; they're less explicit but more dangerous.

And so now that the Russians' attention has been completely drawn, the second act of today's drama can begin. A small group of young men move quietly around the back of the vehicles with the paint pots they've been keeping hidden inside their jackets. A black swastika is daubed here, Dubček's name there in red on the green camouflage metal plating. There's paint on gun sights and periscopes. There are broken bottles beneath the tyres of cars. There are bags of flour in gun barrels. Underground leaflets flutter down into unguarded turrets.

Before long, a couple of lorries arrive from the airport with the soldiers' lunch.

"Bloody soup again, I expect," groans an infantryman, looking up reluctantly from his magazine. Just as he speaks, a single shot rings out a hundred metres away followed by distant cheers. The conversations freeze but the Russian is unconcerned. "It's all right. Dmitri has got another squirrel. They taste disgusting but at least it's meat. Can't be many left now."

But the shot has chilled the Czechoslovaks and broken the atmosphere. The game's over for today, the crowd moves away and the soldiers set about cleaning their vehicles before the afternoon inspection. There might be a musical performance in the children's playground later.

The locals head off to Wenceslas Square to join the few hundred students sitting there on the cobbles around the monument. People come and go here, to eat or to sleep, but the numbers never falter day or night. They've worked out a rota.

At one side of the square littered with wreckage, Eva is standing and talking with a tall man. He's wearing a long raincoat even though the day is dry. Recognising Jan and his brother Gustav approaching, she pulls away and moves towards them.

"Eva!" He runs the last few steps to her and they embrace warmly, then she shakes Gustav's hand and smiles a greeting. "Eva, what are you doing here? We thought at least you were safe."

"I am safe, Jan."

"You know what I mean. In England. Why did you come back? And where have you been?"

"I've been to see my family. Yes, they're all right. I've just got back to Prague. And how is everyone? Have you seen Aleš? It must have been terrible for you all, when it happened. I was still on a train…" The words are tumbling out of control so Jan takes her hands in his to calm her. They look into each other's faces in a new way now. All relationships have changed. Then the three of them begin to walk to nowhere in particular but staying in the Square.

"It was horrible, Eva. Unbelievable." Jan shakes his head sorrowfully. "I'll never forget this as long as I live. None of us will. We're scarred."

"And your arm?"

"Oh, that's nothing. It's all right, just a broken bone. Bones mend. But listen, it must have been almost worse for you, though, not really knowing what was happening."

"I'm back now. And I'm glad. Somehow…" she pauses, choosing the words carefully, "it gives me a chance to start again. All of us must now."

"So you're going to stay?"

"I don't know. No, I don't think so. I think I have to go back, if they'll let me."

Jan beams and slaps an arm around her shoulder.

"Aha! You've met someone, haven't you? Hear that, Gustav? Our little Eva is in love with a capitalist!"

"Don't be silly." She pulls away but smiles.

"Then what about Aleš? You're engaged, aren't you?"

"Yes. No. I don't know. Anyway, I had to come back for the anniversary next month."

"Of course, happy birthday Czechoslovakia! What a joke that is."

They take outdoor seats at one of the cafés. Business continues as well as it can and the people need their cafés and bars more than ever now. The three of them sit in silence over their hot drinks for several minutes, looking out across the crowd, the banners and the discreetly placed groups of armed soldiers.

"Did you hear about Josef?" Jan continues quietly, his head bowed. "You wouldn't believe what he's been doing. I never quite knew what to make of him before but he's a hero now."

"Josef? What do you mean?"

"He was in the Television Centre when the Russians came in and starting shooting the place up."

"My God. Was he –"

"No, listen. He and a few others got out at the back and made off in a truck with some equipment. They hid up for a while then set up a studio in a block of apartments. They've been broadcasting ever since, nonstop. And it's been picked up by the BBC World Service too. The Russians are furious 'cause they can't find them, or the relay transmitter."

"Have you seen him?" She is astonished and has anxiety written across her face.

"Yes, the once. He came to get someone for an interview and I helped him. He told me everything that's going on. Look, I can take you there and you'll see for yourself. It's on Na Petr –"

"Don't tell me," she interrupts quickly. "It's best not. The fewer people know the better. As long as he's safe, that's all that matters." Gustav shoots her a quizzical look now. Everyone's instincts have been sharpened lately.

"Eva, who were you talking to when we met you, the other side of the Square?" She pales slightly but recovers herself before Jan notices anything.

"Oh, no-one important. One of my university lecturers. I have to sort out my course."

"Don't mind my brother," Jan chuckles. "We're all on edge these days. There are probably agents everywhere. You don't know who you can trust. It's hot. A lot of intellectuals are getting out."

"Isn't that what the Soviets want?"

"I guess so," Jan shrugs, "but what can anyone do? We can't fight them. We can't even argue with them. Dubček and Svoboda have caved in – well, I expect you've heard the broadcasts. A lot of people are angry but they didn't have a choice, did they? And it's obvious Dubček's sick now. People may as well go. Better free and weak than a slave, or even dead. Don't you think?"

"So will you go too?" Jan and his brother exchange heartfelt looks.

"Maybe. Probably, yes. They've already got me marked down, haven't they? On a list somewhere. There's no life here now and I may be able to do some good work abroad. Josef knows people who have set up a route into Austria. Can you help me, Eva? I mean, tell me somewhere I can stay in England for a while?"

"Yes, I expect so."

"And will you come too?"

"I don't know. I'm not ready yet."

"It will have to be soon," interjects Gustav. He has been following the exchange carefully, watching their faces while keeping an eye also on those around them, self-appointed watchdog and mentor to his dangerous younger brother. He has promised their mother. "The borders are bound to be sealed off soon."

"Yes, I suppose… oh, that reminds me." She reaches into her jacket pocket for the creased and dirty photograph. "I met a girl on the train in Germany, on the way here. A Czech. She was with her mother who insisted they stayed there when we got the news. The girl didn't want to, she was really upset. I promised to try and find her boyfriend –" Jan takes the photograph and studies it, "– just to let him know she's safe. She was in a terrible state. See, the address is on the back. Do you know it?"

"Sure," says Jan with a sigh, "but there's no need."

"What do you –"

"His name's Tomáš Holub."

"You know him?"

"Everyone in the country has seen this photograph by now. It's been on Josef's television broadcast." Jan's voice has hardened along with his eyes. He tears up the photograph into tiny pieces, leans over and drops them carefully into the nearby drain.

"Jan! What are you doing?"

"He's dead, Eva. Dead. Some Russian shot him for handing out flyers."

Φ

In the huge lecture hall, the young research engineer is saying something about crossbeam stressing and equivalent continuous loading, whilst at the same time making expansive sweeps with coloured pens over the diagram on the board to divert attention from the fact that his sum hasn't worked. But it's late in the afternoon and a Friday anyway so he decides to concede and dismisses them with an assignment.

"Dead giveaway, that," says Roy to Graham as they collect their books and papers together and stand up, stretching thankfully, "packing up in the middle of a problem. He's made a boob somewhere." He squints at the distant board for a few seconds. "Yes, see? He missed out the second pivot." Graham looks at him with a mixture of shock and new admiration. All's well again.

"Good grief, fancy you noticing that. Why didn't you tell him?"

"Don't want to get people talking about me for the wrong reason, do I?"

A few minutes later they're squeezing out of the packed lift and shivering with the sudden cold draught from the open doors, heading for the Union along with a few hundred others newly released from mental toil.

"Talking of boobs," says Graham predictably, "have you noticed that rather lovely brunette who's always reading a book in the coffee bar?"

"Sure, that's Alison. She's on the soup wagon sometimes. Very nice."

"I think I feel my social conscience being pricked suddenly."

"Don't you think of anything else? You've already got half the female population of Manchester sorted by cup size."

"What else is there to think about?" Graham assumes an innocent look. "It is normal, you know, for blokes."

"Yeah. You should meet my friend Paul back home. You make a right pair." Graham nearly falls over laughing. "Anyway, you've got no chance. She's far too intelligent for you. Second year Psychology."

"Mmm, a challenge, I grant you. But not impregnable for a skilled man."

They have to queue up for ten minutes in the coffee bar but it's worth it for the fresh Eccles cakes that are becoming a late afternoon ritual.

"So are you going to the disco in the bar tomorrow tonight?" Graham suggests, sensing a change in his new friend's demeanour. "You know what a disco is, do you? A place with loud music and pretty girls leaping about in tiny dresses and men standing five deep at the side of the room trying not to look lecherous? Psychologically fascinating. Oh, you could invite Alison. Might even enjoy it."

"I'll see. Probably need to do some work, though, catch up a bit."

"Ah, you've seen the light of engineering, then."

"Not really. It's just that sometimes you have to accept things as they are, don't you?"

In the early evening, he stands for a while at the open window of his small, yellow-painted room, looking out over the carpark at nothing in particular as the two hemispheres of his brain do battle over what he should be doing. A passing police car with blue light flashing distracts his eye. He notices with pleasure his own small green car parked below and feels a pang of guilt that perhaps he hasn't been grateful enough for the advantages life has given him. Maybe he should write to his parents. Maybe. He draws the curtains and turns back past the unmade bedclothes to the small desk, where he picks up the heavy red and blue textbook from the pile and opens it at the index. It is Thermodynamics for Beginners. As he picks up a pen, Magical Mystery Tour explodes through the thin wall from next door. Roy thumps the wall.

$$\Phi$$

Mr Carter has shut himself away in the dining room at the back of the house. This is a normal Friday evening. The table is strewn with papers except for the imposing Hewlett-Packard electronic 9100 calculator borrowed from the office. He has a fountain pen in his hand and will probably be here until past midnight. It may be over twenty years since he was demobbed but the work ethic, the drive to provide security for his family, has never dimmed; moreover, you just have to keep ahead of the others.

In the lounge, his wife has turned off the television – the news is always disturbing these days anyway – and picked up her own pen along with the pad of pale blue writing paper. She knows that she should write to her son because he must be homesick and would appreciate some news from home. Except that there isn't any. Life is going on in exactly the same pattern it has done for years now. She gets up first and makes breakfast, kisses her husband goodbye on the cheek, does some perfectly unnecessary housework before a bite of lunch and an afternoon rest, reads a magazine and then begins to think about making dinner. Somewhere in between she listens to Mrs Dale's Diary. Should she get a little job, perhaps? He wouldn't like it. And she can't write any of this to Roy.

What she wants to write is how proud his father is of him, even though he's never said it and isn't likely to any time soon. (Well, he might when Roy gets his degree, the first in the family, but that's a while off.) She wants to write that there are reasons for his father being so, well, intolerant, why he's so conservative. Things happened in the war, and even before that, things he's never talked about to anyone else. There are reasons. There are reasons why she herself objected to Eva back in July. But she can't write any of this.

It ends up being quite a short letter, telling him that they miss him and the house seems very empty, hoping that he's eating properly and not smoking too much, hoping that he'll make it back for a weekend soon even if it is only to bring a pile of washing and maybe he'll get to see that nice girl Kate when he does. It's a letter full of hope. She licks the envelope and goes up to bed.

Kate is sitting on the edge of her own bed in her underwear, listening to Paul Burnett on Radio Luxembourg 208. The reception is crackly and keeps fading but it's worth it. Her favourite song, by the Bee Gees, is at number three. She's thinking back to the evening of the snooker final, when Roy had kissed her and touched her breast but then pulled away and become silent. There's something wrong with that boy, yet… he's different. Maybe he just wouldn't get involved because he knew he'd be going off to university, but then he has to come back in the holidays, doesn't he, and they get plenty of those. So if she maybe wrote him a letter, friendly-like, something newsy, and casually drops in that it would be good to see him when he comes home...? What can she tell him? That Jim Lloyd has gone off work sick and people are saying he won't be back? That she's sure Mr Jackson is having an affair with the Accounts woman, that one with the short red hair that's definitely dyed, because he keeps leaving the office for a couple of hours after lunch? That Nick has started speaking in Black Country dialect to try and fit in but was beaten up last week at the back of the Social Club by a couple of the Foundry men who thought he was taking the piss? No, she can't write any of this. He wouldn't like it.

She slips off her bra and stands in front of the wardrobe mirror for a moment to check her figure, then slides under the sheets and turns off the bedside lamp, leaving the radio on.

Marian has been giving an evening demonstration at the small, white-painted church in Union Street, Stourbridge. Her brief talk about Swedenborg's vision of the afterlife in Heaven and Hell didn't go down particularly well – no surprise there – but even she had been surprised by the clarity of the messages received, even if most of them weren't the least bit spiritual. Then when it was all over and she was sitting in the MG about to go home, there was a presence that she'd never met before, someone quiet and distant yet with strong thought. A monk? It was difficult to make out everything he was saying because she'd already grounded herself after the event, but he just wouldn't go away. It was something about Roy. Some kind of warning…

"Oh, I see," she then murmurs to herself. But she couldn't tell him that.

Φ

In the huge downstairs Union bar, it's Satisfaction. Graham, however, is staring mournfully into his pint as it vibrates slightly on the table. Trying again, he looks across to Alison, wearing a thin white dress and a bored expression.

"The old ones are the best, eh?" He tries to sound bright but the swell of her breasts has him almost tongue-tied.

"I thought you wanted to talk about social work," she says sharply, "not just stare at my tits."

"No, honestly, I wasn't. I mean, yes, they are very… um, well, let me get you another drink anyway." He fights his way through the crush and finds Roy there, deep in conversation with an attractive blonde woman. "Hey, you made it, then," he greets his friend without taking his eyes off her.

"Yeah, hi Graham. You persuaded me. This is Didi."

"Dee dum. Pleased to meet you. Are you an ol… er, mature student, then?" She's had a few drinks already so isn't offended.

"My, Roy, your friend certainly has a way with women, doesn't he? Good with words. Maybe you should bring him along to Poe Soc. He'd fit right in." She gives Graham a playful punch to the shoulder and turns away to order their drinks. The bar staff are working at a hundred miles an hour; it's a special challenge, Saturday nights in the Union.

"Seems it's not my night," Graham grimaces. "And you were right about Alison. I shall trust your judgement implicitly from now on. It's all underprivilege and social deprivation with her, isn't it? My skills aren't up to that sort of thing." He lapses into a moody silence for a while, looking back across the room and noticing with relief that Alison is now dancing with a short, scary-looking chap with thick glasses. "Jeez, where can a chap find some quiet uncomplicated sex these days?" He hasn't noticed that Didi has already turned back to them, a glass in each hand.

"Come with me, boys," she says. "There's a table over there with some of my students. Graham, I'll introduce you to Red. You'll get on very well with her."

"Not too well read, I trust?" he says, perking up.

"Only D H Lawrence."

ACT 7

Moving On

A few weeks later, at the end of October, Czechoslovakian independence is fifty years old and its young people celebrate by burning Russian flags in the street and distributing mocked-up copies of Zprávy, the official newspaper of the occupying forces, printed on an underground press. There's an exclusive interview with Leonid Brezhnev on the front page beneath his smiling portrait, in which he apologises to the Czechoslovak people for his "error of judgement" and urges his soldiers to return home. There's even a crossword in Russian, composed entirely of obscenities, and a report on the back page of the recent soccer match in which AC Sparta Prague beat PFC CSKA Moscow 68-nil. The daily students in Vrchlického Park ensure that each Russian soldier gets a copy.

Charles University is now more than six hundred years old and its haunted eyes have seen many conflicts from the Hussites to the German invasion of 1938. It will survive this one too. On a wooden bench in the grounds of the Faculty of Arts in Staré Město, Eva sits with the same book of English idioms she had taken to Wales open beside her. She can't concentrate. She has tried to resume her course but the department is hardly functioning with half its lecturers missing and most of the students still spending their days or nights in Wenceslas Square.

She has also met with Aleš again and they have tried to resurrect their relationship. But it's not the same. Nothing is, for anyone, and never will be. Life is compromise. Eva has moved into a small two-room apartment on the edge of the city with an old school friend, Irena, who is studying Medicine and has an appropriate, stubbornly cheerful attitude to human suffering. Each evening they take it in turns to cook whatever dinner they've been able to find and then talk about shared memories with cigarettes and glasses of cheap wine until one or the other decides they have to do some study.

Pavla Horáčková is Eva's best friend, though. They share the same course and, because of this, some of the same sensibilities, although Pavla has not been abroad and is constantly pressing Eva for descriptions of Western life. Especially Western men. She is a little younger and, despite everything, full of optimism for a new start one day, probably in America. It's infectious and Eva has always known that she can confide in her. It's a precious gift these days. Pavla moves the book to one side and sits beside her friend.

"You know," she says, "it's been, what, over two months now since you came back. And we've known each other for two years. You're not the same girl you were before you went to England. Yes, a lot has happened. The fucking Russians happened. But I don't mean that. I mean Roy happened. And I don't want to lose my friend – ha, there aren't so many around nowadays – but you have to go back. If you can." Eva smiles and squeezes her hand.

"I don't know. There are things to do here. And responsibilities."

"You mean your family?" Pavla assumes. "You told me your Dad's not well, is that it? So go and see them. Take a week off. Sorry, but you won't be missed by the department, they'll just assume you're in the Square. Go and see your parents. Tell them what you've told me and see what they say."

Eva says nothing for the moment, running the daunting scenario through her mind, unaware that she's begun to suck one finger.

"Look," says Pavla, rummaging in her cavernous bag and withdrawing a thin book with an English title, "they haven't got round to stripping the library yet. I found this the other day. She's a minor poet, Wyn Messenger, not famous, not especially good but I like this." She thumbs through to page twenty-eight and recites slowly.

"'You must decide.
Stand beneath the cherry tree
and lift your eyes
just for a moment
for that's all the world may give you.
This moment rare,
a moment to decide if life is full
or void,
it lasts or like pink blossom falls
when winds of fate blow
cold indifference.
Is there a haze of pink beyond
or do green leaves make sturdy arms
to hold you from your yesterdays?
You must decide.'

"We only have this moment, Eva. Don't let the wind blow you off where you should be."

Next afternoon, Eva is on the train north-east to Trutnov in the Hradec Králové, near the Polish border.

Φ

A few days before Hallowe'en, Roy and Graham are sitting with Didi and Red in the Sunday evening quiet of the Fallow Court bar. They have drifted into feeling comfortable together, content with occasional silences. Roy is seeing Didi once or twice a week and there is no more than gentle affection between them. Sometimes he tries to imagine what more might be like, but he doesn't feel it. That may seem strange to some people – well, definitely to the majority of students judging by the volume of traffic outside his door in the early hours of most nights. He has almost got used to finding girls fixing their make-up when he goes along the corridor to clean his teeth. But what was it Marian had said? Something like, "When you start out on the path, you leave a lot of people behind." He had met Eva and there it was.

Didi doesn't seem to mind and doesn't ask questions. After all, there's a few years between them and an intelligent, if naïve, young man is a refreshing change from the posing intellectuals she's mostly surrounded by. They have kissed a couple of times, but then only lightly.

On the other hand, she had been spot on about Red and Graham. They suit each other beautifully. The rough, exuberant young engineer who used to attack life headlong with eyes firmly shut seems to be settling for the calm romp he finds with this girl that all other male students watch pass by. He can even be quite soft at times, between the blazing rows they both enjoy, the perennial conflicts of art and science, and gets embarrassed when Roy teases him about it. She is nicknamed for her hair, not unlike Marian's but darker, almost burgundy. It's long and thick and when she tosses her head or dances any man within twenty yards will be transfixed by the flood. Her features are thin, classic Geminian like her quick mind and speech, and she has dark gypsy eyes.

"I had a dream last night," says Roy eventually.

"Ah, here we go, this should be good," mocks Graham. He turns to Didi. "Have you heard about this guy's dreams? They're all naked women on white horses flying over deserts. I hope you're not easily offended."

"Shut up," says Red, digging him in the ribs. "Don't be so rude. Go on, Roy."

"Well, I think it might be about Eva. Have I mentioned her?"

"Just the five or six hundred times." He scratches his head. "Always interesting though. Should I get some drinks in now – they'll be closing in an hour or so."

"Shut up!"

"So I was alone on this boat, one of those old sailing ships kind of thing with an acre of sails, you know? And the sea was rough, pitching all over the place. I could really feel it."

"I said you shouldn't have had that biria –"

"Shut up!" Two voices this time.

"Well, I wasn't getting anywhere and the wheel just kept spinning round. It was scary, except you know how sometimes you can watch yourself in a dream like it's someone else? Very weird. Anyway, after a while I realised there was someone else there. More than one, though I couldn't see them. And it was as if they took over the controls because the wheel stopped spinning and everything started to get calmer, the waves dying down. And I could see a beach up ahead in the distance, still a long way off, and a woman standing there." He stops and looks around at them.

"Then what?" prompts Didi.

"Then nothing. I woke up, I think. The boat didn't go any further."

"Bloody `ell, mate, what a let-down. Now we have to wait for the next instalment."

"No, Graham, I don't think so. See, the thing is I was feeling really sad when I woke up, even though things seemed to be getting better in the dream. And what I don't get is that it was me doing the travelling and the woman was waiting for me."

"Still no news, then," asks Didi gently, "from Eva I mean?"

"No, nothing. I've no idea what's going on. I've written to the address she gave me – her parents, I think – but I don't know if any letters get through now."

"Do you suppose," she continues after a thoughtful silence, "that something's happened? To her, I mean." The words send a chill through all of them and Roy sits bolt upright.

"God, I never thought of that. What sort of thing?"

"I've no idea, Roy. It just seems the kind of dream that's trying to tell you something."

"But look, mate," Graham chips in, suddenly much more sensitive and trying to reassure his friend, "you told me yourself how difficult it is to interpret dreams. This one could be about something completely different. I don't know, something like having trouble with the uni work but it all works out in the end. Eh? Or maybe it's nothing at all. It doesn't have to mean anything, does it?"

"Clairvoyance." Three heads swivel round as one to look at Red. "Or precognition. You seem to be pretty psychic after all, judging by other things you've told us."

"She could be right," Didi agrees. "You should ask that woman you mentioned once, the medium. What was her name?"

"Marian. But –"

"I'm very psychic." They swivel back to her. She sounds very definite about it. "I am, I know. My father's a seventh son and he's Irish we've got Romany blood too. I'm always getting strange feelings."

"Yeah, I know. Usually about five o'clock in the mor –"

"Shut up!"

"It's true. Sometimes I just know what someone's going to say or what's going to happen. I get a sort of buzzing in my head, like someone's telling me." Graham lopes around the bar with his shoulders hunched.

"Ze bells, ze bells!" in a French accent. "Grief, we've got a right couple of nutters on our hands here, Didi. Did you realise? This could be dangerous."

She laughs, delighted by these irreverent and bright young people who accept her as an equal.

"Never a dull moment with you guys."

"I'm serious," insists Red. "You don't know, there might be spirits around us all the time, trying to help us."

"Er, you don't mean they're watching us everywhere, do you?"

"Shut up. Look, we could have a séance, you know, the Ouija thing. We can use this." She drains her wine glass and slips it into her coat pocket so the barman doesn't see.

"I know a trick with glasses and spirits, too," says Graham, standing up again and heading for the bar. "My round."

Red has taken charge of this and insists that Hallowe'en is the perfect time, so a few evenings later they meet up again at Roy's room. He opens the door for them with a flourish and heads off down the corridor, calling back over his shoulder.

"Make yourselves at home, if you can all squeeze in. I'll get us some coffee." When he comes back, Graham has brought the chair in from his room a few doors along and pulled the desk away from the wall, whilst Didi is sitting on the bed, leaving a space for Roy and nervously watching her student in her new and unsuspected element and wondering whether she ought to be here. Red is tearing a piece of paper into small squares and writing letters on them, then arranging them in a circle on the desk around the upturned and washed glass. She is in control. Graham is sitting strangely quiet on his chair and doesn't even make any silly noises when the lamp is switched off. The security light outside in the carpark is just enough.

"Put one finger lightly on the glass," she tells them, "and close your eyes." After a minute or so of nothing happening, Roy clears his throat apologetically.

"Er, if there is a message, well, how can we read it with our eyes closed?"

"Oh, yes," she agrees, "I didn't think of that."

"Sometimes it takes a scientist," observes Graham quietly.

"All right. We'll open our eyes but we have to concentrate."

Soon the glass begins to move scratchily across the desktop and its movement jolts them even more alert. It revolves slowly as if familiarising itself with its surroundings until Red asks, "Is there anyone there?" The glass stops immediately, then edges towards the piece of paper with the word 'No' written on it.

"Oh, well that's all right, then. We can stop now."

"Shut up, Graham. Dear spirit, if you are with us please tell us your name."

G... R... A... H...

"Graham!" three voices in unison. "Stop pushing the glass!"

"I didn't, honest," he protests. "Why shouldn't a ghost be called Graham? It's a perfectly good name."

They settle back again and soon the glass begins to move as if of its own accord, picking up speed so they can barely keep their fingers on it. The atmosphere is suddenly charged. Roy's mouth is open, Graham is beaming excitedly and Didi is rigid with fear. Red is frowning with concentration as she tries to call out the letters.

"G... R... A... H... A... M... Yes, Graham... B... A... B... Y... Baby? Graham baby? What the –? C... H... R... I... S... T... H... E... L... Christmas? P... M... E... No, it's Christ help me. R... O... I... That's meant to be Roy. H... E... L... P... Roy help.

Fuck, what's going on?" The glass is racing now and the tension is so unbearable they're forgetting to breathe. "R... O... Y... Yes, Roy, we got that. E... V... A... D... E... A... Evade what? Oh, no, it's Eva. Then what? I missed the next bit. H... E... L... P... M... E... P... L... E... Help me. Shit, how?" But the glass spins from beneath their fingers and slides under its own power to the edge of the desk, falling and splintering on the floor.

"Well, that's that," says Graham, springing up for the light switch. "Great idea, that was, Red. Bloody great." She is sitting as if transfixed, staring at the table whilst Didi is already standing and reaching for her coat.

"Sorry, guys, gotta go, early lecture tomorrow." She's half through the door before Roy comes to and also starts to get up.

"Just a mo, you haven't had your coffee. At least let me drive –" But she's gone.

"No, it's fine, really. Goodnight," she calls back. Roy gathers up the broken glass as best he can while the others sink back exhausted in their chairs. Graham folds his hands behind his head.

"Don't worry, mate. I expect it's just your powerful spirit that's frightened her off."

"Oh, do shut up!" Red almost shouts, angry and worried at the same time. There was something there, but what was it? "You always have to say something coarse and stupid, don't you?"

"Me stupid? All that was your idea, girl. Don't have a go at me, I'm only trying to get things normal again." Red looks sadly from one to the other.

"I'm sorry, Roy, really. Something went wrong. That's never happened before. Don't take it too seriously. And I'm sure Eva's perfectly all right. Have you had any post from her?"

"No, nothing. But don't worry, it's fine." Oddly, he is the most composed of all of them. He knows that it wasn't real, that it came from their own minds, well, his in particular. Although he doesn't understand the first bit, about 'Graham baby'. The rest is because his inner thoughts are locked onto Eva, they will go on haunting him and it can't be helped. Still, this is not the moment for metaphysics so he goes back down the corridor to make fresh coffee.

Φ

Pan Novák looks sternly at his daughter across the solid oak dining table, the evening meal paused. He is at least wearing the denim shirt with the silver buttons. His wife sits quietly at one side, anxiously, knowing full well what's coming and what she'll have to do.

"You're telling us, girl," he almost growls, his voice throaty from thirty years of the flax factory, "that you're going back there to see this… this boy? This capitalist, this boy," he repeats it with scornful emphasis, "that you only met five minutes ago?"

"No, Papa, I didn't say that. I'm here, aren't I? I've come to see you. And to ask for your advice." So far, it's playing out exactly as she'd imagined it.

"My advice, girl?" The voice is rising now. "My advice? I'll tell you what my advice is. You are needed here!" And he thumps the table so hard his wine glass topples over, falling to splinter on the stone floor. He ignores it. "And I don't mean in this house. It's not just your parents who need you, it's your country. Do you actually know what's been happening?"

"Yes, Papa," she speaks softly as if to balance out her father's tone. "And I know people who have been killed. Of course I know what's happening and I do love my country."

"Well, you don't seem to understand it. We have to fight these bastards, drive them out. They'll take us all over, herd us like sheep."

"They won't come here, Papa. You and Mama are quite safe. They can't even control Prague."

"You think they won't come here?" He's standing now as if to fight them all single-handed. "Not here? But as soon as they know there's a damn dissident in the family, they'll be here all right. They'll be here all right. And we'll be in a camp somewhere." His wife lays a hand on his to calm him.

"Come on, Petr, don't exaggerate. Sit down, think of your heart." He sits obediently and turns to her with affection.

"It is my heart I'm thinking of, Amálie. And the heart of our country. Fifty years. Doesn't that mean anything, girl?" He turns back to Eva.

"Of course, Papa. I'm as sad as you. And angry. It shouldn't have happened, not this. But I can't help my feelings. Please try to understand."

"There's nothing to understand, Eva." He only uses her name when he's really upset. "You stay. And what's wrong with Aleš? Fine young man, an engineer."

"There's nothing wrong with Aleš, nothing at all. He is a good man. Roy is an engineer too. Well, he –" That was the wrong thing to say. Pan Novák is angry again. He gets up and tears off the denim shirt, throwing it to the floor, standing there looking foolish with his hairy barrel chest and belly.

"I don't want to hear the boy's name again in this house," he declares with as much dignity as the situation allows, and strides determinedly out of the room and upstairs. There's a deathly silence left behind, broken only by Eva's gentle sniff as she wipes a tear. Her mother reaches across the table to take her hand.

"You know what he's like, Eva. It's all bluster. He was caught off-guard, that's all. I'll talk to him, my dear. Everything will be all right, you'll see." But right now, Eva can't see that anything will ever be all right ever again.

Paní Nováková lifts herself wearily from her chair and comes around the table to pick up the shirt and the silver button that's been torn off. She'll mend it in a minute and he'll wear it again. Then she moves into the kitchen to fetch dustpan and brush. When everything's been cleared up she returns to her chair and watches her daughter, whose head is in her hands, ideologies wrestling with desires within. She looks up after a while.

"I just want to do the right thing, Mama. But I don't know what that is anymore. That's why I came home to see you both. I thought you could help me work it out."

"When did you last listen to us, my girl? Always so independent. That Josef fellow. And you couldn't wait to get off to Prague."

"Well, everyone thinks Josef's a hero now."

"Why, what's he done, shot a Russian?"

"It doesn't matter. Anyway, that's all in the past. Look, it doesn't matter how independent you are, everyone needs their parents sometimes."

"That's as may be." She crosses her arms. "You won't listen anyway. Whenever we tell you one thing you go right ahead and do the opposite. Always have. You won't be told." Eva smiles slightly. That much is probably true. She wants to say, 'So tell me the opposite of what you think', but it wouldn't go down well now. "You have no idea," her mother continues, "how upset your father has been, how much he worries about you. Don't forget his heart." They both know this has always been an excuse – he once had a test for a murmur, got the all-clear and is as strong as an ox – but say nothing.

Eva's mother gets up and looks out of the window at their small yard. She seems to be deciding something much against her own better judgement. The maternal instinct will always win. She turns to an oak sideboard and pulls open a lower drawer, then lifts up a heavy woollen tablecloth and takes out the two white envelopes with English postmarks. Sitting opposite her daughter again, she tosses them over as if to demonstrate some contempt.

"These came," she says, "a few weeks ago."

Eva just stares at the envelopes, her heart thumping, her breath shallow. The surge of happiness is deflated by the realisation that her parents did not intend to let her know. We live and we learn. Or not. The envelopes have been slit open and roughly taped back, but this was almost certainly done by the new controllers of the Post Office; there would be no point in her father doing it since he cannot read English and doesn't know anyone who does.

"Thank you, Mama," she says simply. The time for anger has long passed. She takes the letters upstairs to her room and sits with them, unread, by the open window of her bedroom at the top of the house. It is the best room in the house, with a view across the rooftops to the wooded foothills of the Krkonoše Mountains. A few white clouds drift across an otherwise clear sky and a pair of hook-beaked red kites circle lazily in the distance, looking for supper. Eventually her heart and lungs return to normal and she is able to think clearly. She doesn't yet know what he has written – and if it were 'Goodbye' there would only be one letter – but he hasn't forgotten. It was real. It is real. And surely he must have also received her letters?

She takes a careful look around her room, wondering if this will be the last time she sees it. Trust has been broken. On a shelf are some of her childhood books and toys that she could never bear to let go of, along with more recent classic English novels and volumes of verse. A glass cabinet holds her gymnastics medals and trophies; no, she was never going to be among the best but the training gave her strength of both body and mind, not to mention the flexibility that has put her in this situation. On the bed still lies her worn, patched-up, limp rabbit doll. Of all the precious memories, this is the one thing she now picks up and places inside the suitcase open on the bedside chair.

Eva takes the fawn leather jacket from the back of the door and carefully puts the envelopes into an inside pocket along with a new pack of German cigarettes she'd bought on the train. Then she closes the door and slips downstairs and outside quietly to avoid either parent who may be lying in wait. Beside the Úpa River, she sits on a grassy bank and finally opens the letter with the earlier West Bromwich postmark.

Φ

They drink their coffee in silence, each lost in different thoughts. Once or twice, Graham opens his mouth as if to frame "What –?" but Red simply mouths back "Shut up." Eventually, Roy decides on a change of subject.

"Graham, can you help me with this song I've been writing? I've been trying to work it out for ages but I can't quite get it all."

"Why me, for Heaven's sake?"

"Because you're just about the best bloody guitarist I know. I've heard you along the corridor."

"Could've been a record."

"No, records don't make mistakes and stop then start again. But you're still good." His friend grins with appreciation.

"Thanks. I've heard you too. You're not that bad, if you work at the picking more. Thanks for asking but no. Matter of principle. It's your song so you've got to do it."

When they've gone, Roy rearranges the furniture and gets ready for bed. It's only about eleven but he's exhausted by the emotion of recent events. He lies awake in bed unable to settle or to think coherently as Fallow Court sinks into the night. There is the characteristic low rattle of a diesel engine in the lane outside his open window, a girl's voice and a car door banging shut, followed within seconds by the muted yet unmistakeable roar of Graham's voice along the corridor.

"Christ! Help!"

Roy levers himself up on one elbow to lift the corner of the curtain, just in time to see the figure of a girl with long brown hair, wearing a white coat and carrying a small case, crossing the carpark as the cab makes a three-point turn and heads back towards Wilmslow Road. Bare feet come padding along the corridor and there's a timid knock on Roy's door. Red doesn't wait for an answer and slips inside, closing the door gently behind her. She stands sheepishly in the dark with head bowed, a bundle of clothes in her arms.

"Sorry, Roy, did I wake you?"

"No, it's all right. I couldn't sleep anyway. What's going on?"

"Janet's arrived," she says simply.

"What? Just now? Graham said she'd written to him a while ago but… Ah, sorry, I suppose you didn't know about her."

"Oh, yes. I knew. He has told me. I just never thought that…"

"Right, of course. Come in anyway, sit down. Would you like some coffee?" He sits up in bed and their eyes are adjusting to the dim light.

"No thanks. What a night, eh? I wonder what's going on with those two. And why would she turn up like that, out of the blue in the middle of the night? Something's up."

She's perched on the edge of the bed, her voice quiet and unsteady as if she's been crying and it hasn't quite finished yet. There are footsteps outside, a woman's, and they seem to hesitate for a moment by Roy's door before continuing further along. They hear a knock, a door opening and muffled voices before everything goes quiet again.

"Can I stay with you tonight, Roy? It's too late to go back and I'm all shaken up after everything…"

She doesn't need to finish the sentence. They know each other well enough now. Roy's heart is racing and he doesn't know why; the vein by his mouth quivers once and all his senses are suddenly heightened. He pulls back the sheet without even thinking about it and she sees that he's naked.

"Thank you." Red stands again and drops her clothes in an untidy bundle onto the chair. The soft light from outside picks out her skin as white as chalk as she turns back to sit on the edge of the bed. She is only wearing a thin, Indian cotton shirt that folds against her small breasts and ends just above her hips. She stretches her arms up to lift the shirt off then slips in beside him. It's a narrow bed but they're only just touching. Roy's skin is coursing with electricity firing off in all directions, his mind reeling with the moment and the sudden dissolution of strings. He has never been here before, never thought of this possibility with anyone else, but here it is and the surprise intensifies every nerve. A kind of panic grips him somewhere in the distance at the back of his mind. What comes next? Next her hand strokes gently, slowly down his abdomen to touch him, hard in a moment.

"Sorry," she murmurs sleepily. "Force of habit. Gosh, you're warm. Don't worry. I think we both just need someone tonight." And her arm moves back to lie across his chest as she leans her head against his shoulder and folds one long, beautiful unshaven leg across his. "You can if you like, though. I won't tell any…" Half-paralysed with incredulity, Roy lies motionless for several minutes and then turns his head to kiss her hair. She moves slightly but is already asleep.

In the morning, he opens sticky eyes to find her already awake and dressed, sitting at his desk with two mugs of tea.

"Good morning, sunshine. Welcome to Friday," she says brightly. "Did you know your face tickles?" He props himself up and takes the tea gratefully.

"Trying to grow a beard."

"Thought so. Half the male population of Manchester has got fuzzy faces. It's like some weird disease has broken out. But you do have a nice body."

"Thanks," Roy grins, "years of soccer training." She's so easy to be with, here and now anyway. He gets up, surprising himself that he's not at all shy, and heads off for a shower. A quarter of an hour later they're downstairs in the dining hall, picking at scrambled eggs and bacon; they don't say much but watch one another amusedly. As they light cigarettes with their coffee, Graham and Janet appear and take their trays to a table on the other side of the hall. Graham occasionally glances across at them questioningly but it's lunchtime before there's a chance to talk as they leave the lecture theatre.

"Janet's pregnant," says Graham from the side of his mouth. Roy has never seen him so down.

"Oh no. Sorry, mate. But when? How? I mean…"

"How long have we been here?"

"Not sure. About seven weeks or so."

"Seven and a half weeks or so, then."

"Hey, Graham, I've just remembered. The glass last night. It was spelling out –"

"Yeah, yeah." He's not interested in spiritual advice now. "Well, obviously she can't have it. It's all right, though, 'cause her uncle's a doctor and knows someone. And he'll keep it quiet. But it's going to cost and I'm practically broke, my grant's nearly gone already. I don't suppose you could… could you? You're a bit better off and obviously I'll pay you back, when I can."

They've reached the bus stop outside the Union and have to decide which way to go. Graham's all for heading to the bar and putting off getting back to his room, where Janet's waiting. Roy steers him onto the platform of the next bus and up the stairs.

"Okay, well, I suppose I could. I don't know. Thing is, mate, I don't believe in abortion."

"For fuck's sake, man, no-one does until it happens to you. We all do things we don't believe in, don't we? And by the way, while we're on that subject, what about you and Red last night, then?"

"Nothing happened."

"Yeah, right. Oh look," he points upwards out of the window, "isn't that a Gloucester Old Spot?"

The first couple of months of university have been a welcome release from the tensions and restrictions of home – he has a social life, his hair is longer and in a ponytail now and he is veering towards becoming vegetarian – but they have brought their own stresses. Not least of these has been the work itself. He is conscientious but despite the A Levels and the upbringing among engineers he's like a cat in a pond, furiously paddling with just a small nose above water and surrounded by very large carp. Graham once told him that it was stupid to leave his room in Fallow Court unlocked; the response was that there was nothing there worth stealing but maybe an educated thief would be attracted to the Physics textbooks. The impersonal lecture theatres and the long nights struggling with indecipherable formulae are taking their toll.

Things might be better were half of his mind not permanently switched onto thoughts of Czechoslovakia. Each day he reads the newspaper but there is almost nothing. Except for the borders being closed, the country has all but been dropped from the British press like last year's garden party, something that Roy will never forgive his own people for. A keen empathy for the Slav has begun to grow in his unconscious. He has even been to a couple of Politics Society meetings, something he would never have dreamed of three months ago, but they've been focused on Vietnam and Paris and he's only picked up some titbits that people have heard on the World Service, reporting on some underground radio station in Prague.

It's half-term and Roy decides that a break is desperately needed to touch base with normality, or the old one at least, so he packs a small holdall, slips a note under Graham's door with a cheque for ten pounds, and heads into the evening traffic of the M6.

His mother seems genuinely disappointed that he hasn't brought any dirty washing for her but surprisingly cheers up when he tells her that he doesn't want to eat meat anymore; this will be a challenge but at least she'll be useful. For the moment all she can think of is a cheese omelette and he eats it on his lap in the lounge because his father is working on the dining room table. His mother wants to show him the new television with BBC2 in colour but there's nothing he wants to watch. He answers her questions about Manchester in monosyllables and then goes for his usual night walk around the estate, noticing with a pang of disappointment that Gaynor's house is empty and up for sale.

"By the way," calls out his mother, apparently waiting up for him, as he returns, "did you know that Paul's back? His mother called earlier in the week to say that Alan's very ill."

He hadn't known, this visit being on the spur of the moment and the last (and first) letter from Paul had been a month ago. Roy makes a coffee and goes up to his room, which somehow looks very strange now. There's a bookcase with several of his old children's books still sitting there and a collection of board games on top of the wardrobe. He resolves to have a complete clear-out in the morning after he's `phoned Paul, then sinks into a fitful sleep in which he has the dream about the sailing ship again. Who are these people who've taken over the controls? This time, they get a bit closer to the beach but he still can't make out who the woman is waiting there.

Breakfast is a silent affair, that is after Mr Carter has expressed his thoughts about Roy's hair and refusal to eat the sausages and his wife has suggested that Roy might like to call that nice girl Kate.

Paul's father is recovering well from his minor heart attack so Paul is in buoyant mood when they meet up in town at the coffee bar.

"Great to see you, mate. Groovy hair," he opens with. "Sorry I haven't written – you know how it is, one party after another, one traumatised girl after the other. So what brings you home?"

"No parties to go to and no traumatised girls. Well, there was one a couple of nights ago, no-one special."

They exchange news. It looks like Paul has embraced student life far more easily than Roy, actually enjoying his coursework whilst also making good new friends. He even managed to avoid any conflicts of interest and inappropriate visitors when Sally came to stay for a weekend, and their relationship is still on. Roy asks him what he knows about Czechoslovakia but apparently Modern History is still stuck on World War I. While Paul waits in the queue at the fish and chip shop, Roy finds a `phone box and calls Nick to invite him to come with them to the match; Nick says 'Sorry' but he's not feeling well – he doesn't want to mention the cuts and bruises on his face that still haven't completely healed.

The Albion are playing league-leaders Liverpool and get a decent 0-0, thanks largely to their keeper John Osborne having a good day and centre forward Jeff Astle a bad one. At the end there's a feeble rendition by a group of a hundred or so die-hard fans of Albion Day, the song written for their Cup Final win last May but which most supporters had forgotten within a week.

They arrange to meet for a drink at The Mermaid tomorrow lunchtime before heading off back to their respective new lives, and Roy goes home to clear out his bedroom, stopping off at the local shop on his way to cadge a couple of empty cardboard boxes. Then he `phones Marian. She's "too busy" this weekend.

As the year draws to a close, Manchester is often dull and usually wet. This is just as well for it keeps Roy indoors more and matches the dour sense of application necessary for him to get on top of his work – or at least face to face with it. He has stopped going to Poe Soc as it seems less and less relevant to reality and he stopped going on the soup wagon after Tom was found dead in Alexandra Park. The silver watch was missing but no-one ever knew what had happened and the police didn't devote great efforts to finding out. Jonno, Mary and the rest still hang around the precinct sometimes but they've moved their patch further over towards Stretford. In any case, the city Council has announced plans to 'redevelop' Moss Side.

There are still occasional nights in the bar and at Folk Club, where Roy sits quietly and studies finger styles, but even Graham is more subdued these days. He still sees Janet from time to time, one or the other travelling up or down every couple of weekends, but in between it's evident that his wild streak has been shot down and this relationship may well be too bruised to heal. He still sees Red, too, though more often than not it's in a threesome with Roy and she's as likely to keep herself warm in the one's bed as the other's. Yes, this is odd and many would be baffled or judgemental, but they are young and this is the late 'sixties. In truth, it's much more innocent than that. They each take the strength and comfort they need from these easy, sometimes playful nights, each giving to the other without thinking about it. Red doesn't make love with Roy, knowing that she can never belong to him until he knows for sure that Eva is lost and the mourning is over. A strange fidelity, but none the less for that.

In the first week of December, Roy walks along to Platt Fields on a free afternoon and does a couple of circuits of the small lake, going through the chords of the song in his head. The day is cold but fine, the sky clear, the ducks exactly where they always are. He gets a coffee from the small café and takes it outside, pensively watching shadows move on the water's surface as he smokes. He doesn't hear Didi wander up alongside him.

"Autumn's gone, then," she says, pulling up a metal chair. They haven't seen each other to talk to since Hallowe'en.

"Hi, how are you? I was wondering where you'd got to."

"I could say the same. Anyway, busy, you know. Essays to wade through, tutorials to tute. Red's coming along well, her writing's more… thoughtful. And I got a new fish. Harry. He's quite adventurous."

Neither of them mention the séance. Roy assumes that her religious sensibilities had been offended, her parents being missionaries, or that she'd simply and unsurprisingly been very frightened. In fact it was neither of these things. Like Roy, Didi had felt for the first time the awesome power of the unconscious mind at work; this revelation interests some people and terrifies others. Now, she catches up on the last month's news before eventually reaching into the depths of her shoulder bag and pulling out a thin book.

"You've stopped coming to Poe Soc," she says, "so I've been carrying this around with me in case I ran into you." She could have left a note at his department or at Fallow Court, he thinks, but doesn't say it. "It's the first collection in English of Miroslav Holub's poetry. Came out last year. I found it by chance in that shop on Lever Street – do you know it?" He shakes his head. "Anyway, Holub is probably the best Czech poet of his generation and he's also a scientist, a pathologist or something like that. Or he's a famous scientist who's also a poet. That's why I thought of you." She hands him the Penguin and he studies the abstract purple cover that looks like a brain scan.

"Oh, thank you," he says, with less enthusiasm than her gesture deserves. She pretends not to notice.

"There have been a few scientists who've turned to verse in the past," she goes on, "but it's mostly sentimental crap. The two things are worlds apart. Holub's different because his work is experimental – like science – but also experiential… um, do you know that word?" Roy shakes his head again. "He writes about real life. Ah, I thought that might get your attention! Look, I've marked page thirty-seven for you." Roy opens the book and reads aloud quietly. The poem is called Love.

"'Two thousand cigarettes.
A hundred miles
from wall to wall.
An eternity and a half of vigils
blanker than snow.
Tons of words
old as the tracks
of a platypus in the sand.
A hundred books we didn't write.
A hundred pyramids we didn't build.
Sweepings.
Dust.
Bitter
as the beginning of the world.
Believe me when I say
it was beautiful.'"[4]

---

[4] Selected Poems, Miroslav Holub (Penguin Books Ltd, 1967)

ACT 8

A New Year

The term having ended with a sigh of relief, a bearded Roy returns to his family only to find that the last few months have irreparably and entirely torn his mind free of childhood. He is a young man with new expectations and thoughtfulness. Some things never change, of course, and there are regular arguments with his father about evenings spent with Marian, going to the wrong sort of church and upsetting his mother when he talks about Eva. The Christmas of 1968 is people wrapped up like train sets singing half-forgotten carols and eating silent meals. He thinks he should write a song about it but doesn't bother.

Fortunately, he is obliged to spend a couple of weeks at the Training Centre where the new supervisor, a tall, thin man with a pencil moustache and very few words, sets the apprentices the task of making their own toolboxes. Roy rather enjoys losing himself in these new skills of design, cutting sheet metal, spot-welding and handling metal tools because they bring him down to earth and stop him thinking dark thoughts.

He takes Kate to the works' New Year social evening and afterwards they drive somewhere quiet to touch and kiss. Somehow, her beauty doesn't seem quite so classical now; she belongs even more to the West Midlands and has a coarseness about her that he hadn't noticed before. Her body is lovely, of course, but Roy has been trained in resistance lately. Kate doesn't really mind, she knows the score and can wait.

Jim Lloyd dies peacefully in the first week of January and Roy cries openly at the news, both for the gentle old man and for himself, for all the people who have entered his life in the last half-year and then left it again.

It is with as much relief as the last term had ended that the new one beckons. He drives north a few days ahead and as he turns off the motorway along Dunham Road into Altrincham a few familiar welcoming drops of rain splash the windscreen. Roy smiles to himself, feeling that he's coming home. From this point in his life, he will carry his roots around with him.

Graham isn't back yet so on Saturday he goes to Maine Road on his own to watch City beat Chelsea 4-1, then spends a couple of hours in the evening with Didi at her flat. It's the first time he's been there and he gets to watch Harry's circumnavigations while she talks a lot about nineteenth century Russian literature, as if that was going to cheer him up. They get a Chinese takeaway but he leaves early, some sort of tension mounting inside him and gripping his stomach and a kind of ringing in his head. Back in his room, he puts finishing touches to the vacation work he's done so that the next few days will be free, and falls into an uneasy sleep.

Three-thirty a.m. is called the Hour of the Wolf. Statistically, more people die at this time than at any other. Roy awakes with the bedclothes wet and every hair on his body erect. Something is moving about the room, a vague black shadow between bed and ceiling. He cannot move a muscle yet is unafraid. Very slowly, consciousness returns and he is able to sit up and switch on the bedside lamp. The room is empty but still something moves within it.

It is ages before he notices the pale blue aerogram envelope slipped under the door and his heart almost tears itself to pieces. It is from Eva. She is here. There's a telephone number. She has only written a few lines but they began with 'Dearest'.

He is exhausted but cannot sleep and there's four hours until breakfast, so he sits at his desk smoking, head racing, suddenly terrified of this reunion. Salford in January is a long way from a summer Welsh beach. What if he feels nothing? Will he know what to say? Then he wakes to find himself aching all over and slumped at his desk at half past six, so he gets dressed and forces unsteady legs out into the early Sunday drizzle and across to the newsagents on Wilmslow Road where Aadesh Patel is cutting open the packs and organising a group of young lads for their rounds. There's a queue of insomniac customers already, all parcelled up like the newspapers against the cold but probably none of them trembling for quite the same reason as Roy. Back at Fallow Court, he reads every inch of the sports pages and is still first down for breakfast, hugely pleased to see Graham stagger over to his table with eyes barely open.

"Great to see you, man. Had a good Chrissie? You're up a bit early, aren't you?" Words are rushing out in desperate need of conversation.

"Jeez, my head. Newky Brown's got a lot to answer for. `S all right, I suppose. Yeah, well I had to get up early, haven't done any work yet." He chews toast and marmalade slowly, drains his coffee and fetches more for both of them, and life creeps back across his face like sunrise over mountains. "Hey, just remembered," he offers, lighting the day's first cigarette, "who was that woman you had last night? Sly dog, term's not even started and you've found –"

"That was no woman. That was Eva."

"Christ! Why was she leaving?"

"She didn't even wake me up, just left a note for me to ring her. She's in Salford."

"Well well. Well bloody well."

Back in his room, Roy is aware that he's putting off the 'phone call. It's still early and she'll be asleep and he has no idea what to say and he can't even quite get her face in his mind. But he knows he's fooling himself so at ten o'clock he goes out to the 'phone box in the courtyard and dials the number. A man's voice answers.

"Ano?"

Roy is confused and fumbles with the coin but at last it drops.

"Um, hello. Is Eva there please?"

"Okay, she come." The voice is young and heavily accented. It is nearly three minutes before her soft, sleepy voice is heard. Roy's eyes fill with tears and he has to turn his back to the courtyard.

"Eva… is that really you?"

"It is really me, Roy. Have you got a pencil? I'll give you the address. Would you like to come this afternoon?"

"I can come now, Eva."

"Not right now, I am very tired. I just arrived yesterday."

When at last he puts the receiver down, Roy stands staring at it for a couple of minutes before a knock on the glass tells him that someone's waiting. There's nothing for it but to go back upstairs, have a hot shower and read the rest of the Sunday newspaper until two o'clock.

The car will not start. Luckily, Graham hears the hollow, slow whirring from his open window upstairs and is soon down with Peter from along the corridor to give a push start. It works on the second attempt and the old green Ford sits guiltily belching grey smoke in the lane as Roy tries to compose himself. He doesn't know Salford and it's a tricky journey. Once, as he waits at the lights and pores over the map, the engine dies again and cold fingers grip his stomach. Of all the fucking moments for this. Then it restarts first time, he breathes a prayer to whoever may be listening, and arrives outside the tall Victorian terraced house just before three.

She is waiting at a window and comes to the door with her coat already on before he gets there. Why did she choose this? It seems another intimation, after her brief note and almost formal conversation on the 'phone, that something has moved. She looks different, too, more Czech, her hair shorter. But it is her, and she cannot hide her smile as their hands reach out and clasp each other.

"Eva... Thank God... Are you all right?"

"Of course I am."

"But I've been so, well, afraid." That's true enough, though it hasn't all been for her safety.

"There's no need. Things are all right, more or less. I like your beard."

"But you didn't write. Did you get mine?"

"Yes, yours got through eventually. It seems that mine didn't, I'm sorry. The Russians control everything now. I wasn't sure that I'd be able to come."

"So how did you get out? I mean, they've closed the borders, haven't they?"

"Oh, there are ways."

They walk slowly and in silence along the local streets over carpets of wet, decaying leaves, their fingers linked loosely, each trying to figure out just where they are. When it starts to get colder, they turn back to the house and she opens the door for him. There's no-one in and she makes coffee, bringing it through to sit in front of the electric fire. His head is full of things to say but none of them want to be said with this distance between them. Still, it is enough to be with her; he has taken another step forward, even if he is lost.

"Why did you come back?" he forces himself to say at last.

"For my degree. I told you before, it's one of the conditions to spend time here. I met an Englishman in Prague from Salford University who told me about a language course here I could do." So she didn't come back for him?

"You're going to stay, then?"

"For some time."

"And then? When you've finished the course?"

She lowers her head to hide a small smile.

"We'll see. Haven't we all learned not to think too much about the future?"

She tells him that she has to find somewhere to live. This place is only for a few days while the university Accommodation Office tries to find somewhere for her. There should be some addresses tomorrow. He says he'll come over to drive her around and help her choose.

"It's all right. I'm sure you've got work to do. Won't your lectures be starting tomorrow?"

"Heavens, that doesn't matter. Would you like me to come?"

It's not the conversation of two lovers who have been parted for nearly six months. Perhaps they are not lovers after all. Perhaps it has just been too long, with too little sunlight to see clearly, too little air even for a candle. Yet as Roy drives back across the city in the growing darkness, he knows that he still loves her. It's not that his heart is racing or anything like that. He knows because, being near her, it is as though she had never gone away. As for her, well, he must wait, trying to imagine what she's been through.

Eva doesn't bother to put a light on as she returns to the room, sitting in front of the fire with her own thoughts. It is remarkable how much university – or just living away from home – has changed this boy, yet the part of him that she loves has not changed at all. Despite the ponytail, the beard, the gathering strength within him, it is as though she had never gone away. But that doesn't make anything any easier. She takes out the letter that had already been waiting for her at the Languages office when she arrived and turns it round in her fingers, wondering when destiny will grow tired of playing with her.

The first three addresses they try next day have already been taken, they can't find the fourth and there is no-one in at the next, so they take a break at a small run-down café that smells of fry-ups and hopelessness.

"Who was that who opened the door this morning?" Roy asks. The young man had let him in with a smile, said something in Czech and gone to find Eva. Roy could hear them chatting while he waited.

"Jan's an old friend from Prague. Another engineer. He hasn't been here long – the house is a sort of safe place organised by the underground but we can only stay there a few days."

"What were you talking about?"

"You," she laughs. "Jan thinks you are very young and too hairy."

It is mid-afternoon and becoming gloomy when they reach the last address and are ushered in by an old, hard-faced and silent woman with white hair. The stairs are dark and bare and there is a smell of curry from the lower flat that follows them up. The room has a double bed, a small table with one chair, a wardrobe that leans to the side and a thin, torn square of dark maroon carpet. It might have been the old woman's room, so well does it suit her. A grimy window with one pane cracked and taped up overlooks the Eccles Road and somewhere to the back of the house they hear a mournful siren on the Ship Canal.

"You can't live here," Roy whispers as they inspect the unspeakable bathroom on the next landing.

"I have to take it. The Accommodation Office said there's nothing else. It's all right, it won't be forever. And I've lived in worse places." That cannot be true.

They go back for her suitcase and, who knows, perhaps a final embrace with Jan, and she moves into the hell-hole. After she has urged

Roy to leave, because she can't bear for him to see what she knows is coming, she sits on the edge of the bed beneath the bare yellowing bulb and stares down between her feet. Then she licks the end of a cigarette, even though it's American, and lets all the despair and yearning and fear that her heart has been storing up pour out.

Φ

Three turning points follow on each other's heels in one day later this week.

On Thursday the 16th of January, 1969, Roy's laboratory finishes early so he drives to the Salford Languages Department to surprise Eva. He is still at the age that likes to arrive unexpectedly rather than call ahead, not realising that this is as equally likely to bring sorrow as joy. This time it is just as well. He parks on the muddy waste ground to the back of the Technical College and crosses to the incongruously new, white, multi-storey block. It is the first time he has seen a continuous elevator, the small, doorless compartments gliding quietly into and out of his astonished view. Other students are stepping on and off confidently but he doesn't feel sure about being able to get off at the right level so takes the stairs instead. Having caught his breath at the eighth floor, he discovers that Eva isn't there and hasn't been in all day.

"She had some personal matters to sort out," says the middle-aged secretary, perfectly used to young people's dramas. She is not very efficient but she is friendly and chatty, and therefore sometimes more helpful than she means to be.

"Oh yes?" replies Roy absently, wondering whether he's brave enough to take the lift back down. "Sorting things out for her course, I suppose."

"No, that's all been arranged," the woman says, while continuing her typing. "We had all the documents through from Prague last week, for her transfer. She's all signed up for her three years. I expect… oh, did I say something?"

Roy is already out of the office, his eyes wide and staring, realisation flowing through every nerve. So she always intended to stay. Then why…? Never mind. He jumps into the elevator, idly wondering what would happen if he failed to get off at the last floor, and instead steps lightly out into the afternoon sunshine in search of a florist.

Φ

In the square, students still gather but the numbers have thinned out. Beneath the shadow of the Václav statue, a young student of History and Political Economy at the university sits down cross-legged with a small rucksack from which he calmly takes a petrol can. Then, slowly and deliberately, he unscrews the cap and pours the fuel over himself. Others nearby catch the smell and jump to their feet, shouting at him to stop. For a moment he looks as though he wants to speak, but instead he tosses a piece of paper towards the nearest group, then he's on his feet ablaze among the crowd's screams. The living pyre runs erratically back and forth beneath the statue, flames lighting up the flanks of the great horse so that it almost seems to be stirring from its two-thousand year rest, until he finally topples with arms outstretched.

One woman runs forward to throw her coat over him but it's too late. Everyone else stands shocked and motionless. Perhaps they already know in their hearts that this barbaric self-immolation – and the twenty other suicides that will follow – has been done for them, to atone for their guilt in preferring survival to death, compromise to pride. The nation's shame has been expressed and is staring back at all who watch the grotesque, charred body. The woman picks up the paper he had thrown towards them and reads the three words aloud for the others to hear.

"'Truth is revolutionary.'"[5]

In separate offices, Dubček, Svoboda and Smrkovský each sit back in their chairs, stunned and deeply saddened by the news of Jan Palach's actions, one day before the meeting of the Central Committee that is due to endorse their capitulation to the Soviet terms. Each one searches despairingly for an alternative reason.

"Was he mad?" Not at all.

"Was he unpopular?" Far from it.

"Had he broken up with a girlfriend?" No, sir.

"Had he failed his exams?" No, sir.

"Is his blood on me, then?"

Ф

The news flashes around the world, thanks to Josef, but Roy hasn't heard it when he arrives at Eva's room in the evening. She had been out when he came earlier. There is a light at her upstairs window behind bright new curtains and the front door is open, so he lets himself in to the dull brown hallway. He pauses to tidy his hair before the dresser mirror, but most of the silvering has gone anyway. He runs lightly up the stairs, rehearsing his words.

---

[5] Jan Palach died four days later in hospital, leaving letters explaining his actions. Half a million people attended his funeral and the Týn bells were heard across the city. Then life began again. Another student, Jan Zajíc, burned himself to death in Prague on the 25th February, 1969.

There are two voices in the room, one a man's, deep and unfamiliar, and they stop abruptly at his knock. There is a long pause.

"Come in." Her voice is quiet, strained. She is sitting on the edge of the bed in a black skirt and blue sweater that don't really suit her. There is a colourful chequered blanket over the bedclothes now, a white lampshade, a white lambs' wool rug beneath her feet and a new bedside lamp that has a shade decorated with cartoon characters. A tall man with short hair and defined, confident features stands by the chair. He is late twenties and wears a green corduroy jacket and grey casual trousers. The room has been transformed and its gloom now belongs only to its occupants. Roy catches the mood and freezes for a moment before closing the door.

"Hello, Eva. I… um, I brought you…" He offers the flowers but her hands do not move from her knees nor her eyes from the floor. Instead, he lays them on the table, all his other words forgotten. The man looks at Roy with undisguised anger and begins to speak rapidly and vehemently in Czech, whilst Eva closes her eyes and drops her head a fraction more.

"Roy," she murmurs at last, "this is Aleš, my fiancé."

"Your…?"

He simply does not understand the words but stands there by the door, staring at her as if still waiting to be introduced. The man is speaking again, insistently.

"He says I must interpret what he's saying. He says what do you want? You have no place here. You are a… a child, a… a puppy. You do not understand anything about us… about our lives. You are a… a fool. You must go."

The man has not stopped speaking during this and the two voices, one urgent and scathing, the other soft and flat, are tumbling in an uncontrollable whirlpool around Roy's head as he looks from one to the other. The man then takes a step forward and Roy flinches, expecting to be hit, but instead he picks up the flowers and crushes their stems in his large, workman's hands before throwing them out of the window. In the silence, he glares at Roy, waiting.

"Eva, do you want me to go?" Roy says at last, his voice holding firm as he controls the tremor breaking throughout his body. She doesn't answer. So he lets himself out with false dignity and almost makes it to the car before his legs begin to buckle. The hard-faced ghoul with white hair peers out after him from the open front door while two voices, both now raised, can be heard from the open window upstairs. The flowers have landed beneath the front wheels of Roy's car and are pulped as it leaps out into the traffic and the downpour that has just begun.

Blinded by tears, he drives crazily, the needle quivering near sixty at times as horns blare and headlamps flash. The wipers do the best they can to help but he can hardly see anyway. Trafford Road, past the silent docks, Chester Road, this is the wrong way but by instinct he turns left into Edge Lane and through the neat gardens of Chorlton. The lights are green at Wilmslow Road and the back wheels slide sickeningly as he takes the turn too fast but now he's in the side lane and past the wire mesh gates of the carpark, spitting gravel.

He has no idea at all where he has been or how he got back.

When he finally wakes next morning he is rested and has no idea that Graham held him in his arms for an hour before putting him to bed. Yet he feels strong. Some great machine, the one that no-one sees or can name but which controls every cell of the universe, has shifted gear and moved on to the next stage of its journey.

Φ

A NEW YEAR

"What now, then?" asks a haggard-looking Graham at breakfast on Friday.

"What do you mean?" It's a silly question but it buys a few seconds.

"I mean, what now, then? I gather from your incoherent rambling last night that it's all over. Christ, man, you were in a state. It's lucky I was in my room."

"Oh, did you… did I…? Thanks, Graham. I'm sorry."

"It's okay, we're mates. So?"

"No, it's not over."

"How come? I thought you said he was her fiancé."

"Yes, that's right. But it's going to be all right." He chases a fried mushroom with his fork through the tomato sauce of the beans, taking another piece of cold toast at the same time. "Do you remember that dream I told you about last term, the one with the sailing ship? I had it again last night only this time I got much closer to the beach, not quite there but close, and the woman was smiling. And I glimpsed one of the people – or whatever they were – who'd taken over the controls, just a sort of moving body of white light. So I don't know how, but it will be all right."

"Surely after what happened at her flat…?"

"I said I don't know. But it's not finished, there's ages to come yet."

Graham shakes his head sorrowfully at his deluded friend and passes over a cigarette.

"You're either mad or you're mad, mate. What kind of relationship is this? I don't know, it's… it's unreal."

"And you can't kill something unreal, can you?"

They finish their coffee and pull their coats on, heading for the bus.

"You're coming in?" asks Graham in surprise. "I would have thought, after last night…"

"I'm fine, actually, I feel good. And I've missed most of this week anyway so I need to catch up." They're sitting in the lecture theatre with a hubbub of voices around them, waiting for the young research engineer, before Roy speaks again. "It's funny, you know, what you said before about what sort of relationship is it. It is unreal. In the last, what, seven months or so all these really weird things have happened to me and changed my life completely. I don't recognise myself. No wonder my parents are confused. But look, the things I remember clearly, all the good things, they're the ordinary and unexciting times, the things that aren't so dramatic. They're what's real."

"Like what?" Graham is still only half-awake and struggles with esoteric existentialism at the best of times.

"Well, not so much about Eva – there's a lot I don't even remember very well about when we met. No, things like, well, you –"

"Ah, ordinary and unexciting, eh?"

"You know what I mean. You've been important, down to earth. And there's Red too, of course. I love both of you. Oh, sorry…"

"That's all right, I know what you mean. I think. So if you love two women, why can't Eva have two men? Don't worry," he grins, "I'm not the jealous type. Mind you, Janet is. Jeez…!" The engineer comes in and doesn't apologise for being late. The room quietens. "You've shaved your beard off!" Graham hisses.

"I wondered whether anyone would notice," Roy whispers back. "It'll grow again."

When Janet arrives on Saturday morning, she is taken aback to find the other three waiting impatiently for her beside Roy's car. She is fallen upon and bundled, protesting that she has new shoes and a smart suit on, into the back with Red while her case is wedged into the boot with the two large baskets.

"Where are we going?" she almost shrieks for the third time as they pull onto the main road and head south.

"We're going up the country," the two boys sing out together, "baby, do you want to go?

"We're going up the country, baby, do you want to go?
"We're going some place we've never been before…"⁶
"It's therapy," adds Red.
"It's magic," adds Graham. "That's what we need, some magic."
"But my clothes…"
"You can change when we get there. There's plenty of trees. Take a left up here, Roy." Graham continues to give directions between bursts of song. The front half of the car is in oddly exuberant mood while Red does her best with Janet in the back, introducing herself and chatting; today, she's Roy's girl. It's a crisp, fresh morning although mist is still hanging over the hedgerows half an hour later as they push through Alderley Edge and along Wizard's Way. Janet is not a student and still expects domesticated weekends, but her irritation is soothed when the engine stops, the boys wind down the windows, and a tangible peace wanders into the car. They seem to have the Edge virtually to themselves this morning.

"That's Jodrell Bank over to the right," Graham informs them.

"Can't see a thing."

With only mild complaints now, Janet wriggles out of her things and into jeans, sweater and boots, shrinking below the window as cars flash past on the road while the others giggle outside. She emerges at last with her hair a mess, but she's bright enough to realise that she may as well relax and not spoil the day. With Graham leading the way they clamber over a stile and along a muddy track before turning left down a sharp incline beneath a rocky overhang. A hundred yards further, it is Red who's first to notice the trickle of water on the rock, the etched face and ancient, chiselled words.

"'Drink of this and drink thy fill for the water falls at the wizard's will.' Yuk, don't think I will, thanks," she says, "it looks a bit putrid. Who's the wizard, then?"

---

6   From the album Living The Blues by Canned Heat, 1968.

"That's Merlin," Graham announces. He's been here before and is enjoying playing tour guide.

"Not *the* Merlin, surely?" asks Roy.

"One of them. There've been loads. Practically any magician in legends got called Merlin. This one was a hermit who lived in the caves here. They say there was a great plague in the local village and he popped out to heal everyone."

"Then popped back in again, I suppose." Janet is not impressed.

"'S right. I'll show you his tomb later, it's over the other end."

They retrace their steps and the girls continue along the precipitous top path, gingerly picking their way over gnarled roots and damp earthy steps, while the boys walk quickly back to the car to get the lunch baskets.

"Fancy you knowing all that," observes Roy.

"I'm not a complete peasant," Graham grins, "just sometimes. I take things as they come, down to earth like you said, but that doesn't mean I don't appreciate other ways. I just don't write songs about them."

Roy is touched by his friend's concern for him. He knows that today is for him, a respite from pain and a nod to his alternative beliefs, and he feels a touch guilty for not having recognised Graham's sensitivity. He pauses by the car, key in hand, and defies his whole upbringing to lay a hand on Graham's shoulder.

"Thank you. I'm blessed to have a friend like you."

"Aw, shucks, gerroff." He shrugs it away with an embarrassed laugh. "Come on, the girls will be lost or falling down one of the old mine shafts if we don't hurry." A few minutes later, when they've almost caught up and the bare winter forest of the Edge stretches down below them, he adds, "Remember last term, that Ouija thing? Very weird, but it got me thinking. We should maybe do that again one evening, just the two of us. What do you think?"

They eat their sandwiches sitting above the caves, huddled together for warmth, then run around like children through the silver birches, up and down dirt paths and across streams. Janet slips onto her bottom in the mud and doesn't mind, so this tells them that everything's all right today and they're free of all the grasping emotions of late. Roy and Red run hand in hand, zigzagging along a wide path, kicking up piles of leaves and weaving up towards a sandy-coloured bank. This is a magical place.

They stop suddenly and stand stock still, seeing Graham up ahead and aware of his change of mood. He's beside a huge birch with five trunks, motionless with his arms outstretched towards the weak afternoon sun. Seeing them, he switches to become bright again.

"This is supposed to be the tomb," he says. "It does feel strange. We should come here at night."

"No thanks," Red shivers. "Too spooky. I'm off that sort of thing for a while."

"Well, anyway. Come on, I'll show you the witches' circle. Where's Janet got to?" She's gone ahead of them and found it, sitting silently on one of the stones with her head bowed. "Hey, you shouldn't break the circle," Graham calls out. The others shoot him questioning looks and he shrugs. "Well, that's what they say. There's a proper way to do it. They say this place is still used by a local coven."

In the car on the way back, Janet is still quiet until eventually she gives in to Graham's probing.

"I saw what's going to happen, how everything will turn out." She won't say more. In the front seat, Red leans across to rest her head on Roy's shoulder.

"Do you think they dance round naked?" she whispers, and Roy forces himself to keep his eyes firmly on the road ahead. They get back to Fallow Court tired but restored.

"See you guys for dinner in an hour, then," says Graham as he disappears along to his room with Janet's case.

Roy heads the other way to the showers, to wipe away the streaks of mud and any lingering pain of the last few days, standing with eyes closed under the hot spray. There is a click behind him.

"Room for two?" says Red. She is naked, slim and white and happy. "You really ought to lock your doors, you know."

"Hey, you can't... not here... I'll get thrown out if anyone..." But she simply steps forward and closes his mouth with her own, pressing her body tightly to his. They stand silent and unmoving like this, his head nestled against hers and melting into one another with the heat, sharing the most precious gift of gentle, undemanding touch. That's all. And it will be the last time they are together like this. Creeping back to his room, they can hear the quiet argument coming from Graham's. Although the four of them dance and drink and laugh at the Chicken Shack[7] concert in the Union later, there is a shared and unspoken awareness that it is time to move on.

The 'phone call comes the next Friday, during dinner. Peter is apologetic.

"Sorry, mate, she didn't leave a message," he tells Roy later. "I came to get you but you weren't in your room, and when I got back she'd rung off. Didn't even leave her name."

"Did she have an accent?"

"Er, well, she only said a few words. But yeah, I guess. French, is it?"

Roy has already gone, calling thanks over his shoulder and taking the stairs three at a time. He pulls up outside the house just after eight-thirty to see the upstairs window dark and bare; inside, the blanket, the rug, everything has gone.

"Left this afternoon," says the thin, high voice from the stairs. "Bleedin' students. Mind, she did pay, more'n some do." The ghoul peers at him toothlessly and with the folds of skin around her eyes it's impossible to tell if she's grinning or glaring.

---

[7] The band was formed barely ten miles from Roy's home. Annoyingly, he repeatedly claims them as his own.

A New Year

"Did she leave an address? Please?" Roy asks, but the woman just turns away to her own room.

He sits on the bottom stair to think. She has called so he has the right of reply. There was no message so she was asking a question. It's a question she can't bring herself to ask. What? There can only be one, or she wouldn't bother. So now he has to find her, to prove that he understands. There has to be a clue somewhere...

A door at the other end of the hall opens a fraction and an Indian man looks out hesitantly. He is old and slow with a white beard but his eyes are kind; Roy looks directly into them, thinking fast and drawing on his casual friendship with Aadesh Patel at the newsagent's.

"Are you a Hindu, sir?" he asks. The man nods, taken by surprise. "So you wouldn't tell a lie, would you, sir?" He shakes his head and grins. "Did the girl upstairs leave an address when she left, please?"

"Oh, yes, she did, my friend." The voice is clipped and correct. "And she left instructions too, that it should be given to the tall foreign gentleman with an accent."

Roy stands up, smiles and takes a few steps towards the man but keeping a respectful distance.

"Have you always lived here, sir, in England, I mean?" The man smiles back, ahead of the game.

"Oh no, sir, not at all. But if I had, I would still be a foreigner to you, wouldn't I?"

"Then what am I to you?"

"It's in the top drawer of the dresser, young man."

"Thank you, sir. Would you like an accent too?"

"That won't be necessary, my friend." The old man is already retreating back into his room with a sigh, looking across to his wrinkled wife sitting by the gas fire with an expression that says 'Oh, to be young and in love again'.

Roy takes the paper out and begins to copy down the address, then reconsiders and slips Eva's note into his pocket. He may as well take all the luck going. He is along the Bury New Road within six minutes. She is astonished to see him but lets him in without a word, recognising destiny when it calls. He stands inside the bright, comfortable room, his apparent relaxed air belying the fervour within.

"Hello, Eva. You called." It had been barely an hour ago.

"Yes, I… yes, I did. I'm not sure why." She stares at him, unable for the moment to comprehend how anyone could be like this, feel like this, after all that has happened. "How did you find me?"

"I never lost you."

He moves forward a few inches, which is not easy on his trembling legs, and opens his arms to her. In a moment, she is with him and against him and they are resting in each other as though they have both just awoken from the same awful dream. It is their first embrace since the railway station in Wales and when they kiss it is like some favourite childhood taste suddenly rediscovered in a most unlikely place.

"Don't let me go again," she murmurs into his neck. "I have been so foolish… to think I could live without you… that it was just a holiday romance. You can't imagine how horrible it's been, the last months." She is gripping his shoulders tightly and her head is buried in the collar of his coat, her words muffled, so that he has to lean his own head down to hear her. "Everything's been a nightmare. And in that room, with the old woman downstairs, I just sat there and it was like the walls were moving in on me. Like I was being punished." She pauses and lifts her face to his at last, allowing him to wipe the tear from her lashes. "I've been so afraid. Confused. But you are so much a part of me, I wasn't really alive."

"Then we'll start to live again now," Roy whispers, stroking her hair like a child's.

"Would anyone like some cake? Oops, sorry, I'm always in the way." The cheerful American voice disappears back into the kitchen, but they break apart with a smile and follow her. "So you must be Roy," she continues, looking him up and down. "I'm Maggie. My flatmate moved out this week and anyone could see that Eva needed a break. Oh my God, did you see that room?" She is a genuinely happy, orange-haired girl of about twenty, flat-chested and plain and just now enjoying being mother with a dishcloth over her hands as she leans over the oven. "Banana bread?"

"I beg your pardon?" Roy is taken by surprise at the scene change.

"Jeez, he's so polite. Must be English."

"Maggie makes beautiful banana bread," Eva explains, turning to her with a suspicious look. "Is this one… okay?"

"Sure it's okay. Would I do that to you? So sometimes I add a little something, say, for flavouring, but not this time."

She makes coffee too and they take it into the large lounge where Roy and Eva sit close together while Maggie prattles.

"I'm American, you know? You probably guessed. In exile from Boston, Massachusetts. Eva and I met at the uni. Say, did you ever hear of an American doing Languages? Still, it beats working."

Later, with the record player on quietly and Eva in the bathroom, she leans towards Roy conspiratorially.

"I know I talk a lot but I do see things too. That girl's been through hell so you look after her, you hear?"

"Of course I will. Has she, well, said anything much… about me, I mean?"

"Christ, yes, she never stops. It's you, Roy, so like I say don't let her down – or you'll have me to deal with and Americans fight dirty."

Maggie disappears diplomatically when it's time for Roy to leave. He holds Eva close and has to ask her again, however unknowable it might be.

"Why did you call this evening? After last week?"

"I'm not sure, darling. Maybe…" there's a long pause, "maybe it was your dignity."

"Shall we get married, then?"

"Maybe."

ACT 9

Reality

Roy tears the envelope as quietly as he can and astonishment turns into glee as he reads. His small, strangled gasp is immediately met with frowns and hushings; the great oak-panelled hall of the Whitworth Library is not a place for happiness. Eva looks up at him across the desk with an arched eyebrow and he pushes the piece of paper across to her, but she doesn't really understand it. He motions to her to leave and they pack away quietly, walking as fast as the aged and dignified surroundings allow until they emerge into the light Saturday rain.

"Don't you see?" are his first words as he takes her arm and they run for the Union. "This solves the problem. I was getting so worried."

"What problem?" she protests, a little annoyed at being taken from her books just as the point was becoming clear. He brings the coffees before explaining.

"The car. I told you I was having trouble with it. The starter motor. All its teeth are falling out – happens when you get old. And there's no NHS for cars so it's very expensive. But now this!" He waves the envelope triumphantly.

"What is a Premium Bond?"

"Oh, it's a sort of competition. A lottery. It's the first time I've ever won anything except for a packet of stamps when I was nine. This money will pay for the car with some left over. Isn't it amazing how things turn up just at the right moment? Like the other day, I was stuck on my project – some theory I just couldn't get – and when I turned on the radio later there was a science programme about almost the same thing. Er, you don't seem very enthusiastic."

"It's just coincidence, isn't it? I don't see why it's so important. You can always use the bus."

"I think it's more than coincidence. These things were really important to me and I was so worried. We need the car – it would take ages to get to your place and we couldn't go anywhere, say, in the countryside without it." He says 'we' without even thinking and he cannot consider them as anything but one now. These last three weeks have been as though they were twin souls reunited. Not so long ago, his every thought had been about her but now he barely thinks of her at all during everyday life because she is no longer a separate person. So it stings slightly that she doesn't see his point. "It's as if, I don't know, someone is guiding us and making sure things work out."

"That's silly, Roy. You've just been lucky, that's all. It's a good thing but a lot of bad things happen too. Where were Jan Palach's guides, then, or the ones who were supposed to make sure things worked out in Czechoslovakia? Gone on holiday? I'm going to get a sandwich."

She has a point and he is momentarily deflated. This requires more thought. But as she moves away to the end of the queue he can feel the flow of energy between them stretching across the space. It is an exhilarating and peculiar sensation, feeling that one's very blood is beating with another's, one's nerves are firing in resonance. He has not even been surprised to find that he has begun to know a few minutes beforehand when she is going to call – so he walks down the corridor to the 'phone and waits – and even sometimes what she is going to say. He is as certain of their love now as on that Welsh beach, for what is love if not this atonement? His eye is caught by the large poster of Billy Graham on the wall above the Christian Soc display and he smiles to himself. No, there is no need for suffering. This self-sacrifice is painless. He is absorbed in everything, loving life and at ease with everyone. Things are as they should be.

There is another reason, too. As he watches her shuffle slowly with the noisy queue, he realises that other people do not notice her. Not like they do, say, Red. In no way does she conform to that ideal guiltily anticipated before, the tall and willowy blonde ghost of the mountain lake with sad features. It almost embarrasses him that he doesn't find Eva particularly beautiful. Surely he should? But look: she is medium height with medium brown short hair, her body is strong but not slim. Her features are distinctive and lovely when she smiles (but nobody smiles all the time) but she has somehow begun to look more western in these last few weeks in England. She is older than most of the others around them, too, with a self-possession and experience that most of them will never know. A touch of hardness. Yes, he desires her, he wants to touch and be close to her, but it's not for the way she looks. So it must be for her soul.

Approaching the table again, she catches his intense look and smiles back, lighting up the gloomy February room with a wrinkle of her nose. Yes, it's for her soul.

He realises that he hasn't taken his eyes off her for about five minutes and that makes him suddenly aware of someone else's eyes on him. Turning to his left, he sees that a group of English students have taken a nearby table. Red's face is tragic, and he turns away again quickly before the fact can register on his own. One hand holding her sandwich, Eva reaches the other across to him.

"Where are you, Roy?" But she's still smiling.

"What? Oh, sorry, miles away."

"Are you dreaming again?" His mind switches to sailing ships but he hasn't told her about that yet; in any case, last time he had the dream there was something wrong with the ending that he hasn't understood. No, she must mean something else. "Sometimes I think you're not meant for this world, darling," she laughs. "Your mind is off somewhere else enjoying itself. I've never met an engineer like you."

"Well, I'm not like the engineers you know," he says, rather unnecessarily. "And I'm pretty sure I'm not anyway, an engineer, I mean. My tutor's certainly sure of it."

"What do you expect? You have such strange ideas – wizards and mediums and ghosts who cheat on the lottery! And you spend more time writing songs than on your coursework." She squirms closer along the bench seat until their hips and legs are pressed together, putting on her little girl face and voice that he's powerless to resist. Adrenaline starts to flow and his penis erects. She really can do virtually anything she likes with him. "Do you think they can see us now?"

"Silly. And they're spirits, not ghosts. Not necessarily people either, just spirits. I don't expect they hang about in the Union coffee bar either." Though he can't be sure about that. "I thought your people understood about that sort of thing, myths and magic?"

"You're thinking of Dracula, dear," she whispers, baring her teeth while her fingertips tip-toe along his leg under the table. He won't take much more. "And he's Romanian, anyway." His hand grasps hers just in time and she sighs, resting her head on his shoulder. "Oh well, I suppose I have to wait until the party."

"Party? What… oh, yes, tonight. I nearly forgot." He finishes her sandwich.

"You'd better not, it's mainly for us after all. Maggie's gone to so much trouble, I haven't been able to get into the kitchen for days. Look, I need to go back to the library soon. This course is hard, you know. I have to translate everything twice."

"Yes, of course. I admire you, you're stronger than I would be."

"No, anyone could do it if they have to. And we Czechs are used to hard work and – what's the expression? – keeping our heads down."

They remain in silence for a few minutes, holding hands, as the clamour grows around them. Now that Saturday afternoon has arrived, studies and libraries have mostly emptied and the student mind is gearing up for the evening concert. Tonight it's Fleetwood Mac and Roy almost wishes there wasn't a party. Their guitar blues have become his favourite music and he's confident that Man of the World will always be his personal song. As Eva gets up to leave, she suddenly thinks of something.

"What do you think the rest of the money's for, then?"

"What?"

"The money the ghosts won for you. You said there'll be some left over – do they have a plan for that?" He can't mind being teased by her.

"I hadn't thought about it. Yes, I expect they do."

He decides to go back to the library with her and they leave arm in arm, unaware that Didi is watching them closely, her head on one side and an amused smile playing at the corners of her mouth. She turns to the Chemistry lecturer she's been seeing recently.

"I think I'm going to get another goldfish. Company, for Harry."

By three o'clock he simply can't focus on the book any longer and passes Eva a note as he packs away again. She gives him a little wave and blows a kiss. If he's honest, he only stayed this long to be near her and to encourage her work; continuous binomial probabilities are quite beyond him but at least he's done all he can this week. Besides, he's come to appreciate the simple Saturday afternoon pleasures of coffee and a cigarette in a hot bath listening to the soccer commentary on the radio as rain drums on the flat roof.

He has to wait for the bus and is soaked through by the time he reaches Fallow Court. He turns the taps on and is already pulling off his shirt as he returns to his room, entering to find Red sitting cross-legged on the bed with sore eyes and smudges of mascara. It reminds him that Eva never used to wear make-up until a couple of weeks ago.

"If you could have seen yourselves," she blurts out. "All sheep's eyes and giggles, making an exhibition of yourselves. How do you think I felt? Everyone I was with knew about us and what was going on, trying to be polite and not talk to me about it. But they all knew. I felt so… humiliated." Her eyes are blazing now. "How can you be so selfish?"

"Red… I don't know what… well, I'm sorry." He is still in the doorway, completely nonplussed. This was completely unexpected. Surely she understood?

"Sorry? Is that it? You're just a hypocrite."

That one word immediately fills his mind with all the lonely childhood hours and family arguments and naïve struggles of adolescence. So much criticism. Yet as he has begun to become himself, he has been determined to be honest and open. He has been honest with Red. She's known his inner thoughts.

"I'm a woman, Roy," she goes on, taking advantage of his hesitation. "Did you think I wouldn't feel anything, I wouldn't mind? We've shared something special, haven't we? Not long ago you were kissing me in the shower and –"

"Shit, the bath!" He turns and races to the washroom, snatching at the taps just as the water starts to spill out. "The bloody overflow's blocked again."

"– and you can't get much more erotic than that." She has followed him to continue the tirade as he tries to mop the floor with his towel. A thin student with acne turns from his wash basin with a horrified look towards them, toothbrush hanging from his mouth.

"Who's that? Roy?" says a voice from a toilet cubicle. Roy hurriedly wrings out the towel while grimacing apologetically to the other student as he tries to steer her out.

"And in three weeks you haven't called me or anything and next time I see you you're making love in the coffee bar with someone else." Her voice echoes along the corridor and follows him into the kitchen. He turns the kettle on.

"Red, I'm sorry. Didn't Graham tell you that Eva was here?"

"I should have thought that was your responsibility, don't you?"

"Yes, yes, you're right. Of course. But look, you've always known about her. I've told you everything." That just makes her flare again, cheeks flushed and her hand clenched on a Coronation mug nearby.

"And do you think that didn't hurt too? God, have you got no feelings? I didn't want to know anything. Every time you mentioned her name, a bit of me cracked inside. But no, as far as you're concerned I was just a bit on the side while you waited for the main course. Jeez, you think you're so sensitive and honest, don't you, God's gift to twentieth century women!" His eyes are anxiously on the mug but it's too late. With a stamp of the foot she hurls it past his head to splinter on the wall, just missing the window. The explosion spent, she covers her face with her hands and sobs quietly.

"Hmm, you're making a habit of breaking things round here," he says gently, taking her by the shoulders and drawing her to his chest.

"I thought you loved me," she whispers. "And I know I was supposed to be with Graham, but I was beginning to love you. Now it's all dead."

"Oh, Christine," he murmurs, using her real name for the first time. "I do love you. But it's in a different way. You've been good to me and I do care, but Eva is… well, she's special. I thought you knew that. I don't know how to explain… but don't you see that I can still love you?" She pulls away from him, calm now, looking him in the eyes.

"No," she says, "I don't see."

She leaves the kitchen just as acne student enters, staring after her and then at the shattered pieces of his mug. He looks at Roy like a dog who has been whipped for leaving tooth marks on his master's slippers when he fetched them for him.

"My mother gave me that when I was two," he says flatly.

"I'm sorry, mate," says Roy, shaking his head still full of disbelief. "Perhaps I can get you another one."

"Some things are irreplaceable."

Roy makes coffee for one and turns away towards the bathroom to pull the plug. The water will be cold now anyway. Acne student calls out after him.

"And some people just have no thought for others."

Φ

"You don't seem to be enjoying that burger, mate," Roy says to Graham as he pushes his own plate away. There are only about twenty students in the dining hall this evening, quietly slicing and inspecting each mouthful and giving the place the solemn air of a pathology laboratory.

"I think they've started using horses. That or it's the flesh of old students who've withered away in the library. Your omelette okay?"

"S'pose. I'm sure vegetarians eat other things except omelettes, though. It's turned out a bit of a disappointing day, all told."

"Well, what do you expect? You can't blame her, can you? Women are funny about these things. And Red may be on the fried egg side but she is definitely a woman."

"But there you are, see? You know her as well as me, probably better. She's been in your bed more than mine. And actually, one night she was in both, if you remember. Did we ever get jealous?"

"Ah, but now you're being logical. They're different. Anyway, we're men and we're friends too."

"She could be friends with Eva."

"No, she couldn't. That's the point. And if you don't mind a randy down to earth sod like me giving you a word of advice, you won't say a thing about Red to Eva. Not a word. Or you'll lose her too. Women are a different species to us."

"Hmm, I'm beginning to see that. I've got it all wrong about love and friendship, and just when I thought I was getting to understand life a bit. Thanks. Coffee upstairs?"

While Graham heads off to stack their plates on the trolley, Roy wanders up the steps and waits by the noticeboard. It has started to fill up with pleas for lifts home here and there across the country for the half-term break coming up, and he realises that he hasn't arranged anything with Eva. If everyone agrees, this could be the first time his parents have met her; it's a fearful proposition but one that has to be faced sooner or later. In a corner of the board is a yellow leaflet advertising a Welsh opera company on tour. As he reads it, for something to do, things fall into place in his mind.

"Look," he points it out to Graham, "they're doing The Bartered Bride."

"Someone should."

"Don't be daft. It's Czech, by Smetana. Eva would love that and it's in Aberystwyth next weekend. That's only a few miles from where we met. I'll have the car back from the garage by then."

"Oh, I get it. Second honeymoon and all that. Well, first then. It'll all be a bit expensive though, won't it? And you'd have to find somewhere to stay."

"Not a problem," Roy grins, realising at last what the spirits' plans were for the Premium Bond.

Roy is fingering his guitar as Graham comes into his room with the coffees.

"I've got the verse for that song now, you know, the one I've been working on since the summer. Not sure about the chords after the A minor but I think it's right." He plays it through, slowly, plaintively.

"Sounds good to me. Any lyrics?"

"A couple of lines."

"They ought to resonate with the music."

"'The broken sea… calls out to me…'" Roy sings quietly.

"A bit strange. But it harmonises. Goes into C major seventh, a broken C, right? Try that."

"Yeah, thanks, mate, you're right," he says, playing it through again. "I don't know how, but everything's starting to fit together now."

"So it should," says Graham, pointedly looking out of the window, "when you're in love."

It's after nine o'clock when Roy finally arrives at Eva's flat and he feels a burst of pleasure to see her at the window waiting for him

"Sorry I'm late," he tries to say as she kisses him in the hallway. "Had to wait ages for the bus then I got off at the wrong stop." This is only partly true. The `phone call to his parents had taken over twenty minutes before everything had been agreed and then he'd walked to the city to calm himself down. All is well now because she's telling him that she's missed him since this afternoon.

"Oh, I had a bath and listened to the radio," he says, acutely aware that he has started to tell lies. Still, there are bound to be more.

"Have you noticed anything?" she asks, doing a twirl for him. He had, unconsciously, but now the effect takes hold. She's wearing a soft, bright red blouse with a low, frilled neckline, and tight black satin trousers. Her hair is somehow different too, she has spent time on her make-up and a discreet perfume has begun to envelop him. She has never shown off her body like this before. It's exciting and shocking all at the same time and Roy's body and mind start to argue with each other. This is a different woman and he has no idea what to say, but in her own excitement she doesn't notice. "I bought them this afternoon, couldn't resist. I would never be able to afford things like this at home even if I could find them."

'At home'?

He shakes his head to clear it and decides to relax and enjoy being with her. The music is too loud for serious talk anyway so he allows her to lead him by the hand through to the darkened lounge, full of swaying bodies and chatter. It's an hour later before the volume drops and they're dancing close.

"You haven't arranged anything for half-term, have you?" She shakes her head and looks hopeful. "Well don't, I've got a surprise. I found out what the ghosts were planning." She smiles her happy child smile and tightens her arms around his neck, her breasts pressed up against him. Suddenly he knows the full danger of love and feels a pang of fear. Carol, Kate and even Red pass into closed chapters, for he is holding his woman now.

"Anyone for food?" Maggie's bright voice breaks across the room and a light-hearted relieved cheer goes up. "Help yourselves, children, and don't drop crumbs on the carpet." She and another American girl are carrying plates full of colourful things to a table on one side and soon the music has changed to Leonard Cohen and the bodies are sprawled on the floor filling their faces. Paper cups of wine and cigarette ends are scattered among them.

Jan is here and now he comes over to join Roy and Eva. A tall, giggling blonde girl rather too well-built for her thin, white party dress is with him, hanging on to one arm and staggering slightly.

"Do you remember Jan?" says Eva. "He was here before, at the first house I was in, remember? He came up this afternoon from London to collect his things. He's got a job with a magazine there." The two men nod and smile to each other, unable to converse but recognising one another as friends now. Jan and Eva start to talk rapidly together, laughing and indicating others in the room with their eyebrows. In a few minutes, she turns back to Roy.

"It's so good to speak Czech again. I really miss it. He's telling me about this girl – he has no idea who she is and they can't understand each other, but she's just attached herself to him and won't let go. It's all right, she can't hear us, she's completely drunk." Suddenly she looks at him with concern. "Are you all right, Roy? You've gone very pale."

Roy is suddenly aware that a lot of other people around him are either giggling foolishly or have gone strangely quiet and a light dizziness has started to spread through his head that will certainly turn into nausea before long. He fights to control the rising swell within and gets to his feet heading for the kitchen door, hoping he doesn't stagger. He almost falls over Maggie sitting in lotus position with a bearded Rastafarian man who is soundlessly fingering a flute. He looks impressive.

"Roy, honey, you okay?" she asks.

"I'm not sure," he mutters as he passes. "It's just the banana bread, I suppose. Thought it was straight."

"Well, whoever heard of a straight banana, honey?" she says quite seriously, and the group around her fall apart in delighted hysterics.

"Be cool, man," says flute man, unhelpfully.

Roy throws open the kitchen window to the cold night and gasps in the air but it doesn't help. The nausea is threatening to knock him out. He has no experience of this but suddenly, by pure instinct, he knows what to do. As Eva follows him in, not sure whether to laugh or cry, he is scouring the kitchen cupboards and within a few minutes has eaten the two remaining bananas, a tin of pineapple, a packet of sweets and a jar of raisins intended for the next cake. Finally he sits at the kitchen table taking slow, deep breaths as the storm passes.

"'S all right now, sorry," he mutters. "I guess I can't take it. I'm not an engineer and I'd make a lousy hippy too."

"Don't worry," she says, sitting on his lap, "I love you whatever you are. But there is something strange about you. Everyone else is having a good time." She is soft and warm, relaxed and dreamy, slipping her hand under the top of his shirt to massage his shoulder gently. "I can't keep my hands off you. Come to my room," she whispers, touching her lips to his. But his head is still unsteady, he daren't close his eyes yet and he's beginning to tremble with a cold shiver. After all that's happened, surely it shouldn't be like this?

"Give me a few minutes," he says, lifting her up. "I need the bathroom."

At the top of the stairs, the door is closed but there's no answer to his knock so he pushes it open a few inches. The blonde girl is sitting on the toilet with her head bowed and her hair falling forward; white pants are stretched across her knees and her shoulder straps have slipped, exposing one pink, bulbous breast. She has been sick in the bath and is now asleep. Perhaps he should feel pity but instead cannot help the revulsion and disgust that fills him. He realises, too, that there is nothing exceptional about this scene in student society and that only makes him feel more isolated. The day that began so well has become a disaster and, reminded that he belongs nowhere, he is now completely clear-headed. And cool. He washes his face under the cold tap, runs some bath water to clean it out, pulls up the girl's straps and leaves it at that.

Eva's room is dark when he enters but someone else has got there first. There is a low moan from the bed and two white bodies lie there reflecting the streetlamp, faces buried in each other's hair. Mechanically, he goes back downstairs where the room is alive again with dancing but he can't see Eva so goes to the kitchen to make black coffee. Someone has put on The Beatles' Revolver album and he sings along in his head to Nowhere Man as he stands by the open window with his mug. In the morning he awakes early, cold and cramped in an armchair – it had been too late to get a bus – and grimaces at the awful mess of the room and the stench of stale wine and cigarettes.

With a relief he doesn't quite understand, Roy sees Jan across the gloomy room, still asleep and face down on the sofa with two pink legs behind him still wearing their white party shoes. He sits motionless, adjusting to the fact of Sunday and willing the circulation back into his aching limbs. After a while, flute man appears down the stairs in his underpants, his large hairy head ludicrous on top of a wiry, bony frame, and sleepwalks into the kitchen. When he returns with two mugs their eyes meet.

"Cool, man," he croaks and plods back up.

Roy makes coffee too and then searches out some bin liners to set about the clear-up. When he opens the windows, Jan wakes up and they smile to one another like colleagues in arms who have gone through a war together and survived. He makes coffee for him too and Jan takes it up to the bathroom while Roy finds the hoover – even that doesn't wake the girl. By the time Eva appears at about ten o'clock, the room has been sorted, the kitchen table laid and there's bread in the toaster. She has a hangover, her face is drawn with streaked make-up and she is wearing an old brown dressing gown and pink fluffy slippers. She looks beautiful.

"Hello, sweetheart. Aah… what time is it? I must look awful. Oh, did you clear up everything? What a strange man, you are." She kisses him and he catches an unusual scent of sleep, smoke and soul. So is this what it's like being married?

Before long the others join them and they all sit around the kitchen table, Eva and Roy, Jan, Maggie and flute man. Party girl is still asleep on the sofa. Gradually, the others' senses catch up with Roy's.

"My, what a party," observes Maggie. "Did it all go well?"

"What party?" asks flute man genuinely. Maggie pats his hand fondly.

"Never mind, hun, it's been a long night." She turns to the others. "You wouldn't believe what Jim can do with a flute."

Over more coffee and cigarettes, Eva and Jan begin talking urgently in Czech while the others just listen to the calm, lyrical flow of the language. There are long pauses in the conversation, followed by Eva's serious questions. At length, she turns back to her other friends.

"We are talking about how it is now in Czechoslovakia. Jan is in touch with the underground. Things are very bad. The government has given up and nobody is fighting. Nobody does anything. It's just like before all over again."

"Before?"

"In `thirty-eight and again in `forty-eight. We gave in then, too."

"But it would have been suicide to resist," Jim puts in. "Each time you were betrayed by your allies. You couldn't stand against Hitler or Stalin. And nor Brezhnev." Maggie looks at him with new respect.

"Listen to you. So knowledgeable." It's his turn to pat her hand.

"I don't just eat grass and play flute, Mags. I have a brain somewhere."

"Cool."

"All the same," Eva responds, "the Prague Spring came so close… Many people feel ashamed. That's why Palach –"

"No, come on," Jim interjects, warming to the subject, "that was just pointless. The shame is all on the Western governments."

Jan suddenly gets up and says something to Eva, going out and upstairs.

"He says he has a present for me," Eva explains.

Ф

On a thin layer of crisp snow, Alexander Dubček stands with head bowed, an almost unrecognisable shadow, in front of the Philosophy Faculty of Bratislava University. He has been released from the nearby hospital – some say it was radiation sickness caused by strontium in Moscow – and is recuperating at home as there is nothing else for him to do. So now he walks the streets of what will become Gustáv Husák's capital and reads the gold lettering on the memorial stone, already fading.

'Here, Russian occupiers killed a girl.

She was fifteen. August 21, 1968.'

The story is well known and it runs vividly through his mind while he stands as if mesmerised, shoulders hunched, hands in pockets, before shambling forward around the building.

Along the broad street behind him a convoy of huge green tanks is edging forward having crossed the Danube from Hungary. It is still early morning yet a crowd of hundreds, both young and old, soon gather to sit across the road in a wall of humanity. The first tank simply rumbles straight at them and they scramble clear, shouting with shock and anger. Students emerge from the university and run among the tanks and lorries, smashing lights and daubing swastikas on their metal-plated sides. A small group manages to set an oil drum alight and heavy black smoke hangs over the invaders, but the next tank merely rolls over the drum, crushing it flat beneath its caterpillar tracks along

REALITY

with all the other rubble hurled pointlessly at it. Frustration is all that the Slovaks have now.

A Russian officer, his Tula Kalash over one shoulder, watches the unfolding scene from the turret of his tank with bewilderment, a sickness beginning to claw at the pit of his stomach. Why is this happening? They were told they would be welcomed. What has gone wrong? The tension of screamed insults and figures running everywhere gets into his head and he snaps, letting off a single shot towards the crowd. A girl standing silently watching falls dead. She was a student nurse. The crowd erupts with sheer hatred now and others die alongside her.

Dubček shivers with the cold.

"Comrade," says a voice by his shoulder. He starts and turns towards the young man, never knowing any more whether to expect a needle, a bullet or a simple fist. The student looks into his eyes and holds out a small parcel wrapped in brown paper and roughly tied with string. "This is for you, from all of us here."

He turns away and disappears before Dubček can say a word. Standing on the street there, he unties the string and opens the book of Holub's poems. But the glow of pleasure that he has not been forgotten freezes on his face when he reads the handwritten inscription on the first page.

'From the students of Bratislava.
To Alexander Dubček, the little oak[8] from Mouse Street
who turned out to be a mouse after all.'

One of the pages has been marked with a thin strip of blood-stained material.

Ф

---

[8] The word 'dubcek' means 'little oak' in Russian.

Eva takes the book from Jan with delight when he returns to the kitchen.

"It's my favourite poet," she says to the others. "An English translation." She flicks through the pages and begins to read to herself and then aloud for them. "'…a hundred books we didn't write, a hundred pyramids we didn't build. Sweepings…'"

"'Dust'," continues Roy. "'Bitter as the beginning of the world. Believe me when I say it was beautiful.'" Eva looks up at him in astonishment and he just smiles.

"Hello, who are you all?" The blonde girl is standing in the doorway, rubbing her eyes and squinting in the daylight and ruining the moment. Her dress is creased and stained with red wine, one strap broken, her hair matted.

An excited Roy telephones Eva on Wednesday evening.

"I've got the car back and everything's arranged for the weekend. But we need to leave early on Friday, very early. I want to visit someone on the way. It's important. And bring your smart evening clothes, all right?"

"Visit who?" she is confused. "And we'll miss our morning lectures."

"This is more important, I promise. I'll explain on Friday. See you at eight o'clock."

"So who's more important than our degrees?" she asks as they set off in the thin morning sunshine towards Liverpool. Roy has spent an hour poring over the map and has written detailed notes for himself. The paper sits folded on the dashboard. "We'll be in trouble if we keep missing lectures. And I have so much to do." The dirty city flashes past and away behind them, and despite her reservations Roy is full of a sense of release and hope. This holiday is going to be good. Today is going to be great.

"You can't go through life always doing what you're supposed to. What other people say you have to. Now, remember I told you about Marian, the medium back home?"

"Oh, not this again. You know what I think," she complains. "It doesn't do any good believing in – what do you call them, 'spirits'? It's nonsense."

"You don't know that. Sure, we don't really know what's true. But just imagine it is true, even part of it. It could change everything in our lives, knowing what happens after death, that sort of thing."

"I don't want to know. And I can't see that it does any good. It just gives people false hopes."

"Then what about healing? Some mediums can heal with their hands. I've seen it."

"How?"

"I don't know. Nobody knows, but it happens."

"It's impossible."

"Well, let's not argue. It's a lovely day and we're going on holiday. Our first holiday together. Anyway, Marian wrote to me – and that's pretty unusual for her – and told me about this medium who lives up this way, on the Wirral. That's the other side of Liverpool. She says he's fantastic and I should meet him since he's not that far away. He specialises in psychic art."

"What on Earth's that?" Her incredulity is still tinged with annoyance.

"I'm not sure exactly, but I think he goes into a kind of trance and paints pictures of spirits, like, people's guardians. That's what I've arranged for this morning."

"And you think that's what the extra money was for?"

"Heavens, no. He doesn't charge a penny. We just give a donation. No, the money's for your surprise later."

She smiles at last and puts her head on his shoulder, trying to get him to give away the secret but failing. Before too long they're through the tunnel and away along the back streets of Birkenhead into the countryside. The day is brightening, almost like spring, and they wind down their windows to catch the sea air.

Whatever either of them had separately expected, John Cotton and his wife surprise them. They are ordinary and homely, in their late fifties and cornerstones of their local Anglican church. John is deferential in describing his gifts when Roy questions him. It all began to happen spontaneously. No, he's never had any art training. He hadn't even heard of Perugino before. The two women sit quietly in the kitchen discussing more parochial things and Eva stays there when John and Roy move to the studio.

Later, as they drive south, Roy is very quiet. This is mostly because of the sheer impossibility of what has happened, but also for the way John had looked at him as they left and said, "Take care."

"Well, it is a lovely portrait," Eva concedes, trying to prompt Roy out of himself. They have stored it very carefully in the boot since the paint is still wet, and moved their bags to the back seat of the car. "Nice colours. And the monk has a very kind face."

"Fifteen minutes," is all that Roy can say for the moment.

"Yes. That was surprising."

"He just put some music on, stood still and seemed to go into a kind of trance muttering to himself in Italian, I think it was. Then paints and brushes were flying everywhere and it was finished in fifteen minutes. With his eyes closed."

"Come on, Roy, that's impossible."

"It's true, I was watching him the whole time. It's incredible."

"Well, I agree with that."

She's not good with maps and it's already late afternoon before she realises where they're going next. He's taken the B road from Dolgellau to try and disguise the route but with a small squeal of delight she recognises Talyllyn Lake as they pass it. The fading sun gleams silvery on its still water and even the wildfowl don't disturb the calm surface. They're a million miles from their everyday lives now and she relaxes at last, reaching across to hug him.

"Careful! This pass is narrow. Here." He takes the tickets from the top pocket of his jacket and passes them across. "Tonight. We're going to dress up and do it properly."

"Smetana, I love it. Thank you, Roy. And I thought the smart clothes were to meet your parents."

"Well, that too, I suppose." Although he doubts that her clothes will have much of an effect on his father's thinking.

"But Roy, you don't like opera. What was it you said – 'the ultimate pomposness' or something?"

"Pomposity, yes. I don't like it, but I do love you. And at least this one's in English."

They drop into the town past the turning to the campsite by the station – such mixed memories flash through their minds – and he slows to a crawl along the promenade. The sad, February somnolence of the place is obvious and he wonders whether it was a mistake to come back. The beach is empty down to a grey sea, litter blows around the bus shelter and the putting green is closed up. Outside the Seaview he switches off the engine and musters a smile.

"Now you can speak to Mrs Baggage however you like. I can't wait to see her face. I've already booked but they don't know who we are yet."

This is something that Eva certainly wasn't expecting and as the heavy front door swings back she is about to face some moments of truth and learn who Roy is. The Receptionist raises a sceptical eyebrow but soon recovers his composure.

"Good evening, I'm Mr Carter. I telephoned earlier this week to book."

"Ah, yes, sir." He flicks a page over agonisingly slowly and a small smile plays on his lips, for some personal reason, as he simultaneously glances across at Eva with one eye. "Two single rooms. This way, please."

Eva feels herself melting from the feet upwards and doesn't know whether to cry for joy or disappointment. Single rooms? How can this man refuse himself so much? Refuse her? Roy seems more and more unreal. It can't be for appearances' sake – one look at his ponytail, beard growing back, jeans and yellow Granddad shirt, confirms that he doesn't care what people think. But when they meet in the bar before dinner he is ordering a Martell and wearing a newly-pressed dark blue suit with a black tie. He's playing a part now and enjoying it. She wears a thin, chocolate-brown evening dress that clings to her thighs as she walks so that one could almost touch her skin through it. It is cut low at the front over a shadowy, mythical valley fringed by a cream taffeta shawl. They both stand still and smile at the other, dinner and opera now almost incidental in the face of this most subtle eroticism.

Mrs Baggage does a double-take when she sees Eva on her rounds at dinner and her practised professional welcome is muted with shock. But she is a woman who prefers not to know much about other people's lives and she soon moves off to the next table. It's all they can do to stifle their laughter.

Even Eva agrees that the opera is quite terrible. It's an amateur company whose undeniable enthusiasm still cannot disguise its absence of talent. They still emerge into the cold night under a cloudless sky in good spirits. This is all happy experience to look back on one day.

"Of course, what can you expect?" teases Roy. "He did die in an asylum." Nearly back to the hotel, he pulls to the side of the road overlooking Cardigan Bay outside Aberdyfi and they watch the slow, rolling waves. "There's a buried city out there," he says, "so they say. When trouble threatens, you can hear the bells ringing under the sea." They sit close together, quietly, dreamily, not listening for bells but with minds full of tumbling memories.

"Roy," she asks after a while, "who do you think the monk is, the one in the painting? Is he from your mind, the person you want to be?"

"Who can say?" is all he can say.

They take coffee downstairs, each lost in their own thoughts, and then take the stairs slowly, one at a time, arms around one another. They are exhausted. In Eva's room, the curtains pulled back and moonlight bathing them, they stand close together and help each other to slip out of their clothes. Taking one another's hands lightly, they are naked together for the first time. But they both know that they will not make love tonight, not here, and both are somehow relieved. Perhaps the greatest expression of love is not the act but the acceptance that it is not necessary.

ACT 10

Breaking Down

This is their zenith. On the ceiling above them, slow moving patterns of moonlight reflecting from a turning tide seem to bring this Welsh, second-class Eden hotel room to life with the spirit of July, `sixty-eight. Roy feels like a child, filled with awe by the strength of her athletic body and the way her skin melts into his own. And she, who has already known many sides of love, is touched by this child and also finds herself again a girl, discovering a new side. How many can there be?

When he returns from the bathroom, she is lying on the bed almost asleep, the sheets pulled back. As he sits on the edge of the bed to look at her, his every thought dissolves and the physical world slips quietly away to nothing. He is only conscious of consciousness itself, breathing and chemistry suspended in an altered state where neither are required and where his being has joined with hers in non-being. At his shoulder stand other non-beings, saying nothing but holding the space, taking control. In a soundless nowhere, there is just the faintest low hum of the engine that gives life to it all. No time passes, so that he may know the truth. Will he remember?

He awakes alone in her bed at eleven o'clock to find a note on the pillow. 'Gone for a walk.' There are two kisses. He doesn't have to wonder where she is. His clothes are neatly folded on top of her case, which has been packed, and he creeps stealthily to his own room to wash and dress.

It is almost high tide again as Eva walks slowly along the beach, picking her way over small rocks and the night's seaweed. She wears the fawn, soft leather jacket over jeans and a purple cotton blouse, the gathering breeze no match for the day's warmth. The night is sweet in her, yet she can never shake away her distrust of happiness in this inconstant world.

Up ahead, with feet overhanging the grassy bank near the edge of the campsite, is a figure, bent and motionless. It looks as though it has lost something precious and having searched the sand in vain is now searching the mind. It is Sally. Her hair is shorter and her glow has equally been cut away. She smiles briefly when she recognises Eva but they both know that everything has changed and it is several minutes before they are at ease in their conversation.

"So you don't work at the hotel any more?" asks Eva.

"Not for ages. I was sacked. Mrs B never liked me and told me not to come back when it reopened after the repairs. She found Peter in my room one night – remember, the German boy? – and used that as an excuse. I liked him, not just for the sex, but I never saw him again after." She is still carrying loss around with her, although she's got another job now, at The Willow.

"What about Paul? Didn't you go and see him? You were good together."

"I suppose. But he was never my type, was he, a different world. He hasn't been in touch since Christmas."

"Different worlds can work."

"I don't believe that. Anyway, I was just his holiday tits, wasn't I? It was different for you and Roy. You were in love."

"Was I?"

"'Course. Anyone could see that."

When Roy approaches, she retreats into herself again as if unable to face their togetherness and makes an excuse about her lunchtime shift starting soon. Eva realises that they haven't exchanged addresses but it's too late. She sits holding hands with Roy in their sandy hollow, laughing about the opera and Mrs Baggage, until it's time to go back for a bite of lunch before leaving. He looks back once over his shoulder as they go and frowns; it looks as though the sand has been dug up in one area.

He tries to describe what he experienced in her room last night but struggles to find the words.

"Anyway, life is becoming more and more strange lately. And wonderful. The more happy I am, being with you, the closer I feel to everyone else – and every thing too, like trees and stones and us are all part of one… family. I love everyone. And things work out just as they should, like that money turning up, and I just seem to know things… like, intuition."

"You're in the flow," she smiles indulgently. What kind of man is she going to live with?

"Mmm. And there are signs, too, like someone is guiding me. Okay, you'll laugh at this, but the other week I was driving along, on the way to yours, and thinking about what I should do with my life –"

"Yes, that is a problem."

"– when a car flashed its lights at me from behind and overtook. So I automatically looked at its registration number and for some reason

I read it as a Bible reference. Luke nine twenty-three, I think it was. Well, I couldn't help looking it up later." He pauses, as if suddenly aware that he is opening himself up completely.

"Well, what did it say?"

"Yes, well that's what's so weird. It was exactly what I was thinking about, like an answer to my question. About dedicating yourself to a spiritual path." Even the sea seems to be hushed and listening now, the gulls wheeling around silently over their heads.

"It was just a car, Roy." Her voice is gentle yet firm. "You can't go around thinking everything's significant and spirits are giving you signs. Life isn't beautiful."

"But last night –"

"Last night was love. Aah, I was right about you, wasn't I, not belonging? The monk is you, isn't he? But you can't ignore the real world – what about my family back home, and Prague and the people who were killed? That's what life is." She swings on his arm playfully, breaking the rhythm of their steps and the mood. They are nearing the hotel and can see Mrs Baggage at the front window, waiting with arms folded tightly across herself. Eva stops at the side of the road and looks into his eyes, touching his face. "I'm sorry, darling. Yes, yesterday was lovely, thank you, and last night was beautiful. I love your body…" She giggles. "You're the first man I've known who looks better without clothes."

The phrase thrills him. How incredible it is to be loved.

Just then a car passes and beeps its horn; there's a man driving and the glimpse of his face jogs some memory in the back of Roy's mind.

They've nearly finished lunch when Roy brings up another thing on his mind.

"About last night. I noticed… why have you shaved your legs? And under your arms?"

"What? Well, women do."

"You never did before. You've started to look... well, different recently."

"Maybe. It's not important, is it?"

"I loved your hairy legs." The man at the next table chokes slightly on his food and one of his wife's eyebrows nearly disappears beneath her hair.

For nearly two hours on the road, Eva can't help wondering whether it's such a good idea to be visiting his parents now. True, she finds herself growing helplessly closer to him yet she doesn't share his sense of finality, his apparent knowledge of their relationship. Her own life is not without its signs but they're the sort that are inside and can't be looked up in a book. Dropping down between the lovely stone walls of Bridgnorth, they cross the wide, fast-running Severn and it feels like a point of no return. She knows that childhood has not been easy for him and is not yet quite over, while for her it is; surely the gap will be obvious. On the other side of Stourbridge, she reaches behind to her bag on the back seat and brings out a small parcel to show him.

"I got a small present for your mother. Do you like it? I loved it when I saw it and had to get it." He hardly notices what it is. Somehow, the only thing he notices is that she hasn't asked whether his mother will like it. The thought is put into the small back room of his mind reserved for small things.

They fall silent for the last few miles as dusk begins to settle in. He has timed it carefully so that they arrive shortly before dinner, to avoid any awkward conversation. For Roy, this homecoming is special for at last he has the prize just as he said he would seven months ago. All the same, they are going to be judged: she is foreign, a communist, an older woman, and he is... well, he's not turning out as his parents wished. As they round the last turn and coast onto the gravel drive, Eva's eyes widen in awe.

"Roy, you didn't say your parents were rich. What a wonderful house." It is detached, with a double garage, bay windows with leaded glass and rose bushes edging the front lawn.

"No, not rich," he laughs. "We'd say 'middle class'. Tomorrow I'll show you where the rich people live, up the hill. Even I can't believe those houses." It has been easy for him to take for granted his family's comfort, his own privilege, and he's only not materialistic because he's never had to be. Now, seeing his father in the headlights, clearing away the gardening tools and wearing shabby old clothes, he begins to sense the flaw in his developing spirituality. This has all been the result of hard work.

The tyres crunch to a stop, the engine dies and they sit for a moment shrouded by the beautiful peacefulness of the estate. Then the porch lantern flashes on and his mother is there, smiling with arms outstretched – though not for him, of course. Eva, it seems, is to be the prospective prodigal daughter. Within minutes of their arrival, Roy's preconceptions have been turned on their heads alongside his mother's attitudes: her affection is open, her concern for Eva genuine, and she seems to understand almost better than him what she has been through. When his father reappears, changed and smiling, offering drinks, the production is complete and a flicker of resentment begins to knock on the door of that small back room of Roy's mind. Heavens, whatever else one might expect from one's parents, the least is that they should be consistent.

For her part, Eva settles immediately into the space created for her in the family's bosom. Her natural sophistication, so long repressed, can now flower and within an hour after dinner – with wine, can you believe? – Roy hardly recognises anyone around him. He even wishes that his annoying younger sister, Helen, were there because she sees through everything, but she's at a friend's house. Still, there is a sting in the day's tail that betrays Roy's parents as they prepare to go upstairs.

"You won't be late, will you, my dears?" says his mother. "You know I can't sleep until everyone's settled, Roy. And you'll say 'goodnight' downstairs, won't you?" In his flash of humiliated anger, Roy barely hears Eva's reply.

"Yes, of course, Mrs Carter. I hope you sleep well. Goodnight."

"You see?" he manages when the door has closed. "They treat me like a child."

"Then don't act like one. You didn't even say 'goodnight'. That was rude."

"It means 'I hope you have a good night' and I didn't feel like it."

"It's just a word people say to be polite. Like 'how are you?'"

"Oh, and I always thought that meant 'how are you?'. You mean, nobody actually cares?"

"Don't you think you're being a bit immature? Anyway, you'll always be a child to them. My parents are the same." It's the first time she's criticised him and meant it, and they both need some silence to digest the fact. At length, she stands and says, "I'm going up, too. Goodnight, Roy."

When she has gone he switches off the lights, draws the curtains back and sits with a cigarette in the streetlight by the open window. Having arrived five hours ago, Roy just wants to leave. It's not just that this place represents the old life; the last few minutes have brought to the surface the lingering undercurrents of tension in his new life. However deep his adoration, Eva is different and he can never share in what has made her what she is. On a Welsh beach, he had conceived the possibility of perfection, touching for the first time his burgeoning idealism. Now it appears that human imperfection is too far gone and there will always be too many things over which their relationship can have no control. He lights another cigarette and imagines his parents asleep upstairs in their separate rooms. They must have been in love once, surely? Two by two, he thinks of his parents' friends and his friends' parents – no, perfection doesn't exist. Roy resolves to catch up with Nick this week; of all the people he knows, Nick is the only one who seems content with life's stupidities.

There is the distant click of the bathroom light and light steps are coming downstairs. They hesitate outside the door and he can see her pale outline beyond the whorled glass as her fingers close on the handle. She is wearing a thin, cream gown over a short, white nightdress, the streetlight picking out her body beneath it.

"I wanted to say 'goodnight' properly," she says quietly, head bowed. "I'm sorry. Let's not go to sleep with bad feelings, ever." He stands and they hold each other lightly, her skin so clean and soft next to his that it washes away all the dark thoughts. Lost within each other, they do not hear the other footsteps on the stairs or see the large, dark outline behind the door.

"You're right," he says. "I'm sorry too. Stop now. We'll make this work." She smiles agreement and is already moving towards the door when the light flashes on and cuts them to pieces.

"Have you no consideration for your mother?" growls Mr Carter, looking right past Eva and not including her in his invective. "My God, you're selfish. When are you going to grow up? Well, while you're under my roof –"

"I was just going, Mr Carter," Eva interrupts firmly.

"What? Yes, all right, Eva. Goodnight."

She turns briefly towards Roy and purses her lips in a kiss before leaving. It's not enough. The vein on his face starts to throb and he takes a step towards his father with something very like hatred welling up, a fist clenching.

"How dare you? How dare you misunderstand so complete –" But his father has seen it and has already turned away. In the kitchen, Roy sinks onto a stool waiting for the kettle to boil and finds himself trembling with this awful new emotion that has no place in a spiritual life.

On Sunday morning, Eva gets breakfast in bed and Roy doesn't. He makes his way downstairs to find that everyone is busily avoiding everyone else, so takes himself out for a walk up the hill. The huge, mock-Tudor houses with their tree-lined drives somehow don't seem so impressive today.

"They've started building some new ones up there now, since I was here last," he tells Eva when he gets back. "There used to be a field there with a beautiful white horse I used to talk to when I was a kid."

"I suppose people have to live somewhere," she observes.

"So do horses."

The Mermaid used to be a coaching inn, a long, low, white-washed building with arched wooden doorways and ivy clinging around the windows. There are plans, says Adam, to modernise it. For now, the warped wooden tables still sit outside near the carpark and it's just warm enough today to sit out. When Roy returns with their drinks and a lunch menu, they begin to relax at last.

"Did you sleep well?"

"It was a strange night," she says. "Yes, I slept deeply and I was dreaming something about us... I can't remember it now. But I can still feel, I don't know, waves going through me as if part of me is still asleep. It's odd, I don't usually dream."

"Yes, you do. Everyone does. But maybe you just don't remember."

"Isn't that the same thing? Anyway, it was probably caused by that scene last night. I think I know what you mean now, about your parents. Your father anyway. Actually, I had a nice talk with your mother while you were out. Your father was working in the back room."

"He always is. Every evening, every weekend. So what did you talk about?"

"You, mostly. You'd have been embarrassed. She showed me some old photographs."

"Oh, no. Not the ones when I was a fat kid? Still, I suppose that means she likes you. She accepts you."

"She was nice. And we talked about girly things too, like clothes and make-up. She gave me some good ideas. I like her, Roy, and she cares so much about you. I expect your father does, too, in his way."

"Yeah, right. But last night was… look, shall we go home?"

"I haven't finished my drink."

"No, I mean back to Manchester."

They eat their Ploughman's lunches in silence and are just lighting cigarettes when the red MG pulls into the carpark. Marian climbs out, still turning heads at forty-five, and waves cheerily to them. Roy explains but Eva feels herself bridle instinctively. Perhaps it's because of the woman's attractiveness – is she a threat? – or because she has been ambushed into the meeting. If Marian is aware of the coolness she shows no sign of it and they talk superficially for twenty minutes until Roy goes to get more drinks.

"Who is Tomáš?" Marian asks suddenly, appearing to look at the empty space next to Eva.

"I… er, I don't know what you mean," she answers, taken aback.

"Yes, you know him. He's a young man in spirit – I mean dead. He says something about a poet… is Tomáš a poet? I don't understand… All right, yes. He has a message." She stares past Eva in an unnerving way and nods as though in conversation. "Good heavens," she goes on, "how odd. That's a first. He says you have a message for him. It's usually the other way round. Do you understand, dear?"

Eva has become cold through and through, her body rigid as her mind tells her to run. It cannot be, it simply cannot. Roy must have told her so it's telepathy or a trick… but no, she hadn't told Roy. So it's impossible. Finally she composes herself.

"Yes, all right, I understand. Tell him she is fine, she's safe, but I don't know where she is now." Marian puts her head on one side and considers.

"You will meet her again, Eva. In England. He's asking... no, he's begging you to let her know that he's safe too. He's in the spirit world but he's fine. Will you do that, please?"

"Yes." Her voice is small and hoarse, and she is still pale when Roy returns. He beams when Marian explains and takes Eva's hand.

"Brilliant! Welcome to the club. Now you know what I've been talking about." She can't answer and drinks her vodka and tonic very slowly instead, wishing the whole thing would go away. Marian is watching her closely and gets to the root of Eva's difference.

"I'm not going to go on, Eva. But I have to tell you that your grandmother is with you, your father's mother. She's tall, dark hair, something unusual about her left eye. Her name's Marie. What's that?" She stares at the wall behind them. "I see. She says she had another son, your uncle... I don't know why she mentions that. Anyway, they're with you, to help you, and they love you very much. That's... oh, all right. One more thing. Your father must be careful, it's his heart. He should get it checked." She sits back, apparently worn out, and takes a long slug of her Martini soda. "Sorry about that, Eva, but they just wouldn't let me stop. Quite insistent. It's not usually tiring for me but they were a bit difficult to understand."

Roy has been sitting there transfixed throughout. Somehow, even though it's a belief, one never quite gets used to the enormity of it.

"You know, Eva, that is strange because... well, I didn't like to mention it before because you didn't like the idea... but I had a dream, too, about your father, I'm sure. Is he all right?"

"He did have a problem with his heart years ago. But it was all checked out and he's fine. I suppose he is under pressure now, at the factory. The Russians. But I don't have an uncle anyway." Suddenly she turns on Marian. "Why did you have to say all that? I didn't ask you to."

"No, my dear." Marian isn't offended in the least. "But I had to. It's what I'm for. And I can't order the time and place. In any case," her eyes narrow, "you knew I was going to say something, didn't you? Sooner or later."

"Okay," Eva smiles, relaxing. "I think I did. I've been having a strange feeling that something weird was going to happen."

"A premonition," says Roy triumphantly. "That's what it's called. I get that all the time. In fact, I'm sure that Paul is going to turn up in a minute."

"Paul, coming here? Why would – oh!" She kicks Roy under the table as she sees Paul get out of his father's car and come over to them.

"Hello, Eva, great to see you again. Thanks for `phoning, Roy. Am I late? Oh, did I say something?"

The march of education is taking its toll on their friendship, especially on Paul, and even this has changed in the last two months. Paul has learned that many of the great questions of history have not been answered, let alone learned from, so he doesn't ask many questions himself now. He is learning to dissect words and so doesn't take them seriously. He is finding that things often do not mean what they seem, nor people what they say, so that nothing seems to mean very much any more.

"You haven't written for a while," says Roy, choosing the wrong opening to fill a gap in the conversation.

"Nothing much to tell."

"Are you still writing songs?" He turns to Marian. "We used to play a lot together. It was Paul who got me started on the guitar."

"No, I hardly play now."

"Shall we do something tomorrow, then?"

"I don't know. What do you want to do?"

"Maybe he just felt left out," Eva suggests as they walk back down the road after the pub has closed. "Now we're together and he's on his own."

"Maybe. I just think he's changed. Why didn't you tell him that we saw Sally yesterday?"

"I don't know. Perhaps I didn't think he deserved it."

When they get back to the house, Roy's father is working and his mother is having her afternoon rest. They make coffee and sit drinking it in the kitchen, and Roy asks her what she thought of what Marian had said.

"I suppose it was quite interesting. My grandmother did have a squint in one eye. We were very close when I was small. But I don't have an uncle."

"You could ask."

"I think I ought to know, don't you think? Anyway, I don't know if I'll ever see my parents again."

The next day, Roy shows her around the town. It doesn't take long as there are few points of interest, although Eva wants to look in every women's clothing shop. Then he drives her to the factories where he is supposed to work one day. He does this with an odd sense of pride despite the place seeming ever more alien to him. As they pull away towards home ahead of the evening rush, he catches sight of Kate climbing into Mr Jackson's car, laughing, her miniskirt riding up those long, slim legs. For an instant there's a raw memory of what might have been but then she's forgotten. The perfect body now seems unimportant. By Wednesday they've had enough and make excuses about work to be done in Manchester. Mrs Carter seems genuinely sorry to see them go.

"My mother's become very fond of you," says Roy as they turn onto the M6.

"Mmm, we got quite close. She talked to me a lot, you know, about personal things. I think she's lonely. But she accepts me because she can see that you're happy. I don't know about your father, though… does he think I'm a communist?"

"Probably. I don't care what he thinks."

"Well, I know he wasn't very nice. But you told me on Saturday that you love everybody."

"Yeah, that's going to take a bit longer than I thought."

And when he's finally learned this – even supposing it's a thing that can be learned – will it turn out to feel as he's imagined it? Will the spiritual life be tangible? Right now, he is running from childhood on a crazy paper chase, his mind full of clues that point the way but mean nothing until he finds the cipher. Still, every experience, even the bad ones, pushes him towards the next corner as he chases life's meaning. But then there's sweet Eva – he watches her for several moments as the motorway stretches empty and straight ahead – what has she to do with all of this and how can he share it with her when she comes from such a different world? With an awful lurch, Roy realises that his father may be right after all: what Earthly use is spirituality?

Blindly, though not randomly, by instinct rather than design, Roy has arrived at that extraordinary phase of the chase where alternative worlds meet. Most people never experience it and for those who do it's usually a mere fleeting glimpse of inner cosmos, the distant echo of a majestic chord. Thoughts are mirrored in events. Things happen in union with ideas and needs. Synchronicity. He doesn't realise how privileged this makes him, nor how powerful is this state. It might take the form of, say, money appearing when it is needed – to mend the car and take a special trip – or of knowing what another person – especially Eva – is about to say. Questions answered. Sometimes it is questions asked, like the car breaking down on the wrong side of Stafford.

"I don't understand it," Roy moans to Graham later. It's early evening, they are almost the only ones who have returned early from the break and the corridor is quiet. The dining hall is closed for the week so they are opening tins and packets from home in the kitchen. "I mean, the thing's only just been serviced. It's really upset me – and

God knows how I'm going to pay for the tow. I've used up all the money I got the other week, in fact I overspent a bit in Wales. So I'm flat broke now. Just when I thought things were working out, in tune with nature and all that."

"Then p'raps it's nature's way of telling you that things don't always work out," says Graham, matter of fact. "After all, what's so wonderful about nature? Earthquakes are natural. Tropical storms are natural. Disease is –"

"I get the point."

"That's what engineering is for, to improve on nature." He scoops the last of the beans from the tin with a wooden spoon and they drop in a congealed orange mess onto sausages that are spitting and crackling in the frying pan. Roy has to turn away.

"And another thing," he says. "Eva has started wearing make-up and shaving her legs. That's not natural, is it?"

"So what? Surely that's a good sign, shows that she wants to be attractive for you. Jeez, you should see Janet first thing in the morning. Put the kettle on."

"But she knows I don't like it."

"It's women, mate. Best just to let them be. You know, I read once about some women in a Japanese prisoner-of-war camp. A local trader came round every week with medicines, extra food, that sort of thing. But no, all these women wanted was make-up, the silly cows. And the only men around were the little yellow guards so they weren't trying to attract them. It just made them feel better, I suppose."

"That's obscene," objects Roy. "What's nicer than plain, soft, female skin?"

"Aah, I wish you hadn't said that."

They take their food and coffees along to Graham's room since he's the one with a record player. It's a dark and sensual room with every inch of yellow wall covered by posters, album jackets and flyers. There is a lot of black, red and flesh. On the ceiling above the bed is a tall, slim Jane Fonda in a wet, clinging blouse. Additional Mathematics and Workshop Practice sit side by side with Playboy on the desk. Graham moves them to one side to make room for their plates and puts The Who on.

"Where is Eva, anyway? Had enough of her after your cosy visit?"

"Other way round," Roy grimaces. "We had a row on the way back, sort of. She couldn't see why I was so upset about the car, said it was just one of those things."

"My kind of girl. Why don't we –?"

"Shut up. She said I was being childish and I can't cope with real life, my head's in the clouds –"

"A wet kipper in your trousers?"

"Eh?"

"That's what it all comes down to, isn't it? Let's face it, be honest, you can be a bit extreme at times, all this stuff about spirits and hairy legs when what she wants is for you to give her one. It's been long enough, if you see what I mean."

"Now hang about, she's not –"

"Not like that? Grief, you're naïve, mate. 'Course she is, we all are. We're panting for it. It's what makes the world spin. Sex. Nookey. The other. Jeez, you go on about nature – well, we've got cocks, haven't we? They're not just for peeing with. And Eva's a red-blooded woman, anyone can see she knows what it's about just by looking at her. She's had men before. And she's beautiful, man, a gymnast, right? A supple body, full of energy, spreading her legs over the asymmetric bars and all that. She's a woman, not a princess, and she wants a man, not some kind of messiah waiting 'til we're married. Oh, you're not still a virgin, are you?" He pauses to attack a sausage while Roger Daltrey leads on I Can See For Miles.

Roy doesn't answer, sitting back and toying with his fork. It's never been put to him quite like that before and had it been anyone but

Graham he might have stormed out. But he's a friend and he usually tells the truth.

"I just…," he says hesitantly at last, "I suppose I just want everything to be right. The perfect place and time."

"It never is, mate. And by the time you realise that, she could be gone. You not hungry?" Roy has pushed his plate away hardly touched and now stands, shaking his head as if to dislodge uncomfortable thoughts.

"No. I'd better go anyway, get on with some work."

"Hell, that reminds me. Sorry, I nearly forgot." Graham rummages in the drawer of his desk and brings out an envelope, passing it over. "I was in the department earlier and the secretary asked me to give you this, soon as." Roy stands at the open door, reading the letter. Could this day get worse? "What is it, then? An honorary degree for services to women?" Roy lets that go.

"It's from the Prof. Says my work and attendance are appalling and I could be kicked out if I fail the end of year exams. He wants to see me."

Ф

Eva is reading a different sort of letter, sitting quietly in the deserted departmental library. It had been addressed to 'Eva Nováková, Inglish, Salford University, UK' and was waiting in her pigeonhole when she arrived this morning. It is from Aleš. He does not know any other way to contact her since she moved from her awful room but he is neither angry nor judgemental. He apologises for his behaviour that evening. It had been fear. He still doesn't understand why she went back to England (he doesn't even mention Roy) but he is trying to accept it, that it's something she had to do. He loves her and is waiting for her. As most people agree, Aleš is a good man.

She allows one tear to fall and then wipes her eyes, wondering whether after all she has made a big mistake. The last few days have been the best and the worst of Roy. She had never had such mental struggle and frustration with Aleš, and probably never would. His feet are firmly on the ground. But she had never touched such inner peace, such a sense of life's beauty, either. This is a rollercoaster and, at the moment anyway, it's not much fun; it's like when the car has just crept up to the top of the highest, steepest climb and you know you're about to hurtle down the other side with a sharp turn waiting at the bottom. The race might be exhilarating but there's always the thought that the car might leave the tracks later.

On the other hand, she is finding that she loves England. As much as she also loves her home country, misses her friends and familiar places (and even her parents), and as much as she feels she ought to be there alongside them at this desperate time, there is such a genuine freedom here to be oneself and enjoy living. There are nice clothes and good music, there are cinemas with every kind of film, there are bright young people and you can find good food in so many different places. She has a real opportunity here, to grow and to be successful, with no-one telling her what to think and how to behave. Well, Roy has in a small way started to tell her what to think… but surely they can work through that? He is still young, yet growing fast.

She puts the books away in her shoulder bag, slips the letter into her jacket pocket and steps lightly onto the open, moving lift. What would happen if she didn't get off at the bottom? She is composed again now: for all the reasons to go back, for all the things that ought to be done, it was her trusted intuition that brought her here. No, come on, it was more than that. It was the quiet song in her heart, moving through her like gently rolling waves, and the fact that she could never get Roy's face out of her mind.

Stepping out into the chilly evening, she immediately sees the large, black saloon car without number plates parked a few yards away with a gorilla at the wheel. Inspector Peter Jones steps out of the front passenger door.

"Miss Nováková. Hello again. We need to talk."

Φ

"It was a good idea of yours to come here," says Roy. It is the next night and they're sitting in the car at the Edge allowing the quiet and clean air to seep into them. The car has been fixed. It turned out to be a minor fault. Graham shrugs, pulling on his cigarette.

"You needed a break after the break you've had."

"Sure do. Everyone needs to get away from things sometimes. That's why I got so wound up about the car – I need mobility, space."

It is nearly eleven o'clock, the night sky clear and starry, and ahead of them the trees on the fringes of the Edge are bare and bending over to one side like stooping old men with limbs outstretched in supplication. Maybe this is caused by the magnetism of the mineral deposits deep below. In the centre is the wizard's tomb, or what might be his tomb. They walk there briskly with coats buttoned up, carrying flasks, a blanket and guitars as they kick through piles of wet leaves. Cows in the nearby field watch them pass silently and nothing else is moving. Soon the town lights can be seen below, a soft orange in the mist, and they turn off to the left.

"What did the Prof say, then?"

"Oh, the Riot Act, you know. Must do better. Letting the side down. Obligations. I tried telling him about Eva and how she's needed a lot of help but he wasn't interested. Said that's my affair. I think it was supposed to be a joke. Then he said perhaps I should change course."

"Really?" Graham is genuinely interested by this. "You know, that's not such a bad idea, mate."

"How can I? My Dad's company is paying me to do engineering training – and anyway we're nearly through the first year."

"Only half way, you'd catch up if it was something you enjoyed. Let's face it, Roy, you're not an engineer and you never will be. Don't get me wrong, you're clever enough to do the work but you'll never enjoy it. It doesn't suit you. Perhaps you could do, I don't know, Divinity or Philosophy."

Roy feels a sudden, unexpected rush of excitement at the surprising idea of studying something he actually enjoys. He's never thought of work being like that.

"You could be right. To be honest, I hate what I'm doing. I'm probably only here because no-one ever suggested anything different before. And I've changed a lot this last year. I can't stand that lecture hall, a hundred and fifty students sitting there like blotting paper, and torque stresses and shearing moments are all very well but they don't do anything for me." He's beginning to get fired up but the new mood suddenly deflates. "Anyway, the company would never let me do it. And I can just hear my father…"

"They'd have to," says Graham, warming to his task. "What's the point of paying you to do something you hate when you're only going to leave as soon as you can anyway? I assume you've got a contract? So go for it – as long as it's not Marxist Sociology, that might be a step too far."

Roy laughs and throws an arm round his friend's shoulder.

"What a wonderful, sly, devious, calculating brain you have."

"Aw shucks, I jes' want yer t'be happy, boy."

They sit on the grass beside the great tree on the tomb, sipping coffee. Graham picks out a slow, haunting, resonant sequence of notes on his guitar that die away like footsteps slipping through the shadows. Roy follows with a verse of his song and the first couple of lines of the refrain that have come recently. In D minor it's E... D... E... F..., then D... G... F... D... in G major.

"I'm sorry about what I said yesterday, about Eva," says Graham. "I know she's special. I'm probably just jealous. And I can see that you might get hurt."

"It's okay. You may be right. I am a bit weird about things like that. I want to, sex, I mean, but it's more than something physical for me. I mean, Bardot could walk out from behind that tree naked and I don't think I'd react much. That's what women are supposed to be like, isn't it, with us men randy as hell all the time. I don't know, maybe I've got some genes missing."

"Or they're too tight," Graham grins. "No, listen, don't worry about it. You may not be like me but I'm glad there's you around."

They stay for about an hour, talking very little, until it's too cold and the coffee's finished. The Edge is the sort of place you expect mysterious things to happen at any moment. But as they make their way back past the deserted stone circle, nothing has happened, there have been no strange lights in the sky, no soft spirit voices, no sign of Merlin. Yet as they reach the car, pausing for a moment with hands on the doors before the countryside is shut out for another day, a new mystery is beginning to develop. A new future to be plotted.

Graham quietly wonders what he's done and hopes that things haven't already gone too far.

ACT 11

Spring Rites

The next few days exert a peculiar strain on both Roy's mind and body. First, he sets about finding a new course, which turns out to be a lot easier than he expected. This could be partly because Engineering are quite keen to get shot of him but also because at a redbrick university everyone knows someone who knows someone else. The interview goes well, purely down to his natural enthusiasm even if some of his ideas are rather cranky. When asked about the three most inspiring people he's met, he talks animatedly about an entranced John Cotton, a young Kenyan trainee who has an arranged marriage and his friend Graham who's a guitar-playing engineer. Still, the boy can think for himself and he's unusual in having some experience of international politics. He is provisionally accepted by Philosophy, with a major in the History of Science.

Next day he drives back down the M6 to face Arthur Morris, the Training Director, with one trump card up his sleeve. A few years ago there had been a lad on the estate, older than Roy, who had gone to Cambridge and got a First Class Tripos in Natural Sciences. He was now a highly paid manager, on grounds of intellect, at one of the company's rivals near Wolverhampton. Mr Morris seems even fatter than last summer and sits at his desk, overflowing the padded chair, like a great walrus with slicked down moustache. His bulbous lips are pursed, his elbows are on the desk and fingers touch together lightly to give the impression of great thought, but he really understands very little of what Roy's telling him and has no idea what tripe has to do with it anyway. On the other hand, Mr Carter has considerable influence around this place and the company has already paid out quite a bit on the lad's training… Graham had been right.

Mr Carter himself is, inevitably, less easy to convince. But he's virtually given up on his son already and this is just par for the course. So after the inevitable 'What the hell are you going to do with a degree like that?' and his wife pointing out that they haven't seen their son as happy as this last week for years, he lets it go. If Morris has agreed to it, then more fool him.

Roy leaves within a day, actually looking forward to the work ahead for the first time since coming to university. He's missed a 'phone call from Eva and there's a note under his door, so he showers quickly, changes and heads off again. It is mid-evening and he hasn't eaten yet so she begins to make something for him. He wasn't expected so it has to be cheese on toast; there's half of one of Maggie's cakes left over from the weekend but he declines that.

"So you've decided?"

"Yes. It's for the best."

They're standing close together in the kitchen, she with knife in hand, both remembering the lunch they had prepared together in the caravan on that first day. Somehow those surreal moments have, after all this time, been translated to a flat in Salford. The magical awakening has become almost an everyday, settled relationship. Although this changes things.

"Why didn't you tell me? Talk it over with me?"

"Everything happened so quickly, and I wasn't even sure myself. I did call you before I went home, but I suppose Maggie didn't give you the message."

"She just said you'd called." She puts the slices under the grill and turns to face him, unsure whether to admire his strength of mind or give way to the sense of loss she feels because he didn't involve her. "Are you sure about this?"

"Yes, I am, Eva. Life isn't worthwhile if we just follow other people's expectations, is it, if we're unhappy? And it's just the course that has changed, not me. Everything will soon be back to normal."

"That," she says, turning away to look out of the window, "is what they said at Čierna nad Tisou."

With a light head, he drives back to his room at one o'clock in the morning, hardly noticing the rain, clearing his head of the old life's gathered dust. He can still feel her kiss on his lips, the touch of her body against his, and some other sort of body turning within him, and he holds on to the feelings as he drives to keep her near a little longer. He takes the route through the city centre and in his mind images of Manchester mingle with those of Wales, of smoking factories with those of tumbling pebbles on a moonlit beach. And as he anticipates tomorrow morning, a sudden panic interferes with it all: where is Eva in all of this now? It is the same question she had asked earlier, but he hadn't heard it.

In the last – he calculates mentally – seven and a half months, his entire life to that point has been swept away, dissolved like saccharine in a fresh cup of tea. Yesterday was an eagle, diving down and tearing at the day, preying on confidence; tomorrow is a ghost of itself, almost alive yet still far away. He has to make it real.

He can't sleep. Back in Fallow Court, he makes coffee and sits until first light leafing through Gilbert Ryle's The Concept Of Mind, smoking one cigarette after another and soundlessly fingering his guitar. It's a struggle to disguise his yawns as he sits in the morning's first seminar on Copernicus and the holy soul's trouble with the Ptolemaic system, his conflict of duty and guilt as he embarked on a revolution. But the room is small and informal, the dozen or so students bright and inquisitive, and they accept and welcome Roy easily. He listens to their conversation with interest and feels at home, as though a seat had been kept warm for him all along here.

On the other hand, he has to strain to be worthy of the seat. He is months behind and while concept and argument come easily there is a great gap of fact and detail to fill in. He takes to the reading list hungrily, the handling of these new and precious books giving pleasure in itself. Every character sparks off not only essays and coursework but new songs demanding to be written too. From Plato to Galileo, Marcuse to Koestler, each of them add momentum to the surge of creativity. Roy has never worked so hard nor neglected himself so badly, with no time to study nutrition as well. Graham sees what's happening and keeps up a constant stream of invitations to matches, bars and concerts, nearly all declined.

Roy goes over to Salford three or four evenings a week but most of their time together is spent working. Eva's own course remains hard for her, sapping her energy, and only now does he fully realise how much she has given to be with him. Despite everything, and because her speech has always been good, he has been taking her for an unusual kind of Englishwoman. So he begins to give her more of his time and, because he doesn't have any, he sleeps less and less. With so much taking his attention, he fails to notice his own mounting exhaustion until the wicked spectre of depression has begun to set in. At first the moods hover briefly and can be chased away with the emerging springtime like late flurries of snow that melt as soon as they touch the ground. But within a month a darker shroud is settling about him.

"I don't understand. Everything was starting to go right," he tells the doctor at the university Medical Centre, "but it feels as if I'm wearing a wet overcoat every day now. I love my work, I have Eva, I have money. But I don't have any energy. I find myself wanting to cry halfway through a lecture or while I'm driving home at night. Aah, your hands are cold," he says, lying back on the comfortable couch, his eyes beginning to close.

She is quite young, the doctor, but he hardly noticed even though he has to undress for an examination. Already this year, dozens have been here before him with similar or greater excuses – difficult love affairs and hard work are run of the mill at university – but this one somehow seems different. There's something else, something darker, more intense. She shakes her head to clear the thought.

"You can get dressed now, Roy," she says, already writing the prescription. "Look, you're just working too hard. And getting a reaction to all that anxiety last year."

"Post-natal depression, then?" he tries to joke.

"You need to slow down, have a rest. It's nearly Easter, anyway, so take a holiday. You need to get some proper food in you, too." The last remark destroys any respect he might have felt for her. He takes the Librium for three days then puts the bottle away in a drawer; he knows lots of other students who've been given Librium here and none of them are any different.

Early on Friday evening just before the end of term, there is a light knock on his door. He looks up from The Sleepwalkers, not even recognising Eva's touch, and is astonished to see her framed in the doorway against the bright corridor light wearing her purple winter coat. She seems down and enters quietly, sitting on the edge of the bed and taking in the pile of books and notepads on his desk.

"Every other university student is relaxing and getting ready for the holiday," she says. "We can't go on like this. The more we see each other, the further apart we're getting. And you haven't kissed me yet."

The expression on her face is so transparent that Roy's heart surges and he is unable to hold back the tears. He stubs out his cigarette and comes to kneel beside her in surrender, his head on her thigh, asking to be beaten with her strokes. One hand runs lightly along her calf to rest beneath her black dress.

"I am so sorry, my love. I haven't been looking after you."

"No, it's not that. You have. But… you're so different now. Remote. I mean, you always were a bit out of this world. That's why I love you, if there is a reason. But Roy, when we met… and in January when I came back… your love was so strong and I felt… I felt like a princess. I know you do love me, but…" She leans down to cradle his head and her voice trails off, leaving a question behind.

"And I do love you just as much," he says, looking up into her face. "But things move on. People change and –"

There is another knock, sharper, and the door opens before either of them can react.

"Roy, I wonder… oh, I'm sorry, we thought you were working." Red stands there, her shock matched by Roy's, but he passes the test and his hand tightens on Eva's leg rather than being withdrawn.

"That's okay, Christine," he says. "This is Eva."

"I know. I mean, I've seen you before. Hello, Eva."

"Are you with Graham?" Roy prompts her.

"Oh, yes. We wondered if we could borrow that book you got on meditation. Please."

Roy gets up and finds it for her and after she's gone he suggests a walk down to the bar, since there'll be no more work done tonight.

They hear giggling as they pass Graham's door. On the stairs, like every man, Roy feels the need to explain.

"That was Christine," he begins pointlessly, "Graham's girlfriend, though actually he has another girlfriend back home and –"

"Janet," interjects Eva with a mischievous smile. "But I thought this one was called Red?"

"Eh? How did you know? I didn't tell you that."

"I'm a woman," she replies, as women do, as if this explains everything. She takes his hand and rubs her head against his shoulder as they pause outside the bar. "Don't worry, I'm not upset. Maybe a bit at first, but then I wasn't with you. I suppose a man needs someone. Anyway, I'm with you now."

"Nothing happened," he says, which is almost true. "And yes, I'm with you." He kisses her tenderly, oblivious to the noisy group of students pushing past them into the smoke and music. They find the last two seats, near to the electronic fruit machine, which Roy frowns at with distaste when he brings their drinks.

"I don't understand why you hate gambling," she says, leaning closer to make herself heard. "After all, you take a lot of risks. With me, for example!"

"This isn't gambling, though," he smiles and gestures towards the whirring and clunking behind him. "It's fixed so the machine always makes a profit. If you win it's because other people have lost. Even then, you haven't earned the money."

"But it makes people happy."

"Surely happiness is only real if you've earned it, when you've worked for it." She snuggles up close to him.

"So what did you do to earn me?"

"Ah, well that must have been a previous lifetime. Look, if I take risks, like you say, it's to try and make things better. We make our own future."

"I don't know. Maybe everything's fixed."

"Fate? No, I can't agree with that. There wouldn't be any point in life, would there? It's me who changed the course of my life."

"Mmm, mine too, darling. But maybe it was all meant to be."

And what has fate decided for us next, she thinks? You wanted me and you won me but you could change your mind. You're so engrossed in your ideas, you can't see that nothing is safe. How long can we resist the things that interfere with us, the rest of the world? Isn't it inevitable?

With the second drink, he says again how sorry he is that he's made her feel sad and embarks on a pseudo-psychological argument about relationships getting harder when people get closer.

"When you're first in love, you only see part of the other person, yes, something special that seems to fit with you. Then, when you get closer, you see other dimensions in the other person and they don't fit so well, so there's bound to be some frictions and spaces." He even tries to illustrate this with sketches on a beermat that mean nothing to Eva.

"Why do you have to break things down? Surely the only important thing is the special something you saw in the first place?"

He recognises defeat and kisses her. On the other side of the room, Graham and Red seem to be making a point of dancing very close and for a moment Roy's mind goes back to the time he'd been here with them and Didi, the night of spirits. Immediately, the telepathy flashes between them again.

"I just thought of something," says Eva. "Remember those things Marian said, about someone called Tomáš the poet?"

"Uhu, I didn't understand that."

"I did, though I didn't admit it. I suppose I was a bit frightened. I was going to give this man a message from his girlfriend but he was killed in Prague before I got there. His name was Tomáš Holub, like the poet."

"Yes, fantastic. Didn't Marian say you'd meet her again?"

"That's right. Well, I had a call from Jan in London. He knows her and she's coming to see me soon."

"So what do you think of Marian now?"

"I don't know. But… Roy, I'm afraid. I feel that something's going to happen. That's why I came tonight, to make sure we were all right."

"We are," he says, putting his arm around her tightly. Outside, an aeroplane is passing silently high above Fallow Court, blinking red, and a light breeze stirs the small puddles of afternoon rain settled on broken flagstones. Saplings in the central bed of the courtyard sway slightly, preparing to burst into leaf with the spring. Roy makes coffee while Eva goes ahead to his room. When he pushes the door open with a foot, it is still dark inside and she is lying on the bed.

"Come here," she says, "I'm still frightened." An hour later, as they lie pressed together, most of their clothes on the floor, the coffee cold and their lips aching, a small sentence begins to form in Roy's brain and travel down. It's not so strange but it means more now.

"Why don't you stay tonight?" Her answer takes a full minute, as though she's practising and reforming it in her mind. It sounds ridiculous.

"I can't. I haven't got a toothbrush." He is so surprised that for a moment he takes it literally.

"You can borrow mine."

She kisses him softly and gets up, allowing the blouse to fall, and stands unselfconsciously at the window looking out over the carpark as if to show the world that this is who she is and where she belongs.

"Soon," she says, turning back and smiling down at him. "Very soon. But tonight we're both exhausted and we need to sleep properly. So I'm taking a taxi home, you're going to sleep and then you can work tomorrow before the film."

He does it the other way round, entirely unable to sleep when she has been so very close. When the door has closed, he undresses fully and goes for a shower and fresh coffee. He works long into the night, long after every other bedroom light in the Court has been switched off, and falls satisfied into bed, intellect spent, as dawn breaks on the last Saturday of March.

They've been wanting to see this Bergman film for ages but she's late, and he paces up and down outside the cinema impatiently looking at his watch and getting that knowing look from the doorman. He checks the momentary flash of anger – no, this is what parents feel when their teenager is out late at night and they suspect no good has been going on. Perhaps she's unwell or something has happened, and now he's grateful to her lateness for making him aware of his own emotions and that reason has triumphed. With perverse logic, he decides to buy her a present instead. But look, that must be her bus turning into St Peter's Square now so he only has time to run over to the confectionery counter and get one of those small chocolate eggs in silver paper that she likes. Within seconds she's here, breathless and apologetic, and they go straight in; one can't afford to miss the first minutes of a Bergman or nothing will make sense. After ten minutes they're relaxing into it and turn to one another, whispering simultaneously:

"I got you a present." Their hands meet in the middle and fingers open to reveal identical chocolate eggs in silver paper. The rest of the film all but passes them by, so full are they of the wonder of how two people can be so close. It's the 'something special they had both seen in the first place' on a Welsh beach, now translated tortuously into reality. And it makes what Eva has to say afterwards, when they walk down Oxford Street to a favourite café, so much worse.

"Roy," she begins hesitantly, wrapping the egg's silver paper tightly round one finger in a ring, "that girl arrived today. Tomáš's girlfriend. I wasn't expecting her yet. That's why I was late."

"Oh yes?" He is already sensing the shadow that is about to spill over them. "Did you tell her everything? What Marian said?"

"Yes."

"And?" This isn't coming easily.

"Actually, she was very happy. It was strange. I was amazed at how well she took it. But she seemed… relieved somehow. Not upset at all."

"Has she gone now?"

"Yes, she went back to London this evening."

"What else?"

"What do you mean?" But she knows he's felt it so takes a drink of her coffee and resigns herself. "All right. She gave me a message from Jan. He's heard from Josef, you know, the reporter… I don't know how but they've set up some sort of –"

"Come on, what about him?"

"I'm trying, darling." She takes his hand across the table, sighs and looks into his eyes. "Josef and I used to be, well, close friends and he still keeps in touch with my parents. And… and my father's very ill. He's had a heart attack. All the pressure at work with the Russians there, I expect. Anyway, it's bad. I have to go back and see him before it's too late."

When God performs His wonders, does He realise the agonies He puts His people through? Or is that somehow part of The Plan? Is the love they have forged so well, with such determination, to be torn away? Like a hunter who has tracked a mythical winged beast through swamp and forest, finally catching the first glimpse through overhanging branches and swaying pampas, only to see it soar up and out of sight in a moment, Roy's whole being rages within him. Eva is still looking at him, her eyes pleading with him to order her to stay, to renounce her family and her country, to say that this is what her parents would want for her, to live happily ever after. Because there's no way of knowing whether she'll be allowed back again.

"Then you must go," he says quietly. "It's your duty."

"Yes," she says flatly. "But Roy… I will come back. If I can."

He doesn't see her again before she leaves because she won't let him come to the airport. On Tuesday morning there's a blue aerogram envelope in the rack for him and inside it there's a single slip of paper.

IN T.ME WE'.L ..ERCOM. ...'LL SEE!

Back in his room, he sinks onto the chair at his desk, bemused. From a drawer he pulls out the small box with all the letters and notes she has written to him and puts a hand on top of it as if to draw inspiration. It works. He remembers saying to her on Friday evening that when you're in love you only see part of the other person but when you get closer there's another dimension. So look closer, Roy. What can't you see? Ah, yes, it only makes sense if you fill in the dots with the missing letters I L O V E Y O and U.

This is only small comfort. He looks across at John Cotton's painting of the Franciscan monk propped against the wall nearby and, not for the first nor last time, opens a dialogue.

"I could have stopped her going."

"Wouldn't that have been immoral?"

"It wouldn't really be a betrayal of her family."

"But would you always have felt guilty?"

"If her father dies, she has to be with him."

"Would that really make any difference to him?"

For some reason, this monk only converses in questions. His face is learned and strong, with deep eyes, but a slight smile plays at the corners of his mouth.

The halls of residence are to be used for a conference over the Easter vacation so the students have to pack up everything and take it home. They can leave their posters on the walls, which is as well for Graham. By lunchtime, Roy is ready; it all feels strangely final to be leaving a bare room. He goes down the corridor to say goodbye to Graham.

"Hi, mate. Sorry about Red barging in last Friday. She was really embarrassed. I mean, you weren't… you didn't…"

"No, we didn't. And we probably never will now." He tells Graham what's happened and his friend sinks back onto the windowsill, since it's the only free surface in the room at the moment.

"Jeez, I'm so sorry, mate. What a bummer. Nothing ever seems to work out smoothly does it? Still, I expect she'll be back. And you need a rest anyway – has anyone told you you look dreadful?" He lights up two cigarettes and passes one over. "'Scuse mouth. But it's no worse than kissing, is it?"

"Dunno, I've never kissed you."

"Just as well. It only causes trouble in the end, eh?" He inhales deeply and turns to look out of the window, misting it up with his out-breath. "Red's bloody good at it, though. Can't resist it. I'm like a kitten with elastic knees." Roy has some trouble with this image, but Graham doesn't give him time to consider it. "I'm not looking forward to this vac, seeing Janet. Red and I…" he pauses, gathering courage to say it, "we're thinking of getting engaged."

Roy drops the book he's picked up as a cold fist grips his stomach. It's not that he begrudges his friends their happiness, but this seems like another finality, an option lost, an era over. Then in the evening, back at home with his parents watching television, comes the news bulletin from Prague.

All exit visas have been cancelled.

Φ

Eva receives the news from Josef like a sickening blow to the chest. He doesn't notice, for he is merely reporting a fact, which is his job. They are in a small basement apartment in Prague – Jan had given her the address – where she has gone as soon as she arrived. She needed a friend, some sort of friend anyway, and he's one that knows what's really going on. On the other hand, she's surprised to find him still at liberty. The underground station did get closed down but he says the Russians never found the relay transmitter.

"I wasn't that important to them, anyway," he shrugs.

"That's not what Jan said. People thought you were a hero."

"Well, you don't want to believe anything Jan says. He's hardly reliable, a subversive like that."

A small alarm rings immediately deep within Eva's head, the instinctive signal developed by anyone for whom suspicion is worn like a second skin to be put on as soon as the border is crossed. No-one ever used a word like that about Jan; moreover he and Josef had been friends.

"Well," says Josef, realising that his image needs repair, "they did question me, like everyone. But they had to let me go. Hardly a scratch."

She is too tired to worry about this now; there are still a hundred and sixty kilometres to go and far worse things to consider. It is as though bars have been silently slid around her and locked. Feeling almost defeated, she bends over with her arms around her knees.

"Dear God," she whispers to herself, "why can't they leave us alone? Poor Roy, what are you thinking?" She will not cry, not here, not in front of him. Then in English, "Why didn't you tell me to stay?"

"Who's Roy, then?" Josef asks sharply.

"Oh," she recovers herself quickly, "someone I used to know. I'd better go to my parents now."

But the reunion in Trutnov late this evening only completes her defeat. Her mother opens the door with a huge smile and a hug.

"Eva, my dear, how wonderful!"

She bustles through to the dining room where Eva finds her father drinking and playing cards with Aleš. As Paní Amálie takes up her knitting again by the fire, her husband leaps to his feet and comes to his open-mouthed daughter with arms outstretched.

"My daughter, why didn't you call us? We'd have come to meet you."

She hasn't even put her case down yet, frozen in shock, and her eyes bore into her father's face with incomprehension.

"But… why aren't you in hospital? Josef said…" And then, seeing the satisfied smile on Aleš's face, she understands.

"Hospital? What are you talking about?"

"I thought… your heart…"

"That? Oh, that was nothing. Just another murmur. Anyway, that was a month ago and I'm fine. We didn't want to worry you about it. Everything's good really. The Russians leave us alone, I've even had a promotion. What?" He's seen the tears streaming down her face.

"No trouble, then, with the Russians? No heart attack?"

"Good heavens, no. I've never been a Party man, anyway, so what would they want with me?"

Finally, she drops the case and sinks into a chair, with pounding heart and waves of fear and relief and fury flooding through her.

"Hello, Eva," ventures Aleš. "That's a nice coat. Did you get it in England?" 'Of course I fucking got it in England, you bastard,' she thinks savagely. 'Would I find a coat like this in this God-forsaken…?'

"Why are you here, Aleš?"

"Oh, he's always here," her father interrupts jovially, forgetting the tears already now that they've been wiped. "We play cards, drink some beer, watch the hockey on television. Why, Aleš is like a so –" He stops suddenly as his wife freezes him with a look as only wives can. "Well, anyway, let's celebrate your arrival. I'll get the Šljivovica."

"You haven't answered my question, Eva," says Aleš quietly, his eyes narrowing.

"The coat? Yes, I –"

"Not the coat. Are you staying?"

Well, is she? Since she is caught in this web of lies, since the gods have thus conspired, since this is the reality of Earthly life, perhaps she should stay. A few months ago, Roy might have committed himself to her and, more recently, she to him; but a lot of things have changed. Despite the chocolate eggs in silver paper, perhaps it's too late. In any case, her visa is gone.

"Perhaps," she says, taking the small glass her father offers.

He smiles, having learned to be grateful for small steps. He doesn't question her about Salford, about where she had disappeared to and why there had been no forwarding address. He's playing the long game. And winning.

Φ

In the comfortable and silent lounge of his parents' house – it is no longer 'home' – Roy sits tightly drawn into himself and anything but comfortable despite Marian's hand on his. It is April 3rd, 1969.

"I'm sorry, dear," she says gently, "but there's nothing we can do except pray. You must have faith. You've seen enough already to know that you are on the path. So whatever comes along you have to accept Spirit's will. I've asked for guidance for you, honestly, but there's nothing. The door's been closed. There are times when we just have to face things alone."

"Believe me, I do know how you feel. I've been there too. But you know how I think – nothing but the truth will do, however much it hurts. And it does. As a medium, I can't help you right now. But I am your friend."

"Why, Marian?" he asks weakly. "Why does it have to be so hard? Everything was going really well."

"Sometimes we never know why. But there is a purpose, believe me." It still sounds like a cliché. "Look ahead, Roy. There's no victory without a struggle, without suffering."

"I don't see why we have to suffer. In any case, hasn't there been enough already?"

"It's only just begun," she shrugs, then holds him to her as he cries. It's true, she can do nothing and even her own faith is flickering in the face of his monumental distress. Come on, guys, surely this is too much for one so young? What possible 'purpose' could demand so much? For all her years of experience and for all the conversations with the afterlife, she is shaken by the darkness here.

The door opens suddenly and Mr Carter is there. He hesitates, and realises that this sadness is of a different order to anything else his son has felt. This girl must really mean something. He retreats.

"I'm going to bed," he says. "Goodnight." His wife is already upstairs in her own room, waiting for the house to settle. It won't, not for a very long time. Roy sits back and wipes his face.

"I'm so tired," he whispers.

When she has gone, he smokes another cigarette then goes upstairs without his usual coffee. He is barely conscious anyway, undressing automatically in the dark and falling on top of his bed. It occurs to him that tomorrow will be Good Friday, a time of crucifixion. It is his last conscious thought.

The small room settles heavily, expectantly, around him as night shadows come to life. Through the open curtains, were anybody looking, pale moonlight picks out the orderly garden, the pool and the weeping willow, as cows in a field somewhere beyond stand motionless. Nothing stirs except dreams.

The mist is clearing and he feels the ship pitching beneath him, its heaving rolls rippling through his weak limbs. In gathering light, the forms around him who have taken control now assume shapes and faces, leering and pointing at him. He is suddenly aware of a stabbing pain in his side and realises that he has been nailed up onto the mast, the pain only getting deeper as he struggles. Desperately looking around over the tops of the waves, yes, he can see the beach… but the ship is slipping past and Eva is turning away.

Roy awakes with a small cry, shivering and covered in sweat. Nothing stirs. There's nothing we can do. It's the will of the Spirit. They've closed the door. Alone. It's only just begun. He's tired, so tired. He has to rest. Lifting himself onto one aching arm, he reaches into the back of the drawer of the bedside table for the tablets. There's forty-two left. That should be enough.

Ф

Evžen Plocek was a toolmaker and by 1968 had become a director of Motorpal and a candidate at the extraordinary meeting of the Czech Communist Party. Plocek set himself on fire in Masarykovo nam in Jihlava, in protest at the Soviet invasion, on Friday 4th April, 1969.

In her small bedroom at the top of the stairs, one hundred and sixty kilometres to the north, Eva hears a small cry in her sleep and wakes up suddenly. At the unshuttered window, she's sure she has glimpsed an anguished face, with mouth open and eyes staring. Around the breakfast table six hours later, there is a deep depression and her mother is trying not to cry. Only Eva understands.

"But why, daughter?" her father insists for the fifth time. "Tell us why you're going back. Why so suddenly? Aleš will be heartbroken, and your mother is…"

"I have to. It's not over yet."

"What on Earth does that mean? This is so selfish, you don't even –"

"Petr, that's enough," his wife interrupts. "If she must go, then she must go."

Just a few hours later, she is walking determinedly through Wenceslas Square in long burgundy leather boots and the purple coat that turns the heads of the few students who still keep vigil at the statue. She doesn't notice them. The afternoon air is bright and fresh, sunlight dancing in a patchwork pattern on the cobbles. Work on the subway has resumed now that the tanks have gone but spring in Prague will never be the same again and the Square will never look as it once did to a Czech even if the bullet holes in the National Museum's stone walls get repaired. No-one's in a hurry to do that anyway. She walks out of the Square and alongside the park, its perimeter wire fence still hanging broken, its grass still scarred deeply with the ruts of heavy vehicles. The place has been frozen like this through the winter and will remain so in the memories of many. But without a glance, she makes straight for the narrow, shadowed side streets and turns swiftly into an old apartment block. At the small basement apartment, Josef answers her knock looking as if he hasn't slept since she left, his hair matted, his face unshaven, his shirt drooping over his belt and a cigarette hanging from a corner of his mouth.

"Eva! I didn't –" She pushes past him and turns to face him up close, waiting for the door to close.

"Bastard!" she breathes.

The dark room is in chaos. The curtains are drawn and there is a musty stench of tobacco and sweat. An ashtray overflows on the table beside an almost empty spirits bottle; in a corner, a stained and crumpled sheet is piled on the bed. She turns away, draws the curtains and opens the window, then takes a swig from the bottle without bothering to wipe it.

"Bastard!" she says again. "So, the great Czech hero, huh? The nation's finest son. And Eva's friend, the snake."

"Is something wrong, Evička?" he asks smoothly. But he's wide awake already and silently calculating.

"Don't ever call me that again," she says, her face white with anger. "I should have known not to trust anyone anymore. Even you, my first lover. Especially you. I thought it was strange that you were living here, free as a bird, that the Russians hadn't shot you when they found your station. Now it's clear. You're working for them, aren't you? You never did care who pays you, did you? You never did have any pride." The last word is spat out.

"Well, just a minute," he actually smiles, taking the bottle from her hand and taking a drink himself. "It seems you have a short memory. Not so long ago, you –"

"I was nothing like you," she breaks in, "and it was a long time ago. I made my choice. It seems that you have too."

"Do any of us really have a choice," he shrugs, "if we want to survive? With the country like this, we do what we can. We make deals, we buy, we sell."

"And you would sell any one of us for your own survival."

"If necessary," he observes with an air of innocence. "I'm no different to the rest, the Dubčeks, the Svobodas, the Smrkovskýs."

"How dare you mention yourself in the same sentence as them."

"Well, see things your own way, Eva. After all, you haven't been here, have you, little patriot? Ah no, I believe you switched your course to a western university…"

She stares deeply into his eyes that had once seemed so much warmer, takes off her coat and sits down on the only chair, pushing the pile of newspapers to the floor.

"All right, Josef, we're not going to get anywhere arguing. It's all just too sad. I don't know why you got me back here – perhaps Aleš paid you? It doesn't matter because I'm leaving again. Someone needs me." His eyebrows rise sarcastically.

"Ah, poor little Roy."

"So you're going to get my visa back. After all, it was genuine, for study. I assume you know the right people?"

"I have, um, some influence." He makes a casual gesture.

"Will you do it?"

"Maybe. Why should I?"

"Because if you don't I'll tell the Russians what you really did during the invasion, and before."

"Ha!" He actually laughs. "And do you think they'd believe you?"

"Yes," she says coolly, despite the sinking feeling in her heart that he may be right. Blackmail may not be enough. "They can't afford not to. They shoot anyone they suspect of having links to the West." Impasse.

"Of course," he says slowly, thinking fast, "there may be another way. One service deserves another, don't you think? You're asking for a deal and it's not a small thing. So what do you have to sell?"

She looks back at him sharply, contempt competing with hatred in her mind. Surely not? Surely this nation has not been corrupted so soon? Surely the free spirit of the Czechs has not been completely broken? Roy had tried to explain once that the spiritual way, whatever that is, demands sacrifice; but surely this God cannot be so perverse as to demand the sacrifice of one's very beliefs?

She doesn't think about it any more because it's all quite simple. Even if she cannot live with herself, she now cannot live without Roy. So she gets up and stands in front of Josef and unbuttons her blouse. His face is expressionless, his lips dry, and he waits until she has removed it before laughing again.

"No, Eva, not me. You don't imagine that I would want your body, do you? I've had it. It's used. But there is a comrade in the Emigration Department…"

Just after six-thirty this evening, Leonid Mikhailovich Sokolov checks the corridor outside his office, turns back inside and locks the door. He switches off the main light, leaving just the soft glow of a desk lamp, opens a new bottle of Stolichnaya and fills two small glasses. He is in his mid-fifties and often wonders why he got sent to this hell hole where nobody wants him and the days consist of listing names and pushing pieces of paper around. Eva watches him closely from the armchair. Apart from the uniform, this man looks very much like that Arthur Morris whom Roy had described to her – essentially, a large slug. Leonid Mikhailovich turns to face her and offers a glass, loosening his tie with the other hand. Well, perhaps there are some benefits to this job after all.

Eva herself has discovered just one benefit to this hell hole herself this evening. While the man had been in his secretary's office checking that she was leaving for the day, she has found the Tokarev TT-33 semi-automatic pistol in a carelessly unlocked drawer of his desk. It is now in her shoulder bag, the one that matches the burgundy boots.

Next morning, she buys a nondescript handbag and puts it in a locker at Václavské Náměstí.

Ф

"How can you be so selfish?" says Mr Carter, leaning over his son with the venom of a wounded animal in his voice. "Don't you ever think about other people?" But Roy can't hear him.

ACT 12

Spirit

"Hello, old chap. How are you feeling? You've given everyone quite a turn."

"Mmm… I'm all right. I've been away for a while."

"I should say so. Four days. Did you go anywhere interesting?"

After a nurse has wiped Roy's hands and face and brought him some sweet tea, the thin, white-haired hospital psychiatrist asks him several ludicrous questions about why he did it and whether he considered anybody else's feelings. Roy doesn't answer and soon stops listening. He hasn't the energy for fools yet. Eventually the man gives up, having written half a page of notes, and wanders off. The nurse comes back with a bowl of warm water, flannel and towel, but Roy is already asleep again, drinking in the clear draught of peace. For the next couple of days, he practises appearing to be asleep for when his parents come; they sit there as though waiting for an apology until it's time to go. Roy has more important things to do. Deep inside, his spirit is returning from its journey to other worlds, unpacking itself and preparing for new work. On the fourth day, Marian comes with chocolate and a happy, relieved face.

"Your father only rang me last night. Roy, I've been so worried. Are you all right now, my dear?" He sits up smiling and takes her hand.

"Oh yes, everything's okay. I just needed to sleep. I'll be as good as new soon."

"You did too much, my dear. You went too fast," she chides him gently.

"Maybe. But there's more to do. Who knows how far there is to go?" He lifts the corner of his pillow with a conspiratorial glance around. "They've been giving me these pills but I just pretend to swallow them. Will you get rid of them for me?" With an exaggerated gesture, she reaches forward to hold his shoulder, scooping up the imipramine tablets and smoothly pocketing them. "Thanks. I just need a few more days, then everything will be on track."

Hearing that the stubborn patient has been seen sitting up and smiling, the psychiatrist has another go, asking Roy whether he really wanted to kill himself and if he still does. The first and last boxes on his list are still unchecked.

"I don't really mind," he replies. "It doesn't seem to matter." This doesn't help the man. But there's no point in telling him that, as Roy has regained full consciousness, he's become aware of a certain darkness inexplicably lurking in a corner of his mind. Something has happened somewhere, something nasty, but he can't quite put his finger on it.

On Saturday afternoon, the 12th of April, he listens on the radio his mother has brought in to the commentary of West Brom beating Wolves one-nil, and his reaction convinces the ward Sister that he's well enough to go home. He spends another four days there, grateful for the appropriate deathly quiet of his father being away on business and his mother finding a lot of reasons to go out. The family will never again discuss what happened. For the parents, it's best to think that there wasn't an Easter in 1969, while for Roy there actually wasn't, at least not in this world. He gets down to coursework with real pleasure and has almost caught up by Thursday, deciding to go back to Manchester early. His mind is still working through its gears carefully but he knows that he is drawing strength from someone…

Alexander Dubček resigns from office on the 17th. He will nevertheless be re-elected to the Federal Assembly and soon sent to Turkey as ambassador. It marks the final triumph of the Soviet invasion, almost exactly eight months after it had begun. It was supposed to take four days.

Roy arrives just before the end of dinner on Friday. There are few other students around, which is just as well, for being back in the world is a peculiar feeling and best not overdone. He enjoys the simple task of unpacking everything and rearranging the room, and it takes a couple of hours; it seems especially important now that it should be comfortable and attractive. Still wide awake, he works until the essay on Ludwig Wittgenstein is finished and there is nothing left to do, then sits in the darkness playing silently through the song. It is still good and the next line follows without thought. D… C… D… E…, C… F… E… C… When he finally falls asleep it is six in the morning and spring has arrived in Manchester.

"It's a lovely day. Why are you still in bed, darling?"

The faraway soft voice comes drifting to him on a scented haze through overhanging woodland branches. He searches for it, stumbling through long grasses and violet flowers beside a small stream of crystal water.

"I'm here. Open your eyes."

It has a strange and gentle accent and is so close to his ear that it might be inside his head. He turns over as the trees thin out to glimpse a field and a figure there, still hardly visible yet beckoning. Emerging from the trees, the mist clears and there is Eva's smiling face.

"There you are at last. Welcome back to the world."

It is several seconds before he can answer, stunned by the pleasure and surprise of seeing her sitting there on the edge of his bed. It seems to have been such a long time since… Slowly, he props himself up on an elbow, still not quite out of the wood.

"Eva! Thank God! Where are… I mean… what time is it?"

"About three o'clock. In the afternoon. Were you up all night again?"

"Ah, yes… I think so, yes, working. How long have you been here?"

"I flew in last night, to London. I've been watching you for half an hour." He sits up now and leans forward to kiss her and she cannot help her fingers reaching out to his skin, playing down his chest and counting the ribs, down to his hip. The kiss lingers until they both feel the terrible disease. "Roy, you're so thin. Have you been ill? There was some trouble here, wasn't there? I'm sure I heard… well, something told me."

"Um, yes, I was in hospital for a few days. But –"

"Hospital? Oh, Roy –"

"I'm fine now. Really. That's all over so we won't talk about it. But how did you manage to leave? I heard that all the visas were cancelled."

"Yes. But, well, there's always a way round these things. And my father paid for the flight."

"Oh, I'm sorry, I forgot to ask about your father. How is he?"

"Actually, he's made a remarkable recovery. Let's not talk about it. I'll make you some coffee."

Sleep still plays about his eyes and limbs but his heart is fully awake. Somewhere along the corridor he recognises the faint theme of Dvořák's Ninth Symphony in E minor and he leans over to the radio on the bedside table, turning the tuning control until he finds it. Then he sits up and leans back on the pillows. The room is warm and musty and the blanket is hanging off the side of the bed. As her footsteps reach his door, the horns enter in the Allegro Molto. She smiles broadly when she hears it. Even though it reminds her of home, that was a different Bohemia and another age.

"For me? This music has a special meaning for me."

"Yes? I'm only just beginning to learn about classical music. I don't know much about it. I was never taught."

"There are some things," she says quietly, sitting beside him on the bed and holding out a mug, "you don't need to be taught."

They drink coffee and sit listening to the music for a few minutes, allowing time for its waves to wash through them and for their auras to meld into one another. She watches him lovingly, the darkness at last receding from her mind. Everything that has happened is past, and everything she wants is now. So there is no reason for fear or for waiting. Now that he is here beside her, his body clinging to the clean white sheet, she understands what he has done: the strength that has upheld her, that kept her from him, safe from his strange, naïve world of spirits and ideals, has now been spent entirely. She has given what she thought she never could, so it is natural that he should have the rest. He has won, by simply not trying.

She sets down her mug and takes his, still watching him as though checking for any residue of doubt, then stands and walks across to lock the door. The curtains are still drawn, softening the afternoon sun that filters through. There is nobody else about in the world. In the middle of the room she undresses slowly, nervously, almost like a schoolgirl, while he watches without fully realising yet what she is doing. But his body is responding and has moved across the bed to make room for her. She stands self-consciously for a moment with her back reflected in the wardrobe door mirror behind her, so that now he can see all of her. He draws back the sheet so that they are equal and she comes to sit beside him again, each almost breathing the other's breath, their blood beginning to pulse in resonance.

As the Largo begins, their fingers come to life as though on violin strings, first caressing and then holding firm, dancing to one side or another, awakening every nerve. Then hands grip and pull the other closer until mouths lock and they are lying full length hard against one another as if to become one.

Wherever Roy has come from, it is far too late to return. Whatever plans he had for this moment are forgotten and put away with childhood. Instead, it is dreams that are coming to life. A serpent is on his back and will never rest again. He cannot even speak. She has won.

"Don't worry, darling," she whispers. "I am yours."

The words touch him more deeply than she could know, at the very source of his life, and he begins to cry softly, partly with love but also with loss. How can one own another? What awesome responsibility is this? But when she takes his hand to her labia and touches him with the other hand, he laughs aloud at the ease with which the fears and anxieties fall, fall, fall away. His lips brush her soft breasts and now she laughs too, her head thrown back in joy. She is on a beach again, cartwheeling through the waves that rush through her, her body and mind abandoned to the audience. The years of training and sacrifice have all had a purpose.

Understanding that he knows little about classical music, she opens herself and guides him into her. He's not ready for the pain and surprise creases his brow, but her legs have entwined him and no power in the world could pull him back. He cannot control it and cries once, quietly, as the explosion burns him and is gone. He lies weakly on her with his face pressed into her breast so that no-one can tell the tears from their sweat. Then with the final pounding, triumphant coda of the Scherzo he enters her again and already it hurts less. They sleep locked together for several minutes.

"My woman," he breathes, running a finger gently across her face. "Thank you. Thank you. But I… well, I need more practice."

"That," she smiles, "can be arranged." She runs her hand through his soaked hair and sits up. "Will you fetch me a tissue? They're in my handbag."

With difficulty, he pulls himself away from her and stands, legs trembling slightly, and crosses to the chair where she has put her things, knowing that she is watching the movement of his every muscle. In the early evening shadow, he peers into her bag and the first thing he sees is a white toothbrush.

It has taken almost exactly nine months for this story to be born. All the energy saved up over that time has now been spent and they cannot help falling back into the fitful sleep that overcomes them, lying with arms around one another. Roy awakes first, surprised to find himself untransformed. It is after nine o'clock and he has seen no daylight today. He gets up to light a cigarette before sitting once more on the bed beside her, stroking her hair and running a fingertip along her spine, wondering what happens next. The radio is still on, with news of a `plane crash and a man who shot his wife and young daughter before hanging himself from a beam in his garage. Nobody knows why. He turns it off.

"Hello. Are you hungry?"

In reply she just moans slightly and squirms closer to him before reaching over to take the cigarette from him, draw on it once then stub it out. She throws back the sheet and moves across to sit astride him.

"Don't do anything," she says, smiling at his enraptured face. He looks like a boy again, but then she feels like a girl. Very slowly and deliberately she moves on him until he is ready and then makes love to him until the disbelief creases his face. "We waited so long, now I can't stop. Do you like my body, Roy?"

"It is the loveliest thing I have ever seen," he says. "I have never touched anything so soft. Can I have it?"

She laughs and gets up, moving like a ghost across the gloomy room to fetch a towel to wipe him with. They consider showering but neither of them wants to wash this feeling away, so they dress quickly and walk down to Rusholme to find some food. The bars are closing, the concert at the Union half a mile further along the road is approaching its climax, and the pavements are beginning to fill with feet and voices. He makes do with just a large bag of chips whilst she has a meat pie with hers, teasing him all the while. They walk back slowly towards Fallow Court with the night chill beginning to take hold. Roy checks his watch. Will all this disappear when the clocks strike twelve?

"There's something I have to tell you," she says, pulling him down onto a bench in the courtyard beside her.

"Good God, you're not pregnant already are you?"

"Silly," she giggles. "Listen, it's serious. There's two things actually." She pauses for a moment, uncertain after all if this is the right time or in which order they should come. "When I was at home… well, I asked my mother about what Marian had said. And it turns out that I did have an uncle, sort of. She had a brother but he was — what's the word? — dead when he was born."

"Stillborn."

"Yes. The family never talked about him but what Marian said was true."

"Wow. I bet that was a shock to your mother."

"Not really, she seemed to accept it all quite easily. It seems there's a lot of things we've never talked about. So you see, I think I understand your world, your beliefs, a bit better now."

"Good." But he takes his own world for granted and hasn't realised what a sacrifice she is offering him. "What's the other thing?"

"The other…? Oh, yes. It's my visa. It was, well, very difficult to get it and he… they would only give me a temporary one. For three months. Then I must go back, or…"

"Or what?" He is being slow tonight, not yet back to the world of other people.

"Or stay."

Something heavy and dark falls through Roy's stomach. So, just as the next act begins, a grinning spectre that was not in the script enters stage left. The Holy Innocents Church of England clock begins to strike midnight.

On Monday morning, Roy is happy to rejoin the other students for the seminar on Sartre's Critique of Dialectical Reason, though he struggles to get a clear handle on it. Still, he has good relationships with the others and knows that someone will help him. Nobody here knows anything of what happened during the Easter vacation and he will not tell them. But when Professor Meeks asks to see him at the end of the week, he can't help the sense of foreboding that comes over him. Has his father been in touch, to warn the university about his son's fallibility? Alan Meeks comes out of his office to greet Roy and ask his secretary Nora to fetch two coffees. He is a short, tubby man with silvering hair and bright, round eyes. This Chair is his life and he cares for his students like a father.

"Is it my work, sir? I've been trying hard to catch up."

"Good heavens, old chap, I didn't ask you here to give you a hard time. I'm no good at that sort of thing. If that was the case, I'd get Nora to write a letter to you. She's got quite a way with – ah, here she is." She enters with the coffees without knocking and uncermoniously puts them down on top of a pile of essays. The professor regards the plastic cups with distaste. "I see the machine's working again, then. Did you put extra sugar in mine, Nora?"

"To be sure I did. An' if you're after wanting anything different you'll have to make it yourself, for sure I haven't got time."

"No respect for authority," he smiles when she's gone, "but worth her weight in emeralds. Where were we? Ah yes, your work. Roy, listen to this carefully because very few students hear it and survive to tell the tale. I want to congratulate you. You've done a sterling job catching up, remarkable, and you show genuine ability." Roy can't help beaming and fidgeting with pride as Professor Meeks carefully removes the plastic cups and picks up the top few papers. "Your recent stuff, what you did over the vacation, is excellent. Mind you, I'm inclined to think that your comparison of Bacon's Advancement of Learning with a Noddy annual might be overstepping the mark a touch. Be that as it may."

He pauses and puts the papers down, takes a drink of coffee and grimaces, and is then suddenly serious, his academic eyes piercing into Roy's.

"Now, old chap, I know you've had your worries this last year." He holds up a hand as Roy opens his mouth to speak. "No, I'm not prying. You told me enough when you started here and I can piece much of the rest together from your writing." He smiles at Roy's raised eyebrows. "Well, I'm not completely senile yet. You wouldn't write what you do if you didn't want people to read it. Anyway, like I say, you've been under pressure and you've made a great effort to put things right, I respect that. The point is this…" Of course, the reason he is a professor is the disarming candour with which he gets to a point. "…how are things now? The exams are in a few weeks."

Roy sits back with relief and takes a sip of the terrible coffee.

"Everything's good, thank you. I feel like I've come out of a long tunnel. Honestly, changing course was the best thing I've ever done. Well, almost. I even feel, well, a bit guilty."

"Why on Earth is that?"

"Because I'm so glad to be doing what I do. Not many people can say that, I suppose."

"Right," he nods, "that's all I wanted to know. So let's go over a few points now so you know what to concentrate on. You've got some very strange ideas about Galileo."

When Roy leaves forty minutes later he's exhausted by the effort and level of the impromptu tutorial and deeply touched by the man's concern for him. Nora is putting the cover on her typewriter as he passes with a quiet 'Goodnight' but she still sees the single tear he's tried to hide.

"Holy Mary," she mutters to herself, "what's the ol' fool been saying now? He never does know how to put things."

Roy makes his way to the Union in the early evening drizzle, using it as an excuse to wipe his eyes. He is amazed to feel so clean and free. In the bar he buys himself the first drink and goes to sit alone in a corner, full of love for life, for work and for a short, tubby middle-aged man who cares about him. An hour later, he's had two pints and two whiskies and is beginning to regret it.

"Well, if it isn't the guru of Fallow Court. Oh no, it's not, it's Roy."

Graham is weaving through the crowd and the haze of smoke, followed by Red and Didi and a very sober-looking young man in a tie who looks as much at ease as a turkey on Christmas Eve. They find some chairs and pull them up.

"Hi there." Roy tries to smile from one to the other all at once but he's not focusing very well.

"I haven't seen you for ages," Didi opens. Tie man glances at her sharply, surprised by her familiarity with this bearded, long-haired chap in jeans and floral waistcoat. "It's not like you to be here alone."

"Jus' had t'see the Prof, thassall."

"Oh, not again, mate," says Graham with concern. "More trouble?"

"No, not't all. Quite the oppsit… er, opposite. `S all going well."

"You don't look very well, mate. You know you can't take much booze. I think we'd better get you home." He stands and helps Roy up, winking to the others. "Don't worry, I'll make sure the Guinness Book of Records gets to know about it." Roy has a puzzled expression as he grabs his jacket and allows himself to be led away like a child.

"'S Newcastle Brown actchly."

Didi now takes his arm.

"I'll take him, Graham. It's all right, my car's not far. You stay and enjoy yourselves." Tie man has been hovering behind them like a traffic warden and his curiosity makes way for indignation.

"But Didi, I thought we were going to discuss Browning." She looks over her shoulder and takes him in from large, prominent ears to suede shoes.

"Don't you think of anything but food?"

Back in his room, Roy collapses onto the bed while she goes to make coffee. He hasn't moved a fraction by the time she comes back and she makes him sit up against the pillows; they drink in silence until a flicker of life returns to his pale face.

"It's been a while," she says eventually, "and there's something different about you somehow. I would hardly have known you. You seem much older, as if you've been right through your life and out the other side. You seem, I don't know, very calm."

"I'm pissed, that's all." He drains the mug and takes a deep breath. "No, you're right, things are different. I've started living instead of going round in circles. Like Harriet." She smiles. He reaches over to the table and lights a cigarette, then sits up cross-legged on the bed. "Didi, what was it like the first time you made love? Oh, sorry, I mean, you're not a virgin are you?" Her face darkens briefly and she looks down at her shoes.

"I don't think that's the sort of thing lecturers talk to students about."

"Sorry, I –"

"No, it's all right. There was someone once. I had a daughter."

"What? I had no idea."

"You wouldn't, would you? I don't talk about her much. She was killed, run over by a car. Then we broke up."

"Good grief."

"It all seems a long time ago. You learn to live with things. And without them. There's been no-one since. Sex? Painful and uncomfortable, in the back of his van next to oily spanners and bits of brake pad. Not romantic. Even later it was never what They say it will be. The Earth hasn't moved. Still, one goes on dreaming. There was a time when I thought that… Never mind, it's too late now, isn't it?"

"One week," he says quietly. "Thank you for telling me that. You've suffered a lot, haven't you?"

"There's a lot of it about. God only had six days, remember, and you can't expect a perfect job on piecework. That's why we have ideals."

"Are they all hopeless, then?"

"Probably. But we have to go on trying to finish the job or there's no point, is there?" She gets up wearily and crosses to the window to watch the moon being eaten up by clouds, waving to Graham and Red as they enter the carpark and look up. "How was it with Eva?" she asks without turning round.

"Painful, at first. Surprising. I wasn't expecting it. I even felt guilty – something I'd waited so long for and I didn't feel much. Next time was better, and the next, and –"

"Well, no-one can say you weren't trying!"

"It's like a drug. Once you've tasted it… but now I feel, somehow… trapped. It's hard to explain. I'm confused. Don't get me wrong, I love Eva as much as I always have. But, well, do you remember once saying to me that love is two people getting what they want from each other?"

"Sounds like something I might say, when I'm drunk." She leans back in her chair against the wall, a feminine anger beginning to rise within her as she sees where this is going.

"No, it was in Platt Fields, that first day we talked. Well, I think I understand that now. What worries me is that Eva and I seem to have everything we want from each other now, everything that's been building up since we met. Yes, I'm happy but I feel trapped. And what's next? It's all in the real world and what's it got to do with the spirit?"

Didi's anger finally wells up, darkening her face, and she stands up taking her coat from the back of the chair.

"My God, I was wrong. You haven't changed a bit, just like all the rest. It all comes down to sex. All your philosophy is just balls. You wanted her and now you've had her and she's given you everything you don't want it any more. Eva will end up like every other woman, thrown away."

"Look, I didn't mean –"

"It's quite clear what you meant. Your hypocrisy is luminous. Well, my sex life may not be much of an example to mankind but I have learned one thing. The sex isn't important at all. That's just fucking, or making babies. What matters..." she's crying now, her voice breaking, "is the warmth of someone beside you, a touch when it's cold at night, a friend, another human being sharing your life even when you're alone. Let me tell you, Roy, you get very tired of living on your own. You ring people up. You talk to yourself, just for company." She goes to the door and pauses with a finger on the handle. "You feel trapped? There'll be countless long nights when you'll give anything to feel trapped. Spirit? Ha! God doesn't say words like a woman." She pulls open the door sharply and Graham nearly falls in, one hand raised to knock. She pushes past him. "Fucking men."

"Very apt," he says, staring at her back as she almost runs along the corridor. "Not interrupting, was I? I mean, you –"

"Shut up."

It's the first time Graham has been in here since last term and he notices the painting of the monk, now framed, hanging on the wall above the bed.

"Hmm, doesn't that put Eva off when she's... when you're... I mean, he probably disapproves, being celibate and all. Don't you mind being watched?" He takes the cigarette offered and sits on the chair, still warm. "Anyway, I just came to see if you're coming to that meeting tomorrow. You know, TM. The maharishi guru chap."

"I'd forgotten about that. Yes, I suppose it might be interesting."

Φ

A week later, Roy sits back exhausted in his chair, the table between him and Eva lost beneath books and papers.

"It's no good," he says, "I can't focus on this." She looks up and puts a hand on his arm.

"Take a break. You've been working since seven, mostly helping me. And it's the fifth time you've come round to work this week. You must be worn out. What time is it?"

"Half eleven," Maggie chips in, sitting with her book by the gas fire. Roy lights his last cigarette, screws up the packet and throws it at the bin. It hits Maggie.

"Well, that's enough, then," says Eva, getting up to stretch before sitting astride Roy's lap and kissing him. For the last two weeks she has felt happier than she believed possible, now that they belong to one another. She has made her choice and life has rewarded her. "Let's have something to eat."

"There are cookies in the kitchen," says Maggie without looking up yet seeing everything. "I made them today." Roy tries to get up but she won't let him, playful and loving, hardly allowing him to breathe. "All right," Maggie sighs, going to the kitchen, "I'll go shall I? I know when I'm surplus." As the kettle boils, she calls back. "Say, Roy, how was that meeting you went to? The meditation thing?"

"Quite interesting, I suppose. Not for me."

"Didn't you say Graham was keen, though?" prompts Eva.

"Yeah, odd that, for an engineer. He thought it was the best thing since the Clifton Suspension Bridge."

"I can't quite see Graham as a yogi."

"No, but he's actually a very surprising chap. Very deep, really. Mind you, anyone who can play the guitar like him must be halfway to cosmic consciousness already."

"Cosmo where?"

"Sorry, it means, well, perfection. Nirvana. Paradise. No, it just seems like a psychological technique to me."

"Nothing wrong with that," says Maggie, coming back in with a tray as Eva clears some space on the table. "Sound capitalist principle – the end justifies the means. What does it matter if it gets you to God? It's already big in the States."

"Have you tried it, then?"

"Sure. It gave me a migraine. I'll take weed any day."

"Well, Graham's going for it big-time. He has a 'Do Not Disturb' notice on his door now for half an hour every morning and evening while he does his thing… his mantra. You can almost feel him evolving through the walls. I don't know, it seems unnatural to me, cutting yourself off from people."

Maggie hands round the cookies and edges forward on her seat, facing him with eyes alight, knowing she can win this.

"And what's wrong with that," she demands, "if what you're doing is the right thing? So Jesus walks into the bar asking for volunteers and you'd tell him to wait because you just bought the first round? Shit, Roy, you have to do what's right and to hell with everyone else." Something that Marian once said nags at Roy's mind but he's too tired to remember.

"What did I say? Is this because I hit you with the fag packet? Anyway, how come you're so wide awake tonight?"

"I have jet lag."

"You've been here two years," laughs Eva.

"So? It was a long flight."

Roy's taken the last of the cookies so they move over to sit around the fire with their coffee.

"Are you missing Graham, then?" asks Eva, snuggling closer and laying her head on his shoulder.

"Mmm, I suppose. I mean, we still talk but it's different. The friendship's changed. A lot of things have changed since Easter."

"So why don't you move in here, then?" The simplicity of what Maggie says is staggering.

"Yes, why not?" Eva says excitedly, putting her arms around him. "It makes sense. You're here every day anyway and you wouldn't have to do so much driving. I'm always worried you'll have an accident when you're so tired."

"All the cookies you can eat," offers Maggie. "And it's a double bed."

Despite the exhaustion, Roy is ahead of her this time. He's grateful for this American girl's quiet and unselfish care for Eva and he hasn't forgotten what she said the first time they met. There may be some national guilt, too, about Russia getting off scot-free. So the reparation will be to see them safely settled in together and then she'll move out, leaving them with a home and a future. It's a lot.

"'Course, the kitchen could be a problem," she continues, "you having taken the pledge, and I'm not giving up my burgers for Jesus or anyone else. But people have to live together. You know Jim, my flute man? He's vegetarian only he's not strict about it when he's in company. He says the good karma of not eating meat isn't worth the hassle and bad feelings it gives other people. We have to compromise, don't we?"

"No, definitely not," says Roy, completely missing the funny side of it and falling into her trap.

"You're not going back tonight, are you?" asks Eva later when Maggie has left them alone. The idea of him moving in has only brought her closer to him and she is longing for them to wake up together.

"I ought to. There's a lot to do tomorrow. Anyway, I haven't brought my toothbrush."

"I bought one for you today. And a flannel. They're in the bathroom."

There is a long valley near Heywood, a few miles to the north, through which runs a fresh, clean stream that visits each in turn of a string of ruined stones, the remnants of cotton mills that gave way to time. A century ago these slopes would have been thronged with people, full of determination and believing in prosperity; it wasn't really their fault that they remained poor, since few realise that to gain independence one first needs to be independent. So dreams died and stones fell and the pretty valley is desolate and bare despite its greenery and wild flowers. Roy almost stumbles over the carcase of a dead sheep. It is Saturday afternoon and they have driven out of the city for some time off in country air, but death doesn't take days off. Eva is gathering flowers several yards away and they meet up beside a section of drystone wall that hasn't yet collapsed.

Watching her approach, he realises that his emotion has somehow blunted, being so used to having her in bed beside him now. Or something in his brain has changed since Easter. As she clambers towards him, smiling happily, she even looks so different these days and most people take her to be English. Her hair is shorter and styled, her clothes modern and brightly coloured – today she is wearing hotpants and a shirt tied at the waist, most of its buttons open – her face carefully made-up. Westernised. She kisses him and knots a yellow flower into his hair.

"Do you want to go back?" she asks, jumping up onto the wall beside him so that her bare legs brush his face.

"No," he lies. He looks intently along the valley to where it turns. There are probably more ruins there.

"Why are you so moody, then? I thought you loved nature?"

"I'm not sure this is nature," he sighs. "Somehow it takes your energy instead of giving it, like the Edge does." He turns towards her and leans against her thighs, reaching forward to kiss the top of her breast. "You are nature," he says.

"So why don't you want to move in with me?" It's the first time either of them has mentioned the idea since last night, which seems to her an answer in itself. He doesn't reply straight away, taking time to think about what he wants to say and what he ought to say.

"Eva, it's not the right time, not now with our exams only a few weeks away. We wouldn't do any work. I wouldn't be able to keep my hands off you. Anyway, things are settled just now, we are settled. We don't have to make any decisions before –"

"The exams, yes, I get it. You want to prove yourself. Then afterwards there'll be something else to prove."

"I don't know what you mean."

They amble hand in hand back towards the car and he helps her up the last few steps on a grassy overhang, pausing at the top to hold her and look past her along the winding green valley with its stones melting away into it alongside the chattering water.

"There's another decision we have to think about, too," she says quietly. "My visa runs out before the end of July. I can try to renew it but I'd have to go back. Would you come with me?"

"Of course," he says without thinking, resting his head against hers. "And will you come home with me next week, when we're on study leave?"

"No," she breathes into his neck. "I promised Jan I'd spend a few days in London. Anyway, you need to work."

Instead, Roy spends the first few days of the break working alone in his room at Fallow Court. It is quiet as the grave. He misses her and there is no escape from it: her smile, her skin, her voice have worked themselves like a fifth column into the fabric of his mind and occupied all the strategic positions. He can neither think nor move for their control. He is invaded and is no longer free; welcomed in though she was, he can no longer do anything without reference to her. By Tuesday night he has done all he can, rewriting and cataloguing and colour-coding his notes, so next morning he gives up and is turning off the M6 by lunchtime.

ACT 13

The Examination

Inspector Peter Jones, sans gorilla, settles himself in a plastic chair outside the café on the Euston Station concourse, takes a sip of his coffee and then ignores it. It's foul. He is wearing dark blue jeans and a white casual shirt with a lightweight blue jacket, which he hangs on the back of the chair. He is in his early thirties so can get away with these clothes. He opens his copy of the Evening Standard and holds it just low enough so that he can watch the slim young man in jeans and black rain jacket with the hood pulled over his head and a small rucksack on his back. The young man is standing stock still near one of the platform barriers. Keeping the newspaper in place with one hand, Jones lights a cigarette and settles back to wait. There's a lot of waiting in this job. Anyway, the Manchester train isn't due for another ten minutes and it's never been known to be on time.

The road from the motorway into Wednesbury is clear and Roy is soon into the familiar Black Country environment he left behind such a short time ago. Even in the warm sunshine, the area seems bleak and colourless, the light filtered through an ever-present haze. This is the industrial heart of the nation, full of decent working people, but they seem like incomprehensible aliens. Even with the car window wound down, there is something impenetrable between them and Roy. Yet this is, as his father has often reminded him, the real world.

He pulls into the Social Club car park near the Canteen and only has to wait a few minutes before spotting Nick arriving for lunch. They greet each other with affection. Nick's grey trousers have a sharp crease and he wears a green silk tie on his white shirt. The jacket slung over one shoulder is thread for thread identical to the one that Roy hated ten months ago.

"How good to see you!" Nick enthuses, shaking hands and standing back to study his friend. "Well, we have both changed, haven't we? Where did you buy this?" He fingers Roy's beard lightly and laughs.

"Hello, Nick. The world seems to be treating you well."

"Oh, as well as I deserve, I suppose. I am happy. I did my ONC at college and now I'm spending some time in Systems Analysis."

"Is that computers?"

"Yes, a new department. I want to get in on the ground floor."

A lot of heads turn when Roy enters the Canteen and several conversations change tack as he's recognised, this Cyclops among humans. As they take their trays across to a window table overlooking the sports field, newly marked out for cricket, he catches snatches of their talk but strains to understand the language.

"Are you on holiday, then?"

"Yes, just for a few days. Exams start soon. I changed my course, you know."

"Well, even I could see you weren't an engineer." They eat in silence for a few minutes and Roy gazes out across the grass to where they had first talked, where he had first seen Kate and where so many things had started without him realising it. "There's something on your mind," Nick states the obvious. "Is it serious?"

"I'm thinking about getting married."

"That is serious. Is it Eva?"

"You have a good memory."

"It would be difficult to forget, your feelings were so strong."

"Really? You noticed? Well, I thought I needed to see you again, to ask your advice."

"Me? I'm the last person… I mean, our situations couldn't be more different."

"And that's why you're exactly the right one to talk to. Plus you're a good friend, I believe."

"Thank you, yes I –"

"And I can't stop thinking about it, what you said back then." Roy is becoming animated. "So I have this passion for Eva and you're going to marry someone you don't even know. Sorry, I don't mean to be rude."

"That's all right. I'm not offended."

"Ha, nothing upsets you, does it? You'd make a great snooker player."

"I am. I beat Dave Steel last week. Look, you're wondering whether passion – as you put it – is a good reason to get married, yes? Well, I can't say that my way is right because that makes everyone else wrong. But it's not true that I don't know Asha. We've been brought up with the same culture and beliefs and faith, with hundreds of years of tradition behind us. We know we can trust each other and will do everything we can to make it work. I think that marriage is based on that kind of understanding."

"And what about sex, boys?"

The soft voice makes them both start, not having noticed Kate come over to stand behind them. Roy swivels and finds his gaze drawn inexorably to her bare legs as though she speaks from the thigh. He forces his eyes to move up along her slim body in its thin, token summer clothes to the black waterfall of her hair. She looks as exciting as ever yet she fails to excite him.

"Hi, Kate. You haven't changed."

"I can't say the same. Anyway, Nick, what about sex?" she repeats, pulling up a seat to their table. With the movement there comes the light breeze of a perfume that is not from any bottle. Nick looks at her, unperturbed.

"It's important," he agrees, "but it's not a problem for me. Maybe for you it's a problem, Kate, because you'd probably like to try out every man in the company and then the county before you make a choice. But even that wouldn't be a fair test, would it? He gets one shot with no allowances. Marriage is too serious to depend on sex." He half-turns to Roy. "Or passion."

Roy stares in surprise at the Asian's dry candour towards this minor goddess who could have any other man in the room she wanted. Most of them are already watching her. For an instant she is stung by his words but doesn't show it, instead looking at him with a strange, subtle desire.

"Look, sex should be the result of feelings," he goes on. "It's an effect, not the cause. As soon as it becomes an objective, some kind of prize, then the whole point of the relationship is missed."

"So you just let your parents decide things for you," she challenges.

"I am eighteen. Do I even understand myself yet? It's far more likely that I would mess things up than my parents would. The trouble with the West," he waves a hand between them as though to take in the whole country, "is that you believe you are completely free, that you can choose anyone. But you will never be satisfied. Kate, how many men are available to you? Roy, how many women? Billions. With a bit of patience and effort, you could try out maybe a few thousand. Then would you be satisfied, knowing there are still so many more? Anyway, sex is just a physical pleasure that's not much different from one person to the next and you don't even really need a man for that, do you, Kate?"

She sits back sharply with a flush to her cheeks and looks to Roy for support, but he just shrugs.

"Game, set and match, love."

She stands, tense but still proud and glares at Nick.

"Just you wait until your Asha's got a headache."

"Good grief," says Roy, as they watch her disappear across the room, a hundred eager eyes following, "I thought I was the idealistic one. But I think you're wrong about one thing, mate. Sex with someone you love is special. With Eva… I can't describe how beautiful it was the first time."

"But that's just it." Nick leans forward now and drops his voice, not wanting to be the centre of attention. "The first time. I'm sorry, Roy, but will it be the same the hundredth time, the thousandth time? You asked for my advice and I can't give it, but there's one thing about my family's beliefs that might help. Don't get so hooked up on love. Love is everybody's destiny, it's where we are all going in the end. The important thing is to suffer as little as possible – and cause as little suffering to others as possible – along the way." Across the green field and through the thin haze comes the mournful wail of the factory siren cutting through their thoughts. Nick stands to leave.

"Just a few minutes, mate," Roy protests, "it won't matter."

"No, I am given a fair pay for the hours I work. Look, I hope everything goes well for you and good luck with the exams. It's good to see you again. Try not to think too much!"

He shakes hands and is gone before his friend has time to reply. Roy sits back down again and is already thinking too much. The Canteen empties and soon the figures walking round the sports field have disappeared too, leaving him alone with a whole new outlook to deal with. He gets a coffee from the machine and takes it through to the bar where Harry is already clearing the tables and hanging dishcloths over the beer pumps. The man stops working and squints.

"Is that Roy Carter inside that hair?" he smiles. "Hello, lad. How's life treating you?"

"As well as I deserve, I suppose." He puts the coffee down on the edge of the snooker table, lights a cigarette and sets up the balls, carefully chalking a cue.

"Playing yourself, are you?" observes Harry.

"It's the only way I can win," Roy replies, cueing off with a hollow crack and hitting the pink.

The train glides in only a couple of minutes late and soon Peter Jones spots Eva in her familiar fawn leather jacket, carrying a small suitcase. She embraces the hooded young man warmly and they begin to walk quickly towards the Underground stairs. Jones folds the newspaper and puts it into his jacket pocket, adjusting his dark glasses as he follows at a discreet distance. They take the Victoria Line to Oxford Circus, switch onto the Central Line across to Holborn and change again, taking the Piccadilly Line west to Green Park. Jones is enjoying this, his adrenaline flowing as he hovers just out of sight at each platform and jumps onto the carriage next to theirs just in time. He's worked out that the last stage of the chase will probably be north on the Jubilee Line and he's right. Who would ever think of looking for Czech dissidents in Neasden?

They turn right out of the station and pause to light cigarettes while Jones crosses at the pedestrian lights and appears to head left. Jan and Eva walk down the hill, under the bridge and take the first left, talking animatedly all the while before turning into Selbie Avenue. Jones watches them enter the corner house and before they can get to a window he's at the front door of the neighbouring house, shielded by a large bush. He shows his warrant card to the stunned middle-aged lady who answers as he gently pushes past her and closes the door.

"Sorry, madam, this is rather important. May I use your `phone, please?" The new portable radios are due to come into service any day now but he hasn't got one. "Thank you. Are you alone in the house?" She nods, wide-eyed. "Good, now I suggest that you get your coat and go shopping for an hour. No, make that two."

By the time she returns with three apples and a carton of milk, she's missed it all but her neighbours are all standing in small groups on the pavement, talking in hushed tones. There had been at least six police cars – or was it ten? – and two ambulances and they all had those black uniforms and shields and helmets and guns but actually there weren't any shots which was a bit disappointing and they just took away three young men and two girls.

The next evening, Eva calls Roy from a public box outside Euston Station.

"My parents? Yes, they're fine, actually they're being quite nice for some reason… What? Nothing much, going for walks, reading my notes, you know. I had a drink with Paul but he didn't have much to say – oh, you remember The Mermaid? You wouldn't recognise it, all dim lights and fishnets and cardboard canons hanging on the walls. All fake. Horrible. So how are you enjoying London?"

She tells him that it's been interesting, which is at least true in a way, and that Jan has made some good friends and has settled happily in London, which was true until two days ago. She doesn't mention that he has been interrogated for eighteen hours, looks like death warmed up and has been told that if he doesn't "co-operate" with the British authorities then he will be deported (which translates as shot by the Russians). She doesn't mention that she herself has had yet another searching interview with that nice Inspector Jones, was then released with warnings though without charge and had to find a cheap, seedy hotel for the night in Paddington while she waited for news of Jan. She doesn't say that she no longer knows which fucking side anyone is on.

"Oh yes, guess what? Marian's getting married again. Her doctor. Says she can't stand the pain any longer… What? No, on the 'phone, says she's too busy to see me now."

Five minutes later, Eva has rung off to catch her train but he's still sitting beside the telephone when his mother passes on her way to the kitchen.

"Would you like something to eat, Roy? Your father's having cheese on toast though he really shouldn't. Still, if he wants to kill himself… Did you hear about Geoffrey Mason, you know, came to our party, Lucille's husband? Dropped dead last week. Coronary. All those executive lunches, I expect. Dinner will be in two hours. Are you going back tomorrow?"

"No thanks, no I didn't and yes, I am," he mutters, but she's already in the kitchen listening to The Archers.

Φ

In the small Salford examination hall, Eva sits with her body tensed, one finger playing with her lip. It's her last paper. The more the other students around her seem to be absorbed in their work the less well she focuses on the paper and the less sense even the questions seem to make. Then just as she feels she has a hold on them, her thoughts scramble and reform around Roy. He was so distant at the weekend, locked within himself, concentrating, almost cold. She had been silently pleading with him to hold and reassure her – not just about the exams – but he hadn't noticed. Why has she always been alone when she has needed someone most? And now, after all the months of fear and tension, the nights of torment and days of impossible decisions, it has all come down to these precious minutes ticking by in an examination hall. She thinks of Roy, now writing feverishly in his own exam room and silently whispers "Good luck, darling" as a single tear forms in one eye.

"Are you all right, Miss…?" The invigilator hovers beside her and tries to read the name on her card but decides he can't pronounce it anyway. It brings her back to herself. She nods and smiles, and when he calls time finds that she has filled eight sheets and can't remember a single word on any of them. Outside, Maggie takes her arm and steers her towards the Union bar.

"Jeez, that was rough, wasn't it?" she lies. "Guess that's me for Boston next year. Still, what's done stays done."

Eva allows herself to be carried along and by mid-afternoon they've had several vodkas and Eva has the hiccups.

"Is it really all over, Maggie?"

"Sure ish, honey. Let's shelebrate."

"I think we've had enough. I can't see straight. Let's get the bush… I mean, the bus."

They link arms and sway out exaggeratedly, propping each other up at the bus stop and laughing. Maggie is perfectly sober but plays along because she understands what her friend has been through and how she must be feeling now, however brave her words. She pushes Eva up the stairs to the top deck and they fall into the front seats.

"We should have a party, whadja shay? When's your birthday, li'l Czechi? I've got you down as Pisheesh."

"Last Tuesday," Eva says quietly and Maggie immediately drops the act.

"What? And you never told anyone? Does Roy know?" Eva shakes her head. "Well sod him, the selfish bastard." As they get off the bus and wait at the side of the road, Maggie continues. "Right, well we're going to have a birthday party for you." She disappears into a nearby shop.

"Honestly, I can't drink any more," Eva says when Maggie reappears with a long, thin bottle wrapped in blue tissue paper.

"This," her friend says, "you'll drink." She unwraps it with a flourish.

"Šljivovica!" Eva's eyes light up and she embraces her friend and protector in the middle of the road as they cross to their flat.

Roy sits at his desk, drumming his fingers and checking his watch. She said she'd call when she got back after the exam. He waits for the next move. The last book has been read, the last paper written, and there seems to be a vacuum where his brain should be. He idly turns the pages of the Leonard Cohen songbook she bought for him two weeks ago. On the inside cover she has written that she loves these songs; it didn't seem to matter that he finds them monotonous and has said so more than once. It wasn't thoughtful, but then she's been withdrawn recently, preoccupied. Yes, they've both been tired but does she think he hasn't noticed that these days she wears perfume more often, she uses more make-up and wears shorter, thinner clothes? Does she realise that she's started complaining more, that he snores, that he smokes too much? He turns to look to the monk for support but the man's eyes are painted and blank. Eventually, Roy gets up and walks to the 'phone box in the courtyard. Maggie answers and he can hear music in the background.

"Hi, Roy. We were wondering how long it would be before you called. I had a dollar on it being another half hour yet… What? Yes, she's here… No, I don't think she wants to talk to you right now. You're not our favourite person at the moment… Why? Why? Shit, the kid's exhausted and crying and you didn't even know it was her birthday last week… Well, did you ever ask? Do you ever even listen? Hell, what am I talking to you for anyway? You're full of crap, Roy. So you've got this big thing going for you, you've got her to love you, you got what you wanted – so what's next? And where are you?"

Roy is wandering morosely along the corridor until he hears Chopin coming quietly from Graham's room. He goes in and stands by the window, talking to his own reflection.

"Do I not listen to other people?"

"We all do that. Sometimes it's because we have our own thoughts and they're in a different language."

"Yet we go on believing that we understand each other."

"Just because people know the same words doesn't make up for the differences between them. It doesn't mean they're communicating."

Roy breathes on the window and draws two heads facing away from one another.

"There are so many differences," he says. "How can you get so close to someone and then find that hardly anything fits any more, like you've got to start all over…?" His voice trails off as the thought circles his mind and comes back to where it started. Graham stretches and gets up from the bed.

"Time to learn a new language, then," he says, putting a hand on his friend's shoulder. Roy turns to him with a puzzled frown.

"What does 'schmuck' mean? Maggie called me a schmuck before she put the 'phone down."

"It means we both need a drink," he smiles, "while I tell you my brilliant plan."

Φ

The girls have both been asleep on the back seat for an hour by the time Roy turns slowly through the gates of the campsite at the foot of Glastonbury Tor. It's one week later, after midnight, and the place is dark and silent. He is exhausted by the long drive and strains his eyes to follow the rutted track in the car headlights around to an empty space in the lower field.

"Shall we bother with the tents now?" Graham whispers, half-asleep himself.

"Well, I've been in this seat long enough. Come on, they only take a few minutes."

"In daylight, maybe."

Outside, the air cold and breezy beneath a perfectly clear sky, Roy urges a little more energy into his limbs and unknots the ropes over the roof rack. The first tent takes twenty-five minutes and even then the guy ropes are loose because they daren't use the hammer. He wakes the girls up and they crawl inside with their sleeping bags while Roy and Graham get started on the second tent. Finally it's up and Roy digs out the small gas cooker from the boot and puts a kettle on for coffee. They drink it with hands cupped round the enamel mugs for warmth and that strange sense of pride in their building work that only men have. The huge form of the Tor stands watchfully above them in the moonlight and an airliner blinks green above it with a distant low roar.

"The Americans will be on the moon soon," says Graham, for conversation.

"That'll be a surprise. They think they're going to Heathrow."

"Idiot. I mean the Apollo thingy, Neil Armstrong and his lot. A few more weeks."

"Yeah, s'pose."

"Aren't you interested? It's a brilliant engineering achievement. Fantastic."

"Seems like a huge waste of money to me, just to bring back a few bits of rock."

"Those bits of rock could tell us where we all came from."

"Who cares? It's where we're going that matters. And I," he stands and yawns, "am going to sleep."

"Right. Well, hang on a few minutes, will you? I haven't meditated yet."

"Christ, Graham, does it matter? It's after one o'clock and I've been driving for five hours. It hardly seems worth being saved if you can't just miss one meditation."

"It's important to me, mate. That's why we've come here, after all, 'cause this is a spiritual place."

Roy trudges over to the shower block then realises he doesn't have any shillings for the hot water, so he goes back and sleeps in the car after all. Within another day here he will have caught the meaning of the place.

In the morning there's a gentle knock on the car window. Roy stretches, opens one eye and sees Eva's lips pressed against the glass, leaving a perfect pink kiss as she stands up. He has managed to make his peace with her and with Maggie, with the help of flowers and Bourbon respectively, and perhaps getting away from the old ways and into the New Age will clear their minds. He stumbles out of the car into her arms and allows himself to be led by the hand like a child over to the tents, where Red and Graham are busy over gas cookers. All the equipment as well as the roof rack has been borrowed along the way from Graham's parents, a traditional and conservative couple who have nevertheless held onto the artefacts of a more exciting youth. Roy gratefully accepts cheese on toast while the others demolish sausages and eggs. Farmer Eric, a Scottish refugee with two hundred sheep in the adjacent fields, comes round to take the pitch fees, not even attempting to hide his disdain for colourful clothes and long hair. But the campsite is still sparsely populated so he's glad of the extra money, wherever it comes from. Then, with washing up and showering done, the four friends link arms and set off along Coursing Batch to the town.

Hippy ways have barely reached Manchester yet, let alone West Bromwich, and this Somerset town is the vanguard of the revolution. With broad smiles and wide eyes, they walk the length of the High Street, pointing out this crystal display and that outrageously dressed girl, spending the best part of an hour and more money than they intended in Gothic Image. Three of them are relaxed and feeling like happy tourists; Roy is simply feeling at home, yet with a strange sense of foreboding growing in his guts. In The Courtyard café, they settle down with buns and coffees to exchange paper bags. Graham, now predictably though a few months ago unthinkably, has a book on Buddhist meditation, some sandalwood incense and a small, brass ritual bell, whilst Red, equally predictably, has a skimpy, tie-dyed, rainbow-coloured top and a heap of beaded wristbands. More surprisingly, Eva's prize possession is a thin silver chain bearing a white-spotted, black stone.

"I've never seen anything so beautiful," she says. "It's obsidian. They say it gives you spiritual protection." There's another small paper bag inside the larger one, but she slips this into a pocket without showing it to them. "What have you got, Roy?" It's a book of blues sheet music and a greetings card with an image of exploding flowers for his mother's birthday next month.

"Well, she certainly won't be getting another one like that," grins Graham.

After a while, they turn left down Magdalene Street and are soon walking the neat lawns of the ruined Abbey, once the very seat of English Christianity but most of its stone taken four hundred years ago to build the town itself. Now its few remaining walls stand bare and sterile, defeated first by Henry and later by Aquarius. Since the trip was his idea, Graham has been reading up on the myths and legends and delights in playing tour guide, complete with expansive gestures and dramatic pauses. He points out the Holy Thorn and, way over to the right, its original site on Wirral Hill; there's the apocryphal tomb of King Arthur, the most successful financial scam of the Middle Ages; there are stories of Joseph of Arimathea and his nephew Jesus sailing across The Levels.

Towards late afternoon, they walk back rather more slowly than they had come, heads buzzing with strange histories and new, very modern sights. Sleeping bags are swapped over and the two exhausted couples fall into their tents for a nap.

Graham yawns widely as he scrambles out just before eight o'clock to find Roy quietly strumming his guitar, the new songbook open beside him. The evening is still warm and the sky is clear. He waves cheerfully to another young couple, early twenties, who must have just arrived and are pitching their tent not far away, and puts the kettle on the small cooker.

"I'll make them some tea," he tells Roy. "It's traditional on campsites, to welcome new arrivals. I remember my folks always doing that."

"No-one offered us tea," observes Roy.

"No-one was awake," his friend points out. His gesture is well-received and Roy watches them chat for a few minutes while he struggles with some new chord sequences. "They're from up your way," he says when he gets back. "Stourbridge. That's not far, is it? They've been coming for a few years now, know the area well. The guy said there's talk about a music festival somewhere near here, maybe next year. That'd be cool, huh?"

Graham can't be bothered to cook – it's his and Red's turn today – so he offers to buy a takeaway. The girls' orders are taken and they are left to the essential business of hair and make-up while the boys drive into town to the Chinese restaurant at the top of the High Street.

While they eat, sitting on the grassy bank at the edge of the field, the new neighbour comes over to return the mugs. He is shy and softly-spoken, tall and thin with jet black hair pushed behind his ears and held by a purple band. With some kind of intuitive inner recognition, Roy watches him carefully as he shares some joke with Graham and notices that Eva is doing the same, even as he gives them all a small wave and wanders back to his own tent.

In The Rifleman's Arms down the road, they receive the usual stares and tuts from the local farmers who haven't yet quite got used to their town being peacefully invaded. Roy and Graham take over the table football while the girls make friends with a group of bald middle-aged men by being hopeless at darts.

"Eva seems happy today," says Graham. "You two have made up then?"

"Yeah, I think so. We're all right. It's weird though, how she seems so completely at home in the West now when less than a year ago… She loves this place. She even loves rainy Salford."

"She loves you."

"I s'pose. Take that! Two-nil to the Baggies. She's changed a lot."

"That's a good thing, then, if she's happy. You're a lucky beggar. Except… two-one."

The pub still keeps its old-fashioned charm, which is to say no repairs or modernisations have been done for a generation, and it's quiet except for the murmuring of deep voices and an occasional brief laugh. They sit around an oak table in one corner and talk over Graham's legends. Of course, it's the nature of legend to be perhaps five per cent true and the rest wild exaggeration, whether for social or political reasons. Eva is listening to the others but quietly withdrawn, wondering what legends will be told by Russian soldiers to their families and what of Communism itself when it is finally a thing of history, centuries hence.

"What do you want to do tomorrow?" Graham asks brightly.

"I don't know. What do you want to do?" Roy says automatically, without thinking, the words suddenly transporting him to a caravan in Wales where it all began.

"The Chalice Well," Graham says firmly. "Remember, we passed it up the road on the other side?"

"What's there?" asks Red disinterestedly.

"A well." Three voices reply in unison.

"Ah, but it's a holy well," Graham goes on. "The water's got a ruddy colour so they say it's Christ's blood from the Holy Grail."

"Iron oxide, mate," chips in Roy, whose insistence on truth can be quite annoying when everyone else is caught up in myth.

"Actually, it is rather a nice place," Red concedes the next morning as the three of them sit on the upper lawn in the orchard. Graham is meditating underneath the votive yew below, cross-legged with eyes closed and thumbs to forefingers in the prescribed pose. Other visitors recognise this and tiptoe around him. "I'm going to buy a bottle of the water from the shop on the way out. Maybe it's magic and will turn Graham into a human being again."

"It's free, actually," observes Roy unnecessarily, "except we didn't bring anything to put it in."

"Do you really think it will work on these men?" asks Eva impishly, giving Roy a nudge. It takes him a few moments to realise what she meant. He stands and turns towards the Tor, looming high above them, the fourteenth century St Michael's Tower standing brightly in a shaft of sunlight against darkening clouds.

"Shall we go up there tonight?" he suggests. "Should be a spectacular view. And Graham says it's very spiri… ah, perhaps not." The first heavy spots of rain hit the roof of their shelter and within a minute they're having to run for the car, a dazed, other-worldly Graham staggering behind.

By the evening, however, summer has been restored, the air is warm and the grass is glistening like a field of pearls. The tents have only leaked slightly. Roy and Eva cook rice with tinned peas and sweetcorn and, in a separate pan, three burgers. They smile to each other and share a kiss, remembering the first time they made a meal together.

It's nearly ten o'clock by the time they're climbing over the stile at the far edge of the site and trooping along Basketfield Lane to the nearest entry point.

"Whose idea was this?" Red complains as she slides back for the fifth time on the wet grass. The slope is terraced and there's a well-trodden narrow path, but it has turned to mud with the afternoon downpour. Roy leads the way in a spiral route to save energy, walking carefully to keep the guitar balanced on his back. Later, he will wish that Graham's research had uncovered that there's a well-constructed, gentler path on the other side of the hill and also that Farmer Eric's sheep use these slopes for their toilet.

It takes about twenty-five minutes to reach the plateau and discover that a dozen others, including their campsite neighbours, have had the same plan. But it's worth it. When they finally stand upright at the top, they find that a beautiful mirage has formed around them. An evening mist has followed them up the slope and now hovers some fifty yards or so below, uplit by the sunset. To the west can just be seen the top of Wirral Hill, all the ground below swallowed up by a gently swirling primaeval sea just as it must have been two millennia before. The lights of the town below glow a ghostly orange while above them the sky is perfectly clear and full of stars. Roy and Eva stand with arms around each other, transfixed and slightly breathless in a moment of timeless silence.

They go over to join the others, huddled in groups near the base of the tower and talking quietly among themselves in the strange new language of the `sixties. One mentions a spiritual renaissance, another a Second Coming, yet another the renewal of Gaia. Sweet-smelling cigarettes are being passed around – politely refused by Roy and Eva – and someone starts to improvise quietly on a flute. Knowing full well that Graham is the real guitarist here, Roy passes the instrument to his friend and he plays along, effortlessly understanding where the theme is going as Red gazes lovingly at him.

"What do you think of all this?" Roy whispers to Eva, sitting close to him with knees drawn up and head on his shoulder.

"I'm not sure," she says. "A little while ago, I couldn't ever have imagined…. There's nothing like this back home." That word again. It touches a deep spot inside his brain. "But I'm glad we came here. Thank you. It's like… like I'm seeing the world for the first time… at least, so many things I never thought about before. So many new stories, even if they are only stories."

"But what do you feel?" He emphasises the last word.

"Feel? Well, when there are so many new things you always feel a bit… uncomfortable, I suppose. England hasn't been easy." He doesn't know the half of that. "But yes, I'm beginning to feel more peaceful, more accepted. At least," she laughs quietly, "until we get our exam results at the end of the week." There's reality again, always hovering just behind the door.

Roy ignores the spectre. He is not on the top of a hill but visiting a new planet, peopled by strange and gentle creatures whose unspoken thoughts he intuitively understands and whose beliefs he has always shared. He might even sabotage the ship that brought him so that he can stay. On cue, the girl who arrived yesterday with purple hairband man gets up and begins to sway with the music, dancing with slow, light steps out onto the hilltop, turning and flexing with arms outstretched. Roy's eyes follow her, framed against the mist as though on the far shore of a lake. She is tall with long, straight blonde hair, willowy and with gentle, almost sad features, yet with an athletic body…

Eva's closed hand is resting on his.

"Roy? Where are you? Look, I got something for you yesterday. A souvenir of this trip." She opens her hand to give him the small paper bag she had kept in her jacket pocket for the right moment. He opens it to find a small, heart-shaped rose quartz crystal. He finds it sentimental. Wouldn't it have been more appropriate to give him the obsidian and keep this for herself? But he manages to smile and kiss her happy face.

As they silently drink coffee from the flasks they have brought with them, Roy remembers something that Nick had said. What was it? Something like, "Don't get hooked up on love… the important thing is to suffer as little as possible…"

ACT 14

Family

A frog plops noisily from its lily pad and the fish scurry away. Roy stands by the small garden pool, a small vodka in one hand and willow leaves trailing over the other shoulder, watching the guests in their threes and fours like grotesque, thin mushrooms planted by his parents in carefully chosen groups. The sun is shining warmly, as always on these birthday parties, and his father is circulating with a tray bearing a punch of his own invention. Yet there is one significant difference this year.

Eva is wearing a thin, short, lilac dress with a bold purple floral pattern and Roy watches the gentle movement of the curves of her hips and breasts through it as she glides up to him, smiling.

"It's a nice party," she says, taking his arm and leaning into him. "Your father says you should mix more with these people. Why are you standing here on your own?"

"I like the pond," he says pointlessly. "I was just thinking. One year ago I was here in exactly this spot, wondering if you were really true, if you really happened, if I'd ever see you again." She snuggles closer to him as he bites on the ice in his glass. "They all thought I was crazy."

"Here I am," she whispers.

"Yes." But his voice is flat. "It seems like a lifetime ago. We've been through so much…"

"Roy," his father has suddenly interrupted their thoughts, "Paul's arrived. Will you get him a drink?"

"Sure, Dad. Is the food ready?"

"Your mother's seeing to it in the kitchen."

"I'll go and help her," says Eva brightly, taking Mr Carter's arm and steering him back across the lawn. Roy can't take his eyes off them and doesn't notice Lucille Mason sidle up to him. As usual, she can be relied upon to put into words what others only dare to think.

"They go well together, don't they? Could be your mother thirty years ago." She sighs wistfully, taking Roy's arm in a practised, casual way. "Happy families. You've made a good choice there, love. She's charming, everybody likes her, fits in perfectly." She says it with satisfaction, as if it had all been her own work, and pats his hand. "Yes, I made a good investment there." Her point escapes him.

"Hello, Lucy. I was very sorry to hear about your husband. It must have been…"

"A terrible shock? That's what everyone says. No, not really. It was always coming. But look," she brightens, "life goes on, eh? And I hear you did well in your exams, Eva too. Congratulations. Onwards and upwards."

"Thanks, it was a relief."

The afternoon passes respectably well, as this annual event always does, and Roy even allows himself to be drawn into a few brief conversations alongside Eva. It is very noticeable that the males, company directors to a man, visibly flush slightly and stand straighter when she comes near while their wives discreetly look her body up and down and paint on forced smiles. But Roy's younger sister Helen, now sixteen and normally far too sophisticated for these occasions, does give him a wink and a thumbs-up for the first time in their lives. When the last tipsy and perspiring guest has gone, the glasses are draining by the sink and the lawn has been picked clean of cocktail sticks and cigarette ends, he stands on the terrace with Paul watching Eva and his mother talking over coffee in garden chairs beside the pool.

"She looks lovely today," observes Paul. "Who would have thought it, eh? A berk like you catching her." He's right, she is slim and fit, rested and radiant. The day is at peace and family tensions have dissolved, at least for now. "Have you got your visa and everything?"

"Yeah, we're off next week. My parents have been very kind, given us the money for the flights. And they've invited Eva to stay here when we get back." She knows that he's talking about her and glances across the length of the garden towards him with contented love in her eyes. "But... I don't know why, Paul, but I can't help feeling... afraid, somehow. Something's going to happen."

Something does. The absolute calm of an early English summer evening is broken by a low drone, which becomes a spluttering roar as a remote controlled model aeroplane swoops out of the sky, loses height, and crashes into pieces just beyond the end of the garden.

'Why,' Roy says to himself, 'can't they just leave us alone, for God's sake?'

Φ

The Ilyushin Il62 lumbers across the quiet night sky and flops like a tired goose into Ruzyně International Airport. It taxis up towards an old diesel bus and within a few minutes the handful of tourists and returning émigrés emerge into the shadows. In the departure lounge overlooking the tarmac, an old man sweeping around the empty seats stops to watch the figures file onto the bus. You don't see many tourists here, not real ones at least. The bald man in a white apron behind the bar goes on absently polishing the glasses. In the control tower they relax and return to their newspapers; nothing else is expected tonight.

Roy and Eva, both half asleep, bump along the eighteen kilometres of the Lenin Road towards Prague in an ancient taxi that smells, like the airport, of dark Bulgarian tobacco. At the Čedok Palace Hotel on Panská, she checks him in, gives him a goodnight kiss and then takes the taxi on to the small apartment she shared with Irena. She had warned him it would have to be like this. All the same, alone and exhausted in the tiny, musty room, he feels utterly lost and unwelcome, further from home than he has ever been. He draws back the curtains and opens the window to look out over the night city, the little that can be seen. He's read the newspapers, listened to the World Service, heard Eva speak of home. But none of it had touched him. Now he is actually here, a player in international politics. This, Dad, is reality. And it's quite impossible to obtain any food or coffee in a Category B hotel after eight o'clock at night. Without even the energy to wash, Roy falls into a restless sleep and dreams that the ship reaches harbour but somehow the sea is even rougher there.

In the morning there is no hot water and the cold water that eventually arrives is brown. He opens the door to find the chambermaid just outside his room apparently devoting minute attention to the worn, green carpet there. As he's about to leave, the `phone rings but no-one speaks when he picks it up. Roy becomes aware that he is already shrouded by the thin, grey cloud that hovers over half of

Europe, seeping into the pores so that one never feels entirely clean, getting into the mouth so that one can never say exactly what one is thinking. He stands for a moment, then pulls out a single hair and fixes it with spittle across the lock of his suitcase, like he saw someone once do in a film. It drops off in the draught of the door as he goes out.

He has to help himself to a cold breakfast because they stopped serving five minutes ago although by means of elaborate mouthing and gestures he does manage to get some coffee. It's the end of July but he's shivering as he waits in the lobby for Eva to come and show him her city.

"I had some naïve idea," he says as they step out into the sunshine, "that Westerners would be welcome here, at least by ordinary people. The hotel staff aren't friendly at all."

"You're welcome if you have dollars," she replies, adding as an afterthought, "and anyway, there aren't any ordinary people anymore."

They turn a corner and there it is, Wenceslas Square, a long strand of cobblestones and trees and number eleven trams and trolley wires, grey facades and expressionless faces. A queue stretches across the front of the Jalta Hotel for more than fifty yards to a small kiosk. Eva peers into it as they pass, the housewives eyeing Roy with sullen interest.

"German biscuits," she says.

"What? They're queueing for biscuits?"

"German biscuits."

"Are there any cafes?" he asks tentatively. "I need some more coffee to settle my… my stomach." She smiles and takes his hand, leading him to the pavement tables near the statue. Glancing across to the museum, he can see the shell damage. So, it really did all happen. He tells her about the telephone.

"Do you think my room's bugged?"

"Are you important?" she laughs.

After his second cup, he's relaxed enough to realise what's been mystifying him for the last twenty minutes.

"There must be at least five hundred people in the Square, probably more. But it's so bloody quiet."

"It's normal," she shrugs. "What is there to talk about at this time of the year?" She leans back in her chair, also uncomfortable. The city that she loves is seeping back into her but perhaps it's too late, it can never be the same now that you can buy German biscuits and a couple of newspapers that say different things. "Look around, Roy," she says. "How many men can you see wearing light raincoats?" There's at least ten, all medium height with bland faces.

"Good heavens, yes. You don't think it's going to rain… oh, I see."

"There is much misunderstanding about the term 'Romanesque Prague' for example." The young guide in a neat white suit speaks clipped and correct English and has the full attention of the ten or so shirt-sleeved and striped-trousered Americans in the castle. In turn, they have the intense attention of four Czech teenagers propped against a stone wall, smoking. "It is generally thought to include all the relics from the tenth to the thirteenth century, but this is a simplification. On this site we see many relics which are properly the heritage of earlier cultures. You must take great care in the interpretation of cultural phrases."

Roy and Eva pass the group by and continue on their own way beneath the high, flat brick walls topped by narrow windows. The place has an air of disuse, of thoughts long abandoned.

"What a cheat," he observes, studying the official guidebook. "That woman's lifting everything from this book, practically word for word." But no-one speaks for themselves in public these days. "Let's go through to the second courtyard. There's a sanctuary there, what's left of St Mary's church. It's the –"

"– oldest building in Prague, yes. I didn't know you were so interested in old stones."

"But it's where Bohemia started." Soon they are emerging back into the sunshine and looking out across the Vltava at the city panorama. Two castles, either side of the river. Two ways of looking at everything.

They leave by the Renaissance Gateway under the Black Tower and head to her apartment where Irena welcomes Roy and then leaves to stay with a friend. With windows open to the cool of early evening and shadows already beginning to swallow the room, the remains of their meal left on the table beside a flickering candle, they are lying together on her hard, narrow bed.

"You know what was on the hotel menu for tonight?" he says. "'Goast beef' followed by 'fruit stew'. Isn't language fascinating, especially the mistakes you can make." He is lying on one arm, the other hanging over the side of the bed holding a cigarette while she is against the wall. He doesn't notice the moisture in her eyes. "The Bible's full of it, so many things misinterpreted. If you take the Gnostic version, the whole Church goes down the drain."

"How do you know one's right and the other's wrong?" she murmurs. "People just choose the one that fits their own ideas. None of it makes any sense to me – I wasn't brought up like that. I don't know what you're talking about, or why. I mean, do you know where we are right now? Do you know what we've just done? You and me, your body and mine. What's the Bible got to do with it?" She clambers over him and stands, wrapping a sheet about herself as she crosses to the window so that he doesn't see her tears.

"God is love," he mutters. The candle burns out with a hiss, sending a thin stream of grey smoke curling up to the ceiling.

In the morning she collects him again from the hotel and he follows dutifully, subdued. They turn towards the Old Town Square where they find the same guide at the head of the same Americans.

"I'm sorry about last night," he whispers. "It's… it's just the way I am. I wasn't taught that. It's just in me."

"No," she replies quietly, "you build it up for yourself. You create such elaborate thoughts for yourself, all… spires and arches…"

"…political change took the form of Gothic art due to the introduction of the Franciscan monks…"

"It's all stones, Roy. A building. But it's not one we can live in. It's not real, it's a dream."

"Love is a dream. We create it in our souls and –"

"Crap, Roy. You talk such crap sometimes. Last night after dinner you made love to me like an animal." A very large American woman in a particularly ghastly trouser suit turns to stare at them, confused by the double stream of voices. "You couldn't wait. You – what's the word? – you screwed me. My blouse was torn, my shoulder was bruised…"

"…and the Saint Vitus basilica became the cathedral we see today…"

"I'm so sorry. It must have been the slivo… the brandy."

"But I enjoyed it, Roy. It was human. It hurt. It was love. You still don't understand, do you?"

"…and the fourth university of Europe was founded…"

"I'm sorry." He is utterly crestfallen. "I didn't mean… it shouldn't hurt."

"Why not?" she insists. The fat American woman turns round again with a look of disdain. "Why not? Life does. Why can't you accept that you're an animal like everyone else? Why can't you come down to earth?"

Roy's head has begun to spin with the wind rushing through the cracks in his mind.

"Sorry. Sorry. I… I've lost my confidence. Please stop." She takes his hand and her mood softens, remembering her own sense of loss and despair that first day on Victoria Station, and many other days since.

"All right. But ask yourself, Roy. How can you live two different lives?"

"…now we shall see the period's ultimate masterpiece, the Old Town Tower of Charles Bridge, symbolically unifying the two settlements…"

As the group moves off, Eva and Roy stand apart as two people do when they don't know what to say. The square suddenly seems empty despite the others gathering by the Old Clock a little distance away. She watches it, waiting for the little figures to perform for her as they had done on her own first visit to the city so long ago. Roy comes closer and holds her from behind with both arms around her, kissing her neck.

"I want both," he whispers. "I want you and… I will try. Will you help me?" Her reply, if she makes one, is drowned by the metallic chimes and the delighted gasps of the tourists as the puppets dance for them.

Ф

The old train bumps and rattles its way steadily, hypnotically through the bare countryside of old Bohemia in the late afternoon. As far as the eye can see, the fields are flat and populated by horses, men and women, preparing for the harvest. Many rest on their tools for a moment to watch the carriages trundle past. This is not rich Somerset land or Welsh mountain, there are no tors or broken cotton mills or Edges. The compartment is less than half full, the travellers silently reading books or simply facing one another when not taking glances at Roy and drawing their private conclusions about his hair, beard, jeans and canvas shoes. Eva tried to persuade him to wear a suit for her parents but he said he's already uncomfortable enough and anyway he should be himself. After an hour he can bear the oppressive silence no longer.

"What are you thinking about?" As one, the other passengers look across quickly at him and then away, as though speech is forbidden here, especially in a foreign language.

"About Sally," she almost whispers, "something she once said in Wales when we were watching people go past the window."

"What was that?"

"Nothing really. She was trying to imagine who they might be – you know, film stars, secret agents…" She glances at the likely candidate in the raincoat at the other end of the compartment; he shifts slightly in his seat and looks out of the window but her eyes meet his in the reflection.

"Yes, I suppose we never know," he agrees. "We all look ordinary." Well, hardly, in this case. "But you never know what momentous events they could all be involved in."

At Trutnov's small provincial station, Pan Novák has been waiting for them eagerly and his smile only slips for a moment when he sees Roy beside his daughter. She runs to him as though she had never expected to see him again. Roy's hand is almost crushed by the smaller man's grip when they shake, but then he may as well not be there as they drive across town, the other two talking and laughing constantly. Eva's mother has tears in her eyes when she embraces them both, presumably for joy. It's late in the evening so they just share coffee and cake before bedtime. Roy is surprised to find his suitcase has been put in Eva's room and her father has not suggested that they say 'Goodnight' downstairs.

Next day, they walk through fields towards the Krkonoše Mountains and circle back to sit beside the Úpa River, close to where she had read Roy's letters, the day her parents had lost her trust. Now she is back in a very different time and they are trying hard. She is trying hard too. But in the evening, while everyone makes an effort with the small talk, neither smiles nor clear spirit can disguise the tension that binds them all. Nobody is going to ask the question.

The end comes suddenly, at dinnertime. As soon as the soup is put in front of him, Roy's fear breaks onto his face and he looks anxiously to Eva.

"Didn't you tell them? I mean, that I'm vegetarian? I'm sure this…"

"It's good," she says simply. "Try it."

"But…"

"My mother made it for you. It's a speciality. Try it."

They watch him expectantly as he weighs his karma in the balance of human relationships, desperately trying to remember what flute man and Maggie said about compromise. In this small, cosy, very foreign room with heavy curtains drawn across wooden shutters, an open fire dances in the grate. The old settee has been patched and draped with a thick, blue woollen blanket. A clock on the sideboard ticks very slowly as though to suspend time. As far from home as he could be, Roy decides with his mind and hesitantly takes up the spoon. After all, he could always be wrong.

Body disagrees.

After two mouthfuls, he has to leave the table hurriedly in shame and despair and get to the bathroom. On his return, six family eyes look at him accusingly and then drop to the table. There is little of the rest of the meal that he can eat either, and as little is spoken. When they are finally alone, he struggles to free himself from these binds that have enclosed his life.

"I'm really sorry, Eva. Honestly, I…"

"Couldn't you make an effort? For them? For me? Is it really so important?"

"I did try. I did. It's just… how I am."

As they prepare for bed, she goes over to stand by the open window and look out over the rooftops of her home town.

"I'm not going to come back," she says, without turning round.

His legs no longer work and he sits heavily on the quilt with head bowed, unable to voice even one of the questions pouring through him.

So this pure ideal, this mystical belief, this new life, this greatest love the world has ever known, has lasted barely thirteen months. Where the armies of the Warsaw Pact failed, there is after all no cure for the cancer of intolerance and the weakness of human flesh.

Ф

The Ilyushin Il62 lumbers across the quiet night sky. Roy sits alone next to a window, looking out at vague shapes below picked out by moonlight, watching life pass him by through the tears that stream his face. There is a deep, agonising pain in his gut, a pain that will never leave him, the pain that reminds you of when you made a terrible decision that changed the very course of your being.

Eventually, rocked by the continuous light turbulence, he falls asleep. He dreams that he is asleep, alone in a caravan. It is the hour of the wolf. He wakes to the sound of clouds, stands, and walks over to his clothes, his feet leaving white shadows on the threadbare carpet. As he dresses, he watches the dissolution of the mistiness above the bed where she had lain with him, like two raindrops in an ocean. He takes his guitar out across the grasses, shimmering silver in the early dawn, and sits in the hollow of the dunes. Everything is silent except for the low breathing of the watching mountain above the town.

Waves whipped by a gathering wind now rush in to caress the beach as the tide turns. Stones scatter as water breaks on the sand, destroying its identity.

Of course she was right. How does one marry the spirit of a waterfall?

Eva takes a taxi from the airport back to the apartment but cannot sleep for the deep, agonising pain within. In the morning, she walks to the university to find her friend Pavla Horáčková, the only person left she can trust. She gives Pavla the small key to the locker at Hlavní Nádraží, telling her, for her own safety, that she must not look inside the nondescript handbag inside but simply bring it back on her arm.

Φ

One early summer morning, a young woman in a fawn, soft leather jacket walks casually across the cobbles of Václavské Náměstí and stands beneath the statue. A large group of students sits quietly to one side and there are perhaps thirty others in the Square, a couple of them wearing light raincoats. A single shot rings out but few heads turn.

After all, it is the 21st of August.

Broken Sea

Verse One
The broken sea calls out to me,
waves whipped by wind caress the beach,
as I begin to feel the end –
the tide has turned, you're out of reach.

Verse Two
A mellow moon, a haunting tune,
as night begins and waves rush in.
Somehow I'd known I'd be alone
with just the sea for company.

Chorus
Why should it be, when love has gone,
one gets the blame though both are wrong?
Why should one lose more than was won at the start?
And like waves breaking on the sand,
must we forget where we began?
Is all that's left a memory, a broken sea?

Verse Three
Now you have gone and I am left
carried along upon the ebb.
And so it seems my life will be
an echo of the broken sea.

With gratitude to Dr Toby Young.

The Players

The United Kingdom

Roy Carter – 18, has just finished A Levels, then reading Engineering at Manchester University

Paul – Roy's best friend from school, reading Modern History & French at university; his father is Alan, his Uncle Harry owns the caravan in Wales

Graham – Roy's university friend in Engineering

Janet – Graham's girlfriend at home

Mr & Mrs Carter – Roy's parents, living near Sandwell Park, West Bromwich

Helen – 15, Roy's younger sister

Carol Reeves – Roy's first, now ex-girlfriend

Lucille Mason – a friend of Mrs Carter

Marian – 45, a Spiritualist medium and Roy's friend

'Nick' – Roy's Asian friend from Kenya, to be married to Asha

Arthur Morris – company Training Director

Jim Lloyd – company Trainee Supervisor

Kate – secretary to Mr Jackson, company director

Adam – landlord of The Mermaid Inn

Sally – Paul's girlfriend in Wales

'Mrs Baggage' – owner of the Seaview Hotel in Wales

Phil – landlord of The Willow pub in Wales

Carl and Peter – young German men in Wales

Red – an English student at Manchester University, real name Christine

Maggie – Eva's American flatmate in Salford, reading Languages

Deirdre Scott – known as Didi, an English lecturer at Manchester University

Nurse Mary Mallory – Eva's friend in Liverpool

Inspector Peter Jones – early 30s, British secret service police

John Cotton – a psychic artist and Anglican

Czechoslovakia

Eva Nováková – 21, a student of English at Prague University. Her pet name is Evička.

Pan Petr and Paní Amálie – Eva's parents, living in Trutnov in the Hradec Králové district near the Polish border

Josef – Eva's first lover, a journalist

Aleš – an engineer, Eva's next boyfriend and then fiancé

Jan Hájek – Eva's friend, a dissident and engineering student

Gustav – Jan's brother

Pavel Dušek – a student of English, a demonstrator

Tomáš Holub – shot dead for handing out flyers

Irena – Eva's friend, sharing a Prague apartment with her, a medical student

Pavla Horáčková – Eva's good friend at university

Alexander Dubček – First Secretary of the Communist Party (KSČ) of Czechoslovakia until forced to resign in April, 1969

Gustáv Husák – successor to Dubček when the Soviet Union takes full control

Gabriš – lifelong companion of Dubček, murdered during the invasion

František Kriegel – a member of the Presidium of the Central Committee of the KSČ, Jewish, the only reformer who refused to sign the Moscow Protocol

Josef Smrkovský – Chairman of the National Assembly and supporter of Dubček

Hradčany Palace (Castle) – offices of the president

Oldřich Černík – Prime Minister

Ludvík Svoboda – President

Antonín Novotný – ex-leader of the Communist Party

Alois Indra – author of 'the Invisible Letter' (with Drahomír Kolder, Secretary of the KSČ), a traitor, Chairman of the KSČ

Jozef Lenart – ex-Premier

Václavské Náměstí – Wenceslas Square (Wenceslas = Václav)

Miroslav Holub – Czech immunologist and poet

Stepan Vasilievich Chervonenko – Soviet ambassador to Czechoslovakia

Leonid Mikhailovich Sokolov – Russian emigration officer

The Soviet Union

Leonid Brezhnev – General Secretary of the Central Committee of the Communist Party of the Soviet Union

Nikolai Podgorny – Chairman of the Presidium of the Supreme Soviet, later succeeding Kosygin

Alexei Kosygin – Soviet Prime Minister

Alexander Shelyepin – Soviet trade union leader

If you have enjoyed this book...

Local Legend is committed to publishing the very best spiritual writing, both fiction and non-fiction. You might also enjoy:

AURA CHILD
A I Kaymen (ISBN 978-1-907203-71-8)

One of the most astonishing books ever written, telling the true story of a genuine Indigo child. Genevieve grew up in a normal London family but from an early age realised that she had very special spiritual and psychic gifts. She saw the energy fields around living things, read people's thoughts and even found herself slipping through time, able to converse with the spirits of those who had lived in her neighbourhood. This is an uplifting and inspiring book for what it tells us about the nature of our minds.

A SINGLE PETAL
Oliver Eade (ISBN 978-1-907203-42-8)

Winner of the national Local Legend Spiritual Writing Competition, this page-turner is a novel of murder, politics and passion set in ancient China. Yet its themes of loyalty, commitment and deep personal love are every bit as relevant for us today as they were in past times. The author is an expert on Chinese culture and history, and his debut adult novel deserves to become a classic.

PATHWAYS OF THE DRUIDS
Christopher J Pine (978-1-907203-61-9)

Christopher J Pine's wonderful debut novel is an exciting blend of fantasy, myth, magic and history. A true adventure story for all ages. In AD 60, the Roman Empire occupies Britannia and the ancient culture and freedoms of the Celts are being destroyed. Guided by the Druid priests, Boudicca leads the Iceni in an uprising against Nero's forces. It's a losing battle. However, the Druids have a mastery of nature, and skills far beyond those of the Romans. They devise a final desperate strategy to avoid slavery, and summon their greatest magic yet to open a portal into the alternative world of Triannaib. One last Celtic tribe, the Ordoveteii, race to cross the threshold…

5P1R1T R3V3L4T10N5
Nigel Peace (ISBN 978-1-907203-14-5)

With descriptions of more than a hundred proven prophetic dreams and many more everyday synchronicities, the author shows us that, without doubt, we can know the future and that everyone can receive genuine spiritual guidance for our lives' challenges. World-renowned biologist Dr Rupert Sheldrake has endorsed this book as "…vivid and fascinating… pioneering research…" and it was national runner-up in The People's Book Prize awards.

REDEEMING LUCIFER
Lennart Svensson (ISBN 978-1-910027-20-2)

This extraordinary novel is a tale in the finest tradition of legendary deeds, a blend of esotericism, pure imagination and acutely observed historical fact. A Russian army captain and his trusted striker find themselves journeying through parallel, mystical worlds in an epic quest to find Lucifer, no less, and to heal the world of its ills. But first, an ultimate, cosmic battle must be fought… This book challenges each of us to examine our life's purpose. Lennart Svensson is a Swedish academic and this is his debut novel in English.

5IGN5 OF L1F3
Nigel Peace (ISBN 978-1-907203-20-6)

What's it all about, then? Life. Why does stuff happen and is there any point anyway? Does anybody have a Plan? Well, actually, they do. But it's not as well thought out as you might hope. Unfortunately, it turns out that Heaven is uncomfortably like Earth, with a lot of the same idiotic people, and ridiculously bureaucratic. Of course, the angels mean well but their Grand Plan is just begging to be sabotaged… This hilarious novel takes us on a breathtaking journey involving lost identities, car chases, the delivery of fish, some SEx and a few Good Guys. Oh yes, and a nice dog.

These titles are available as paperbacks and eBooks.
Further details and extracts of these and many
other beautiful books may be seen at
www.local-legend.co.uk